A GAME IN THE NIGHT

When the Duke of Candover asked to accompany Maggie into her house, she had no choice but to agree. After all, how could she pretend to the world to be his mistress if she did not admit him into her private quarters to complete an evening of entertainment.

Once inside, she said, "How long will you have to stay to preserve your reputation?"

"It would be a blow to both our reputations if I left too soon," the duke replied. He spied a chess board set up with pieces. "Shall we have a game to pass the time?"

As Maggie looked into the duke's piercing eyes across the table, she felt a trembling sensation go through her as she wondered if chess was the only game the most successful womanizer in the *ton* intended to play that night. . . .

MARY JO PUTNEY was graduated from Syracuse University with degrees in eighteenth-century British literature and industrial design. She lived in California and England before settling in Baltimore, Maryland, where she is a freelance graphic designer.

The Controversial Countess

by
Mary Jo Putney

A SIGNET BOOK

NEW AMERICAN LIBRARY

NAL BOOKS ARE AVAILABLE AT QUANTITY DISCOUNTS
WHEN USED TO PROMOTE PRODUCTS OR SERVICES. FOR
INFORMATION PLEASE WRITE TO PREMIUM MARKETING
DIVISION, NEW AMERICAN LIBRARY, 1633 BROADWAY,
NEW YORK, NEW YORK 10019.

 SIGNET TRADEMARK REG. U.S. PAT. OFF. AND
FOREIGN COUNTRIES REGISTERED TRADEMARK—
MARCA REGISTRADA HECHO EN CHICAGO, U.S.A.

SIGNET, SIGNET CLASSIC, MENTOR, ONYX, PLUME,
MERIDIAN and NAL BOOKS are published by NAL PENGUIN INC.,
1633 Broadway, New York, New York 10019

First Printing, January 1989

1 2 3 4 5 6 7 8 9

PRINTED IN THE UNITED STATES OF AMERICA

To Nic, who may well be
the only professor of economics in America
who reads and enjoys my books

Of the many books consulted for the background of this story, the author wishes to acknowledge particularly *Wellington: Pillar of State,* by Elizabeth Longford, *The Foreign Policy of Castlereagh, 1812–1815,* by Sir Charles Webster, and *The Reminiscences and Recollections of Captain Gronow* (Viking Press edition, 1964).

Chapter 1

Rafael Whitbourne, the Duke of Candover, was enjoying the kiss. Lady Jocelyn was a delightful armful and the tentativeness of her embrace was sweetly stimulating. Rafe was in no hurry; he had waited three years hoping she would marry and become eligible to be his mistress. He didn't doubt that he could have persuaded her sooner, but it was strictly against his code to tamper with innocents, and that is what Lady Jocelyn Kendal had been under her facade of sophistication.

The pleasant moment was destroyed by an explosive entry into Lady Jocelyn's drawing room that caused her to jerk away from Rafe and turn to the intruder. For a charged moment Jocelyn stared at the new arrival, a man as tall as Rafe himself and of similar age, somewhere in his mid-thirties. Under other circumstances he would have been pleasant-looking, but as he stood frozen in the doorway the newcomer looked ready to do murder.

The duke was startled and not pleased; he preferred to conduct his *amours* lightly, with mutual pleasure and no recriminations. However, if the man in the doorway was not an angry husband, Rafe was prepared to eat his expensive top hat.

Lady Jocelyn cried out "David!" and moved toward her husband with pleasure, then stopped dead at the expression on his face. The tension between them was so strong the air seemed to pulse.

The silence was broken when the man said in a tight, angry voice, "It's obvious that my arrival is both unexpected and unwelcome. I presume this is Candover? Or are you spreading your favors more widely?"

As Lady Jocelyn rocked with the impact of the words,

Rafe nodded coolly to the intruder and said, "Servant, sir. You have the advantage of me." The man's green eyes were as bright and hard as emeralds and the duke could see him visibly wrestling with the urge to throw his wife's guest out. Fortunately, discretion won. Rafe was a noteworthy Corinthian, expert in all manner of gentlemanly sport, but fighting a furious husband of military bearing was not high on his list of pleasures.

Having won the battle for control, the man said tightly, "I am Presteyne, passingly the husband of this lady here." His gaze returned to his wife, and his words were only for her. "My apologies for injecting my presence where it is so clearly unwanted. It will take only a few moments to remove those of my belongings that are still here. Then I will disturb you no more."

Then Presteyne was gone with a wall-rattling slam of the door quite at odds with his controlled speech. Lady Jocelyn folded onto a satin chair, oblivious to the fact that she was not alone in the room. "Do you know, Lady Jocelyn, from the look on your husband's face, he does not share your belief that your marriage is one of convenience."

She turned to look blankly up at him but said nothing. Rafe was irritated to find himself caught in the sort of ill-bred emotional scene he detested and he was unable to keep a hard edge out of his voice. "If you will forgive a personal observation, you don't look precisely casual yourself. Just what kind of deep game are you playing? I can tell you right now he's the wrong man to manipulate with jealousy. He may leave you or he may wring your neck, but he won't play that kind of lover's game."

There was a look of stark tragedy on Lady Jocelyn's beautiful face, and her voice was a whisper as she said, "A great deal of stupidity and confusion is afoot, all of it mine. I have been trying to understand my heart, and I have done so too late."

The duke felt his anger dissolve in the face of her youth and vulnerability. Rafe had once been equally young and confused and the sight of her pain was a too-vivid memory of the disasters romantic love could bring. Since sympathy might cause her to break down entirely, he said crisply, "If you are the romantic I take you for, go after him. You won't get what you want from me, I promise you. I gave my heart away many years ago to someone who dropped and broke it, so I have none left to give.''

Remembering the pain on Presteyne's face, Rafe continued, ''On the other hand, if you throw your charming self at your husband's feet with abject apologies, I have every faith in your ability to bring him around your finger, at least this once.''

As Lady Jocelyn's hazel eyes widened in astonishment, he added dryly, ''A man will forgive the woman he loves a great deal. I would not, however, recommend that you ever let him find you in anyone else's arms again. I doubt he would forgive you a second time.''

Her voice was on the verge of hysterical laughter as she said, ''Your *sang-froid* is legendary, but even so, the reports did you less than justice. If the devil himself walked in, you'd ask him if he played whist.''

''Never play whist with the devil, my dear. He cheats.'' Rafe picked up his hat, mildly pleased that he didn't have to eat it, then lifted Lady Jocelyn's hand to give it a light farewell kiss. ''Should your husband resist your blandishments, feel free to contact me if you wish to resume our . . . discussion. However, I shall not expect it.''

As he looked into the lovely face that usually sparkled with bright life, he found himself saying involuntarily, ''You remind me of a woman I once knew, but not enough. Never enough.''

Then he walked out the door, nodded at the staring butler, and stepped into the civilized confines of Upper Brook Street. Within moments, his groom brought up the ducal phaeton and Rafe climbed in and took the reins. It had been an odd, unsettling experience, and Candover was grateful that he had been able to maintain his aplomb. The part of him that could laugh at his own vanities was amused at the pride he took in adding to his own legend for imperturbability. Not that Lady Jocelyn was likely to spread the story, and Rafe certainly had no intention of doing so. He had shown a bit more of himself than was comfortable and would just as soon forget the whole matter.

As he crisply turned into Park Lane and headed toward his home in Berkeley Square, he congratulated himself on a narrow escape from what could have been a sticky affair. He should have known better than to get involved with a bantling-brained romantic like Lady Jocelyn. He *had* known better, but she was really quite delectable, the most appealing woman he had met in years. She reminded him of . . .

He cut the thought off sharply. How fortunate that Lord Lattimer had summoned him for a discussion; it was bound to mean something interesting, and he rather thought he would like to get out of England for a while.

It said much for Edward Lattimer's good nature that he felt only a mild twinge of envy as he watched the Duke of Candover's progress across the crowded drawing room. The duke was almost theatrically handsome, so exactly fitting the part of an aristocrat that he might have been an actor rather than the genuine article. Tall, lean, and lithely athletic, his clear gray eyes were a startling contrast to the black hair and dark skin inherited from an Italian grandmother. Impeccable evening dress discreetly complemented his figure and his breeding, and the eyes of every woman in the room followed him. The soirée was very select and a number of the ladies present had been his mistresses at one time or another; most would be pleased if that were still the case. While Candover had sometimes been called arrogant, the term was unjust. Rather, his air of cool control came from bone-deep pride and confidence that was as much a part of him as his marrow. The duke's manner invited no intimacies, but it was devoid of the hauteur that created enemies, and men liked and admired him as much as women did.

As the duke worked his way through the crowd toward his host, Lattimer wryly told himself how lucky he was to be short, stocky, and balding. Had he been as handsome as Candover, he would automatically have sought a woman of matching beauty and never noticed his shy, plump Elizabeth. True, it would be gratifying if other women watched him as they did Candover, but Elizabeth *did* look at him that way, and she had given him more happiness and contentment than all the duke's glittering mistresses combined had brought him.

Lord Lattimer was a product of the middle classes but his

brilliance and administrative skill had made him a top official in the Foreign Office and brought him a title as a reward. While his background and concerns were quite different from Candover's, they had struck an unlikely friendship a decade earlier and found pleasure and intellectual stimulation in each other's company.

When the duke finally reached Lattimer, his social smile warmed. "Good evening, Edward. Will Elizabeth object if we disappear into your study for a while?"

Lattimer laughed, then replied in a voice pitched below the sound of the crowd. "Good evening, Rafe. Don't worry, Elizabeth knows you would never attend one of these musical evenings if we didn't have something that needed to be discussed discreetly."

"Excellent." The duke said no more until they left the room for the peace and mild clutter of Lattimer's study, where Rafe accepted a cigar from his host and they puffed in quiet pleasure for a few minutes while exchanging desultory news.

Lattimer was pleased the duke had been able to return to London from his country estate so quickly and his shrewd eyes observed that Rafe had the fine-drawn look that meant he needed to be traveling and doing again. Candover's rank assured him entry to the highest levels of society wherever he went, and Lattimer occasionally asked him to do a bit of unofficial government business abroad. Diplomatic channels were not as private as a government minister might wish and Lattimer knew he could rely on his friend's discretion and restless intelligence.

Eventually the duke grinned, flicking the ash from his cigar as he said, "Enough pleasantries, Edward, you didn't invite me here to discuss my racehorses. How might I serve you?"

Lattimer smiled in answer, tobacco smoke wreathing his round face. "I'm sure you're familiar with what's been going on at the peace conference in Paris."

"I've followed it, of course. But I thought that most of the issues had been settled at the Congress in Vienna?"

"Everything would have been fine if Napoleon had stayed put in Elba, but his return to France and the battle at Waterloo put the cat back among the diplomatic pigeons."

Lattimer pulled the cigar from his mouth and eyed its glowing tip with disfavor. "Now there's another Treaty of Paris in the works, as well as negotiations for a formal alliance between Britain, Prussia, Austria, and Russia. A year ago the Allies were willing to blame the wars on Napoleon's ambition, but considering how France supported him when he returned from exile, most of them are out for French blood. The German states in particular want to punish the whole country—France will end up in worse shape than she was before Napoleon's Hundred Days."

"That's common knowledge, along with the fact that Lord Castlereagh wants a moderate settlement. Where do I come in?"

Lattimer pulled a deep draft of smoke into his mouth, then let it trickle out slowly as he decided how much to say. Not that he didn't trust his friend, but there was no point in telling any more government secrets than necessary. "There is a tremendous undercover struggle for influence in these months until the new treaties are settled. It wouldn't take much to upset the diplomatic equilibrium, even to the point of war. Information is critical. Of course, we have our unofficial sources—also known as spies."

Lattimer ran his hand through his thin hair distractedly. "You know that one of the things I do is read and evaluate the intelligence reports that come in."

He seemed disinclined to continue and finally Rafe prompted, "What have you heard that's so disturbing?"

"Hints of a plot to disrupt the peace negotiations, possibly end them all together," Lattimer said bluntly.

Rafe thought carefully about his friend's words. What single deed could be so disruptive that the Allies would be thrown into chaos? "An assassination attempt on one of the leaders? All the Allied sovereigns except Prinny are there, as well as the chief diplomats of most of the rest of Europe. If any of them is killed, it would create quite an uproar."

"Very good," Lattimer said, as if the duke were a bright schoolboy. "I hope to God I'm wrong, but my sixth sense says something is brewing that could cause a great deal of trouble."

"Who is the assassin, and who is the target?"

"If I knew *that,* I wouldn't need to be talking to you

now," Lattimer said with a return to gloom. "I really only have hints to work with, gleaned from half a dozen sources. If I had to guess, I would say that French revolutionary elements might want to cause trouble. If the Allies impose too harsh a treaty on France, the country might rise up in arms, which is what the radicals want. As for possible targets . . . there are too many."

He ground his teeth into the cigar butt, then said thoughtfully, "Alexander of Russia, for example. Or either of our own chief negotiators; Castlereagh is the main voice of moderation in Paris, while Wellington's prestige is phenomenal after Waterloo. You may not know this, but there was an assassination attempt on him in Paris last winter. In fact, that was the main reason the government sent him to the Congress in Vienna: to save his life. The 'Savior of Europe' may lead a charmed life on the battlefield, but no one is safe from a determined assassin. And besides the targets I just mentioned, there are plenty more, like Metternich and the Austrian emperor."

Rafe contemplated his friend's words. A conspicuous assassination at this point could be a disaster for a war-weary Europe; beyond that, he knew and respected both Castlereagh and Wellington and would hate to see anything happen to them. He found himself hoping that if there was a conspiracy, it was aimed at someone else. "This is all very intriguing, but what do you think I could do about it? Surely your existing spies would be the best source of more information. I have no underground connections in Paris."

"True. But I need someone to work with my best agent in Paris, who is being difficult just now."

"Why not have one of your diplomatic people who is already there deal with your spy?"

"Because I can trust you."

"What do you mean by that cryptic comment?" Rafe drawled.

Lattimer sunk lower in his chair. "I have reason to believe one of our delegation in Paris is . . . unreliable. Someone may be taking bribes, or perhaps has misplaced revolutionary ideals. At any rate, secret information has been getting out of the British mission. I don't know who it could be—they are all hand-picked men. Maybe I'm seeing shadows where none exist and there is no traitor, merely carelessness, but the business is too vital to risk working through unsafe channels.''

"So you want me to tell your pet spy what you've just explained to me, then invoke his aid to investigate this plot?''

"Exactly, except that it's 'she,' not 'he.' ''

More and more interesting! "You said this person has been difficult lately. Do you have reason to doubt her loyalty, too?''

Lattimer was silent so long that Rafe was sure that was the problem until he said, "That is a possibility, though my own feeling is that she's reliable. More about that later. The major problem is that she wants to retire and leave Paris as soon as possible, before the negotiations are finished.''

"Offer her more money," the duke suggested.

"We have: she's not interested. One reason I want you to meet her is because of your . . . persuasive abilities with women.''

"Why, Edward, you shock me!" Rafe said with an amused gleam in his eyes. "Are you suggesting I sacrifice my fair white body on the altar of British interests?''

Lattimer looked uncomfortable. "Not necessarily—I'm sure you have other means of persuasion. You are a duke, after all; she may be flattered that we are sending you to France just to talk to her. Perhaps you can appeal to her patriotism.''

"Oh . . . I just have to talk to her. For a moment you had me worried. I do have my standards, you know.''

Ignoring Rafe's amusement, Lattimer said testily, "I've sometimes wondered. Although you might find Maggie to your taste—she's undoubtedly the most beautiful spy in Europe.''

With eyebrows raised, the duke murmured, "Fascinating. What is the evidence of her disloyalty that you don't want to credit?''

Lattimer chuckled ruefully. "I've always thought her an Englishwoman; certainly she speaks like one. I know nothing of her background, but it was obvious that she hated Napoleon and looked on her work as a personal vendetta.

For those reasons, I trusted her without thinking much beyond that. After all, her information was always good."

"What changed your mind?"

"As I said, I always assumed she was English, until I recently had contact with some gentlemen who have known her at previous stages of her career." He halted a moment, then said, "The French royalist thought she was French, the Prussian says she is a Berliner, and the Italian is willing to swear on his sainted mother's grave that she is from Florence."

In spite of his friend's glum look, Rafe couldn't help laughing. "I see. You are no longer sure where the lady's loyalties lie, if she can be dignified as a lady."

"She's a lady, no doubt about that," Lattimer snapped. "But whose lady is she?"

His friend's vehement reaction to an implied slur said a great deal about how he felt about this Maggie. The duke was surprised, but said mildly, "You said yourself she has given you no reason to doubt her."

Lattimer sighed. "It's hard to believe Maggie would betray us, but one of the reasons she is so effective is precisely because she can convince a man of anything. With the situation so grave, we can take nothing for granted, including her loyalty.

"Now that Napoleon is on his way to St. Helena, suppose she is feathering her nest by selling information about England to the other Allies? Perhaps she's in a hurry to leave Paris because she's earned a fortune through double- or triple-dealing and wants to escape before she is caught."

"And if she has been betraying you, what should I do, assassinate her?"

"Good God, of course not!" Lattimer looked at the duke suspiciously, not sure if the remark had been a jest. "It's not a killing matter. If she's untrustworthy, just tell Castlereagh so he won't rely on what she says. He may want to feed false information through her to her other masters. Besides, even if she *is* selling information, she may still be able to help us ferret out a conspiracy."

"So my mission, should I accept it," Rafe said thoughtfully, "is to seek the lady out and convince her to use her abilities to uncover a plot. In addition, I ascertain where her loyalties lie and if there are grounds for suspicion, I warn the head of the British delegation not to rely on her information. Correct?''

''Correct. You'll have to move quickly, though; the negotiations won't last much longer, so any conspirators will have to strike soon if they want to cause trouble.''

''I can leave day after tomorrow. The prospect sounds quite stimulating. You say she's the most beautiful spy in Europe?'' Rafe mused, a gleam in his eyes as he stubbed out his cigar. ''I promise, I shall do my utmost for king and country.''

After a day of frantic preparations and consultations with his staff, the Duke of Candover was ready to leave England. He would be traveling fast, taking only one carriage, his valet, and a wardrobe that would do justice to his rank in the most fashionable capital in Europe.

The last evening, he was quietly sipping brandy in his study and rustling through the day's mail when he came upon a note from Lady Jocelyn. In it, she thanked him for his good advice in sending her back to her husband, extolled the joys of a happy marriage, and urged him to try it himself. He smiled, glad to hear matters had worked out; underneath her beauty, famous name, and extravagant fortune, Lady Jocelyn was also a very nice girl. If she and Lord Presteyne were both raving romantics, perhaps they would stay happy indefinitely, though Rafe had his doubts. He raised his brandy glass in a solitary toast to her and her lucky husband, then smashed the glass into the fireplace.

The toast to her happiness came from the heart. Still, his smile went awry as he contemplated the shattered results of his uncharacteristic gesture. A man known for cool *savoir faire* would have been better advised to refrain; all the duke had to show for the moment was one less crystal goblet and a mild feeling of depression. He rose to pour himself a fresh glass of brandy, settling back in the wing chair to survey his library with a jaundiced eye. It was a beautifully proportioned room, one of Kent's finest efforts, a symphony of Italianate richness. In all of Rafe's vast holdings, there was no spot he enjoyed as much. In that case, why the devil did he feel so restless?

Stretching his long legs out in front of him, he decided to cure the morbid mood by giving way to it. Lady Jocelyn wasn't the issue; if he had wanted her that much, he could have married her. What disturbed Rafe was the extent to which she reminded him of Margot, beautiful, betraying Margot, dead these last dozen years. The two women were not physically similar but both had a bright, laughing spirit that was irresistible; whenever he had been around Lady Jocelyn, he found himself remembering Margot.

As he sipped his brandy, he tried to think objectively about Margot Ashton, but it is impossible to be rational about one's first love. First and last in Rafe's case, the experience had cured him forever of romantic illusions. *But while it had lasted, it had been a very convincing illusion.*

Margot was not the most beautiful woman he had ever known, and certainly wasn't the best born or the wealthiest. But she had warmth and charm in lavish abundance, and she sparkled with a vitality that shone through the dawn mists of Rotten Row like a sun even when she and Rafe had danced until three in the morning. She had moved him in ways no other woman ever had, and since he could never be that young again, no other woman ever would.

Rafe's real regret came from the knowledge that it was his own jealousy and anger that had ended their engagement. If he had possessed at twenty-two the cool aplomb he developed later, if he had been able to accept her roving eye, he could have had her friendship over all these years.

Because when all was said and done, her companionship was what he missed most. He knew time had enhanced her sexual appeal; no woman could possibly be as desirable as memory painted her. The irreplaceable loss was how Margot had shared his laughter, and the way her changeable eyes would meet his across a room with such intimacy that he forgot the rest of the world existed.

The duke's reverie ended when the stem of the goblet in his hand snapped, cutting his fingers and broadcasting brandy across his lap. Scowling at the mess, he stood up. He'd had no idea the stems were so fragile, and the butler would sulk for days when he discovered the set of goblets was now two short.

Rafe rose and headed upstairs to his bedchamber. A little

self-indulgent melancholy was poetic, but he was beginning a hard journey early the next morning and it was time he got some rest.

Chapter 2

"No!"

Though the perfume bottle whizzed by his handsome head with no more than two inches to spare, Robert Anderson made no attempt to dodge, knowing that Maggie had an excellent aim and no real desire to damage him. She was merely, so to speak, sending him a message. With her usual good sense, she had chosen to throw the bottle of cheap scent given to her by a purse-pinching Bavarian with poor taste.

Robert grinned at his companion. Her magnificent bosom was heaving and her eyes flashed sparks; gray ones today, he noted. "Come now, Maggie, what is so terrible about the prospect of meeting with this duke that Lattimer is sending? You should be flattered the Foreign Office is taking such an interest in you."

A spate of Italian profanity was his answer. He tilted his blond head to one side and listened critically. When her outburst was finished he said approvingly, "Very creative, Maggie, love, but it isn't like you to slip out of character. Surely Magda, Countess Janos should swear in Magyar?"

"I know more profanity in Italian," she said loftily, "and you know perfectly well I never slip out of character with anyone but you." Her look of aristocratic dignity gave way to an impish chuckle as she added, "Don't think you can change the subject, which was the Most Noble, the Duke of Candover."

"So it was." Robert blinked his blue eyes ingenuously. He and Maggie had known each other for a long time, and while the relationship was no longer as intimate as it had been, they were still the best of friends. It was most unlike her to be temperamental, even when she had been acting the part of a volatile Hungarian noblewoman for nearly two years. "What do you have against the duke? I assume you met him sometime in your checkered past and he rumpled your fur."

Maggie had been dressing for dinner when Robin called and had dismissed her maid when he appeared. Sitting down at her vanity table, Maggie lifted a silver-backed brush and began pulling it through the tawny waves of hair that fell over her shoulders. Scowling artistically into the mirror, she said succinctly, "The man's a prig."

"Does that mean he failed to show adequate appreciation of your charms?" he asked with interest. "Strange, the duke has the reputation of being quite a lady's man. I have trouble imagining he would ignore a tasty morsel like you."

"I am nobody's tasty morsel, Robin! And rakes are the biggest prigs of all. Pious hypocrites, in my experience." She tugged viciously at a knot in her hair. "Don't try to pick a new fight with me until we've finished with the current one. I refuse to have anything to do with the Duke of Candover, just as I have no desire to continue spying. That part of my life is over, and neither you, the duke, nor Lord Lattimer are going to persuade me otherwise. As soon as I can take care of a few matters of business, I will be leaving Paris."

Robert came to stand behind her, taking the brush from her hand and starting to gently pull it through her thick, dark gold hair. It was odd how they shared some of the intimacy of a married couple, though they had never married. He had always enjoyed brushing her hair, and the faint sandalwood scent released took him back to the years when they were happy young lovers, challenging the world with few thoughts for the future.

Maggie was looking stonily into the mirror and her eyes were now a cold gray, not sparkling as they had earlier. After several minutes of brushing, she began to relax and he asked quietly, "What's wrong, Maggie? Did Candover do something despicable? If it upsets you to see him, I won't mention it again."

She chose her words carefully, knowing that Robin was all too adept at picking up hidden meanings. "He *was* rather despicable, actually. It's ancient history now, and it wouldn't really upset me to see him. I just don't want someone else nagging me to keep doing what I'm tired of."

Robert smiled, his gaze meeting hers in the mirror. "Then why not meet him just once to tell him that? If you want to wreak a little vengeance for past injuries, wiggling your lovely body just out of his reach would be a fitting punishment. It would certainly drive most normal men mad with longing."

She looked startled, then thoughtful. "I'm not sure that would work. We parted on rather poor terms."

"Being angry then doesn't mean he hasn't been thinking lustful thoughts of you since," Robert said firmly. "Half the diplomats in Europe have let state secrets fall from their lips while struggling for one of your smiles. All you have to do is wear that green ball dress of yours when you meet him, palpitate as you refuse his request, then slink out of the room. I guarantee it will cut up his peace for at least the next month."

Maggie regarded her reflection contemplatively. While she had a great deal of whatever it was that drove men mad, she was not convinced that Candover would succumb to her charms. Still, anger and lust were closely related, and Rafael Whitbourne had been very angry indeed at their last meeting. . . .

A slow, wicked smile curved her lips, then she threw back her head and laughed. "Very well, Robin, you win. I'll meet with your ridiculous duke. I owe him a few nights of ruined sleep. But I guarantee he won't change my mind."

Robert dropped a quick kiss on the top of her head. "Good girl." In spite of her protests, if she saw Candover there was a chance she could be persuaded to continue in her work for a while longer, and that would be a very good thing.

When Robin left fifteen minutes later, Maggie did not immediately summon her maid to complete her toilette. Instead, she crossed her arms on the edge of the vanity and laid her head on them, feeling sad and tired. It had been

20

foolish to agree to see Rafe Whitbourne. He *had* behaved very badly but even then she had seen how his cruelty had come from pain, and she had been denied the pleasure of hating him.

Nor did she love him—the Margot Ashton who thought the sun revolved around his handsome head had died over a dozen years before. Maggie had been many different people in the ensuing years, as Robin had taken her under his wing and given her a reason to go on living. Rafe Whitbourne was no more than a bittersweet memory, of no relevance to her present self.

Love and hate are indeed the sides of the same coin because they both mean caring; their true opposite is indifference. Since indifference was the only feeling Rafe could rouse in Maggie now, minor forms of revenge were hardly worth the effort. She just wanted to be done with this phase of her life, with deceit and misdirection and informers.

Most of all, she wanted to accomplish the task that had been deferred for years, and to go home—to England, which she hadn't seen in thirteen years. She would have to start over again, this time without Robin's protection, but even that aloneness would contain relief; the two of them knew too much about each other for Maggie to reinvent herself when he was around.

She lifted her head and propped her chin on one fist, studying her face in a mirror. Her high cheekbones made her a convincing Magyar and she spoke the language well enough that no one ever doubted her Hungarian identity. But how would Rafe Whitbourne see her after so many years? A faint smile touched her full lips, the lips that had had at least eleven pieces of bad poetry dedicated to them.

Apparently the man could arouse *some* emotion in her, even if it was only one as ignominious as vanity. She surveyed her image critically. Her face lacked the classic restraint of true beauty: her cheekbones were too high, her mouth too wide, her eyes too large. Maggie had never been a great fancier of her own appearance but at least she didn't look that different from when she was eighteen. Her skin had always been excellent and the amount of riding and dancing she did kept her figure intact; the only change was a bit more fullness to the curves, and no man had ever objected to *that*. Her hair had darkened a bit, but instead of becoming dull tan as blond hair often did, it was now the shade of rippling, golden wheat. Actually, she looked better now than when she and Rafe had been engaged.

It was tempting to imagine that he was fat and balding, but the damned man had the sort of looks that would only improve with age. His personality was another matter; his father had been alive then so Rafe had been merely Marquess of Wilton, but he had always been aware of his consequence and the intervening years of being toadeaten would have made him quite insufferable. It would be rather fun to pierce his complacency. Certainly, Maggie thought mischievously, she could try. But she could not help wondering: what kind of man had Rafael Whitbourne become?

The Duke of Candover had not been in Paris since 1803 and there had been many changes in both streets and atmosphere. Even in defeat, France's capital was the center of Europe, with four major and scores of minor monarchs present to glean what they could from the wreckage of Napoleon's empire. In spite of the plethora of rulers, "the king" always meant Louis XVIII, the aging Bourbon whose unsteady hand held the French throne, and "the emperor" always meant Bonaparte. Even in his absence, the emperor cast a longer shadow than the real presence of any other man, and danger pulsed beneath the surface gaiety. Its presence made Rafe feel wholly alive and ready for what might come.

The Prussians wanted revenge, the Russians wanted more territory, the Austrians hoped to roll the calendar back to 1789 or earlier, the French wanted to save themselves from any massive reprisals after Napoleon's insane and bloody Hundred Days. And the British, as usual, were trying to be fair-minded. It was like trying to mediate a discussion between pit bulls.

The duke took rooms at a hotel whose name had changed three times in as many months to reflect changing political currents. Now it was called the Hotel de la Paix, since Peace was an acceptable sentiment to most factions. In the evening he went to an Austrian ball where Lord Lattimer had arranged for him to meet the mysterious Maggie. Rafe dressed carefully, mindful of Lattimer's suggestion that he charm the lady spy. Experience had taught him that he could generally get what he wanted from women with a debonair smile and some intent conversation; frequently, they offered a good deal more than he desired to accept.

The Austrian ball was a glittering assemblage of the great and notorious of Europe, including all the important monarchs and diplomats as well as the lords, ladies, sluts, and scoundrels that were always drawn to power. It was easy to believe dangerous plots swirled under the surface and Rafe hoped this agent was as good as Lattimer claimed; Paris was a powderkeg and the wrong spark could set the continent ablaze once more.

The evening was well advanced when he was approached by Robert Anderson, who had some undefined role with the British delegation. It was Anderson who had arranged the meeting with Maggie; he was a good-looking chap, shorter and younger than Rafe, with fair hair and a slight, elegant figure. He looked vaguely familiar; not surprising, since the British embassy was staffed by aristocratic relations and younger sons. Nodding briefly, he said, "If you'll accompany me, your grace?"

As they snaked their way through the crush, Rafe surreptitiously examined his guide, wondering idly if this man was the weak link in the delegation. Anderson was so good-looking as to be almost pretty; impossible to imagine him as having two brains to rub together, much less to be a spy. He looked neither more nor less suspicious than any of the other members of the delegation Rafe had met.

Anderson led him out of the ballroom and up a stairway to the next floor. There were a number of doors along the corridor they entered; the open doors led into empty rooms, and Rafe wondered cynically what he would find behind the closed ones. Stopping outside the last door in the corridor, Anderson said, "The countess will be waiting for you, your grace."

"Do you know the lady?"

Anderson said cautiously, "I have met her."

"Tell, me what is she like?"

The blond man looked blank, then shook his head. "I'll let you discover that for yourself." He opened the door and

23

said formally, "Your grace, may I present Magda, the Countess Janos?" Then bowed briefly to the lady and left.

The room was richly furnished, with elaborate Louis XIV moldings, two chairs, and a velvet couch designed for dalliance, but Rafe was aware of none of that. His eyes were fixed on the woman standing opposite, her lush figure lovingly defined by a green satin evening gown with a froth of embroidered net floating over it. The decolletage was low enough to catch the attention of any man not yet dead and one wheat-gold curl fell charmingly over her shoulder, but that was not why his heart hammered with stunned shock. It was said that everyone had a double somewhere in the world; if that was true, he had just met Margot's.

As Rafe studied the woman, his face showed none of his surprise. Margot had been reported dead a dozen years ago; was there any possibility the report had been wrong? News was often mangled as it traveled. He pulled back from his chaotic emotions to compare the countess to his memories. This woman appeared to be about twenty-five years old; Margot would be thirty-one but it was not impossible that she looked younger than her age.

Surely this woman was taller than Margot, who had been only a little over average height? But Margot's bearing and vitality had made her appear taller than she was; it had been a surprise how far he had bent over the first time he had kissed her . . .

Sharply he forced himself to continue his analysis. This woman's eyes appeared green and she had an exotic, foreign air. But she was wearing a green dress, and he recalled how changeable Margot's eyes had been, shifting from gray to green to hazel with her mood and costume. And if Margot had been living on the Continent all these years, she might look un-English now.

There were no differences that could not be ascribed to time or faulty memory; the only real question was the countess's behavior. If she were Margot, she *must* recognize him, for Rafe had hardly changed out of recognition. The last scene between them had been an angry disaster, but even so, he would think she would acknowledge him, even if it was with a curse.

Instead, the countess stood with an amused smile during

Rafe's lengthy inspection, her posture both relaxed and provocative. Clearly she would not speak first, as if they were competing to see who could be most casual. Well, Rafe was the supplicant so it was up to him to initiate the discussion. Bowing deeply, he said in French, "My apologies, Countess. I had been told you were the most beautiful spy in Europe but even so, the description did you less than justice."

She gave a rich, intimate laugh. Margot's laugh, but she answered in English with a strong Magyar accent. "Spies are not noted for beauty, so you are forgiven your surprise." Fluttering her fan, she added, "I have heard of you, too, your grace."

Rafe decided it was time to use some of his alleged charm. Drawing near the countess, he smiled down at her and said, "You know why I am here, and it is a serious business. Let us not stand on formality. I would prefer you use my given name."

"Which is?"

If she was Margot and this was an act, she was doing it well. Rafe's smile was showing signs of strain as he lifted her hand and kissed it, then said, "It is Rafael Whitbourne, though I prefer my friends call me Rafe."

She snatched her hand back as if he had bitten it and said sharply, "It must have been singularly inappropriate to name you after an archangel."

When she said that, Rafe's doubts were abruptly laid to rest. In a wondering voice, he said, "So it *is* you, Margot. You are the only one who ever dared mention my lack of affinity for archangels." As she gazed blandly up at him, he continued, "It was a good quip; I've used it myself many times. But how in God's name did you come to be here?"

Laughing, she said with Magyar overtones, "Who are you talking about, your grace? Some little English girl who resembles me?"

Her denial produced a flash of anger greater than any he had known in years. Rafe could think of one absolutely guaranteed way to determine the identity of the woman in front of him. Stepping forward, he put both hands on her shoulders and kissed the mouth that was laughing at him.

It was Margot; as he held her, he recognized an elusive

essence that was not that of a stranger. Even without that sense of familiarity, Rafe would have been sure because he had never met another woman whose touch produced such a flare of desire.

From the way she quivered under his hands, Margot felt that attraction as strongly as he did. After yielding initially she tried to pull away but he held her still, exploring her mouth and marveling at how little she had changed in this particular way.

When he released her shoulders, she stepped back sharply, her eyes blazing with such rage he thought she might strike him. On the whole, she was entitled and he would have made no effort to avoid a blow. Instead, in one of Margot's mercurial shifts of mood, she laughed, a bubbling laugh with no conscious provocation, and all the more attractive for that. When she spoke it was with her own natural English accent.

"I had you guessing, didn't I? But really, *cher* Rafael," she pouted, the naturalness disappearing behind practiced flirtation, "I am distraught that you had forgotten me. After all we had meant to each other." She added a soulful look.

Rafe was glad to see a flash of the old Margot but her worldly mask was less appealing. He drawled, "Please excuse the liberty I took, but it did establish your identity."

Maggie had been infuriated at the kiss, but Candover's look of cool self-satisfaction was worse. Of course a kiss meant nothing to him, he must have participated in thousands over the years. Probably *hundreds* of thousands, to the point where kisses were meaningless currency. She was even more furious that she had unwittingly responded.

To steady herself, she crossed to the sideboard where two glasses and several bottles stood. She had opened a bottle of Bordeaux earlier and now poured two glasses, handing one to the duke before saying, "Our kind hosts have provided us with everything a mischievous couple might want. A pity to waste it all. Pray be seated." She sat on one of the solitary chairs, pointedly ignoring the velvet couch.

When the duke had also settled himself, Maggie said lightly, "Why should I have been hard to identify? I am said to be well preserved for a woman of my advanced years."

"Age cannot wither her. . . ?" He smiled faintly as he quoted the line. "That in itself is a cause of confusion—you scarcely look older now than at eighteen. But the real reason I had trouble deciding if you were Margot Ashton was that she was supposed to be dead."

"I am no longer Margot Ashton." Her hard tone softened when she asked, "Why did you think I was dead?"

His voice expressionless, he said, "It was reported that you and your father were in France when the Peace of Amiens ended, and that you were both killed by a group of French rabble on their way to offer their arms to Napoleon."

Her smoky eyes narrowed with an expression he couldn't interpret. "The news of that reached England?"

"It was something of a *cause célèbre* at the time—the public was outraged that a distinguished Army officer and his beautiful daughter were murdered simply for being British. However, since we were already at war with the French, no special diplomatic sanctions were possible." He studied her curiously as he drank more wine. "How much of the story is true?"

"Enough," she said shortly. "None of that is to the point. You are here to convince me to continue my services to England. You will appeal to my patriotism, then you will offer me a substantial amount of money. I will refuse both. Since the outcome is already determined, I see no reason to go through the motions. Now if you will excuse me. . . ?"

She stood and started toward the door but stopped at his raised hand. Rafe was uncertain how to proceed; given the resentment Margot obviously felt for him, Lattimer could not have made a worse choice of envoy. Now that he knew "Maggie" was Margot, Rafe also knew that part of his job was done—she was certainly English, not French, Prussian, Italian, Hungarian, or any other role she chose to play. Beyond that, he flatly refused to believe she would ever betray her country; if British state secrets were being sold, it was not by her.

In an effort to accomplish the rest of his assignment, he said, "Is it that hard to listen to me for a quarter of an hour? I may surprise you with something you don't expect, Margot."

"I am not Margot. I am Maggie." Her tone was hostile but she sat down again, her face blank and impervious.

"What is the difference between the two?"

"None of your bloody business, your grace. Please speak your piece so I may leave."

It was hard to continue in the face of such hostility, but he made himself say calmly, "Why is it so necessary that you leave Paris at this particular moment? The new treaty will be negotiated and signed before the end of the year. It may be just a few more weeks."

She shrugged, but her answer was matter-of-fact. "That argument was used on me at Boney's first abdication. The Congress of Vienna was supposed to be six or eight weeks, and lasted nine months instead. Before it was over, Napoleon had returned and once more my services were indispensable."

She sipped her wine, savoring the complex flavor, then said with a trace of weariness, "I am tired of postponing my life. Bonaparte is on his way to St. Helena to preach his destiny to the sea gulls and I have some business that is long overdue."

Rafe's voice was soft as he asked, "What kind of business?"

Hesitating, she poured more wine though her glass was not empty. Her face averted, she said, "I will go first to Gascony."

Rafe felt a prickle at the base of his neck and guessed what she had in mind. Nonetheless he asked, "Why?"

She turned to face him, her face expressionless. "To find my father's body and take it back to England. It has been twelve years . . . it will take time to find where they buried him."

He had guessed correctly but took no pleasure in it. The wine tasted bitter on his tongue; he must now speak of something he would have preferred to keep private. "There is no need to go to Gascony. You won't find him there."

As she stared in puzzlement, he continued, "I was in Paris when news of your deaths arrived, so I went to Gascony and arranged to have the bodies returned to England. They are buried in the family plot on your uncle's estate." When she continued silent, he added, "I was told that two fresh graves belonged to *"les deux Anglais,"* and never thought to question it. Also, I was in some hurry to be on my way."

The striking face was shocked and vulnerable, the worldly veneer dissolved, and she sank back into her chair and briefly buried her face in her hands. Rafe was painfully reminded of the warm, laughing girl she had been and had to restrain himself from going to comfort her; he doubted the gesture would be welcome.

Rafe had envied the friendship between Margot and her father, which was quite unlike the distant politeness between Rafe and his own sire. Colonel Ashton had been an affable, honest soldier, less interested in seeing his daughter a duchess than in seeing her happy.

Maggie raised her head, her face composed but her voice unsteady as she said, "The second coffin must have been Willis, my father's army batman and valet. The two of them . . . gave a good account of themselves when we were attacked."

She could hear the edge of tears in her voice and she stood and crossed to the window, pushing the heavy brocade drapery aside to look into the dark boulevard with its flaring lamps. She should have known this interview would not go according to plan; Rafe Whitbourne had always been able to find the vulnerable spots in her. That ability had been welcome when they were young and in love but it was intolerable that he could use that to manipulate her when the love was gone. Perhaps it wasn't manipulation, merely a recitation of the facts; either way, she hated losing her control in front of him.

When she was sure her voice would be even she said, "Willis was a small man. It would have been easy to assume his coffin was mine." She could see her reflection in the dark glass. Willis had taught her how to shoot dice; she had called him Uncle Willy when she was a child. "I'm glad he's in England—he would have hated the thought of being buried in France. I was going to take him back too, but you have made that unnecessary."

She turned to face him, leaning against the windowsill, no longer hostile but her eyes searching. "Why did you do it? It couldn't have been easy."

Indeed, it hadn't been easy, even for a man of great wealth and influence. He had come to France with the unexpressed hope of meeting Margot again and had postponed his departure to the point of endangering himself. When the news came that it was forever too late, he abandoned his plans to return to London and instead had gone alone into Gascony, using his excellent French to pass as a Frenchman. It had taken weeks to locate the bodies; then he had taken the lead-encased coffins over the Pyrenees into Spain rather than risk crossing France again.

When the two coffins had been buried again at the Ashton family estate in Leicestershire, with his own hands Rafe had planted daffodils on the smaller grave, because he had met Margot in the spring and daffodils always made him think of her. He said nothing of that; it was not only maudlin and sentimental but vaguely laughable since hindsight now showed that he had acted under a misapprehension.

Where had Margot been when he was in Gascony? Injured perhaps, or held captive in the local jail? If he had searched, could he have found her and brought her home? But that too was irrelevant now so he said merely, "There was nothing else I could do for you. It was too late for apologies."

"Why did you feel it was necessary to apologize?"

"Because I behaved very badly, of course." He shrugged. "The more years pass, the worse my behavior looks."

Maggie felt the ground getting very soft underfoot and decided it was time to head for firmer territory. She looked directly at him and said, "I am obligated to you."

She wondered if he would use that obligation to compel her to stay in Paris. Instead, Rafe replied in a neutral voice, "There is no obligation. I suppose I did it for myself."

If he had tried to use her gratitude to force her to stay, she would have rebelled, but his quiet disclaimer bound her as nothing else could have. She said, "You can tell Lord Lattimer that I will stay here and continue working until his treaty is resolved. Is that satisfactory?"

She was glad that the duke refrained from any show of triumph when he answered. "Very good, especially since there is more at stake here than routine information gathering. Lord Lattimer charged me to discuss a special task with you."

"Oh?" Maggie returned to her chair and with a casual gesture totally at odds with her formal gown, she twisted crosswise in the chair, draping her legs over one arm while she leaned against the other. Realizing what she was doing too late to stop, she cursed herself silently. She maintained ladylike posture except when she was alone or with Robin; exasperating to slip into her old hoydenish behavior with a man she hadn't seen in thirteen years. He had always been amused at the restless way she couldn't sit still long, and had claimed Margot could not be ungraceful no matter how she twisted herself around. Well, if he wanted her help, he could jolly well put up with her idiosyncrasies. "What does Lattimer wish me to do?"

The duke looked at her thoughtfully, his long elegant hand lightly clasped around the stem of his wineglass. "He has received several hints that there is a plot afoot to assassinate one of the major figures here at the peace conference. He would like you to investigate as quickly and thoroughly as you can."

"Indeed?" Maggie frowned, personal unease forgotten as she considered what Rafe said. "Just three weeks ago a plot to assassinate the king, the tsar, and Wellington was exposed. Could that be what Lord Lattimer has heard rumors of?"

"No, Lattimer was aware of that affair and apparently this is separate. What makes this new conspiracy so dangerous are indications that it originates in the highest diplomatic circles of the conference. That makes it more difficult to detect and gives the conspirators better access to their target or targets." Rafe reached inside his coat and pulled out a slim envelope. "Lattimer sent this to explain what he knows."

Maggie accepted the envelope and made it disappear. "Have you read what he wrote?"

"Of course not—it was sent to you."

Maggie snorted. "You'd never make a spy."

Rafe's voice was silky but for the first time emotion showed through. "Quite true. I could never match your talent for deceit and betrayal."

Maggie whipped herself upright in the chair, her silk slippers slapping to the floor as the room pulsed with the unspoken past. She was too well trained to let anger run hot and uncontrolled, so after a moment of furious internal struggle she answered dulcetly, "No, I'm sure you couldn't. When your fairy godmother waved her wand over the ducal crib, the special gifts she bestowed were stubbornness and self-righteousness."

Their eyes locked together, two angry, passionate people determined to give nothing away. Rafe counted to ten in English, then French, then Italian, reminding himself that for all the haunting flashes of Margot Ashton, this woman was a stranger, hardened and unpredictable in ways he would never understand. He was not in Paris to romance her, reminisce with her, or to make childish taunts, no matter how great the provocation.

And who was doing the provoking that time? He put the thought aside and shrugged away the insult. "No doubt you are right. To return to business, do you think Lattimer is right to be concerned? He is working mostly on guesswork." He drank a deep swallow of wine. "Of course, he is a brilliant guesser. In your professional opinion, do you think he might be right again?"

"It's entirely possible," Maggie said, happy to leave the charged emotionalism that kept surfacing in their conversation. "I have heard nothing in particular, but there *has* been a curious silence from the radicals. It isn't like them to give up as long as there are still young men left to be sent out to die for some insane revolutionary ideal."

She shook her head before saying aloud, "I'll start investigating immediately. If I hear anything I'll contact the British delegation." She stood and shook her tawny hair back as if freeing it from some tangle. "I hope you enjoy your stay in Paris, your grace. Now if you will excuse me, there are some people I must talk to."

He stood also, carefully keeping his distance. "There is one more thing: Lattimer wants you to work with me on this, not with the delegation."

"What!" Maggie was outraged. "Why on earth should I waste time dealing with an amateur? If there is a conspiracy afoot, time is critical, and at the risk of insulting your grace's consequence, you would only complicate matters."

Rafe could feel his lips tightening but his voice was level as he replied, "Lattimer fears that someone in the British delegation is either careless or treacherous and this is too important to risk. He wants you to report to me. We've set up a temporary courier service between here and London, and if events warrant, I'm to contact Castlereagh or Wellington directly."

"How nice to know that Lattimer trusts them," she said with heavy sarcasm. "However, I still prefer to use my own channels."

The duke said gently, "I am not in a position to compel you, but for the sake of the task at hand, do you think you could manage to choke down your repugnance and work with me? It shouldn't be for very long."

Maggie glared at him, suppressing the desire to pour the rest of her wine over his head to see if that would disturb his impenetrable calm. Unfortunately, there was no compelling reason not to work with him except for her personal distaste, and like it or not, she was under a heavy obligation to him. Through slightly gritted teeth, she said, "Very well, I will contact you when I have something to report."

After she set down her wineglass and opened the door to leave, he said, "Let me give you my direction."

She smiled at him wickedly. "No need. I already know where you are staying, the name of your valet, and the number of pieces of luggage you brought." Having finally managed to produce a surprised look on the Duke of Candover's face, she added sweetly, "Remember, information is my business."

Maggie felt rather pleased as she left. At least she had gotten the last word for tonight; a pity it wasn't the last word with the duke forever.

Chapter 3

Before proceeding to her next rendezvous, Margot stepped into a dark side passage for a moment to regroup her forces. Leaning against the wall and closing her eyes, she mentally went through the profanity that she knew fluently in five languages and adequately in seven more. *Damn* Robin for talking her into meeting the duke, damn the Duke of Candover for his impossible, impenetrable coldness, and damn Margot Ashton for not being as dead as Maggie had thought. Most of all, Maggie damned herself for the faint, irrepressible anticipation she felt at the thought of seeing more of Rafe Whitbourne.

She was all the way down to Slovenian curses before she could laugh and resume her journey to another assignation room, a near-twin of the one she had just left. Maggie entered without knocking and found Robin languidly reclining on the velvet sofa with a glass of wine in his hand, for all the world like a lover awaiting a lady. Which after all, she reflected, was more or less the case. More or less.

He glanced up at her, the look of fatuous vacuity he cultivated changing to amused intelligence. "Dare I ask how your confrontation with the duke came out?" he inquired lazily.

Maggie scowled, then poured herself some wine and moved Robin's feet from the sofa so she could sit down. "If you had any sense you wouldn't ask, but unfortunately I have to tell you about it. You and he win—I'll be staying through the end of the peace conference, no matter how long it takes."

Robert gave a soft whistle of surprise. He had hoped for this outcome but had considered it unlikely. "How on earth did Candover accomplish that? If he has developed some miraculous technique to handle you, I should ask him what it is."

Maggie laughed and reached over to pat his hand. "Don't waste your energy, Robin. His method was not one that anyone else could use." Her brief amusement faded and she drank deeply of the wine before saying with studied neutrality. "He had the bodies of my father and his man sent to England. They have been buried at my uncle's estate the last dozen years."

Robert looked at Maggie sharply. He had respected her reasons for leaving Paris, and while it was good that she was staying, this new fact suggested a myriad of interesting questions. How well had Maggie known the duke, and were there implications here that might affect his own plans? Keeping those questions to himself, he asked aloud, "Is it possible that he lied about that, to convince you to stay here?"

Maggie was startled by the question; it had never occurred to her to doubt Rafe's words. She did not even pause to reconsider before shaking her head. "No, he's one of your proper English gentlemen, without enough imagination to lie."

Robert smiled, looking irresistibly boyish. "Haven't I convinced you yet that not all Englishmen are gentlemen?"

"You, Robin, are *sui generis,* absolutely one of a kind. The fact that you are English is a mere accident of birth." Maggie smiled at him affectionately. In spite of all strenuous objections to the contrary, Robin was completely a gentleman, more so than Rafe Whitbourne had proved to be. Occasionally Maggie wondered idly about Robin's English background; she suspected he was the illegitimate son of a noble house, raised and educated among gentlemen but forever an outsider in the ranks of polite society. That would explain why he showed no desire to return to his native land, but she had never asked for confirmation and Robin had never volunteered.

"Your suggestion to tantalize the duke with my irresistible body was a dead loss, by the way," she added wryly. "It wouldn't have mattered if I was Helen of Troy or as ugly as Madame de Staël; the duke's noble mind is above such crass matters as lust, at least when he is engaged on His Britannic Majesty's business."

"He merely has superhuman control. Seeing you in that gown tempts me to lock the door and overpower you with kisses myself." Robin's flippant tone was belied by the serious expression in his blue eyes.

"If it's green gowns you want, mention it to that ravishing ladybird of yours and I'm sure she'll oblige," Maggie chuckled.

At Maggie's laughter, Robert withdrew his searching gaze and returned to a question he had been pondering. "Why did Candover do something as extraordinary as returning your father's body to England? It must have been very difficult to arrange."

"I imagine it was." Maggie was reluctant to tell even Robin her history with the duke. Choosing part of the truth, she said, "He and my father were friends." Before Robert could inquire further, she went on, "For your sins, you can now help me with the urgent project Candover dropped onto my plate."

Quickly she outlined what Rafe had said about a possible plot hidden in Parisian diplomatic circles. At the end, she produced the envelope Rafe had given her and drew out two sheets of closely written paper. Maggie read the first sheet, then passed it to Robin while she perused the second.

After he had looked at both papers, Robert said in a voice devoid of his earlier bantering, "This could be very serious, even more so than Lattimer could guess in London. There have been other conspiracies, but always by insignificant people far from the centers of power. This looks different."

Maggie agreed gravely. "I know. I can already think of several names to put behind this conspiracy."

Robert sighed. "So can I, all men who will be impossible to accuse without rock-solid proof, even if we were sure."

"After you and I have both checked with our informants, it may reduce the number of possibilities," Maggie suggested.

"Or it may increase them," Robin said ruefully. "Well, all we can do is get to work and hope for the best." He laughed suddenly. "You're disobeying orders—according to this, you should have nothing to do with anyone in the delegation save Castlereagh and Wellington. What if I'm Lattimer's weak link?''

''Nonsense,'' Maggie scoffed. ''he means the regular delegation, not you.''

Robert shook his head with mock sorrow as he stood. ''I can see that all my lessons have been wasted. How many times have I told you not to trust anyone, even me?''

''If I can't trust you, who can I trust?''

He stood and dropped a light kiss on Maggie's golden head. ''Yourself, of course. I'll leave first. Shall I come by tomorrow night so we can discuss our findings?''

She nodded and watched him don his low-level diplomat's face. Every delegation was cursed with junior officers who had better family connections than wits and Robin looked like one of those. Really, he seemed too good-looking to have a brain! In reality, of course, he had a mind like Saracen steel, highly polished and razor-sharp. It was he who had taught her how to gather and analyze facts that might be of value, as well as how to cover her own tracks and avoid suspicion.

But he was wrong on one count, Maggie thought as she finished her wine. At the moment, she was not at all sure she could trust herself. Her life was no longer entirely under her own control, and she didn't like it one damn bit.

After Maggie had gotten the last word and swept out of the room, the Duke of Candover gazed after her in bemusement. He had cherished romantic memories of the girl he had loved and lost, with occasional reminiscences about what might have been. It was jarring to have that nostalgia shattered by the very real presence of the former beloved, now alive, impudent, and dismayingly competent.

Rafe emptied his wineglass and set it carefully on the table. It was obvious that the girl he had loved no longer existed. Moreover, he wasn't at all sure he liked this new woman, this Maggie with her cool, polished surface and her prickiliness. She acted as if he had been the one to betray her so many years ago, not vice versa. He sighed and stood up. Most truths had more than one aspect; perhaps her memories of the incident were different from his. It didn't matter now. It takes youth to risk the appalling dangers of total love, and Rafe knew he was no longer capable of that. From all appearance, Maggie was equally incapable of such feelings, if indeed she had ever had them.

But Rafe's memory had been wrong on one point, he mused as he stepped into the corridor to return to the ball. He had thought no woman could be as desirable as his memories of Margot. As it turned out, Maggie was even more captivating than he remembered, with a sensuality that had made it hard for him to keep his hands to himself even when she was spitting insults. If they had to spend much time together, it would be difficult to maintain a proper distance.

Downstairs the ball churned on exactly as he had left it, a noisy battle of languages echoing off the high ceiling and a miasma from the hot, eager bodies hanging over the room. With his height advantage Rafe could look over the heads of most of the other guests; seeing nothing that encouraged him to stay, he started working his way across the room toward the exit. It was a crush that would have gladdened the heart of a London hostess, and his progress was slow. Because of the crowd, it was a complete surprise when he came face to face with Sir Oliver Northwood, and there was no possible way to avoid the man.

Northwood's face lit up happily but Rafe was temporarily paralyzed by shock. *Bloody hell, it only needed this!*

"Candover! Wonderful to see you! I had no idea you were in Paris, but of course, half the *ton* has come over. Too many years trapped on our island, don't you know." He laughed heartily at his own wit and offered his hand, which Rafe accepted without enthusiasm. Northwood was a beefy blond man of medium height, a younger son of Lord Northwood and almost a stereotype of the hearty country gentleman. They had been part of the same loose circle of young bucks years earlier, until Northwood's disastrous contribution to ending Rafe's engagement. He doubted the man even knew what he had done, but Rafe had avoided him with great success for most of the intervening years.

"Good evening, Northwood. Have you been in Paris long?"

"Why, I'm with the British delegation, been here since July. M'father thought I should get some diplomatic experience." Northwood shook his head mournfully. "Wants me to settle down and take a seat in Parliament, make myself useful, you know.''

The man was close to Rafe's own age and had been wasting his father's blunt for years, so Lord Northwood could be forgiven for insisting that his least rewarding son do something for the family fortunes, or so the duke thought. Given the closeness of Parisian diplomatic society, they would be running into each other often, so Rafe resigned himself to putting a good face on the relationship. He asked, ''Is Mrs. Northwood here with you?''

He was unprepared for the ugly glint that came into Northwood's eyes as they flicked across the room. ''Oh, she is here, right enough,'' he said shortly. ''She wouldn't miss the opportunity to . . . make so many new acquaintances.''

Following the direction of the glance, the duke saw Cynthia Northwood at the edge of the ballroom, in earnest conversation with a British infantry major. Even at this distance Rafe could see the tension in their bodies, the air of being alone in the room. Feeling as if he was eavesdropping, he returned his gaze to Oliver Northwood. It was time to start gathering information, so Rafe asked, ''How are the negotiations going?''

Reverting to his normal joviality, Northwood laughed. ''Hard to say. Castlereagh plays everything very close to his chest, y'know, don't let us underlings do much except copy documents. But I'm sure you've heard that the first problem has been taken care of—what to do with Napoleon. They were thinking of exiling him to Scotland but decided it was too close to Europe.''

''St. Helena is certainly far enough away to reduce the opportunities for mischief,'' Rafe agreed. ''Though it might have simplified things if General Blücher had captured Bonaparte and shot him out of hand as he wished to.''

Northwood laughed. ''It certainly would have, but once the emperor surrendered to the British, we were stuck with preserving his unworthy hide.''

''One has to admire the man's effrontery, not to mention his cunning,'' Rafe agreed. ''After calling Britain the most powerful, steadfast, and generous of his enemies, there was no way the Prince Regent could throw him to the wolves, even though most of the British people would cheerfully see Boney in hell.''

''Instead, he retires at British expense to an island that is supposed to have one of the best climates in the world,'' Northwood said grumpily. ''Still, if he'd stayed on Elba I wouldn't be here in Paris now,'' he added more cheerfully. He gave a man-to-man chuckle and said, ''It certainly is true what they say about the Parisian ladies, isn't it, Candover?''

The duke favored him with one of his coldest stares. ''I have only just arrived and have no opinion on the subject.''

Immune to setdown, Northwood glanced toward a side door in time to see Maggie return to the ball, her golden hair shimmering above the provocative green gown, looking every inch the high-born trollop. Northwood stared at her, his jaw slack, then whispered reverently, ''Say, would you look at that blond doxy! Must have been upstairs with some lucky devil. Think I'd have any success if I asked her for an encore?''

It took Rafe a moment to realize that Northwood was referring to Maggie. He had never thought of her as blond, a word that conjured up thoughts of pale anemic maidens. Maggie's glowing cream and gold vitality was too vivid to be called merely ''blond.'' Once he realized who Northwood meant, the duke felt a distaste so strong that he was tempted to practice his boxing. Instead, he said only, ''I doubt it. I met the lady briefly earlier and she struck me as particular in her tastes.''

The implied insult bounced off Northwood's impenetrable skin. ''You met her?'' he asked eagerly. ''Tell me about her. Though you know,'' he said with a frown as Maggie disappeared into a clump of Austrian officers, ''she looks familiar but I can't place her—I have it!'' he said with a snap of his thick fingers. ''She reminds me of an English girl I knew years ago. Margaret, no, Margot, something.''

''Do you mean Miss Margot Ashton?'' Rafe said icily.

''Yes, she's the one. You were after her yourself, weren't you? How was she?'' The coarse laugh left no doubt as to the kind of relationship Northwood assumed Rafe and Margot had had, and was exactly in keeping with the rest of his conversation.

"I wouldn't know," the duke said shortly. "Miss Ashton died the year after her come-out, I believe. I can see some resemblance to the lady you were admiring, but this woman is Hungarian. She's Magda, the Countess Janos."

"Hungarian, eh? I've never had a Hungarian. Will you introduce me?" Northwood said gleefully, admiring the way Maggie's gown plunged down her back.

Deciding that he had had more than enough of this mawworm's company, the duke said, "Unfortunately I am leaving for a pressing engagement, but I'm sure you can find some other mutual acquaintance. If you will excuse me. . . ?" He was on the point of breaking away when someone latched on to his right arm and he looked down into Cynthia Northwood's wide brown eyes.

"Rafe!" she said enthusiastically. "How delightful to see you here. Will you be staying in Paris for a while?"

Her firm grip on his arm prevented the duke's escape; since she had been his mistress and they had parted on friendly terms, he could hardly repulse her. Cynthia was a pretty chit, with dark curls falling around her heart-shaped face and a look of misleading innocence. As he studied her, Rafe realized that her attention was not on himself but on Oliver, as if she was fawning over the duke as a way of spiting her husband.

Gently disengaging his arm, he said politely, "Yes, I've taken apartments and intend to stay through the autumn, perhaps longer. But while I appreciate your enthusiasm for seeing an old friend, pray have a thought for my valet. He is so protective of my coats that I'm surprised he actually lets me wear them."

Cynthia released him apologetically. "Oh dear, I'm sorry. It comes from being in Paris, you know. People are so much more demonstrative here and I'm afraid it is contagious."

"Is *that* your excuse?" her husband said in an ugly voice.

Rafe could feel the undercurrents as the two glared at each other and decided that he absolutely must escape before they started a public scene of the sort he most detested. After making the barest of farewells, he slid away through the crowd, making sure that no one could catch his eye again.

Outside in the warm night air, he gave a sigh of relief.

Since he hadn't brought his carriage and it was still early, Rafe decided to walk a bit before returning to his hotel. It would be interesting to see what Napoleon had done to the city and it would give him time to get his disordered thoughts under control.

First Margot—it was hard to think of her as Maggie— whose very presence was a disruption and a reminder of things best forgotten. And then, on top of her, the Northwoods. He shook his head ruefully; the evening might have been designed by the devil in a farcical mood. But it was hard to be amused by a farce that made him feel as if he had been kicked in the stomach. As he walked obliviously toward the Tuileries, the duke was remembering it all with the sharp clarity of an event that had happened yesterday rather than thirteen years earlier.

Rafe had loved Margot Ashton with uncritical adoration, awed and humble that a woman who could have her choice of London's most eligible men had chosen him. They had behaved with circumspection in public since their engagement had been unannounced, but he had spent every possible moment with her and she had seemed as happy in his company as he was in hers.

Then had come that fatal bachelor party in June. He could remember the name of every young man in the group that night, could see with excruciating accuracy the expression of drunken delight on Oliver Northwood's face as he lovingly detailed how he had relieved Margot Ashton of her unwanted virginity in a garden during a ball some weeks earlier. Most of the young men present knew Margot and one had quickly shushed Northwood, saying it was inappropriate to mention the girl's name, but by then the damage had been done. No one present knew of the engagement, so they were unsurprised when Rafe had excused himself; the green tinge to his face was attributed to the quantity of claret he had drunk and he was forgotten as soon as he left the room.

Outside, Rafe had made it no farther than the street when he fell to his knees and began retching. Feeling as if his very guts would spew out, he thought of Margot's body under that drunken sot, her full lips kissing his, her long legs entwined . . . The vision burned on his brain with nauseating clarity, and he had no idea how long it was before someone said, "You all right, lad? I'll call a chair for you." The Samaritan helped him to his feet, but Rafe refused further aid, heading blindly down the street as if he could outrun his imagination.

The rest of the night was spent walking the streets of London, heedless of his direction. More than once lurkers in the shadows considered the richness of his attire, balanced it against the expression on his face, and decided to let him continue unmolested on his journey. The young gentleman might be worth a pretty penny but his dead gray eyes threatened disaster to any thief foolish enough to try to collect it.

Inevitable that he would end up at Margot's house early the next morning, just before she left for her dawn ride. They had no plans to meet but he had joined her unannounced before and she greeted him with surprise and delight despite his disheveled evening attire. An emerald-colored veil had floated over her wheat-gold hair as she danced across the salon for a welcoming kiss, her changeable eyes green-gold in the early morning, her laughing face brimming with vitality.

Rafe had pulled violently away, unable to bear her touch. Then he told her what he had learned, heaping abuse on her golden head. He knew her passionate nature and only his idealistic desire to bring her a virgin to their marriage bed had prevented him from taking what she had so casually given Oliver Northwood.

Besides him, how many? She was much sought after; had he been the only one too foolish to taste her luscious flesh? Had she accepted his offer among so many because he was heir to a dukedom? On those early morning rides, could he have ridden her as well as his stallion if he had had the temerity to ask?

She made no attempt to deny any of it. Had she offered the feeblest of defenses, he would have grasped it with passionate gratitude; had she wept and begged his forgiveness, he would have granted it, even knowing that she was unlikely to be faithful in the future. He would have beggared himself of his whole life's pride if she had given him the barest reason to do so.

Instead, Margot merely stood and listened, her creamy complexion turning dead white. Then she had said calmly how fortunate it was that they had discovered each other's true nature before it was too late. It had confirmed Rafe's worst fears, for he had maintained a desperate hope that the story was untrue.

Though they were not officially engaged, Rafe had given her a Whitbourne heirloom ring, which she wore on a chain around her neck. She pulled it from between her breasts, breaking the gold links in her eagerness to be free, hurling the ring to the floor at Rafe's feet with such force that the large opal cracked. Murmuring that she did not wish to keep her horse standing any longer in the cool morning, Margot had walked out with her head held high, no emotion visible.

That was the last time he saw her. The short-lived Peace of Amiens had been in effect and within days she and her father had left for the Continent. As the months passed, Rafe's fury and sense of betrayal were overcome by his longing and he found himself waiting with hope and pain for the Ashtons to return to England. After almost a year of agonizing, Rafe had gone to France, hoping to meet Margot again. If he had found her he would have begged her to marry him, even if she would accept him only for his fortune and title.

But then in Paris the news had come that it was forever too late, and the only thing left was to bring the bodies of her and her father back to England. As time passed, Rafe had convinced himself that it was fortunate that she had died before he could abase himself to her; the thought of being married to a woman before whom he was so helpless was not a pleasant one.

The Seasons and the Beauties had come and gone since then, and few remembered the glorious Margot Ashton who had been so briefly the toast of London. Rafe had learned to take his pleasures from the skilled and willing married women of his set, kissing lightly and letting go gracefully. Not for him the tawdry problems of getting birds of paradise out of the loveliest when they were loath to go; he saw no reason for a man to pay for a mistress when there were so many volunteers available for the price of a few compliments and an occasional bauble.

He had taken particular pleasure in cuckolding Oliver Northwood. Cynthia Browne had been a pretty, happy girl, the daughter of a prosperous country squire, and marrying the son of a lord was considered an excellent match. Oliver had been attractive in a bluff, blond way, and Cynthia had not realized the kind of man she was getting, with his gambling, drunkenness, and continual womanizing. Being a girl of spirit, she had decided to play her husband's game and began taking lovers of her own. The duke had been more than willing to cooperate, enjoying Cynthia's attractions and concealing his ignoble desire to revenge himself on her husband. Northwood would never know how his indiscretion had shattered Rafe's illusions, but there was still satisfaction in paying the man back in his own coin.

Cynthia was not promiscuous by nature and she had sometimes complained about Northwood's behavior. It was tragic, really; with a loving husband she would have been the most devoted of wives and mothers. Instead, she gave herself to any man who wanted her and she rapidly became embittered. Rafe had withdrawn from the affair quickly, uncomfortable with her desperation.

In the years since, he had seen Cynthia occasionally and was glad to see that she had regained her equilibrium, no longer holding herself as cheaply as she had. There had been recent rumors linking her with a soldier and the duke wondered idly if that had been the major Cynthia had met at the ball, and if she really loved the man or was using him as still another weapon in her war with her husband. Her tactics seemed to be working; Oliver Northwood was apparently the sort of man who would chase anything in skirts but was infuriated that his wife claimed the same freedom to amuse herself. One of them would probably end up murdering the other. As he went up the steps to his hotel, Rafe swore he would not let himself get caught in their crossfire. Paris promised to be unpleasant enough without that.

Chapter 4

Even before her eyes opened the next morning, Maggie remembered her encounter with the Duke of Candover with a shudder. Impossible man! Odd how in general she admired the calm control of most Englishmen but the same trait infuriated her in the duke. Whatever warmth and spontaneity he had had as a young man had obviously dissipated over time.

Lying in her bed she could hear the first early morning street noises outside, the creak of a cart, occasional footsteps, the cry of a distant rooster. Ordinarily she got up at this hour, had a cup of coffee and a hot croissant, and went for a ride out at Longchamps. This morning she just groaned and pulled the covers over her head, burrowing further into the feather mattress as she planned a busy day of spying.

Half an hour later, Maggie rang her maid Inge for breakfast. As she sipped strong French coffee, she jotted down the names of the informants she wished to contact first. While it was popularly supposed that a female spy gathered information on her back, Maggie scorned that method as too limited, tiring, and indiscriminate. Her technique was entirely different, and as far as she knew, it was unique: she had formed the world's first female spy network. When men talked of their secrets, they might be cautious in front of other men but were often amazingly casual in front of women. Maids, washerwomen, prostitutes, and other humble females were often in a position to learn what was going on, and Maggie had a talent for getting them to confide in her.

Europe was full of women who had lost fathers, husbands, sons, and lovers in Bonaparte's wars; many were easily persuaded to pass on information that might contribute to peace. Some of them wanted revenge much as Maggie did, many were impoverished and desperately needed money. Together, they made up what Robin admiringly called "Maggie's Militia."

Pieces of vital documents could be put together from scraps in trash baskets, important papers were sometimes left in the pockets of clothes sent for washing, men bragged of their deeds to their conquests. Maggie cultivated the women who had access to such data, listening to their joys and sorrows, sometimes giving them money to feed their children even when they had no information to sell. In return, they gave her loyalty beyond anything that could be purchased. She was reasonably sure that none had ever betrayed her and many had become friends.

Since losing her father, Maggie had spent about half her time in Paris, most of it disguised as a humble widow with brown hair and a padded figure. When the Congress of Vienna was called, Maggie had become the Countess Janos and resumed her natural appearance so she could move among the diplomats at their social level. Then Napoleon had returned from Elba for his Hundred Days and she had left Vienna, still in her countess guise, and come back to Paris to send what information she could to the Allies.

Over the years Robert Anderson had played many parts. He was the spymaster who gave her the money to live comfortably and to pay her informants and he had helped her establish her network and her lines of communication, a difficult task when Napoleon's Continental System had closed almost all European ports to the British. At various times intelligence had been sent through Spain, Sweden, Denmark, and even Constantinople. Many times Maggie suspected that Robin himself had carried it to England, traveling secretly with smugglers. It was dangerous work and she was always relieved when he reappeared, jaunty and intact. He spent about a third of his time with Maggie, though sometimes months would pass between visits.

For many of those years they had been lovers until suddenly, three years before, Maggie had felt it was no longer the right thing to do. Robin had accepted her decision with good grace. He had offered to marry her once, shortly after he had saved her life, and had certainly been relieved to be turned down then. Perhaps he feared she would ask him to repeat his offer and he would be honor-bound to marry her.

Maggie smiled over the list of names she was compiling, wondering if Robin really thought she would hold him against his will. He was her best friend, the man she trusted most in the world, the brother she never had, and she would never trap him into a marriage that might destroy their friendship. But still, her bed had been cold and lonely these last years. With all she had been through one would think that Maggie should have outgrown her proper English upbringing, but she could never be casual about where she gave her body.

Robin had recently emerged from the murkier pools of spying to attach himself to the British embassy in an unobtrusive secretarial position. Maggie assumed that his identity was known to Lord Castlereagh, but the rest of the mission probably thought he was an agreeable rattle of no particular value. She took comfort in the fact that he was nearby, not hundreds of miles away, amid unknown dangers.

After assuming her inconspicuous widow costume, Maggie set off to learn what her women knew and to instruct them on what to look for. With luck, her friend Hélène Sorel would soon be back in Paris and able to assist in the task.

Over *pot au feu,* a long *baguette* of bread, and a jug of wine, Maggie and Robert discussed their discoveries. Splitting the last of the wine between them, Maggie said, "We are agreed then?"

"Yes, the three men we have decided on are the most likely masterminds behind this, though we'll have to watch half a dozen more. Even then," Robin sighed, running his hand through his fair hair, "we may not have the right man."

"Well, it is the best we can do. I suppose we could warn the guards around the most important persons, but there have been so many other plots that most are already cautious."

"True." Robin sipped his wine while he studied Maggie's face. There were shadows under the changeable gray-green eyes, as if she had slept badly. He said slowly, "I have an idea you are not going to like."

Maggie's mouth quirked up. "I have disliked the majority of your ingenious ideas over the years so don't let that stop you."

Refusing to respond to her teasing, he said, "I think that you and Candover should pretend you are lovers."

"What!" Maggie banged her glass down so sharply the wine sloshed out. "Of what possible value would that be?"

"Hear me out, Maggie. Most of our suspects are senior aides and divide their time between fighting over the treaty and attending salons and balls with the rest of the diplomats. The best way to approach them is by going to the same places."

"Can't you do that?" she asked mutinously.

"I am not important enough. A junior clerk would look out of place at the more exclusive functions."

"Why can't I go to them alone?"

Robin said patiently, "Maggie, you're being difficult. It was bad enough going to that Austrian ball alone; if you make a habit of that, you'll be too conspicuous. It will be assumed you are looking for a lover and you'll spend all your time fighting off men who are interested in you for nonpolitical reasons."

"I have had ample experience dealing with that!"

Ignoring her interjection, he continued, "Candover is a perfect escort: he's important enough to be invited everywhere and is not known to be political. And, of course, he's a friend of Lattimer's and is here to help investigate this conspiracy. If you and he go around making cow-eyes at each other, you can go anywhere and talk to anyone without rousing suspicion."

"Do you think it is really necessary that I do this, Robin?" Maggie said, fighting a valiant rear-guard action.

"Yes, your intuition is the best weapon we've got." He caught her eye, trying to impress his opinion on her. "Time and again you have felt there was something wrong about a person we had no reason to suspect, and have been proved right. In the absence of hard evidence we are going to need every advantage we have, which means you must get well enough acquainted with our suspects to develop an opinion and perhaps pick up some clues. But you can't do that unless you get close."

"No, you're right. If I knew them well they wouldn't be on the list because I would already have an excellent notion of their innocence or guilt," Maggie admitted. "But I don't know if I can make convincing cow-eyes at Candover. I am more likely to throw a glass of wine in his arrogant face."

Robert chuckled, knowing he had won his point. "I'm sure that someone of your magnificent acting skills can do a good job of draping yourself over the duke. In fact, I should think most women would envy you the job."

Ignoring her snort, he added, "Besides . . ." He hesitated, then continued when she looked at him curiously. "This could be very dangerous, much more so than the sort of work you usually do. We are talking about desperate men, and time is running out for them—the Allied monarchs are all anxious to finalize the treaty and get home to their kingdoms. They should be gone by the end of September at the latest, so if anything is going to happen, it will be in the next two or three weeks."

"So?" she prompted.

"If someone suspects you, your life could be forfeit," he said bluntly. "Candover might not be a professional spy, but he looks like a good man in a fight. I won't be near you most of the time, so it will be good if the duke is."

Her cheeks reddening, Maggie snapped, "Since when have you decided I am incapable of taking care of myself?"

"Maggie," he said gently, "there are times when no one person can do it all, no matter how clever he or she is."

Her face whitened at the reference. Robert didn't like reminding her of the circumstances of their first meeting but wanted to ensure that she was cautious; he knew from experience that Maggie was brave to the point of foolhardiness.

After a moment Maggie smiled and said with resignation, "Very well, Robin. Assuming the duke can be convinced, he and I shall become an *on-dit* for a while. We will be seen everywhere, and will appear so enraptured that no one will suspect us of having a useful thought in our heads."

"Good." He stood. "I must leave now. There is someone I must meet who can never be found by the light of day."

Maggie rose also. "Since time is in short supply, I will pay a visit to Candover and explain his dire fate to him. But if he objects, I will give you the job of convincing him."

Robert shook his head. "I think it better that he not know of our connection. You know the first rule of spying."

She nodded. *" 'Never tell anyone anything they don't need to know.'* No doubt you're right; he is an amateur at these games."

"Yes. Let us hope that he proves a talented one." After a quick kiss on her cheek, Robert was gone. Maggie looked after him with vexation. Here he was, worried about her safety, when she expected that what he was doing was twice as dangerous. She shrugged and climbed the stairs to her room. If she had been of a worrying disposition, she would never have lasted long in the spy business. Far better to spend her time wondering how she was going to tolerate so much time around Rafael Whitbourne.

The Duke of Candover had attended the theater with a group of English visitors and found the evening disquieting. The Parisians were passionately devoted to the theater, and the many playhouses were a barometer of society. The performance had been good but there were odd, dangerous undercurrents. An order had been given to the managers of all city theaters to admit free of charge a certain number of soldiers from the armies of occupation; what was intended as a good-will gesture had tonight resulted in brawling in the pit between Frenchmen and Allied soldiers. Fortunately, no one had been seriously injured but the play had been disrupted for almost half an hour.

On returning to his rooms, Rafe was lost in thought when he entered his bedchamber. He was about to ring for his valet when a cool voice emerged from a shadowed corner. "I'd like a word with you before you retire, your grace."

The voice was unmistakable—honey with a touch of gravel—and he knew who it was even before his eyes had adjusted to the dim candlelight. Maggie was casually sprawled across a chair, dressed entirely in dark men's clothes, her bright hair covered with a scarf and a black cloak tossed across the bed. Rafe wondered how the devil she had gotten in but refused to give her the satisfaction of asking. Instead he said, "Are you practicing to be a Shakespearean heroine—Viola, perhaps?"

She gave an unexpected peal of laughter. "Actually, I rather fancy myself as Rosalind."

He removed his coat and dropped it over the sofa. "I assume you have a reason for being here that is different from what a gentleman usually expects on finding a lady in his bedchamber."

The remark was a mistake; she gave him a dagger look and said, "You assume rightly. There are a number of things we must discuss and this seemed quickest and most private."

Rafe nodded in acceptance and said, "Care to join me in some cognac?" Pouring them each a glass from the decanter his valet had placed on a sideboard, he sat in a chair at right angles to his visitor. "What have you discovered?"

She swished the brandy around in the glass before taking a sip, then said, "My sources indicate three principal suspects and several minor ones. They are all prominent men, the kind usually considered above suspicion, and all have the ability and the motivation to plan this kind of conspiracy."

Her high cheekbones were impossibly dramatic in the candlelight, and strands of golden hair escaped from the scarf to glow around her face, softening the starkness of her garb. With an effort Rafe forced himself to concentrate on her words.

Maggie said, "In no particular order, the prime suspects are a Prussian, Colonel Karl von Fehrenbach, and two Frenchmen: Count Armand de Varenne and General Michel Roussaye."

Sipping the brandy, he asked, "What would be their motives?"

"The Count de Varenne is an Ultra-Royalist, a close associate of King Louis's brother, the Count d'Artois. As I'm sure you know, d'Artois is a fanatic reactionary. He and his emigré friends want to wipe out every trace of revolutionary spirit in France and take it back to the *ancien régime.*"

She shrugged and made a French gesture of exasperation.

"Of course that is impossible—one might as well try to hold back the tide—but they won't accept that. Varenne has spent the last twenty years skulking around Europe on dubious royalist business. Some of his . . . past projects qualify him for our list."

"I see," Rafe said, stretching his long legs out before him and crossing them at the ankles. It was interesting to hear Maggie's analysis of the local situation and he was beginning to enjoy himself. "If this plot comes from the Ultra-Royalists, who do you think it would be aimed at?"

She paused, then said, "This may sound far-fetched but perhaps Varenne might try to assassinate King Louis himself so the Count d'Artois would become king. D'Artois would never condone having his brother killed, but it is not impossible that Varenne would take matters into his own hands."

Rafe whistled softly at the idea. It would never have occurred to him but in the context of present-day France anything might happen. "What about the other Frenchman?"

"Roussaye is a Bonapartist who was born the son of a draper and fought his way up to being one of Boney's top generals. If the wars had continued he would have ended up a marshal, if he hadn't gotten killed first. He is tough and brave and absolutely dedicated to Napoleon and the revolution. He is on Talleyrand's staff, dealing with questions relating to the French army."

"Who would be his most likely target?"

Maggie shrugged. "From his point of view, almost anyone important would do. The militant Bonapartists are convinced that the quickest way to make the French people rise up again would be to humiliate them with a harsh treaty, and they are probably right. Our British negotiators, Castlereagh and Wellington, are very aware of that and have been doing their best to ensure a moderate settlement. If anything happened to either of them, particularly Wellington, the revolutionaries will certainly get all the humiliation they could want."

Rafe frowned. "And Europe might be at war again within a year or two." Wellington was the hero of Europe and his prestige was immense. He had never been defeated in battle and the British considered him a demigod. "There have been other attempts to assassinate Wellington that have failed.''

"Even a charmed life may eventually run out," Maggie said dryly. "Personally I think he is the most likely target, but it is impossible to get him to take precautions. He is not vainglorious but thinks it cowardly to appear to value his own life too much. If anything happens to him, Britain will be baying after France's blood as much as the Prussians are.''

"Speaking of Prussians, what about Colonel von Fehrenbach?''

Maggie finished her cognac, then got up to replenish the two glasses. Rafe admired the way her skin-tight pantaloons fit; he had never realized quite how shapely her legs were. Perhaps women should be encouraged to wear men's clothes more often.

Oblivious of the duke's scrutiny, Maggie sat down again and said, "The colonel is a typical Prussian and hates the French in a pure, uncomplicated way. Von Fehrenbach was an aide of Marshal Blücher's and is now a military attaché with the Prussian delegation.''

She stared down at her brandy as if divining the past, then said slowly, "It is much easier for the British to behave with restraint than the other Allies. Considering how horribly the nations of Europe have suffered, it is no wonder the Prussians and Russians and Austrians are determined to make France pay. France has sowed the wind and is reaping the whirlwind.''

"How do *you* think France should be treated?" Rafe asked softly, knowing her personal reasons for hatred.

Maggie looked up at him, her gray eyes cool and steady, and said, "If Napoleon stood before a firing squad, I would pull a trigger myself. But someone must stop the hating or there will be no end to it. Castlereagh and Wellington are right: destroying France's pride and power will create another monster to rise up and fight again. If anything happens to either of them . . .'' She shrugged eloquently and looked back into her brandy.

Rafe took her meaning. "They and the tsar are really all that stand between France and a vengeful Europe. Do you think von Fehrenbach might want to assassinate one of those three?''

Maggie frowned. "I think he would be more interested in getting rid of Talleyrand and Fouché. They are Frenchmen who served both the revolution and the royalists and they lead the French negotiations against the four Allies. An honest Prussian would despise them for being turncoats and von Fehrenbach might want to kill them simply because they are who they are."

"Now that you have given me a lesson on the politics of the conference, what do we do about it?"

Rafe's voice was a lazy drawl and Maggie studied him without enthusiasm; the time had come to present Robin's plan. "It is necessary to meet the men I have described and to observe them more closely. I have a talent for spotting villains and once I have talked to our possibilities I might be able to guess which one is our man. Even if we can't prove it, it will give us an idea which direction the blow is likely to fall."

She paused, then said levelly, "Distasteful as the idea is, it is expedient that the two of us act as lovers. That way we can mingle with the diplomatic corps inconspicuously, going to all the salons and theaters and balls. You are prominent enough to be invited everywhere, and you can take me as your mistress."

Maggie resented the way his eyebrows rose with ironic amusement. "That seems a reasonable plan, but do you think you can bear that much of my company?"

"I can bear whatever is necessary," Maggie said shortly, "no matter how distasteful I find it."

Her mood was not improved when Rafe laughed aloud. "A palpable hit! But it illustrates my point. Do you think you can restrain yourself from sinking your claws into my unworthy flesh?"

Maggie stood and said blandly, "In public, my behavior will be all one could expect of a brainless, infatuated female."

He stood also and looked down with a smile lurking in his gray eyes. "That being the only kind that would be interested in me?" As her eyes sparked, he added softly, "What will you be like in private?"

Maggie was furious with herself for leaving such a wide opening. Until this moment, she had thought strictly as a professional spy dealing with another such. Now she suddenly felt like a woman who had invaded a man's bedroom, and it was not a comfortable feeling. The duke stood no more than two feet away and he towered over her, but it was not a physical threat she felt; the damned man would never have had to use force in his life. All he need do to persuade a woman was to smile that lazy, entrancing smile, exactly as he was doing now. . . .

She stepped away from him abruptly. "There won't be any 'private.' This is strictly a business arrangement." Pulling a paper from an inside pocket, she handed it to him and said, "Here are the names and a brief summary of seven other men who are possible suspects. Read it and destroy it before you go out tomorrow morning. I didn't mention them because I don't want to confuse you with too much information, but all are possibilities and should be observed carefully if you chance to meet one."

As Rafe took the paper, she added, "There is a reception tomorrow night at the British Embassy for the Prussian delegates and von Fehrenbach should be there. I live at 17 Boulevard des Capucines. Will you be able to call for me about eight o'clock?"

Rafe nodded, then asked, "By the way, what does your husband think of your activities?"

"My *what?*" Maggie stared at him in surprise.

"Why, the Count Janos, of course," he said in a dulcet tone.

The question tickled Maggie's sense of humor and her eyes brimmed with laughter as she clasped her hands before her heart. "Oh, my darling Andrei!" she sighed with a nostalgic flutter of her lashes. "He was matchless—utterly beautiful in his Hussar uniform, and *such* a pair of shoulders!"

"Is the matchless count still among the living?"

"Alas, his noble life was lost at the Battle of Leipzig. Or perhaps it was at Austerlitz."

"Over nine years lay between those two battles. Did you misplace him for all that time?" Rafe asked with interest, "or merely decide that you didn't suit?"

Maggie waved her hand airily and lifted her cloak, swirling the dark folds around her shoulders. "Ah, well, they say that spending too much time together is bad for a marriage."

"Do they, indeed? Why do I have the feeling that you are no more a countess than I am?"

Maggie was heading toward the window but she flashed an impish smile over her shoulder. "I, at least, have the possibility of becoming a countess, which is more than you can say," she said flippantly.

As she pushed the drapery aside, Rafe chuckled and said, "Wouldn't it be easier to leave by the doorway?"

"Easier," she admitted, "but I have a reputation to maintain. Good night, your grace." As the dark figure slipped behind the draperies, a faint breeze eddied into the room.

Rafe walked leisurely to the window and looked out. She had vanished, but there was some very stout vine growing up the wall; it would present no great challenge to an active person. He shook his head in amusement and dropped the drapery. She was quite right; while he had an earldom among his titles, he would never be a countess. So she didn't have a husband, he mused, and they were going to be spending a good deal of time together, acting the part of lovers. He could feel his lips curving into a smile. It promised to be a most interesting few weeks.

The Englishman had been blindfolded for his trip through the Paris streets, and he suspected that the carriage had driven in circles to confuse him. His mouth was dry and he swallowed hard, anxious about this upcoming meeting. The man who had summoned him was known only as *Le Serpent,* and like the snake he was named for, he was regarded with fear and loathing by those few people who knew of his existence. The Englishman had no desire to make *Le Serpent*'s acquaintance, but had no choice in the matter.

The carriage rumbled to a halt. It was a common, shabby hackney and the silent man waiting inside had blindfolded the Englishman as soon as they had picked him up. How long had they been circling—fifteen minutes? thirty? Time was curiously hard to judge when one was helpless.

A whiff of fresher air entered the malodorous hackney as the door was opened, and the silent escort grasped the Englishman's upper arm to jerk him out of the carriage and across a narrow strip of pavement, indifferent to the fact that his blindfolded charge stumbled and nearly fell. In seconds they were inside a building, down a stairway, then walking along a narrow, echoing passage. After a very long walk and a climb up more stairs, the escort stopped, there was the sound of a turning knob, then the Englishman was thrust into a room. He raised one hand to remove the blindfold but stopped at the sound of a sibilant voice.

"I would not advise you to do that, *mon Anglais*. If you saw my face, I should have to kill you, which would be a great waste, as I have better uses for you."

The Englishman dropped his hand, demoralized by being blind and alone. He tried to speak bravely, but feared that the result was closer to bravado. "Don't waste my time with threats, *Le Serpent*. You must like the information I supply you or you would not be paying me for it. What is so important that you decided to meet me in person for the first time?"

There was a throaty chuckle. "The tidbits you gave me in the past were useful, but they are trivial compared to what I need from you now. Over the next few weeks, I want complete information on the movements of Lord Castlereagh and the Duke of Wellington, plus daily reports on what the delegation is doing."

"I'm not in a position to know all of that."

"Then find someone who is, *mon Anglais*."

The menace in the silky tone was unmistakable even though *Le Serpent* apparently spoke in a disguised voice. The sweating Englishman realized that he didn't even know the nationality of his dangerous employer. Considering what a political stew Paris was, the wretched man could be anything. Not for the first time, the Englishman wished he had never gotten involved in this, but it was too late for regret: *Le Serpent* knew far too much about him. Sullenly he said, "It may cost extra to learn more. Most of the staff won't talk at all, and those who do are expensive."

"You will be reimbursed for expenses, as long as they

are legitimate. I will not pay for your whores and gambling.''

Sweat formed under the blindfold as the Englishman wondered if *Le Serpent* knew about the money skimmed from the sum provided to pay lesser informants. It had been unwise to appropriate some for his own use, but if he hadn't paid that particular gambling debt, he might have lost his position with the delegation, which would have been disastrous. Keeping his voice as steady as possible, he said, ''You need have no fears on that score.''

''How comforting,'' *Le Serpent* said with unmistakable irony. ''You may send me your reports the usual way. Remember, I want daily information—matters are becoming critical. You will be informed when I need to see you in person again. Now go.''

As the escort came and led him from the room, the Englishman speculated about what was brewing. If he knew what *Le Serpent* had in mind, the information could be very valuable. The danger lay in the fact that he wouldn't know where to sell it unless he discovered who the snake was. But when was profit without danger?

Chapter 5

After Inge had dressed her for the reception, Maggie dismissed her maid and studied her reflection with clinical detachment. This evening she wore a low-cut, coral-pink gown that guaranteed that she would be noticed. Gold chains wound around her neck and her shining, wheat-colored hair was twisted into an elaborate knot high on her head, with ringlets falling over her bare shoulders.

Since her appearance was satisfactory, Maggie was free to think about the Duke of Candover. It was important to understand her feelings before they began their charade, because she found that her emotions fluctuated wildly when she was near him, from exasperation to amusement, and the project they were embarking on was too important to be endangered by personal issues.

Granted, Rafe had acted very badly when he ended their engagement, but she had not been without blame in the affair. He had made amends for that particular sin when he had taken the bodies back to England. It was a strange, generous gesture to make on behalf of a woman he had claimed to despise, but whatever his motives had been, he had balanced the scales between them.

On the whole, perhaps it would be best to pretend they had met just two days before. She would accept him as an attractive, enigmatic man who shared her desire to uncover a dangerous plot: no more, no less. A pity he was so handsome; it complicated matters. The duke was used to getting what he wanted, and he would probably want Maggie herself, simply because she was there, and because he had *not* had her all those years ago.

Maggie knew the duke's type; a complete lack of response would intrigue him since he was accustomed to women falling into his arms. Therefore, her best approach would be friendliness, tempered with a wistful regret that business prevented her from getting on closer terms with him. That should flatter him enough so that he wouldn't feel compelled to prove his masculine powers.

Her reflection looked back at her, cool, glamorous and self-possessed. That image was her armor in the covert wars she had fought, and it was very effective. Though the features were identical, it was not the face of Margot Ashton, daughter of Colonel Gerald Ashton and fiancée to Rafael Whitbourne. Where had she gone, that impetuous girl who had been so disastrously honest, and who had been so unable to control her temper when it mattered most? Gone to where all youth and innocence went.

Fortunately, Inge entered to say that her escort had arrived and Maggie was able to turn away from her mirror. After living so long among the French, she was developing their deplorable habit of morose philosophizing. Thank God she had been born an Englishwoman, with all the pragmatism of her race.

The Duke of Candover looked impossibly handsome, and he wore his impeccably tailored black evening clothes with the same graceful unconcern that he would have bestowed on his oldest riding clothes. If he was impressed by Maggie's flamboyant appearance, it showed only in the faint lift of a dark eyebrow. Offering his arm, he murmured, "Is this the same urchin who scrambled out of my bedroom last night?"

Maggie found herself smiling at him. It shouldn't be so very difficult to stay on amiable terms with the duke. "You have urchins in your bedroom, your grace? Of which sex?"

As they stepped out through the door a hint of smile played around his mouth. "It was hard to say, and alas, I did not have the opportunity to investigate more carefully."

Outside, his carriage waited, resplendent in gleaming black and burgundy, the four black horses perfectly matched and the Candover crest lacquered on each door. The duke handed Maggie in, then settled on the seat opposite as the carriage set off. After a few minutes of unstressed silence had passed, Maggie said, "You had best call me Magda. I suppose you could get away with Maggie, since you are English, but never, *never* call me Margot. It might raise questions, which would not be wise."

"Odd, really," he remarked. "When you were English, you had a French name, now that you are claiming to be Hungarian, you think of yourself as a good British Maggie."

"If only that were the least of my oddities," she replied with an exaggerated sigh.

"Dare I ask what the others are?"

"Not if you value your longevity, your grace," Maggie said in a voice dripping with mock menace.

"You really must call me Rafe, my dear, since we are supposed to be on terms of intimacy."

"Never fear," Maggie laughed. "I will be so convincing that even you will have trouble remembering that this is a charade. Just mind that you *do* remember," she added with a trace of acid in her voice.

Rafe was unsure what had caused her change of attitude, but it was a relief to find Maggie in this relaxed, teasing mood rather than bristling defensively.

"We should speak French now," Maggie said in that language.

Rafe listened with interest. "Is that French with a Magyar accent that you are speaking?"

"Of course! Am I not a Hungarian countess?" Maggie laughed, then continued with a different accent. "Do not answer that, Rafe, it was an entirely rhetorical question. Of course it is a pity to waste my pure Parisian," then she shifted again, "but as long as I don't speak with an English accent, I will not disgrace myself."

It was startling to hear her shift through three completely different modes of speech. Rafe could tell that the Parisian and English-accented versions were flawless and was willing to take the Magyar one on faith. "How on earth do you do that?"

Maggie shrugged. "It is a knack I was born with, like musical pitch. I can duplicate any accent after hearing it spoken for a while. Then I will continue to speak it without thinking until I consciously choose to use another. Here, of course, I will restrict myself to Magyar-accented French, since that is how people know I speak."

"That is quite a gift," the duke said admiringly, "and it explains why a Prussian, an Italian, and a Frenchman all swore to Lord Lattimer that you were one of their nationals."

"Really?" Maggie asked with delight. "I wonder who they were. Though perhaps I could guess. That shows the drawback of an ear for languages. It is not a good thing to have too many identities, you know; there is always the risk of meeting someone from an earlier incarnation."

"I can see the problem," Rafe agreed. "You could not afford too close an investigation of your activities."

They halted in the line of carriages waiting to discharge passengers in front of the torch-lit British Embassy and soon they were among the crowd in the receiving line. The building was magnificent; Rafe remembered that the Duke of Wellington had bought it a year earlier from the Princess Borghese, Napoleon's notorious sister Pauline. As Rafe and Maggie progressed down the line, she snuggled close to him, and whispered seductively, "A sculpture of the Princess Borghese was done by the great Canova. When one of her friends asked how she could bear to pose in the nude, she smiled innocently and said that it was no problem at all because there was a fire in the studio.''

Rafe laughed, then whispered into one elegant ear, ''Were all the stories about the princess true?''

Maggie chuckled richly and fluttered her eyelashes, ''Very true. They say she conquered as many men as her brother, but her methods were much more . . . shall we say, intimate?''

Lightly touching the back of her slim waist to guide her forward, Rafe was aware that to many watchers they must present a perfect tableau of intoxicated new lovers. As Maggie continued her scandalous commentary, he admired her sparkling eyes and full, kissable lips and began to wonder just how far she would go in the interests of verisimilitude. Not as far as he would like, regrettably; she had made that quite clear.

The duke was interested to note that everyone seemed to know Maggie and there were numerous salutations and kisses for the dearest countess. After exchanging greetings with Lord and Lady Castlereagh, the Duke of Wellington, and other dignitaries, they plunged into the chattering crowd in the main reception room. Maggie stayed close, one arm tucked possessively in Rafe's as they made their way around the room. He knew most of the British aristocrats present, and she seemed to know everyone else.

The better part of an hour was spent in meeting people and sipping champagne. Rafe was amused to see how the men looked at him with curiosity or envy to determine how he had won such an enchanting creature. It was equally amusing to see how the women would look Rafe up and down, then give Maggie the same kind of look. Gratifying to know they were both considered such prizes.

How did Maggie contrive to look so exotic and un-English? Certainly, she had those bold eastern cheekbones, and she used her hands with continental verve, but it was more than that. When she pressed against him in the crush, he could smell her scent very clearly. That explained part of it; not for Maggie the delicate floral fragrances of England. Instead, she wore a complex, spicy blend that hinted of silk roads and China routes. Scent was a primitive but powerful form of identification, and to be around her was to think of the mysteries of central Asia.

Maggie had been quite accurate earlier when she said she would be convincing; she very nearly had Rafe himself thinking they were engaged in a torrid affair. When the changeable eyes, brimming with mirth, met his, or when she snuggled against him, he was tempted to whisper in her ear that surely they would enjoy themselves more in a place of greater privacy. He would have suggested that to any other woman who was making his blood race like Maggie was; that coral silk dress caressed her magnificent figure so lovingly that he desired to do the same.

But it was all charade, and when he looked away long enough to cool his rude male instincts a bit, he realized there was a method to the way Maggie was steering him across the room. Though she stopped to introduce Rafe frequently, they were drawing ever closer to a tall, pale man in the uniform of a Prussian colonel. He stood unmoving in a circle of silence, his back against the wall. Occasionally he nodded to someone but he made no attempt to participate in the frivolity around him.

Rafe bent his head to ask, "Is that von Fehrenbach?"

"Yes." When she lifted her head to reply, their lips almost met and she flinched her face away from him slightly. Obviously there were limits to how far she was willing to take acting.

Ignoring that brief, telltale withdrawal, the duke asked, "Do you know him?"

"Not really. I was introduced to him once, but he avoids most social gatherings. He wouldn't be here tonight if this affair wasn't in honor of Marshal Blücher."

As they drew closer, Rafe could see that the colonel had the dueling scars so dear to the heart of German military men, and his blond hair was so fair that it appeared almost white in the candlelight. He would have been handsome if his face hadn't held chilly distaste for the people around him.

When they drew close enough, Maggie gushed, "Colonel von Fehrenbach! What a pleasure to see you again." Extending her hand, she said with a twinkle, "I am the Countess Janos. We met at the last Russian review of troops, you'll recall.''

It was by no means clear that the colonel did recall it, but he was not devoid of manners and he bowed punctiliously over her hand. As he straightened up and got a better look at the plunging coral neckline of her gown, Rafe was glad to see the colonel's expression thaw a bit; it proved the man was human.

When Maggie introduced her companion, the colonel gave a slight, stiff bow. His pale blue eyes were exactly level with Rafe's, and the duke felt a faint chill when their gazes connected. Von Fehrenbach looked as if he had gone into hell, and not come all the way back.

Maggie glanced across the room at Marshal Blücher and said artlessly, ''What a privilege it must be to serve the Field Marshal. We shall not see another like him.''

Von Fehrenbach nodded gravely. ''Indeed. He is the bravest and most honorable of men.''

Delicately baiting, Maggie said, ''Such a pity that people do not fully appreciate the part he played at Waterloo. For all of Wellington's brilliance, who knows what might have happened if Marshal Blücher hadn't arrived when he did?''

Rafe wondered if Maggie might be overdoing her enthusiasm, but von Fehrenbach looked at her with definite approval.

''You are very perceptive, Countess. After all, Wellington had never faced the Emperor before; it is not impossible that Napoleon might have turned defeat into victory.''

Rafe felt a prickle of chauvinistic irritation. Wellington had never been defeated in his entire career, and the battle of Waterloo had already been won by the time Blücher had arrived at seven in the evening. However, he wisely kept his mouth shut while Maggie continued her admiring chatter.

''They say the Marshal was told he would never reach Wellington in time, and that he should not even try.''

''That is true,'' the colonel confirmed with signs of animation. ''But the Marshal refused to listen to such talk. Though ill, he led the march, swearing that he had given his word to Wellington, and nothing in heaven or hell would stop him.''

"Were you with him?" Maggie said, her eyes wide.

"I had that honor. The Marshal was an inspiration, a true soldier and a man of complete integrity." Von Fehrenbach's eyes chilled. "Not like these despicable, lying French."

Maggie gestured vaguely. "Surely not all the French are devoid of honor."

"No? With a king who fled his own capital and slunk back in the baggage train of the Allies? With turncoats like Talleyrand leading them? France rose up behind the Corsican when he returned from Elba, and she deserves to be punished. Her lands should be divided up and given to other nations, her people humiliated, her very name wiped from the map of Europe."

Von Fehrenbach's words were an angry torrent, and Rafe was shocked by his intensity. This was a dangerous man, and he looked quite capable of destroying any Frenchman that crossed his path.

Maggie said softly, her eyes locked with von Fehrenbach's, "But have we not learned anything in two thousand years? Shall there be only vengeance, with no place for forgiveness?"

He shrugged dismissively. "You are a woman. It is not to be expected that you would understand such things."

Deciding that he had been silent long enough, Rafe interjected, "I do not suffer from the countess's failing in that regard, but I agree with her that vengeance may not be the best course. To humiliate a losing opponent is to make an implacable enemy. It is better to help him rise and keep his dignity."

The pale blue eyes shifted from Maggie to Rafe. "You English and your obsession with sportsmanship and fair play," he said with contempt. "That is all very well with boxing and games, but we are talking about war. It was the French who taught my people what we know about savagery and destruction, and it is a lesson we have learned well. Would you be so fair-minded if your lands had been burned, your family murdered?"

There was such sharp anguish in the colonel's voice that Rafe backed away from what he might have said. Instead, he replied quietly, "I would like to think that I would try, but I don't know if I would be successful."

The tension eased and von Fehrenbach retreated behind his impassive mask. "I am glad to hear you admit doubt. Every other Briton in Paris seems to think he has all the answers."

It could have been taken as an insult but Rafe let the comment pass. He touched the back of Maggie's right arm, silently questioning whether it was time they left, but before either of the three could move, a woman joined them. She was small and had a sweetly pretty face framed in soft brown curls. Her rounded body was more sensual than elegant, but her blue satin gown showed the unmistakable flair of a Frenchwoman.

"Hélène, my dear, you are looking very well. It has been too long," Maggie reached her hands out in delighted greeting.

The newcomer kissed Maggie's cheek and smiled. "My dear countess, it is a pleasure to see you again. I have only just returned to the city."

Her voice had the same sweetness as her face, and Rafe did not miss her slight flickering glance at the colonel. Maggie introduced her to the two men as Mme. Sorel. After offering her hand and a curtsy to the duke, the Frenchwoman turned to the Prussian and said, "Colonel von Fehrenbach and I are acquainted."

The colonel's face pokered up even more, if that was possible, and he said, "Indeed we are," in a voice that could only be described as forbidding. Rafe sensed undercurrents and wondered if Maggie knew what, if anything, lay between the two.

Before Mme. Sorel could reply, von Fehrenbach said, "If you will excuse me, I must go attend Marshal Blücher. Ladies, your grace." He nodded coolly, then escaped, his back ramrod straight.

Turning to her friend, Maggie exclaimed, "What on earth did you do to the man, Hélène, to make him bolt like a cavalryman?"

Mme. Sorel shrugged, the movement causing a charming ripple of curves. "Nothing. I have met him several times at various functions. He always glares at me as if I were Napoleon himself, then walks away. Who knows what might be on his mind? Except that he has no use for anything or anyone French.''

Studying her friend with shrewdly narrowed eyes, Maggie said, ''But he is a fine figure of a man, no?''

Hélène said dryly, ''He is not a man, he is a Prussian.'' After exchanging a few more remarks, she took her leave with a charming smile.

With male appreciation, Rafe watched her walk away as he asked, ''What was going on there that I did not understand?''

''I'm not sure,'' Maggie said thoughtfully, ''though I might hazard a few guesses.'' Glancing up at the duke, she said, ''I will be back in a few minutes.''

As she headed for the ladies' retiring room, Rafe compared her walk with Mme. Sorel's, and decided that while the Frenchwoman was well worth watching, it was amazing Maggie didn't have crowds of men following her down the street. His pleasant thoughts were interrupted by the regrettable Oliver Northwood.

''Congratulations, Candover, you *are* a fast worker. Three days in Paris and you've captured the countess.'' Northwood's words were jovial but his beefy face was malicious as he added, ''Not that she's hard to capture, for a man who has the price.''

Turning to give Northwood his coldest stare, Rafe said, ''I thought you were unacquainted with the lady.''

''After you told me her name, I made inquiries. No one knows much except that she's a widow, she's received everywhere, and she has expensive tastes.'' Laughing coarsely, he continued, ''She's very good at getting others to pay for her pleasures.''

Instead of burying his fist in Northwood's gut, Rafe hated himself for asking, ''What else did you find out about her?''

With a leer, Northwood said, ''She's said to be worth every penny of her price, but then, you would know that better than I, wouldn't you?''

It was the vulgarity that disturbed him, Rafe decided. After all, Maggie was a spy, and what better way to get men to talk than over a pillow? She had to support herself, and it was doubtful that the British government paid her enough to maintain that house or that wardrobe. Behaving like any other high-born tart who expected jewels in return for her favors was a splendid way of concealing her deeper purposes.

Odd how it was easier to think of Maggie as a whore than to believe she would betray her country.

Maggie was seated at one of the mirrored vanity tables when the only other lady in the retiring room said in English-accented French, "Isn't the duke a splendid lover?"

Maggie swiveled around in astonishment to stare at the young woman sitting at another table a few feet away. In her frostiest tone, she said, "I *beg* your pardon."

The girl shrank back and said remorsefully, "I'm sorry, that was dreadfully forward of me. But I saw you with Candover and it seemed from the way you were acting that, well . . ." She finished with a vague wave of her hand. Her guileless face was flushed, as if she was only now realizing how outrageous her comment was.

Amusement replaced Maggie's irritation. "I assume from your comment that you have personal experience of his grace's skills?"

The girl ducked her head in agreement. "Yes. My name is Cynthia Northwood. Rafe was . . . very kind to me earlier in my marriage, when I needed kindness."

Intrigued, Maggie asked, "And now your marriage is better and you no longer need kindness?"

"No," Cynthia said, her wide brown eyes hardening, "now my marriage is nothing to me, and I have found kindness elsewhere."

Maggie sighed inwardly; it was one of the curses and blessings of her life that people felt compelled to tell her their innermost secrets. Even total strangers like this artless chit seemed to assume that she would offer good advice or at least an understanding ear. A talent for getting people to talk was an asset to a spy, but did she really want to hear about the Duke of Candover's amorous prowess from his former mistresses?

In an effort to head off any more confidences, Maggie said, "I am Magda, the Countess Janos, but perhaps you know that already."

The girl nodded. She must be at least twenty-five, not

really a girl, but her air of innocence made her appear younger. "Oh, yes, everyone seems to know you. I've been admiring you since you came in. You have such presence."

How could one possibly be insulted by such a naive tribute? Cynthia Northwood was a pretty little thing, Maggie decided after a critical survey, though it was doubtful that intelligence would be high among her attributes. Of course, most men had no desire for brains in their bedmates, and it was unlikely that Rafe Whitbourne was any different from his fellows. Apart from Robert Anderson, Maggie had never found a man who actually seemed to like the fact that she was intelligent; most of them never got beyond staring at her bodice.

Oblivious to the older woman's thoughts, Cynthia was saying, "You and the duke are the handsomest couple here, and he seemed so absorbed in you, not like he is with most women."

Maggie straightened up. "Mrs. Northwood, do you have any idea just how improper such remarks are?"

Cynthia flushed again. "My wretched tongue! My mother died when I was very small, and my father always encouraged me to speak my mind in the most unladylike manner. And . . . and my friend Major Westford likes it, too. He says I'm not missish, like most women. Truly, I mean no insult," she said earnestly. "But I am very fond of Rafe, and he looked happy with you, and I don't really think he is happy very often."

Intrigued against her better judgment, Maggie said, "Surely the duke has everything a man could want: birth, wealth, intelligence, enough charm and address for three men. What makes you think he is not happy?"

"I don't know, really. Perhaps it's that he always seems a little bored. Perfectly polite, but not really caring about what he does. Of course," she added sadly, "perhaps that was just how he was with me. I know he never thought I was interesting, I was nowhere near intelligent enough for him. He just got involved with me because he had nothing better to do at the time."

Maggie listened to Cynthia's speech with horrified fascination and a certain respect. Perhaps there was more to the girl than had been first apparent. She said gently, "Mrs.

Northwood, you really should not say such things to a stranger.''

"No, I shouldn't,'' Cynthia agreed. "But I have been doing wrong things ever since I arrived in Paris.'' With a lift of her chin, she added, "And I have every intention of getting worse before I get better.''

She made a slight curtsy. "Countess, I am sincerely sorry if I have embarrassed you. I hope you will believe that I wish both you and the Duke of Candover well.'' Rising, she continued, "In fact, I wish everyone well, except my husband.''

Then she turned and left, not without a certain dignity. Maggie shook her head as she thought over that strange conversation. If ever she had seen a young woman headed for trouble, it was Cynthia Northwood.

Chapter 6

The Duke of Candover was entirely capable of administering a setdown that would dismiss even so thick-skinned an oaf as Oliver Northwood. Nonetheless, he refrained, idly discussing the treaty negotiations with his companion. Northwood was obviously waiting in hopes of an introduction to Countess Janos, and Rafe found himself with a perverse, unhealthy desire to see how Maggie would react when unexpectedly confronted with her first lover. Assuming that Northwood *had* been the first, as he had claimed.

With his height advantage, Rafe could see Maggie making her way through the swirling crowd, stopping sometimes to greet acquaintances. It was all casual, until she talked to a fair-haired man in the middle of the room. Rafe would have thought nothing of it if his perceptions had not been heightened by his present mission. Just for a moment, he saw Maggie's social mask slip and intense concentration showed on her face as she talked.

Then she continued her progress. The fair-haired man had been turned away from Rafe, but now he looked after Maggie, his expression blank and unrevealing. It was Robert Anderson, the British delegation underling who had taken Rafe to the mysterious lady spy. Lattimer had told Maggie not to deal with anyone in the delegation except the men at the top, so why was she talking to Anderson with such earnestness? Rafe wished he could remember who the blond man reminded him of; Anderson had struck him as negligible on their first meeting, but for a moment he wore an air of shrewd capability at odds with his usual appearance.

As Maggie rejoined him, Rafe wondered if this foray into spying was making him overly fanciful; soon he would be suspecting everyone and everything. No wonder Maggie had been prickly and suspicious in their first few meetings; after years in the shadowy world of intelligence gathering, she must have forgotten what normal life was like. Ignoring his companion, Maggie laid one hand on Rafe's arm and raised her smoky eyes to his as she purred, "Are you ready to leave, *mon cher?* Things are sadly flat here, and I can offer better amusement at home."

"Anywhere you wish to go, Magda, my love." Rafe covered her hand with his own and continued smoothly, "May I introduce you to one of your admirers? This is Oliver Northwood, of the British delegation. Northwood, the Countess Janos."

Maggie's control was admirable. Apart from a slight tightening of the lips at the sight of Northwood, she showed no sign of recognition. Of course, she may have known he was in Paris and that they would meet sooner or later, so she was ready for this encounter. Or had she had so many lovers that meeting the first meant nothing? Very few of Rafe's old mistresses could have disconcerted him; why would Maggie be any different? Why indeed, except that he wanted her to be different?

Ignoring the countess's lack of enthusiasm, Northwood bowed and said ingratiatingly, "It is a great pleasure to meet you, Countess. I have indeed been admiring you from afar."

Maggie acknowledged his words with the coolest of nods. It had taken her a few moments to recognize Oliver Northwood. As a young man he had not been without a certain boisterous charm, but the years had coarsened him. No, the coarseness had always been there, but with time his actions had written it on his face in a way impossible to conceal. Oliver must be Cynthia Northwood's husband, and Maggie felt sorry for the other woman. Cynthia would have been too young and innocent to realize the kind of man she was marrying. Northwood's eyes reminded Maggie of slugs—cold, damp, and slimy—and he was staring at her with the crudest of appraisals. She did not offer her hand.

The man's words were fulsome as he shook his head and added with heavy gallantry, "Our little northern island is incapable of producing beauties such as you."

From the twitch of Rafe's lips, Maggie gathered that the duke found amusement in the wrongheadedness of Northwood's compliment. Smiling sweetly, she said, "You are too hard on your countrywomen. I have just met one who is the fairest of English roses. Such a complexion, and such sweetness of manner!" Drawing her brows together, she added, "But surely she said her name was Northwood, Cynthia Northwood?"

The heavy brows tightened. "My wife is held to be a well-looking female."

"You are too modest on her behalf, monsieur." Smiling brilliantly, she said, "It has been a pleasure to meet you. I trust our paths will cross again. But if you will excuse us now?"

Taking his assent for granted, she deftly removed Rafe and herself from the reception. The duke said little until they were in his carriage, then he offered sardonic congratulations on her skill. "It's a pleasure watching you at work, whether it is coaxing a man to talk or depressing someone's aspirations."

"Your Mr. Northwood is a common type. Unfortunately." After a moment's reflection, Maggie added, "His wife offered her felicitations on my choice of lovers."

If she had been hoping to discomfit the duke, she failed. He merely said blandly, "I'm sure she meant well." Willing to leave the topic of the Northwoods, Rafe asked, "What does your intuition tell you about Colonel von Fehren-bach?''

In the brief flare of a street lamp, he could see the grave expression on Maggie's face as she considered. After a long pause, she said, "It should be obvious why we consider him a major suspect. What were your impressions?''

"He certainly hates the French enough to be dangerous, and with his military background he would be a skilled, formidable adversary. And yet,'' Rafe paused, trying to define his perceptions. Finally he said, "He makes no attempt to disguise his feelings. Surely a conspirator would be more circumspect?''

"Perhaps. Perhaps not.'' Maggie's tone was detached. "He may be so angry that he does not care about his fate after he has accomplished his task.''

"Do you think he is our man?''

This time the pause was so long that Rafe wondered if Maggie was going to answer. With a thread of steel in his voice he said, "Margot, for the sake of our mission I will let you drag me around like a fur muff to disguise your interrogations, but do not treat me like a backward child when we are alone. Like it or not, we are in this together and there is a greater likelihood of success if we share our information and surmises.''

"Is that an implied threat, your grace? If I don't choose to lay bare my thoughts, will you beat me until I change my mind?'' Maggie's voice was lightly mocking. Since he knew she disliked being called Margot, no doubt he would use that name whenever he wanted to put her in her place.

"I have a better way of persuading you than that,'' he replied with deliberate ambiguity.

"If Cynthia Northwood was correct in her praise of your abilities, I suppose that means you intend to overpower my feeble female brain with kisses.'' The sarcasm was unmistakable.

"Not at all. I trust that all I need do is appeal to your sense of fairness, the inbred Achilles heel of Britain.''

After a moment of surprised silence, Maggie laughed out loud. "Your grace, your talents are wasted. You should have become a negotiator like Castlereagh. You certainly know how to best take advantage of an opponent.''

"Remember that we are not opponents. We are partners."

"You are quite correct, I do have trouble remembering that." After a moment, she said, "For all the abundance of motive von Fehrenbach offered, I don't think he is our man. He is not the sort to plot in secret; he would think it ignoble. He might walk up to Talleyrand and shoot him in the heart, but he would not lower himself to conspire with others. The colonel is like a wounded, dangerous bear but he is not, I think, the one we seek."

"Who is Madame Sorel?"

"Hélène is a widow. Her husband was a French officer who died at Wagram." She was also Maggie's best female friend and one of her most reliable informants. Maggie mentioned none of that; fairminded or not, she would not go out of her way to give the duke information that didn't bear on the matter at hand.

"Would you care to guess why the colonel reacted to her presence in such a way?" Rafe asked.

"I think the reason is very simple, and not really political," Maggie said with amusement.

Rafe accepted that without comment before returning to his speculations. "If you are right about von Fehrenbach, one of the Frenchmen is the most likely villain," he said thoughtfully.

"If I am right." Maggie's voice took on a note of bitterness. "But it is not unknown for me to be wrong."

Things can be done in the darkness that would be impossible in the light. Rafe impulsively reached across to take her cool, tense hand in his own, not knowing or caring what memories brought that tone to her voice. All that mattered was that Margot had carried burdens too heavy for even the broadest of shoulders, and that she was feeling that weight. She accepted his hand with a convulsive gesture, making no other acknowledgment. Her fingers warmed, became more relaxed. After a few quiet minutes, they reached Maggie's house and she released his clasp to pull her cashmere shawl about her shoulders.

As Rafe helped her from the carriage, her mouth quirked up and she asked, "A fur muff? That is how you see yourself?"

He grinned, his gray eyes sparkling, and said, "It seemed a suitably discreet garment. Would a necklace, worn for display, be a better simile?"

Maggie was glad to see him relaxed once more, after that curious tension at the reception. Perhaps it was simply that the repellent Mr. Northwood had raised the duke's hackles. Rafe dismissed his carriage for the night but remained silent until they were private in her salon. Before she could comment on the carriage, he forestalled her by saying, "If we are to maintain the illusion of an affair, I can't just drop you at your doorstep and leave. After a discreet interval, I can walk back to my hotel. It isn't far from here."

Maggie wrinkled her nose a bit. She had known this would be necessary but had avoided thinking about it. Still, in his present mood the duke shouldn't be a difficult companion. After pouring them each a glass of brandy, she kicked off her sandals and curled up on one of the delicate-legged sofas, very much at ease in her own home. Teasingly she said, "Should I have asked Mrs. Northwood how long you would need to stay in order to uphold your reputation? Or should I just make up a bed in one of the spare rooms since no one would expect to see you before morning?"

He refused to be drawn. "If that is the best accommodation available, I will slip out the backdoor in an hour or so. It would be a blow to both our reputations if I left too soon." Wandering across the room, he found an antique chess set on a small game table. The chess pieces were designed as a medieval court, the smooth enameled figures nearly three inches high, each a sculpture with individual, hand-drawn features. Rafe picked up the white queen, an exquisite golden-haired lady riding a white palfrey, then glanced at Maggie without comment. The set was too old for her to have modeled for the part, but the resemblance was undeniable. The queen, the most powerful figure on the board.

Setting the queen down, he lifted the black king from the opposite side of the board. The king brandished a sword from a rearing charger and his dark face was arrogant and hawklike. Rafe studied the figure for a moment, wondering if he imagined its resemblance to himself. The kings were the ultimate objectives in chess, but had relatively little power themselves. It was not unlike the game he and Maggie were playing, with the white queen in charge and the king standing by. But they were on the same side, were they not? He looked at the fair-haired white king; it took little imagination to see him as Robert Anderson.

If it was an omen, it was a disturbing one. Glancing up at his hostess, the duke asked, "Care for a game of chess? At the reception, you promised me better amusement at your home."

Maggie laughed and rose gracefully to cross to the chess board. "If you wish. You will find my playing has improved a bit. Shall we toss a coin to see who plays white?"

Traditionally, white moves first, an advantage, but Rafe picked up the white queen again, admired the proud chin, then handed it to Maggie. "She could only be yours."

They sat down and began. In younger days, Maggie had played with a wild brilliance that occasionally brought victory but more often led to defeat against Rafe's more thoughtful style. Now they were evenly matched. The duke was interested to see that she still played boldly, but with a much keener eye for strategy.

An hour passed where the only words were an occasional compliment on a good move. When the clock struck eleven, Maggie looked up in surprise. "At the risk of seeming a poor hostess, I must ask you to leave. We can finish the game another day. I doubt that anyone is watching the house, but just in case, I'll show you to the rear door where you can slip out unobserved."

As he followed her through the high-ceilinged halls, Rafe admired the house. It wasn't really large but was designed to feel spacious, and every detail was perfect. It was very much the house of a gentlewoman, reinforcing the idea that it was not supported on a spy's wages, and he wondered how many lovers were contributing to the establishment. When Maggie turned to face him at the backdoor, Rafe was surprised to find how small she was in her stocking feet, the top of her head barely reaching his chin. She looked young and soft and utterly desirable, and he would have liked nothing better than to kiss her, but it took no very great intuition to decide that would not be well received.

Instead, Rafe just nodded good night and walked down

the steps, crossing the stableyard and turning left into a narrow, deserted alley. It wasn't really late and he felt far too restless to retire tamely to his apartments. He considered going to the Palais Royale to find a card game or a woman but the prospect did not appeal, so he headed toward the Place Vendôme.

Maggie was irresistibly on his mind. It was strange how an idealized view of her innocence still affected him after so many years. Even when she was eighteen her innocence existed only in his mind, so it should be no surprise to learn that she had joined the company of women who collected expensive tributes in return for their favors. It was very common where women had greater beauty than fortune; Maggie at least had goals beyond her own pleasure. He had to admire her efficiency; no doubt she chose her lovers both for their wealth and the information they would supply her. In bed with a woman like Maggie, a man might say anything and not care, nor remember it later.

At the Place Vendôme, Rafe found himself staring at the enormously tall pillar that Napoleon had erected to commemorate the Battle of Austerlitz. The bronze spiral that swirled up the column had been made by melting down the twelve hundred cannon Bonaparte had captured at that battle; the Prussians had wanted to pull the column down. He glanced around the octagonal plaza, nearly empty at this hour, then turned decisively and headed back toward Maggie's house. Why didn't he just admit to himself that he wanted her for a mistress? She was the most alluring woman he had ever met, he would swear she was not indifferent to him, and it might simplify their mission if the charade became reality. All they need do was put aside the memories of their past and enjoy each other as they were now, without recriminations or complications. It made perfect sense, and Rafe was reasonably sure that he could convince Maggie to add him to her circle of lovers. He had never failed yet with a woman he wanted.

It was probably too late to call again tonight but he found himself returning to the alley behind her house, hoping for some sign that Maggie was still awake, perhaps as restless as he was himself. As he paused in the shadows and scanned her windows, he saw a figure coming along the alley from the other direction.

Pressing against the wall of the building, Rafe watched warily as the other man looked around, then climbed the steps and knocked at Maggie's back door. It swung open immediately and the duke saw Maggie standing inside, illuminated by a lamp in her hand. She had changed to a flowing dark robe and her bright hair was loose around her shoulders, like the white queen. Her visitor bent to kiss her and Rafe stayed to watch no more.

In the candlelight it was easy to identify her visitor as Robert Anderson, the white king himself. No wonder she had talked to him with such intensity at the reception; they had been setting up an assignation. Rafe found himself coldly furious without quite knowing why. He knew that Maggie had lovers, so why should it anger him to see one entering? It certainly wasn't jealousy; he hadn't been jealous of a woman since . . . since he was twenty-two, and Maggie had betrayed him with Northwood.

He swore out loud, rejecting the idea. His anger was not from jealousy, but from concern for his mission. Maggie had been told not to associate with the lesser members of the British delegation, and yet she was defying Lord Lattimer's orders.

This was a dangerous, complicated business, and getting more so by the hour. Rafe stalked the streets until long after midnight, thinking hard about the new development. He had unthinkingly trusted Maggie, and he saw now how careless that was. While he still flatly refused to believe that she would deliberately betray her country, from now on he would be more wary of her judgment. Her affair with Anderson might be irrelevant to the business at hand; it was also possible that it was a casual coupling, but Rafe doubted both those conclusions. Even in the brief glimpse he had had of them, he could see the air of settled comfort, as if they were long-established lovers.

The danger was that if she was in love with Anderson, it would certainly affect her judgment, and if the blond man was a traitor, Maggie might be blind to that fact until it was too late. It would be ironic if she who was so expert at using men was herself being used, but the world was full of such ironies.

By the time the duke returned to his hotel, he had decided on a strategy. For the sake of their mission, Rafe must win Maggie away from Anderson. Even if the other man was not involved in a conspiracy, he represented an unknown and possibly dangerous quantity. If the duke told Maggie not to see Anderson again, she would laugh in his face, but Rafe was confident that once they became lovers he would have more influence with her. Too many women had done exactly as he wished for him to doubt his persuasive powers, and in this matter, he would use every weapon he had to gain the upper hand with Maggie. How convenient that in this instance, duty would march with pleasure.

However, until he had secured Maggie's cooperation, it might be well to develop his own sources of information. A wealthy duke has many employees; it took Rafe only a few minutes to think of three Frenchmen who worked for him who were clever, discreet, and trustworthy. Before going to bed, he had written a letter to his agent, summoning all three to Paris immediately.

After giving Robin a welcoming kiss, Maggie offered him a midnight supper and soon they were sitting at the kitchen table, working their way through pâté, sliced squab, and sundry other delicacies left by Maggie's cook. Robin looked both tired and worried, which was unusual, and feeding him seemed a good idea.

A half hour later, he pushed the remnants aside and said, "Now that the inner man is satisfied, what did you learn?"

Maggie quickly described her encounter with Colonel von Fehrenbach, ending with her conclusion that he was probably not the man behind the conspiracy. Then she said, "Out with it, Robin. What has happened to worry you?"

He sighed and ran his right hand through his hair. It was a paler blond than Maggie's, silvery by candlelight. "An informant told me that someone has been making discreet inquiries for a brave fellow who would like to bring down 'The Conqueror of the Conqueror of the World.'"

Maggie whistled softly; the Parisians had hung that nickname on the Duke of Wellington after his victory at Waterloo. It was appropriate, since Bonaparte had gotten into the habit of thinking himself the Conqueror of the World, and Wellington had most certainly cleared up that bit of hyperbole. "So they really are going for Wellington," she said with depression. "They could hardly make a better choice for stirring up a hornet's nest. Were there any indications about who was making the inquiries?"

Robin shook his head. "Only that it was a Frenchman, which fits with the conclusion you reached tonight." After a moment's pause, he asked casually, "How are things going with Candover?"

Maggie shrugged and traced a pattern on the table in a few spilled drops of wine. "You were right, he is an excellent cover for my inquiries. He's perceptive, too; he reached the same conclusion about von Fehrenbach that I did. But, I'm concerned . . ." Her voice trailed off.

"About what?"

Maggie hesitated, then said slowly, "The duke is cooperative so far, but he made a remark tonight about me dragging him around like a fur muff to conceal my activities." Robert chuckled, but she continued, "For the moment it amuses him to play this game. I don't doubt his patriotism, but I'm afraid of what he might do later, when he is no longer amused."

"What do you mean?" Robin asked, his eyes narrowed.

"Just that he is used to being in charge, and doing exactly what he wants. The man is no fool, but if he gets all lordly and pig-headed at the wrong time, it could cause serious problems."

Robert's blue eyes crinkled slightly around the corners. "I rely on you to keep him in line."

Maggie leaned back in her chair, suddenly exhausted. "You overrate my abilities, Robin."

"I doubt it." He rose and gave her a quick kiss. "I'll be going along now. Who will your next target be?"

"I hope to intercept the Count de Varenne within the next day or two. The count lives outside of Paris, but he is a *habitué* of the king's court and attends many social events. I should be able to further my acquaintance with him soon."

Maggie stood to let her visitor out, but for a moment she

leaned against him, her head on his shoulder, and said quietly, "When will it be over, Robin?"

He was touched by the note in her voice. For a moment, Maggie sounded like the girl she had not been able to be for too many years. He gave her a hug, holding her tight for a moment longer than was wise, and said, "Soon, my dear. Then we can all go home to England."

She looked up at him then, her eyes widening a little. "Do you want to go back to England, too?"

He smiled teasingly. "Perhaps. I shall lie down until the feeling goes away."

Then he was gone and Maggie was bolting the door after him. It was the first time Robin had ever shown the least desire to see his homeland. Even he, with his eternal energy and good nature, must be tiring of the endless tension. In that case, she was quite justified in having a few tears of exhaustion in her eyes, wasn't she? After all, she was just a woman.

Chapter 7

The next afternoon was hot and most of the fashionable ladies who had come to St. Germain lolled under shade trees, leaving the walks private for Maggie and Hélène. The Frenchwoman had requested this meeting, and Maggie had accepted with alacrity, knowing they would have much to say to each other. They spent some time exchanging the usual pleasantries of friends who hadn't seen each other in a while.

Hélène had just returned from taking her two young daughters to their grandmother's home near Nantes, where she had stayed several weeks before returning alone to her Paris home. She wanted her daughters out of harm's way, but Hélène herself felt an obligation to contribute what she could to the cause of peace. Until terms for a treaty were settled, information was critical, and the Frenchwoman was well-placed to hear rumors. Hélène knew that what she discovered was passed to the British, and her love for her country and its future was so strong that she chose to do what she knew could be considered treason.

The two strolled along the garden paths in their wispy summer dresses, for all the world like any other ladies of leisure. Only when they were well clear of possible eavesdroppers did Maggie ask, "Have you heard anything of special interest? Your note implied urgency."

"Yes." Hélène's brow furrowed. "I have heard that someone is plotting to assassinate Lord Castlereagh."

Inhaling sharply, Maggie asked, "Where did you hear that?"

"One of my maids has a brother who works in a gambling hell at the Palais Royale. He heard two men talking very late last night, careless from too much wine."

"Could the brother identify the men?"

Hélène shook her head. "No, the light was poor and he just overheard a fragment of conversation while serving someone at the next table. He could say only that one was a Frenchman and the other was a foreigner, with a German or possibly English accent. The Frenchman asked if the plan was set, and the foreigner said that Castlereagh would be out of the way within a fortnight."

Maggie was silent as she tried to assimilate this new piece of information. Was this the same plot that she was pursuing, or a separate one? She wished she knew if the second man had been a German or a Briton; the information could be valuable. Or perhaps not; the men involved might be mercenaries who would turn their hands to anything profitable. There were many such about, drawn to the crisis and confusion of Paris by hopes of gain. As they entered a new path between bright flowerbeds, Maggie spent a few minutes outlining what little she knew of the conspiracy.

Hélène's face was bleak when Maggie finished speaking. "It sounds very dangerous. With so many troops of all nations around, the slightest spark could set France in flames again . . ."

"I know," Maggie said grimly. "But other such plots

have failed, and God willing, this one will, too." Shifting the subject, she asked, "What do you know of Colonel von Fehrenbach?"

Hélène's softly rounded face was shadowed under her lacy parasol and her voice gave no clue to her thoughts. The two women were friends, but each had her secrets. "Not very much. I have met him several times. He is like many of the Prussian officers, angry and determined to see France suffer."

"Forgive me if I seem to pry, Hélène," Maggie said hesitantly, "but is there anything between you two?"

In a colorless voice, her friend said, "He sees me and thinks of everything he hates. Apart from that, there is nothing."

"Do you think he might be involved in this plot?"

Without hesitation, Hélène said, "No. He is an uncomplicated man and would have no use for plots." With a wintry smile, she added, "Not unlike my late husband Etienne, going forward bravely, unperturbed by doubt or common sense. Do you have reason to suspect the colonel?"

"Not really," Maggie shrugged. It was interesting that her friend mentioned the Prussian in the same breath with her husband. "He is well placed to do mischief, but my assessment agrees with yours. Still, if you should see him again and observe anything suspicious, you will let me know?"

"Of course." Hélène smiled serenely, then gestured at an unoccupied bench under a chestnut tree. "Shall we sit while you tell me about that magnificent Englishman you have attached?"

Maggie felt strangely unwilling to discuss Rafe. "It is of no importance," she said as she brushed a stray leaf from the wooden bench before sitting. "He is rich, bored, and in Paris. For the moment he fancies me. What else is there to tell?"

Hélène's wide brown eyes studied her shrewdly for a moment, then she said softly, "What else, indeed?"

It was time to change the subject again. Maggie asked, "Do you know anything about Mrs. Cynthia Northwood? Her husband Oliver is a member of the British delegation."

Waving her flat reticule like a fan to stir the heavy air, Hélène thought for a moment before replying. "Yes, she is one of life's heedless innocents. She is having an affair with a British officer, a Major Westford of the Guards, and she doesn't care who knows it. Having met her husband, I can see her point, but she shows no discretion whatsoever. Why do you ask about her?"

Maggie sighed. "No reason, really, except that yesterday she was telling me a great many things one doesn't usually say to a complete stranger. She is a wild card, and since she is connected to the British delegation she might somehow become involved in something she doesn't understand."

"Hm-m-m," Hélène said thoughtfully. "I see what you mean. Mrs. Northwood is just the sort to babble out secret information in the middle of something else. But if she and her husband are on such terms, she would have no access to anything important."

"True, but we can't afford to ignore any possibility. Can you find out something about her associates, besides her major?"

At Hélène's nod, Maggie continued, "Also, do you know anything about the Count de Varenne?"

Hélène gave her a worried glance. "Yes, and none of it good. That one is dangerous. Is he involved with your plot?"

"Possibly. Do you know where I might casually meet him?"

"He is often at Lady Castlereagh's evenings. Be careful, my friend, when you meet him. They say he writes his name in blood."

Although it was a hot afternoon, Maggie felt a shiver along her spine at the words, and she wondered if her intuition was trying to tell her something important. Rafe was taking her to the theater tonight, and after they could go to the salon at the British Embassy and hope that the Ultra-Royalist count was there. For the sake of thoroughness she wanted to meet him, even though the direction of the plot eliminated the count from the likely candidates. Still, if Varenne was uninvolved, why did thinking of him give her a nagging sense of danger?

* * *

When Rafe called to take Maggie to the theater, her smile was welcoming as she entered the salon in a shimmering, silver-gray dress that reflected hints of blue and green in its folds. Once Margot Ashton had greeted Rafe in a very similar dress with just such an expression in her eyes, and for a moment the duke's world tilted as the past and present crashed together. Suddenly he desired her with all the passionate intensity of twenty-two, wanted to bury his face in tangles of golden hair, to discover one by one the mysteries of Margot's laughing, elusive spirit and lush body. It was a painful moment of disorientation, and his only salvation was that the present-day Maggie was unaware of it.

"I'm sorry to keep you waiting, your grace. Shall we be on our way?" The honeyed voice was friendly and intimate.

With an effort, Rafe buried the effects of that moment of shocking desire, and he was impressed at how calm he sounded as he said, "You are looking particularly lovely tonight, my dear. I shall be the envy of every man in Paris."

With a sorrowful shake of her head, Maggie replied, "I am disappointed, your grace. Surely a gentleman with your reputation for address can offer more imaginative flattery."

"I offer fact, not flattery, countess," Rafe replied with a lift of his eyebrows. "Spanish coin would be useless with a woman of your acuity."

Maggie laughed and floated toward the door. "My apologies for underestimating you. Clearly you flatter on a higher level. A woman who is often complimented on her appearance much prefers to hear lies about her intelligence."

As he helped her into his carriage, Rafe wondered if Maggie would take anything he said seriously; her defenses were formidable. On the other hand, his desire to win her grew stronger every time they met. It would take every ounce of wit and charm he possessed to seduce her, and he hadn't felt so alive in years. Having more money and more women than he knew what to do with had become a bloody bore, and the harder Maggie made him work, the sweeter the prize at the end. He flatly refused to consider the possibility of failure.

As the carriage began rattling down the Boulevard des Capucines, Maggie interrupted the duke's musings to say,

"The plot is thickening. I have a reliable report of a threat against Lord Castlereagh within the next fortnight."

"The devil you say!" Thoughts of lechery vanished as Maggie outlined what had been overheard. Rafe briefly wondered who her informant had been—another patron of the gambling hell, over a pillow this afternoon?—but shoved the thought aside for more serious considerations. "Perhaps I can visit that club later this evening, after I leave you off."

"It is not likely to do much good," Maggie said doubtfully. "You can hardly ask the people who work there the names of the two men discussing assassination last night."

"True. But there is a possibility that one or both of the men may be habitués of the place. It is not inconceivable that one might strike up a conversation with me, particularly if I make a few critical comments about Castlereagh or Wellington."

At Maggie's continuing silence, he added, "I am not wholly incapable of subtlety, you know."

"I suppose not," Maggie said with a sigh. "I presume you know enough to go armed? There are a number of French officers who make a point of insulting foreigners in the hopes of starting a duel, and as an Englishman, you will be fair game. Not as good as a Prussian, but still appealing to a belligerent Frenchman."

"I am touched by your concern for my continued existence."

"Don't flatter yourself, your grace. I merely dislike losing a chess partner in the middle of a game." He couldn't tell whether it was sarcasm or humor that laced her voice. She added, "If you do get forced into a duel, pistols would probably be a better choice. Most of the French officers are capital swordsmen, and it is a rare foreigner who can best them."

Rafe was about to ask why she had faith in his marksmanship when he remembered a long-ago afternoon when they had shot at wafers together at a friend's private pistol gallery. She must remember his skill; surprising that he could have forgotten that Margot had been equally good, the only woman he had ever met who could hold her own shooting against a man. It was one of many things her father had taught her, treating her as if she had been a son instead of a daughter. One of the many things that made her different from any other woman he had ever known.

They pulled up before the theater and Maggie attracted a great deal of attention from gawkers as Rafe helped her from the carriage and escorted her upstairs to their box. It was indeed an excellent play and for whole minutes at a time Rafe would forget serious thoughts in the humor of Molière's *Tartuffe*.

Nonetheless, in the hot, stuffy theater he was sharply aware of the exotic scent Maggie wore as she sat mere inches away, and he casually laid his arm across the back of her chair, not quite touching her but close enough to feel warmth from her skin. He was pleased to see her lean forward a trifle, pretending absorption in the play. Rafe was willing to wager that she was as aware of him as he was of her, and that she didn't trust herself to relax with him. When he had kissed her as a means of identification, she had responded wholeheartedly before anger had pulled her away. If she had responded then, she would again.

The disturbance started just before the second act ended. First there was a murmuring, growling sound from the pit, then shouting broke out and shoving could be seen below them. The actors tried to continue their lines over the increasing noise, but cries of *"Vive le Roi!"* began warring with *"Vive l'Emperor!"*

The next actor who spoke was pelted with pieces of fruit and the whole cast retreated to the wings. In the pit, the noise was getting louder and white banners, signifying support for the king, began to appear. A full-scale riot was in the making, with Bonapartists bringing out violet flags and brandishing them between attacks on their opponents. There were more royalists, and from his vantage point in the box, Rafe could see the violet flags being ripped apart. One brawny fellow with an imperial eagle banner was dragged down, disappearing under brutal kicks and punches. A woman screamed, her voice abruptly cutting off. Rafe had been caught in a London street riot once and the mob below was heading in the same dangerous direction.

The cries of *"Vive le Roi! Vive le Roi!"* had become a harsh, threatening chant that made the walls and ceiling vibrate, and Rafe looked across to see Maggie silently staring down. She was utterly impassive, only the tight set of her lips indicating concern. As he studied the calm profile and flawless golden hair, he had a sudden, horrifying vision of Maggie surrounded and pulled down by rough men. She would be fighting, but there were too many attackers, and with shocking vividness he saw her disappearing beneath harsh, greedy hands. The fearsome image sparked a frantic urge to get her away before violence engulfed the whole theater. Grabbing her upper arm, he half-lifted her from the chair and pulled her toward the back door of the box.

In the tumult it was impossible to make his voice heard, and for a moment Maggie resisted him, her face stubborn. Rafe was on the verge of swinging her off her feet and bodily carrying her through the corridor when she capitulated. Other patrons were beginning to empty out of the boxes but Rafe was quicker, looping his arm around Maggie's waist and hustling her down the stairs.

Halfway to the ground floor, two roughly dressed men blocked the way, eyes gleaming at the sight of Maggie. With a short, savage punch that did credit to his training at Jackson's salon, Rafe knocked the first man against his fellow, pulling Maggie past while the ruffians struggled for balance.

Even outside the building, hoarse shouts from within made it difficult to be heard, and both aristocrats and common people were pouring from the theater. Someone from the manager's office ran down the boulevard screaming for the Guards. Fortunately, Rafe's carriage was waiting nearby and within a few moments they were both inside and heading away from the theater.

Rafe could hear Maggie's quickened breathing but her voice was quite collected as she said, "Your reaction was excessive, your grace. If we had stayed in our box and waved white handkerchiefs, we would have been quite safe. Such scenes are not uncommon, with the royalists trying to intimidate the rest of France now that they have the upper hand. They call it the white terror. Matters are much worse in the southwest of France, and many Bonapartists have been killed."

"While I admire your aplomb, no one is ever entirely safe during a riot," Rafe said dryly. His heart was still pounding and it took an effort to match her calm. "Since it is obvious that you have more courage than sense, I feel a responsibility to keep you intact, at least until you have found our assassin."

The threat to Maggie's safety had roused the most primitive of protective responses in him, and he still felt shaken on her behalf. If she had been alone, a white handkerchief would have been a poor defense against two such men as those on the stairs.

Maggie gave an elaborate sigh of resignation. "How fortunate that I have seen *Tartuffe* before. Still, this means we can get to Lady Castlereagh's evening salon in good time."

"What, no need for a vinaigrette, no maidenly vapors?" Rafe said as amusement began to replace anxiety.

"They would be singularly inappropriate since I am not a maiden," Maggie said sharply. He could hear her drawing a deep breath before continuing steadily, "I've heard that the Count de Varenne often attends Lady Castlereagh's evenings. While it is unlikely that an Ultra-Royalist would be behind our plot, I would still like to meet him." After a moment's thought, she added, "I was warned that he is a thoroughly dangerous man."

"I'll bear that in mind," Rafe said lazily. "Is he likely to challenge me to a duel, too?"

"No, he is more the knife-in-the-back type, I understand. Varenne is prominent among those urging reprisals against Bonapartists. If he had his way, every man who ever held office under the Emperor would be sent to a firing squad."

"Sounds a charming fellow. Remind me to keep my back to a wall if we encounter him." Stretching his long legs as far as possible in the limited space, he added, "Lead on." He hoped Lady Castlereagh had a good supper planned; nothing like a riot to make a man peckish.

Chapter 8

Maggie's hands were clenched in her lap as the carriage rumbled down the boulevard toward the British Embassy, and she wondered if her voice had betrayed her near-panic at the theater riot. It had brought back all her worst nightmares in grotesque detail, and she had been so paralyzed by fear that she could hardly move when Rafe had dragged her from the theater. She knew that there had been little real danger—she had even had a white handkerchief in her reticule—but panic was immune to reason.

While she would have forced herself to stay in the theater rather than give in to her fears, it had been a relief to go along with Rafe. Most of the time Maggie would fight hammer and tongs if a man tried to compel her against her will, but not tonight, not in the face of that seething brawl of mad humanity.

It had been thoroughly comforting to have his strong arm around her, and pure pleasure to watch him dispatch those two ruffians so deftly. All in a day's work for the Duke of Candover, of course. He hadn't even wrinkled his perfectly tailored coat, and he had betrayed no more concern at the riot than if a mule cart had blocked his carriage. She admired his imperturbability. Most of the time she could match it, but not when a mob brought back the horrifying scene that had killed her father and his man Willis, and changed her life forever.

Her hands had almost stopped trembling and Maggie brushed one over her hair, checking that it was still in place. She didn't seem to have any visible signs of that flight from the theater, and in the dark she schooled her face to unconcern.

Rafe's cool gray eyes studied her intently as he helped her

from the carriage on the Rue du Faubourg St. Honoré. He might have an endless river of women flowing through his life, but he maintained the courtesies with the one he was escorting. Maggie smiled up at him and took his arm, saying in heavily accented English, "Lady Castlereagh's evenings are very splendid, with some of the best conversation in Paris. One may see anyone here."

Inside, Lady Castlereagh herself greeted them. Emily Stewart was not renowned for beauty or wit, but she was a kind woman and she and her brilliant husband were devoted to each other. Smiling, she said, "Good evening, Rafe, how charming to see you. I hope Magda has been making you feel welcome to Paris?"

The duke bowed over her ladyship's hand. "She has indeed. The countess even found a theater riot for me this evening, so I should be well informed about events in Paris."

"Unfair, your grace," Maggie said with mock indignation. "Yours was the choice of theater. I thought perhaps you arranged the riot as an alternative to the farce."

Lady Castlereagh smiled wryly. "Unfortunately, one needn't look far for disorders. Nightly mobs in the Tuileries gardens, duels almost daily between French and Allied officers. There have been disturbances at each of the four theaters where I have boxes, and they are the staidest playhouses in Paris." She glanced at the door and saw another party arrive.

"I must excuse myself now but I hope to speak more with you later. Was there anyone either of you particularly wished to meet? There is quite a crowd this evening."

"Is the Count de Varenne here, Emily?" Maggie asked.

A small line appeared between Lady Castlereagh's brows but she said merely, "You are in luck; he arrived a few minutes ago. Over there, in the far corner, talking to the Russian officer." She nodded farewell and left to attend to her hostess's duties.

The splendid reception room was crowded with people and a dozen languages could be heard, though French predominated. Lord Castlereagh and the British ambassador, Sir Charles Stuart, were part of a group that included Prince Hardenburg, the Prussian foreign minister, and Francis I,

Emperor of Austria. Maggie reminded herself that Francis was nominally her sovereign, as long as she was in her Hungarian countess guise, and it would be preferable to avoid a man who might ask awkward questions. Negotiations were at a critical phase now, and the key figures were striving night and day to reach agreement. With the support of Wellington, Lord Castlereagh's plan for an army of occupation was slowly coming to be accepted among the Allies.

Maggie's eyes lingered on Castlereagh for a moment. He was a tall, strikingly handsome man, reserved in public but generous and unassuming in private. The foreign minister was known for both intelligence and irreproachable integrity, and his death would be a tremendous loss. Her jaw tightened; he would not become a victim of political terror if she could do anything to prevent it. She glanced at her escort and found the duke also gazing at the British minister, thoughts similar to hers reflected in his face. Sensing her regard, he glanced down and for a moment their eyes met in perfect agreement as they silently pledged to do whatever was necessary to uncover the conspiracy that threatened their countryman as well as the peace of Europe.

There were a number of Britons present and Rafe knew them all, so it was easy to progress indirectly toward their quarry while they exchanged greetings with fellow visitors. Maggie studied the count surreptitiously as they drew closer. He was in his late forties, a powerfully built man of middle height with an air of command and great elegance. Maggie mentally reviewed what she knew of him. He was the last of an ancient family and was in the process of restoring his estate outside of Paris to its former splendor. He had great influence with the Ultra-Royalists and might be tapped for an important government post soon.

Though he was unlikely to be involved in the plot they were now investigating, the count was a devious and dangerous man, and it was advisable to learn more about him. He had led two different royalist attempts to invade revolutionary France, and he had been governor of a Russian province for the tsar for the last decade. For over twenty years he had been involved in royalist plots against the revolutionary French government, and there were indications that he had arranged assassinations. Certainly he had the knowledge to organize a conspiracy.

As they drew nearer to the count, Maggie was pleased to see that the Russian he conversed with was Prince Orkov, whom she had met several times before. Tucking her hand firmly in Rafe's elbow, she drew him up to their quarry at a lull in the conversation, cooing, "Prince Orkov, so delightful to see you again. Surely the last time we met was at the Baroness Krudener's?"

Prince Orkov's eyes lit up with uncomplicated male pleasure at the sight of Maggie, and he bent gracefully over her extended hand. Introductions were performed all around, but Maggie found that her bright social smile froze when her eyes met those of the Count de Varenne. Most men stared at her with some degree of lechery; occasionally that was a nuisance, but lust was normal and passion is warming. Varenne's gaze was pure ice, the cold, dispassionate evaluation of a buyer contemplating a possible acquisition, wondering if it would prove worth the effort.

For a moment she was off-balance. She could deal with any variety of passion, whether love or anger or hatred, but the count seemed a man who stood apart from such human weaknesses, and she was unsure how best to question him. Plunging in, she smiled and said, "I have often heard of you, *Monsieur le Comte*. It must give you great pleasure to be restored to your country and your estates after so many years of exile."

He paused, his black eyes flatly opaque, then said in a dark, whispery voice, "Satisfaction, perhaps. Pleasure may be too strong a word."

She nodded sympathetically. "France must have changed out of all recognition, but now you and your royalist compatriots have the opportunity to recreate what has been destroyed."

The count shook his head. "We shall never be entirely successful with that. Too much has changed in the last twenty-six years. Jumped-up bourgeois pretend to be aristocrats, the true nobility has been decimated or impoverished. Even the king himself is only a shadow of his distinguished ancestors. Who could look at Louis the Eighteenth and see the Sun King?"

His hoarse, whispery voice was peculiarly commanding, and Maggie wondered if she imagined the undertone of threat. "You seem very pessimistic for a man of the ruling party. Do you think matters are truly so desperate?"

"Difficult, Countess, but not desperate. We have waited a long time to reclaim our patrimony. We shall not lose it again. Now if you will excuse me, I am expected elsewhere." With a polite nod he left the group.

Rafe and Prince Orkov had been discussing horses, that topic of universal and unending interest to the male half of the species. When she turned back to them, Rafe caught her eye and said, "The prince has invited us to a ball he is giving two days hence. Are we free to accept?"

The duke gave her a speaking look so Maggie assumed that someone on the guest list would be of particular interest. General Roussaye, perhaps? She smiled and said, "We accept with pleasure, your highness. Your entertainments are legendary."

The prince took her hand and caressed it in a way that warned Maggie not to let him get her alone. "Your presence will add to its luster, Countess."

After a bit more gush, Rafe and Maggie departed. They chatted with a few more guests so that they would not appear to have lost interest after talking to Varenne, but within half an hour they were on their way back to Maggie's townhouse.

As soon as they were alone, Rafe asked, "What is your judgment on the count?"

"Well, he is certainly capable of anything," Maggie said, "but considering who the targets are, he is unlikely to be our conspirator. I'm glad of that—he seemed utterly ruthless, as dangerous as his reputation." After a brief pause, she asked, "Who is going to be at Orkov's ball?"

"General Roussaye for one, our Bonapartist suspect." Thinking of a way to use the ball as part of his pursuit of Maggie, Rafe said, "Wear that green ball gown again, unless it would ruin your reputation to be seen in it again too soon."

"I think my credit will stand it," Maggie said with surprise. "After all, I am but a poor Magyar widow. People will make some allowances." She couldn't imagine why

Rafe should care what she wore, but she saw no harm in indulging him in something so unimportant. Besides, she did look rather well in that gown.

Rafe accompanied her into her house, this time without dismissing his carriage, and they settled down to continue their chess game, which had devolved into long pauses and steely contemplation. Maggie wondered if there was anyone in Paris who would believe she spent private moments with the duke playing chess. Probably not; she had trouble believing it herself. After a slow hour, Rafe stood and said, "I'm off to the Palais Royal to see if I can find the mysterious conspirator. You said the conversation was overheard at the Café Mazarin?"

Maggie nodded, then looked up hesitantly. The Duke of Candover towered over her, strong, confident, and utterly in control, and he would probably feel insulted if she betrayed a lack of faith in his abilities. Nonetheless, she had the most absurd desire to tell him to be careful and it was hard to keep her tongue between her teeth.

Uncannily, Rafe seemed to be aware of her thoughts, for he said just before he stepped outside, "Never fear, I shan't stir the hornets up." Then he lifted her right hand and kissed it, not with a light, formal brush of his mouth, but seriously, his lips warm and sensuous against her fingers.

Then he was gone and Maggie involuntarily curled her hand into a fist, as if to ward off the tingles of pleasure his kiss had sent up her arm. She smiled a little shakily; after all, hadn't she guessed that he would be interested in adding her to his conquests? No doubt he had notches cut in the post of his bed as a way of keeping track of the ladies he bedded. Or would the post be whittled away to nothing by now? Abruptly she whirled and headed upstairs to her chamber. For once, her sense of humor wasn't giving her any perspective or amusement at all.

The Palais Royal had a long and checkered past. Cardinal Richelieu had built part of it, and sundry royal relatives had lived there. Shortly before the Revolution, the Duc de Chartres had built a huge addition around the gardens, renting out the lower levels as shops and the upper as apartments. These days, the Palais Royal was the very heart of

French dissipation, with every manner of vice available to the hopeful bucks who swarmed there. Externally it was the only really well-lit place in Paris and idlers of every nation could be seen drifting under the arcades and clustering by the columns. The only ladies visible were of the more public sort, and one of these approached Rafe as he alighted from his carriage. He wondered with some interest what kept her low-cut gown from falling off. A fortunate thing that the evening was mild or she would be courting pneumonia.

"Is the English milord here for pleasure?" Her husky voice had a provincial accent, and the heavy mask of makeup couldn't conceal the lines in her face. She had plied her trade long enough to size up a man's dress, nationality, and wealth quickly.

The duke nodded courteously and said, "At the moment I am interested in the pleasures of the *tapis vert*. I understand the play is good at the Café Mazarin."

Losing interest in him as a potential customer, the prostitute gestured vaguely to her left. "It is that way." Tossing her head coquettishly, she added, "Perhaps later you will wish a companion to celebrate or commiserate with?"

"Perhaps." None of Rafe's distaste showed in his face. She was a coarse, unattractive creature and any man sampling her charms risked the pox, but she was no better or worse that half a hundred other women wandering the arcades and gardens. For that matter, she was little different from many of the great ladies of society except for her price, which was lower and more honest.

Making his way through a crowd of Allied officers, Rafe soon found a sign for the Café Mazarin. On the ground floor was a jeweler's shop, still open at this late hour in the hope that a lucky gambler might wish to buy some bauble to bestow on his lady. Beside the shop a grimy staircase led up to the café where a flamboyantly dressed woman presided over the counter, her dark eyes shrewdly assessing new customers. She liked what she saw of Rafe, for she came around her counter to greet him in person.

"Good evening, milord. Are you here for dining or gaming or perhaps to go upstairs?"

Upstairs would mean ladies of a higher grade than the streetwalkers outside. With any luck, they would be pox-free and not steal the customers' wallets. "I've heard that the play is very good here, Madame. Perhaps later I will dine as well."

The woman gave a pleased nod, then led him through the dining room to the gambling salon. It looked like any number of other gambling hells Rafe had been in. In one corner was a *rouge-et-noir* table, in another a roulette wheel. A scattering of tables contained card games such as faro and whist. The atmosphere was smoky and dense with the desperate excitement of serious gamesters, and the patrons ran the full range from innocent young pigeons to the Captain Sharps that preyed on them.

The low murmur of voices was punctuated by the rattle of dice at the hazard table and the soft slap of cards on green baize. All in all, a typical den of iniquity, and not the sort of place that Rafe had ever found attractive. Still, he was here for information, not pleasure, so he spent the next two hours playing at different tables. Whist was the only game he would have enjoyed, because it was more a test of skill than chance, so he avoided the whist table lest it prove too absorbing. Over dice, cards, and wheel, he exchanged casual comments with most of the other gamblers, listening more than he spoke.

Much of the talk was political, hardly surprising given the ongoing peace conference. However, he heard only the talk that could be heard anywhere in Paris. This particular establishment was patronized by a mixture of Frenchmen and foreigners, but if any were extremists, they kept their mouths discreetly shut.

An hour past midnight Rafe was preparing to call it an evening and find some fresh air when his attention was drawn by a thin, dark-haired man at the *rouge-et-noir* table. The man had been winning earlier but luck was running against him now and the bank had taken all his winnings. A wide scar across his cheek shone livid in the candlelight as he reached into an inside pocket to draw out what must be his final stake, then slapped a pile of notes on the red diamond. In the hush that sometimes falls on a crowded room, it seemed that everyone was watching. Rafe was too far away to see the cards dealt, but when the scar-faced man whooped a moment later, it was obvious that he had won.

It would have meant nothing, except that the Frenchman next to Rafe said, "It looks like Lemercier is in the money again. The man has the devil's own luck."

The name was familiar, and after a moment the duke remembered why. There was a Lemercier on the list of secondary suspects that Maggie had given him, a Bonapartist officer if he recalled correctly. Rafe studied the scar-faced man carefully as he rose from the *rouge-et-noir* table. He seemed to have a military bearing. If he was Captain Henri Lemercier, it might be worth improving their acquaintance. As Lemercier crossed the room, Rafe lazily intercepted him. "May I buy you a drink on the strength of your beating the bank?"

The scarred man looked suspicious for a moment, then smiled jovially. "You may. Lost a few to the bank yourself, eh?"

In a few moments, they were sharing a bottle of bad port in the café part of the establishment, and it was obviously not Lemercier's first drink of the evening. He was very well to go, and it took no encouragement for him to talk of the numerous times that his iron nerve had caused him to win when lesser men would have withdrawn from the game. Over the next quarter hour, Rafe learned that he was indeed Captain Henri Lemercier, that he despised all Germans, Russians, and Englishmen, present company excepted, and that he was a devil of a fellow. All in all, not an enlightening conversation, though Rafe was interested to learn that Lemercier was a regular patron of the Café Mazarin. ("At least the tables are usually honest, my English friend.")

Lemercier had the nervous gestures and darting eyes of a ferret and was an addicted gambler, the kind of man who would do anything for money. If he had political convictions, they would easily be subordinated to personal gain, and he might well be the Frenchman Maggie's contact had overheard here the night before. If so, who was the German or Englishman he had been talking to?

After half an hour of listening to the man's ramblings, Rafe decided he was unlikely to learn anything tonight and took his leave with assurances of esteem and hopes of meeting at the Café Mazarin in the future. If he did seek Lemercier out again, Rafe made a note to do so earlier in the evening, when the man was more likely to be sober. He was not an interesting drunk.

Rafe paid the bejeweled woman behind the counter for the port and turned to go downstairs, pausing for one last glance across the room. A blond man was taking the empty chair opposite Lemercier. In spite of the dark smokiness of the room and the man's distinctly French way of dressing, the duke had no trouble identifying the newcomer who was talking so earnestly to Lemercier. It was Robert Anderson, the ubiquitous underling from the British delegation. Maggie's lover.

The Englishman was tense even though he had made this blindfolded journey once before. The summons from *Le Serpent* had been curt, with no explanation of why his presence was needed. Once again a hackney had circled through Paris and the silent escort refused all conversational overtures. However, this time when he was brought into *Le Serpent*'s presence, the sibilant voice instructed him to remove his blindfold.

The Englishman felt a stab of fear that the order meant he would not be leaving, but a hoarse chuckle allayed that. "Don't worry, *mon Anglais*, you will not recognize me. You will need your eyes for what you must tell me tonight."

Pulling off the blindfold, he found himself in a dark room lit by the feeble glow of a single candle and furnished only with a desk and two chairs. *Le Serpent* sat behind the desk, his face masked and a black cloak disguising his body so thoroughly that it was impossible to tell if he was tall or short, fat or thin.

Without wasting time in preliminaries, the dark figure said, "Draw me a detailed sketch of the British Embassy stables. There have been repairs since the Princess Borghese sold it to Wellington, and I need to know about changes. I am particularly interested in where Castlereagh's horses are kept, and I want you to describe his cattle exactly, in both looks and temper."

The Englishman's eyes widened. "Are you plotting against Castlereagh? If anything happens to him, there will be hell to pay. Wellington is his best friend, and he would put the whole British Army to searching for assassins if necessary.'' And a diligent investigation might uncover matters to the Englishman's detriment; only a complete lack of suspicion had made it possible for him to pass so much information.

Reading his mind again, *Le Serpent* chuckled nastily. ''You needn't fear for your worthless neck. Whatever happens to Castlereagh will seem like an accident. Soon the illustrious Duke himself will be in no position to investigate anything.''

As the Englishman started sketching floorplans of the stable and its yard, his mind was racing. It sounded like his repellent host wished to eliminate both of the top British officials, a fact that had interesting ramifications. Clumsy attempts had been made on Wellington's life before, but there would be nothing clumsy about an attempt by *Le Serpent*. The question was, how could this information be turned to account?

Le Serpent asked a number of questions about the routine of the stables and the grooms, curtly demanding that his visitor find the answers to anything he couldn't answer immediately. After covering the stables, he made exhaustive queries about both Castlereagh's and Wellington's daily routines and habits. Tiring under the interrogation, the Englishman snapped, ''Surely you know that the Duke prefers low company and doesn't even live at the Embassy. How am I supposed to know about all his movements?''

''I am quite aware that Wellington lives at Ouvrard's Hotel,'' *Le Serpent* said coldly. ''Nonetheless, he is often at the embassy and if you have the brains of a rodent you should be able to learn what I require. I will expect a report with the answers you could not supply tonight within forty-eight hours.''

''And if I decide I no longer wish to be in your employ?'' It was an ill-chosen time for defiance, but the Englishman was too tired and irritated to be wise.

Le Serpent slapped his hand on the desk and pushed himself to his feet, looming over his visitor. In a voice heavy with menace he hissed, ''Then you are ruined, *mon Anglais*. I can have you assassinated, or I can let Castlereagh know of your duplicity and your own people will destroy you. Publicly, so every one of your relatives and friends, if you have any, will know of your humiliation. Do not think you can buy your life by informing against me, because you know nothing.''

His eyes glittered behind the mask as he continued with deadly emphasis, ''You live on my sufferance, you dunghill cock. I *own* you, and you are fortunate that I am a man of honor. If you serve me well, you will prosper, unless you are caught through your own stupidity. If you try to betray me, you are a dead man. Those are the only choices you have.''

The Englishman's eyes fell before *Le Serpent*'s, and then he had his stroke of luck: the hand that slapped the desk bore a heavy gold ring with a complicated crest on it. He knew better than to stare, but a quick glance showed that the crest was twined by a three-headed serpent. It would take time to identify the owner, but for the first time, the Englishman had a clue. Slumping in pretended defeat, he controlled his inner exultation. He'd find out who *Le Serpent* was, by God, and then the bastard would be sorry for his insults. If he played his cards right, he might be able to come out of this as a hero—a *rich* hero.

Chapter 9

The next morning Maggie received a note from Hélène Sorel describing how a discontented French officer had asked a group of idlers in front of a café if anyone wanted to earn some money by shooting the Duke of Wellington. Since the idiot had made his offer before a dozen witnesses, he had been arrested within the hour. Maggie chuckled. There was plenty of grumbling and discontent in the city, but most of it was as harmless as this. It wasn't men like those that were the problem.

Her amusement faded rapidly as she considered her own

investigation. Robin had stopped by the night before and they had stayed up late talking, but without finding any new insight. Maggie felt tense, and vastly frustrated as well. Too many possibilities, too little time . . . She spent the day pushing harder, looking at the information she had and trying to see some pattern, but without success. She could only continue as she was doing, and hope that General Roussaye might hold the key.

As she dressed for Prince Orkov's ball, even her favorite green satin ball gown failed to improve her mood and she was silent as Inge styled her hair into a tumble of golden curls. Privately, Maggie wondered how much the Duke of Candover was adding to her tension, because of the unsettling undercurrents of attraction and wariness between them. She trusted his good intentions about their mission, but that was all she trusted.

As a spy, he was an untested amateur, and on a personal level he was like a loose cannon on the deck of a ship: uncontrolled and dangerous. Maggie could pretend to a sophistication that played at love without being burned, but she knew how perilously thin her facade was. For her, lack of deep feeling was an act; for Rafe Whitbourne, it was the real thing.

When Inge announced that the duke had arrived, Maggie schooled her face to pleasantness and went to join him. When she entered the salon, her attention was distracted from the concerns of spying by Rafe's admiring expression.

"Thank you for wearing that dress, Countess. It will go very well."

"Go very well with what?" Maggie asked politely.

The duke offered her a velvet-covered box. "With this."

Glancing in the box, Maggie gasped at the contents. It contained an emerald necklace and earrings of dazzling beauty. Delicate gold settings entwined with flawless stones to create jewelry that looked light and airy while at the same being indecently sumptuous. Staring, she said, "For heaven's sake, Rafe, what are these for?"

"For you, of course," he said, a smile quirking.

"I can't possibly accept anything this valuable. People would think . . ." Maggie stopped.

"That you are my mistress? That is the point, my dear."

His voice was deep and caressing, and for one perilous moment Maggie considered what it would be like to be his mistress in fact as well as fiction. Then her jaw stiffened. Attractive as he was, she'd be damned if she would let this unreliable nobleman conquer her, no matter how much they would both enjoy it. Conquest was still conquest, and she was no man's trophy.

She snapped, "I hardly imagine that a queen's ransom in gems is necessary to our little charade, your grace." Picking up the box of jewels, she closed the lid sharply and handed it back.

Undeterred, Rafe said equably, "But it is necessary. Half of the London *ton* is in Paris, and my habits are not exactly a secret. I have always given bits of trumpery to the ladies I am . . . involved with. Someone would think it strange if I didn't do the same now."

"Bits of trumpery!" Maggie said with exasperation. "You could buy half an English county with the value of these."

"You exaggerate a little, my dear. No more than a quarter, and it would have to be a small county at that."

His grin invited her to be amused, and suddenly Maggie could not resist laughing with him. "Very well, if you insist, I will accept the loan of these until our masquerade is done. Then you can store them away for your next mistress."

Taking the box from her hand, Rafe steered her over to a pier glass hanging between two of the windows. He stood behind her and deftly unhooked her simple jade necklace.

"But these emeralds wouldn't be appropriate for just any woman, my dear countess. They will look best on one whose eyes will turn green to match." He lifted the necklace from the box. "Someone with the style and countenance to wear what you call a queen's ransom without being overpowered by it. Offhand, I can't think of another woman they would suit as well."

Rafe placed the necklace around her neck. Her ball gown was cut very low, exposing her neck, shoulders, and a dramatic expanse of bosom, and Maggie felt suddenly naked as his warm hands touched her bare skin and lingered while he fastened the cool gems around her throat. The rush of desire she felt was stronger than any she had known since she was eighteen and had explored the nearer edges of sexuality with this same impossible, attractive man. Glancing up, her eyes met Rafe's in the mirror. His hands still rested on her exposed, sensitive shoulders and for once there was no teasing undertone in his voice.

"Margot, why can't we forget all the complications of our past and just be ourselves? You are the most irresistible woman I have ever known. Being so close to you without touching is in a fair way to driving me mad." His thumbs massaged the back of her neck as he continued, "I want you, and I think you want me, too. Why can't we be lovers in truth? We are both adults, old enough to know what we want. No one would be hurt, and I know we would find a rare pleasure together."

Bending over, he kissed the lower edge of her ear where it showed beneath her golden hair, then moved his lips expertly down her neck. His hands slid down her bare arms, then wrapped around her waist to pull her back against him.

Maggie gasped and tried to ignore the fiery reaction his touch aroused in her. "No, blast you! Nothing is that simple."

Rafe's right hand brushed upward across her breast with a feather-light touch, invoking a deeper level of response, and his deep voice was as rich as velvet as he asked, "Do you really mean no? Your words say one thing, but your body says another."

There was too much truth in what he said, and it produced a torrent of angry confusion in Maggie. Of course she wanted him. She was weak with longing, and dared not admit how perilously close she was to consigning past and future to the devil and letting him make love to her in the intoxicating present. But she had learned self-control in the hardest of schools, and even now she knew he was wrong to claim that no one would be hurt by what they did. Maggie would be more than hurt; she would be devastated if she fell in love with Rafe again. Losing him once had nearly destroyed her, and no handful of days as his mistress could compensate for the danger and pain intimacy would bring.

Maggie jerked away and whirled around, unconsciously raising one arm defensively. "No means *No!* If I'd meant yes, I would have said yes!'' Her elbow smashed into the duke's solar plexus with a force that knocked all the wind out of him, causing Rafe to stagger back, wrapping his arms around his midriff. Aghast, Maggie stared at him, backing up until she was pressed against the pier table under the mirror. In a stifled voice, she said, ''I'm sorry, I didn't mean to hit you.''

He straightened up, fighting for breath. His gray eyes weren't cool now; they blazed with anger, and something more. Maggie had never felt physically afraid of Rafe, but now she was acutely aware of the height and breadth and sheer, athletic strength of him. She had wounded his pride, and that was a far graver blow than an accidental elbow.

The moments it took for Rafe to regain his breath gave him time to grab the last shreds of his temper, and his voice was furious but level as he said, ''It is fortunate for you that I was taught never to strike a woman. If you were a man, I would give you a lesson you would never forget.''

Maggie inhaled deeply, struggling with her ragged emotions. ''Surely if I was a man, this situation would not have arisen.''

Rafe's face remained rigid for a moment, then slowly softened. With a hint of a smile, he said, ''No, I suppose it wouldn't have. I am rather conventional in my preferences.''

Rafe was furious with an intensity he hadn't known in the last dozen years, but his anger faded before Maggie's shocked, unhappy expression. Once more the worldly countess was gone, exposing the girl she had been. Maggie must be deeply affected to lash out like that, and that was promising. She was also more loyal to her other lover than expected, and that presented difficulties. Rafe had thought she would yield to the passion of the moment, like most of the society beauties he had known, and he had been wrong.

He felt a touch of guilt at having made her unhappy. It was true that he always gave his mistresses expensive gifts and the necklace had been intended more to put Maggie in a receptive mood than to support their charade. It was a rare woman that would not be flattered and softened by such a costly, beautiful gift, but Maggie *was* a rare woman. More than ever the duke wanted her, and nothing tonight had changed that desire: quite the contrary. Rafael Whitbourne was unaccustomed to failure, and did not accept it now. Still, the woman who had been Margot Ashton represented the greatest challenge of any female he had ever known, and seducing her was proving far harder than expected.

Then cool strategy and analysis disappeared as Maggie raised her beautiful gray-green eyes to his. There was infinite courage and vulnerability in those smoky depths, and with a surge of unexpected emotion that left him shaken, Rafe realized that he didn't actually want the elusive countess; what he really wanted was to have Margot Ashton back. At that moment, he would have given his title and half his fortune to turn back the clock to the uncomplicated love they had shared when they were young. That was impossible, but surely the girl he had loved still lived somewhere inside the lady spy. If it were humanly possible, he would call Margot forth again. Without thinking, he asked, "Why don't you like to be called Margot? Once you liked your name."

She gazed at him for a long, long time, her changeable eyes now unfathomable. Finally she answered as if the words were being torn out of her. "Being Margot hurt too much."

It said everything and nothing, but intuition told Rafe not to ask for a clearer explanation. Instead he said, "It is time we were off to Prince Orkov's ball. We have a general to hunt."

Maggie's face became that of the Countess Janos once more. "Very true." She turned to the mirror, replacing her jade earrings with the emerald ones, then walked across the salon to lift her long cashmere shawl from the chair where she had dropped it earlier. Wrapping it around her shoulders with casual artistry, she turned to face him and said, "Shall we be off?"

Rafe offered her his arm, pleased that he did not give in to the nearly overpowering desire to embrace her again. Still, as he helped her into his coach, he found himself reaching out silently to touch her silky golden hair, wishing he could bury his hands in it. The duke could only hope that his powers of seduction were as good as was generally supposed. He was beginning to fear that he might be unable to change her mind.

Prince Orkov's ballroom was decorated with barbaric mideastern splendor, including footmen dressed as Turkish harem guards, and an Egyptian belly dancer performing in a side room. Even the jaundiced tastes of Paris society admitted that it was a bit out of the ordinary. In spite of frustration with their lack of progress in uncovering the plot, Maggie was enjoying herself.

Their host had held her hand and gazed into her eyes with Slavic soulfulness, but fortunately he was too busy to seek her out. For the first part of the evening, Rafe stayed close to Maggie's side, playing the part of the devoted lover, as if there had been no traumatic scene earlier. But no doubt for him it had not been traumatic; there were plenty of women available to relieve his physical frustrations later this night.

Fleetingly, Maggie toyed with the idea of letting him have his way with her so she would no longer have the cachet of being unavailable. After a night or two, surely he would grow bored and try his luck elsewhere. With a wry smile she repressed the thought, recognizing it for the outrageous rationalization it was. No matter what reasons she concocted to allow him into her bed, the emotional repercussions would be disastrous. He was upsetting her quite enough as it was. Every time she glanced at Rafe she could feel his lips moving sensuously down her neck, and her knees would start to weaken. It was very hard indeed to keep her mind on the business of the evening.

Although General Roussaye was supposed to be present, Maggie couldn't locate him, and in such a crush she was beginning to fear that they would be unsuccessful. After an hour, she and Rafe agreed to look separately and hope for the best.

Midnight came and went, supper was served, and the dancing resumed, and still she hadn't found the man. Exasperated, Maggie drifted into the room where the belly dancer was performing. As the woman undulated in veils and bangles, three musicians sat on the low dais behind her and played minor-key music that sounded strange to European ears. There were only a handful of other guests watching and as her eye accustomed to the dimmer light, Maggie realized that she had found her quarry.

While Maggie had never been introduced to the general, he had been pointed out to her once and now she recognized him. Michel Roussaye was below medium height and wiry in build, but at first glance he reminded her of Colonel von Fehrenbach. Physically the two men were entirely different, but both had the tough watchfulness of the professional man of war. The blond Prussian was an aristocrat who had been bred to the trade while the dark-haired Frenchman was a commoner who had achieved his rank by merit. Nonetheless, even in this dim light, it was clear that they were brothers under the skin. Would Roussaye have as much anger in him as von Fehrenbach did? Of all their suspects, the Bonapartist had the best motive for creating disruptions.

Maggie crossed the room to take a seat near Roussaye, wondering how she might strike up a conversation since there was no one to introduce them. The general was intent on the dancer and her eyes followed his. Then she blinked and concentrated harder on the performer. Was it really possible for a woman to make her breasts twirl in opposite directions? Improbable as it was, the evidence was before her eyes. The spinning tassels heightened the effect. The dancer was heavier than European tastes usually preferred, but there was a large amount of her visible, all of it superbly trained. Maggie had never seen a belly dancer before, since the few places where they might be seen were off-limits for females. She must have made some sound of surprise, because a soft tenor voice sounded in her ear.

"She is a very talented performer, do you not agree?"

Maggie turned and saw that Roussaye was looking at her with amusement. She smiled and said, "Indeed, monsieur, I had no idea that it was possible for a human body to do such things."

He gestured at the stage. "Orkov hired her as a curiosity, but she is an artist of great skill."

"Is artistry what a man sees when he looks at a belly dancer?" Maggie asked with a deliberately provocative glance. Her reward was a smile acknowledging her hit.

"That may not be the first thought in most men's minds,"

he admitted, "but I have spent time in Egypt and have some appreciation for the fine points of the art."

"She does does have rather fine points," Maggie agreed, remembering that Roussaye's first military experience had been in Napoleon's Egyptian campaign of 1798, when he was scarcely more than a boy. The music ended and the sweat-drenched dancer took a bow before retiring for a break. Focusing her attention on Roussaye, Maggie asked, "What was Egypt like?"

This time his smile was warmer. "A splendid place. The temples and art are almost impossible to believe, even when they are right before you. We look at a cathedral five hundred years old and think it ancient. *Their* temples are many times that age. And the Pyramids. . . ." He was lost in memory for a moment before saying softly, "Bonaparte spent the night in the largest. The next morning when he was asked what he had seen, he said only that no one would believe him." With an undertone of sadness he added, "In the history of Egypt, the brief French occupation is less than the blink of an eye. In the history of France, Napoleon may be of no more importance than that."

Maggie said dryly, "A thousand years from now, people may be that detached. In our time, Napoleon appears as the greatest and wickedest man of our age."

Roussaye stiffened and she wondered if she had gone too far. While she wanted to stimulate responses from him, it was preferable not to alienate him entirely.

"You are not French, madame," he said coldly. "It is not to be expected that you would see him as we do."

Maggie gave him a challenging look. "How *does* the French nation see Bonaparte? I am one of many who paid a high cost for his ambition. Can you convince me there was any value to it?"

The general's dark eyes held hers steadily. "You were right to say that he is the greatest man of our age. In his younger years, to be around him was to feel . . . . to feel as if a strong wind was blowing. The emperor had more force and vitality than any man I have ever seen, more strength and more vision. We will never see his equal again."

Leaning forward, he said intensely, "After the Revolution, the hands of every nation in Europe were raised against us. France should have been destroyed, but we weren't. Bonaparte gave us back our power and pride. We were everywhere victorious.''

"And in his later years, your emperor lost whole armies. Hundreds of thousands of soldiers, countless civilians, died for France's glory. Did he not once say that the lives of a million men were nothing to him?'' Maggie could not keep bitterness from her voice. "When Bonaparte came back from Elba, were you one of those who forgot his vows to Louis and followed your emperor?''

"I was.''

His voice was quiet in contrast to hers. Maggie realized that everyone else had left the room and they were alone in their discussion. Quite apart from her desire to find an assassin, she wanted to know what motivated men like this. Controlled again, she asked, "Do you think it was right to rally to him?''

His answer surprised her. "No, I don't suppose it was right, but that doesn't matter,'' he said gravely. "Napoleon was my emperor, and I would have followed him to Hell itself.''

"Then you got your wish. They say that Waterloo was a close approximation of Hell.''

"It was.'' Roussaye's face was stark. "The emperor was not the man he once was, and fifty thousand soldiers paid the price. Perhaps I should have been one of them, but God had other plans for me.'' He sighed, then said with a lightening of his expression, "I have learned that there is life beyond war. It is a salvation I do not deserve.''

An odd, mystical statement for a warrior. Maggie was saved from further comment when two people entered the room. Glancing up, she saw Rafe accompanied by a tiny, exquisite woman with raven-black hair and the swelling figure of mid-pregnancy. Roussaye rose, a smile transforming his serious expression.

Rafe said smoothly, "Magda, my love, permit me to introduce you to Madame Roussaye. She has been kindly showing me some of our host's paintings.''

The raven-haired woman smiled at Maggie warmly. In the exchange of greetings and introductions, Maggie discovered that Roussaye's wife Filomena was an Italian aristocrat, a distant cousin of Rafe's through his Italian grandmother. Judging by the way the Roussayes looked at each other, it was easy to guess that his wife was the salvation he had referred to; the bond between them was almost tangible. Was the general an ardent enough Bonapartist to risk his personal happiness in a treacherous plot? Unfortunately, Maggie feared that he was.

The intensity of the earlier discussion disappeared in a general conversation. All four had an interest in art, and before the couples parted they made an engagement to visit the Louvre together three days hence.

Back in the main ballroom, a waltz was playing and Rafe swept Maggie into it without asking her permission. As they whirled across the floor, she decided ruefully that conservative opinion was right; even though he held her at a perfectly proper distance, the waltz was still altogether too erotic to be decent. With her awareness of him heightened by their encounter earlier in the evening, it was all too easy to notice how much the closeness and rhythms of the dance were like making love.

It was not entirely a relief to discover that the duke's purposes were strictly business. With so much sound around them, the waltz was a perfect opportunity to talk privately. He asked, "What is your judgment of General Roussaye?"

She hesitated for three complete circles as she marshalled her thoughts and impressions. Finally she said, "He is devoted to France and the emperor, and I'm afraid he is quite capable of participating in any plot that might restore Bonaparte to the throne. He has the best motive of all our suspects, coupled with the intelligence and conviction to achieve his ends."

"But you have reservations," Rafe said, reading the undercurrents of her speech.

Maggie sighed. "Only that I liked the man. Starting with very little, he has achieved a great deal on pure merit. Beyond his military skills, he has taste and sensitivity. I wish that Varenne was our villain, but Roussaye is more likely.'

"If so, my newfound cousin may be a widow in short order," Rafe said, his gray eyes thoughtful. "Since Roussaye has already broken his oath to Louis once, the slightest hint of evidence that he is involved in a plot will put him in a cell next to Marshal Ney, waiting for execution.''

The statement was depressingly true. ''Men are such fools!'' Maggie said with exasperation. ''He has a beautiful wife who adores him, he has earned enough legitimate wealth to live a comfortable life, yet he would throw that all away.''

''Are you sure it is he?'' Rafe looked at her searchingly. He, too, had been impressed by Roussaye, and the discovery that the general's wife was a distant relation made him hope that the man was not involved in treachery.

She shook her head regretfully, her eyes unfocused. ''Not entirely, but I fear that Roussaye is up to something he shouldn't be. Though I have only my intuition, I would wager money that all is not completely above board with the general. Perhaps he is not involved in our particular conspiracy—but I fear that he may be.''

She sighed again. ''We should pass our speculations on as soon as possible. Lord Lattimer may know something that will corroborate them.'' This was one of the times she disliked being a spy. If she were wrong, she might contribute to the ruin of an innocent man. At this moment in time, all the important Bonapartists were on dangerously thin ice, and even a hint of suspicion could ruin a man, perhaps send him to the firing squad. She reminded herself that the stakes were higher than one person's life; the successful assassination of an Allied leader could throw Europe into another war.

Rafe said, ''I'll send a courier to Lattimer tonight, but I think the time has come to talk directly to Lord Castlereagh.''

Used to working indirectly, Maggie was momentarily startled. Still, the foreign minister knew who she was and had reason to trust her guesses. If she and Rafe talked to him in person, they might be able to impress on him the seriousness of the situation. ''We would have to meet with him in a way that would not arouse comment,'' she cautioned.

Rafe smiled. ''That will be no problem. Lord and Lady Castlereagh often entertain distinguished British visitors, which, in all modesty, I can claim to be. As my companion, a woman already known to them, you would be equally welcome. I will contact him and ask that a private breakfast or lunch be arranged.''

It was a perfectly sensible approach. As one of Britain's preeminent noblemen, Rafe was exactly the sort of visitor the Castlereaghs honored with private invitations. "Best make it as soon as possible," she said darkly. "I feel in my bones that something is going to happen soon."

The music stopped and they moved toward the edge of the ballroom. Maggie was about to suggest they leave when the orchestra struck up another waltz and Robert Anderson approached them. He nodded to Rafe, then bowed before Maggie.

"Countess, would you grant me the honor of this dance?'' As he straightened up, his eyes carried a message.

Tired as she was, and even noting the steely glint in Rafe's eyes, it never occurred to Maggie to refuse. Publicly she and Robin were only the most casual of acquaintances, and he would not ask her to dance if there wasn't something he needed to discuss with her. She smiled and extended one hand. "It would be my pleasure, Mr. Anderson."

She blew a kiss to Rafe as Robin took her in his arms and carried her away in the rapid turns of the waltz. With a bright, careless smile on her face, she asked urgently, "Is something wrong, Robin?''

His smile was equally facile, as was his dancing. For all the years they had known each other and as intimate as they had been, they had never waltzed together. Maggie was not surprised to discover that he was an excellent dancer, and they knew each other too well to need to concentrate on footwork.

"Not really wrong, Maggie. It is just that I heard something that I wanted to pass on to you in hopes that your informants might be able to make something of it.'' His grave blue eyes contrasted with his frivolous mien. "One of my disreputable informants has given me a name to put behind the conspiracy. Not a real name, unfortunately, but it is something to go on. The man is called *Le Serpent*.''

"*Le Serpent?*'' Maggie's brows wrinkled in concentration. "It is unfamiliar to me.''

"And to me,'' Robin admitted. "There is no one in the

Parisian underworld by that name. My informant could not even say if the man was French or a foreigner. Apparently, *Le Serpent* has been recruiting criminals to carry out a plot against some of the Allied leaders."

Maggie thought about what he had said, but the information rang no bells. She said, "I will ask if any of my women have heard of such a man. Were there any other clues?"

"Not as such. But I have wondered . . ." Robin's voice trailed off as he deftly negotiated them out of the path of a drunken Russian officer whose enthusiasm for waltzing exceeded his skill. When they were safely clear, he continued, "Is it possible that the name might come from a family crest or some such? The man we are after is certainly someone of power and position, and would most probably have a coat of arms."

Maggie felt a tingle at the words. In his own way, Robin was as intuitive as Maggie herself and it would not be the first time that a small fact triggered a mental leap to something quite different. When inspiration struck, he was usually right.

"It is certainly possible," she exclaimed. "I'll ask around to discover whose arms involve any kind of snake. There can't be too many." It was good to have something concrete to investigate after all the days of frustration.

During the latter part of the dance, Maggie described her meeting with General Roussaye and her suspicions of him. Robin listened intently, and when she had finished, he said, "I will see if I can find any snakes in his background."

With a devilish gleam in his eye he said, "I think we are on the edge of a breakthrough, Maggie. But for God's sake, be careful. My informant seemed to think *Le Serpent* is a direct representative of Satan. Whoever he is, the man is dangerous."

The music ended. Robin had maneuvered so that the last bars brought them to the Duke of Candover. Gracefully handing Maggie back to Rafe's keeping, he bid them good night, then disappeared.

Maggie's worried eyes followed him. Robin must be as tired as she was but if she knew him, he would spend half of the remaining night in Parisian stews and gaming hells looking for further traces of *Le Serpent*. And he told *her* to be careful!

Intent on her friend, she didn't see the black look on Rafe's face as he observed her preoccupation.

Chapter 10

Maggie spent the next morning initiating inquiries about snakes and related heraldic creatures. In addition, there was a fragile old lady in the Faubourg St. Germain who had lost all her male descendants in Napoleon's wars. Mme. Daudet longed for peace, and she also knew the history, marriages, and arms of every important family in France. Maggie had done her a great favor once and the old lady was eager to repay the debt, promising that within forty-eight hours she would have a detailed list of possibilities among both the old and the new French aristocracy. With luck, it would provide some clues.

Around noon, a note was delivered from Rafe saying they would lunch with the Castlereaghs the next day. Maggie breathed a silent prayer of gratitude that the event had been arranged so promptly, and prepared to call on a gossipy woman who was an expert on the upper levels of Bonapartist society.

Her departure was delayed when the butler brought in the card of an unexpected visitor. *Mrs. Oliver Northwood.* Maggie tapped the card thoughtfully, curious what Cynthia Northwood might have to say, then ordered her butler to admit the visitor.

The young woman looked tense and nervous when she entered, her pretty face pale against the dark curls. "I am glad to find you without other company, Countess," she faltered in French. "I wish to discuss something with you."

"But of course, my dear," Maggie said with her best

grande dame manner. She spoke in Magyar-accented English, assuming that Cynthia would prefer it. "Would you care for some coffee?"

At her visitor's automatic nod, Maggie gave orders to the butler, then seated herself, gesturing Cynthia to a sofa near the window where it would be easy to read her expression. Maggie made general remarks and received monosyllabic replies until coffee and delicate pastries were served. Finally she said, "My dear, if you have something to discuss with me, perhaps you had better just come out with it."

Cynthia's wide brown eyes met hers, then slid away. "It is harder to say than I thought it would be. You scarcely know me, and have no reason to listen to my troubles. But . . . but I needed another woman to talk to."

"And you chose me because our mutual relationship with Candover makes us sisters?" Maggie asked with amusement.

Cynthia looked startled, then smiled faintly. "Perhaps that is it. Since we have a . . . mutual friend, and you listened kindly once, I thought I could talk to you." She drew herself up with visible effort. "When we talked before, I told you that I was unhappy in my marriage."

Maggie nodded encouragingly. "Yes. I met your husband later that evening." She gave a small moue of distaste, then let curiosity overcome politeness. "Why did you marry him?"

Cynthia spread her hands wide in despairing gesture. "I fancied myself in love, of course. Oliver was handsome and dashing and lived such an exciting life compared to Lincolnshire, where I grew up. The aunt who presented me was impressed that he was the son of a lord and told me what a splendid conquest I had made. I didn't look beyond his lineage and tailoring."

She smiled wryly. "He *was* handsome seven years ago, before his indulgences caught up with him. I was only eighteen, dazzled that such a man of the world should court me. It never occurred to me to consider his character." She shrugged. "I got what I deserved. It is incredible that we choose our life's companions on a handful of meetings, usually under the most artificial of circumstances. Since Oliver came of a good family, my father saw no reason to deny his suit. I was so pleased by my good fortune that I never asked what he saw in me.''

''You are too hard on yourself. You are a very attractive woman, one any man might fall in love with,'' Maggie said.

''Perhaps,'' Cynthia said, unmollified. ''More to the point, I had a very fine dowry. As a younger son, Oliver would have needed to marry well in any case, but his gambling debts made the situation urgent.'' She sighed. ''It took very little time for me to realize what a poor bargain I had made. I come from simple country folk who believe in old-fashioned things like fidelity. I won't bore you with how I discovered about his women, but it shattered all my illusions. When I confronted him, he mocked me for being a provincial little fool.''

Until now she had been speaking with commendable restraint, but now her voice filled with pain. Ever practical, Maggie poured more coffee in Cynthia's cup. The girl choked a bit as she sipped it, then continued her depressing little tale.

''I decided to pay him back in his own coin.'' She flushed and stared into the depths of her cup. ''It was foolish. Women are not the same as men, and it was a poor form of revenge. Except for Candover, I have few good memories of that time. Rafe was always kind. He told me to put a higher price on myself.''

She glanced up again. ''I didn't know what he meant at first, but I did eventually. I started behaving in a way that would not shame my father if he knew of it, and I found it much easier to live with myself.''

''What has gone wrong?'' Maggie coaxed gently. She was beginning to be impressed by Cynthia's insight. The girl had more wisdom than was first apparent, but she would not be here talking to a virtual stranger were she not in trouble.

Cynthia's eyes were bleakly unhappy. ''I fell in love, and was happier than I had ever been, and now everything is much, much worse.'' She swallowed hard before continuing. ''Gregory is everything I should have sought in a husband but was too foolish to appreciate. He doesn't look at all like a Greek god, but he is kind, reliable, and honorable. Most of all, he loves me. I don't know why, but he does.'' Her voice faded to a whisper.

Maggie looked at her with compassion. No wonder the poor girl looked so wretched. She was in a situation where there was little prospect of a happy resolution.

Cynthia put her cup down and toyed nervously with a ring. "I want to marry and settle down somewhere in the country with Gregory and raise lots of babies and get plump and warm my feet on his back in the winter. That is what he wants, too. He hates the dishonesty of what we are doing."

"But as long as you and your husband live, that is impossible," Maggie said softly. "I understand that in England divorces are virtually unobtainable, that perhaps one a year is granted. Even if you had the money and influence to get a bill of divorcement through your Parliament, you would be an outcast."

"There is no time for that," Cynthia said grimly. "I am with child."

Maggie inhaled sharply. That *did* complicate matters. "It is not your husband's?" she asked delicately.

Cynthia shook her head. "No. Oliver was never very interested in me and we have not been man and wife for years. Unfortunately, while he doesn't want me for himself, he doesn't want anyone else to have me, either." She shuddered. "I am frightened about what he will do when he learns I am increasing."

"And it is not the sort of thing one can conceal very long," Maggie said sympathetically. "What does your Gregory think?"

Cynthia started twisting her hands together. "I haven't told him yet. When I do, I know he will insist that I leave Oliver and go live with him."

"It will be a scandal, but hardly unique," Maggie pointed out. "Perhaps that would be the best solution."

For the first time, Cynthia's voice became uneven. "You don't know my husband. Oliver is horribly vindictive. He would sue Gregory for criminal conversation. Gregory is not a rich man—he would be ruined. His military career would be over. Both our families would be disgraced."

With a catch, she finished. "It would break my father's heart." She buried her face in her hands as sobs overcame her. Between gulps for breath, she managed to say, "The worst is that I fear Gregory would come to hate me for ruining his life.''

Maggie crossed quickly to sit next to her guest on the sofa, putting one arm around her with what silent comfort she could offer. Young Mrs. Northwood was in a ghastly bind, and it was hardly surprising that she was distraught. In fact, given the circumstances, Maggie thought the girl was holding up rather well. Fiercely, she cursed the inflexible marriage laws that kept husband and wife tied together no matter how miserable they were.

When Cynthia's sobs abated, Maggie produced a fresh lawn handkerchief and said prosaically, ''Your choices are limited. You can stay with your husband or leave. If you leave, you can return to your father, live with Gregory, or perhaps set up an independent establishment.''

Cynthia straightened, wiping her eyes with the handkerchief ''It sounds quite simple when you put it that way. Certainly I want to leave, but it will be very difficult. Oliver would be injured in his pocketbook as well as his pride— my father's money supports us. My dowry is long since gone, but Papa sends an allowance that I use for the household expenses. That would cease if I left.'' She shook her head with bemusement. ''With the amount that Oliver loses gambling, he would be unable to maintain an establishment if I wasn't there.'' She lifted a nervous hand to brush a loose piece of hair from her face. ''Perhaps he could manage. Certainly, he always seems to have money.''

An alarm bell went off in Maggie's mind. Northwood was an inveterate gambler with unexpected financial resources? They had concentrated on investigating the assassination plot since that was most urgent, but there was also the matter of a possible spy in the British delegation. If there was such a person, the mysterious *Le Serpent* might be using his services. Since Maggie heartily disliked Oliver Northwood, she was quite willing to believe him a villain, and if he was in contact with the master conspirator . . . Controlling her excitement, she commented casually, ''His salary from the Foreign Office must help.''

''It is a mere pittance, only two hundred pounds a year,'' Cynthia said, then frowned a bit. ''I really don't know where his money comes from. He must pay off most of his debts or no one would continue to gamble with him." She shrugged indifferently. Her husband's finances were not of great interest to her.

Choosing her words carefully, Maggie asked, "Is it possible that Mr. Northwood might be involved in something he shouldn't be?"

Cynthia looked surprised. "Why would you ask such a thing?"

Maggie put on her innocent face. "It was just a hope. If your husband had some secret, he might be more easily persuaded to let you leave without causing trouble." With a roguish smile, she added, "I assumed that part of the reason you wished to talk with me was to get the ideas of a wily European who was not raised with your English sense of fair play."

Cynthia's shock melted to embarrassment. "Perhaps it was, without my being aware of it." Her expression became withdrawn as she thought about what her hostess had said. With a touch of excitement, she said, "Do you know, there may be something that he is concealing. He seemed to change when he joined the Foreign Office, and it has become more pronounced since we came to Paris. He has had more money since then, too. More than can be accounted for by his salary, I mean." She thought a bit more.

"Do you suppose he might be taking bribes of some sort?" she questioned. "Though he hasn't much influence to sell."

"He might pretend to more influence than he has," Maggie suggested. Bribery was frowned upon but common. In fact, in some jobs it was endemic. Many people would accept bribes who would never consider spying against their country, and Northwood might be one of those. Still, it was worth pursuing.

Her eyes shrewd, Cynthia said slowly, "Several weeks ago I was writing letters and looked in Oliver's desk for wafers. He came in and was furious. In fact, he struck me." She continued as if being abused was not that uncommon. "Since then, he has locked all his papers up. Do you think it might mean something?"

"Possibly," Maggie said. "Perhaps not. Some men are naturally secretive. But if he has some guilty secret that you discovered, it might give you some ammunition." She caught Cynthia's distant eye with her own and said seriously, "It is not a nice thing that we are talking about. Are you truly willing to behave in a way that is dishonorable?"

Cynthia took a deep breath, but her gaze was unwavering. "Yes. We women have few weapons at our disposal. It would be foolish to waste one. Perhaps I can stop some greater tragedy, like a duel. I don't think Oliver would fight one, but I could be wrong." She trembled as if a cold draft touched her. "I could not bear to have either his or Gregory's life on my shoulders."

Satisfied, Maggie said, "If you are sure. Do you think you could unlock his desk and investigate his private papers?"

Cynthia gulped a little but nodded her head.

"If you do, you must be very careful, you know. Your husband has a violent temper and if he caught you, he might do you a serious injury. You have not just your own life to consider." Maggie put as much earnestness in her voice as she could. She was not particularly proud of herself for setting a wife to spy on her husband, but the opportunity was too good to pass up. Moreover, if Oliver Northwood really were a spy, that fact might make it easier for Cynthia to escape him.

Her visitor nodded calmly. "I know. I promise I will be careful. I know better than anyone what Oliver might do."

"If you discover anything suspicious, bring it to me first," Maggie added. "I have considerable experience of the world, and I might have a better understanding of what you have found."

Cynthia nodded again as she stood. "I can't thank you enough, Countess. Talking to someone has helped enormously."

Maggie rose also. "Perhaps you should call me Magda since we are going to be co-conspirators. Or Maggie, if you prefer."

"Thank you, Maggie. And please, call me Cynthia." Leaning forward, she gave the older woman a quick, grateful hug.

After cautioning her once more to be very careful about investigating her husband's private papers, Maggie showed

Cynthia out. Then she sat down to think about what she had learned. Quite apart from her dislike of Oliver Northwood, her instinct said that he was capable of treachery. It would be for greed, not ideological reasons. Of course, he might be innocent, or guilty of no more than minor corruption. Still, given the volatile situation here in Paris, information was tremendously valuable, and a weak man might succumb to temptation.

The next question was whether to tell Rafe. Maggie frowned. While the duke and Northwood were not really friends, they had known each other forever, at Eton and as part of the same circle when they were young men about town. It would be very hard for Rafe to believe that someone from that group of bluff, honest Englishmen was a traitor. Much easier to suspect a stranger than an acquaintance.

Under the circumstances, Maggie should not tell the duke of her suspicions unless Cynthia discovered some concrete proof. For the sake of all of them, she hoped that would happen soon.

That evening Rafe went to the Salon des Étrangers, the closest thing to a gentlemen's club in Paris. It was a rendezvous for confirmed gamblers, and many of the richest and most influential men in Paris were regular customers. He had visited several times in hopes of hearing something useful, but without success. Standing at the entrance to the main gambling room, the duke surveyed the sizable crowd for familiar faces. The Salon was far larger and grander than the modest Café Mazarin but the signs of gambling fever were the same. Within a few moments the proprietor, the Marquis de Livry, came forward. The marquis bore a remarkable resemblance to the Prince Regent, both in girth and grandeur of manner.

Smiling graciously, the host said, "How delightful to see you this evening, your grace. What is your preference tonight?"

"I'll wait to see what table calls me," Rafe said.

The marquis nodded, accustomed to gamblers who looked for some magic sign that fortune favored them. After urging the duke to partake of the complimentary wine, Livry left to greet a party of Austrians. Taking a glass of excellent burgundy from a footman, Rafe strolled through the crowd. He had no particular object in view, but it was better to be doing something than nothing.

It was with a feeling of inevitability that Rafe saw Robert Anderson sitting at the faro table. The blond man had a talent for turning up in unexpected places. Was it coincidence, or was Anderson also involved in the murky shadows of intelligence gathering? And if so, for whom did he work? Shielded by a Corinthian column, Rafe sipped his wine and took the opportunity to study the younger man. Once again, he felt a tantalizing sense of near-recognition, but could not identify it. His attempts to remember were interrupted by a jovial greeting. "Good evening, Candover. Good to see you again."

Rafe turned without enthusiasm to greet Oliver Northwood, surprised to find his old acquaintance at a place where the play was so deep. Men of much greater fortune than Northwood had been utterly ruined in the Salon des Étrangers. Still, a gambler who knew when to stop was safe anywhere. After a few minutes of desultory conversation, Rafe decided to ask about Anderson, since Northwood had worked with him for some time. With a vague gesture, the duke said, "Your colleague Anderson reminds me of someone, but I can't remember who. What is his background?"

"Hasn't any," Northwood said, then drained his own glass of burgundy. "Fellow just appeared in Paris in July and Castlereagh took him into the delegation. Must have had a letter of recommendation, but I don't know who from. Says he isn't related to any Andersons I know." He hailed a footman and exchanged his empty glass for a full one, adding, "Comes here often."

"Really?" Rafe asked. "Then whatever Andersons he comes from, they must be well off."

Northwood scowled, giving the appearance of a man coming to a decision. "Perhaps I shouldn't say this, Candover, but there's something dashed smoky about Anderson. Sprang from nowhere, always poking into things that don't concern him, then disappears like a bloody alley cat. Has more money than he should."

"Interesting. Have you spoken to Castlereagh about your suspicions?" As he spoke, the duke watched Anderson push half the counters in front of him across the table after losing a bet, as imperturbable in defeat as in victory. The man looked as blond and angelic as a choirboy. Was that what Maggie saw in him, that handsome face? Or did she fancy herself in love with him? *What the hell did Anderson have that Rafe didn't?*

Rafe was shocked by the surge of jealousy that engulfed him. It was an unfamiliar emotion, and not one that he liked. The duke had always been willing to bid a graceful farewell to women who developed other preferences, and the anger he felt at the memory of Anderson slipping in Maggie's back door was a serious blow to his view of himself as a civilized man. Trying to control his primitive emotions, Rafe reminded himself that Anderson was merely one of many men Maggie had had in her life. There was no point in being jealous of the blond man merely because he was the only one of her lovers that Rafe knew.

That reflection was a singular failure at calming him.

His turbulent thoughts had taken only a moment, and now Northwood answered Rafe's question. Looking around first to assure that no one was within listening distance, he lowered his voice and said grimly, "I've talked to Castlereagh, all right. That's why I'm here—the foreign minister asked me to keep an eye on Anderson. Informally, you know." At Rafe's questioning look, he added, "Just to see if he talks to anyone suspicious. Shouldn't be telling you any of this, but I know you can be trusted, and wanted to put you on your guard. You know what the situation is here in Paris. Can't be too careful."

Northwood looked as if he was weighing whether to continue, then added in a voice almost inaudible in the hub-bub of the salon, "Confidential information has been getting out of the British delegation. Don't want to slander an innocent man—but we're watching Anderson very closely."

It was the most serious Rafe had ever seen Northwood, and he wondered if he had misjudged the man. Perhaps the hail-fellow-well-met demeanor was a deliberate disguise. He looked at his old schoolmate lounging against the pillar and tried to be dispassionate. They had never been close, but they had been friendly in a casual way. Apart from Northwood's connection with Margot so many years ago, the duke had no reason to distrust him, though he could not like his vulgarity of manner. The affair with Margot had been more her fault, since few hot-blooded young men would have refused such a temptation if she offered herself. Had irrational jealousy been coloring the duke's judgment of Northwood ever since? Very likely.

That same jealousy would make it all too easy to believe the worst of Anderson, and Rafe had to remind himself that he was in Paris to help his country, not to pursue personal intrigues. But if the blond man was a traitor to Britain, it would be a great pleasure to see him caught and punished. The duke said, "I'll keep my eyes open, and perhaps I'll remember why Anderson looks familiar. It might be significant."

The duke would certainly be watchful, though he would not pass any observations on to Oliver Northwood. He was feeling more in charity with the man, but any information should go to Lattimer in London or Castlereagh here in Paris.

With a nod of complicity, he drifted away from Northwood, ending at the *rouge et noir* table. It was a game that involved more luck than skill, so Rafe was able to monitor what was happening elsewhere in the room. He noticed when General Michel Roussaye took an empty chair at the faro table next to Anderson, noticed the intent words the two men exchanged, which might or might not have anything to do with faro. Noticed and pondered.

Chapter 11

Maggie and Rafe were both silent on the way to lunch with the Castlereaghs next day. She had been tempted to tell him of her suspicions of Oliver Northwood, but the duke was too much the cool, remote aristocrat today, his dark face impossibly handsome and detached. When they entered the British embassy, Maggie looked around appreciatively. Her other visits had been during large receptions, when the public rooms were crowded. Now she could see clearly the superb proportions and decorations. They ate in a private dining room and the excellent luncheon was served on Pauline Bonaparte's own plate, which Wellington had bought along with the house the previous year.

Looking every inch a duke's mistress, Maggie wore sky blue with matching ostrich plumes in her hair and kept up a light stream of amusing chatter. Here in private, Lord Castlereagh was relaxed and witty and the meal was an enjoyable one. The talk did not turn serious until a silver pot of coffee was placed on the table and Lady Castlereagh signaled for the servants to withdraw. The foreign minister started the discussion by saying, "Have you heard the latest news from the Tuileries?"

Both of his guests shook their heads. The French king's court at the Tuileries was a whirlpool of rumor and gossip as factions of royalists struggled for ascendancy, but there had been no hard news from that quarter. With unconscious showmanship, Castlereagh paused before saying, "Fouché has been forced out of the government, and Talleyrand will be gone in a few days also." With amusement, he added, "Prince Talleyrand loftily offered his resignation. Much to his surprise, the king took it."

Maggie drew her breath in sharply as she considered the implications, then glanced at the duke. His eyes were cool and grave and his thoughts must parallel hers. Talleyrand was difficult and unpredictable, but also brilliant and a force for moderation; his departure might increase the danger for other moderates. She asked thoughtfully, "Who will replace him?"

"The tsar used his influence to ensure that it would be one of the royalists who governed for him in Russia, the Duc de Richelieu or the Count de Varenne. Louis has agreed to accept Richelieu." The minister added speculatively, "The consensus in the diplomatic corps is that he will last only a few weeks."

Maggie shook her head. "Don't be too sure of that, your

lordship. I've met the man and he may provide some surprise."

Castlereagh regarded her keenly; he must have hoped for such information. He asked, "What is your evaluation of Richelieu?"

She considered a moment before saying, "Absolute integrity, capable of being forceful if necessary. He will be a strong advocate for France, but I think you will deal well together."

Castlereagh nodded. "That confirms my own impressions. The negotiations are going well and the other Allies have finally agreed that reparations and an army of occupation will serve Europe better than more punitive measures. The monarchs should be returning to their own countries in another fortnight or so." He glanced reassuringly at his wife, who had been silent for some time. "There are a number of details to be worked out over the next several months, but I think that the worst is over."

Rafe spoke up now. "I hope you are right, but we are afraid that the next two weeks will be very dangerous for you personally, Lord Castlereagh." Briefly he described the rumors that he and Maggie had been pursuing, and their suspicions.

The foreign minister took the news of threats calmly. "Lord Lattimer has informed me of what you say. I realize that there is some danger, but it is not the first time I have been threatened, and God willing, it won't be the last."

Maggie thought with exasperation that stoicism was all very well, but a little fear could be a useful thing. She glanced as her hostess and saw that Lady Castlereagh's round face was tense and her fingers had tightened around a silver spoon. While her husband was being heroic, Emily was dying inside. However, she had been a political wife too long to make a fuss in front of anyone, and perhaps only Maggie really noticed her anxiety.

They talked a few minutes longer, until the dining room clock struck two. Glancing up, Lord Castlereagh said, "I must leave now for a meeting with the French and the tsar at the Tuileries. I expect it will be rather lively."

He and Rafe talked about the tsar's Holy Alliance as they headed to the stables where the duke's carriage waited with the embassy horses. Lady Castlereagh accompanied her guests to the rear door, and Maggie lagged behind for a moment to say, "There is some danger, Emily, but I'm sure he will come through safely."

Emily sighed. "I can only pray that my husband has the same magical ability to avoid bullets that Wellington does. We're been talking about putting guards on all the embassy doors, and now I will insist on it." She swallowed before finishing calmly, "I'll be glad when this is over and we are back in London." She glanced at her handsome husband and said ruefully, "Sometimes I wish Robert would have been content to stay in Ireland and raise sheep. It would have been much easier on my nerves."

Maggie shook her head. "Yes, but he wouldn't have been the man that he is if he had done that."

"True. I remind myself of that." With visible effort, Lady Castlereagh schooled her face to that of a calm hostess. "So pleasant to see you and Candover, Magda. We must get together again soon." Then she re-entered the embassy.

Going down the steps into the yard between the embassy and the stables, Maggie was some distance behind the two men. Candover's carriage had been called, along with a restless bay gelding for Castlereagh to ride to his meeting. Maggie frowned, her instinct for danger tugging her. She scanned the yard and the windows that overlooked it but saw nothing suspicious.

Castlereagh's horse fidgeted and tossed its head, and Maggie could see the way its eyes rolled even from across the yard. The gelding seemed a bit wild for city riding and she wondered that the groom was not holding it in better. The stableyard was a confined place; an out-of-control mount could be dangerous. Her gaze sharpened on the groom, a thin, dark man with a scarred face. Something about him was subtly wrong.

The two men were absorbed in their talk and only Maggie noticed the gelding's behavior. She was staring at the horse when it neighed, a furious sound that echoed harshly between the stone buildings. In horrible detail Maggie saw the bay jerk free of its reins and rear, then twist around, its back arching. In less than a second the gelding had its head between its front legs and was kicking back. The two men were standing too close to the horse to escape and the wild, iron-shod hooves smashed into Lord Castlereagh, hurling him into Rafe so that both men were knocked to the ground.

As soon as the bay jerked loose Maggie cried out a warning and raced down the steps toward the men as the horse plunged and kicked, neighing in frenzy. A wall was behind the animal so it couldn't easily bolt and it continued bucking and rearing over the foreign minister's unconscious body. Apparently uninjured, Rafe grabbed Castlereagh under the arms and began pulling him backward out of danger. The horse reared again, one pawing hoof just missing the duke's head, grazing his shoulder instead. Rafe was jarred sideways but maintained his grip, steadily dragging his burden backward.

Maggie swore out loud as she reached them. Where the devil had the groom gone? The man had disappeared as soon as the horse went out of control. Pulling her feathered bandeau from her head, Maggie waved it at the maddened gelding in an attempt to drive it away from Rafe and Castlereagh. The horse neighed violently again, its eyes rolling wildly and flecks of foam around its mouth, but Maggie stood her ground, the fluttering plumes in her hand causing the bay to back away from her along the wall of the stables.

When it was clear of the humans, the horse whirled and thundered cross the stableyard. The yard was a dead end, and a young red-haired groom ran out of the stables and cornered the frantic animal, attempting to catch it before it could harm itself. Behind Maggie, she heard cries from the embassy.

Dropping the feathered headdress, Maggie turned back to where Rafe was kneeling by the foreign minister's side. "How is he?" she asked breathlessly, dropping down in the dust beside the duke. Castlereagh was unconscious, a bleeding gash on the side of his head, but she could see that he was still breathing.

"I'm not sure," Rafe said grimly. "The first kick caught him full in the ribs, and another hoof grazed his head." As he talked, he was expertly checking out the damage. People were pouring out of the embassy, including a white-faced Lady Castlereagh. Rafe automatically took command, ordering a litter and sending a footman for a physician. Maggie put an arm around Emily and said, "That was a bad kick but he should be all right."

Lady Castlereagh nodded, her eyes terrified but her self-control holding. Two footmen returned with a hastily improvised litter and carefully lifted the foreign minister onto it, then carried him into the house. His wife followed and Maggie went with her to offer comfort while they waited for the physician.

As the procession entered the embassy, Rafe turned and entered the stables. The young red-headed groom had caught the gelding and taken it inside to a box stall, where it danced in agitation, wild-eyed and tossing its head. The bay still wore saddle and bridle, and the groom stood outside the stall, wary of venturing nearer until the horse was calmer.

Rafe asked, "I'm Candover. Tell me, has Lord Castlereagh's horse always been this wild?"

The young groom gave the duke a worried glance. Like all of the embassy staff, he was British and he answered in a broad West Country accent. "Nay, your grace. Samson is spirited, but a better-tempered horse you never saw. Is his lordship hurt bad?"

"We won't know until the physician has examined him, but I think he will recover."

"Will . . . will they destroy Samson, your grace?"

"I doubt it." Swinging open the door of the stall, Rafe entered and walked over to the nervous horse. "I want to look at him more closely."

Candover was said to be one of the finest horsemen in England and years later the young groom would still be telling the story of how quickly the duke calmed a terrified animal, like he'd magicked it. As Samson jerked his head back and flattened his ears, Rafe began murmuring a string of nonsense words and soon the horse let him near enough to stroke its neck. The duke had scooped up a handful of oats before he entered the stall and as the bay's breathing slowed and the agitated movements stopped, Rafe had Samson literally eating out of his hand.

After the horse had finished the oats, Rafe reached up and cautiously slid the bridle off, then nodded with grim satisfaction. It was as he had guessed; the bridle had a cruel cutting bit, and the least pressure against Samson's tender mouth would have caused the horse considerable pain. The young groom looked at the bit, then at the duke, his eyes wide with questions. "Your grace, why would anyone do that?"

Rafe shook his head. "I can guess but I won't. This explains why Samson reared in the first place, but something more would probably be required to make him kick like that. Shall we see what else we can find?"

Uncinching the horse's girth, he lifted off the saddle and cloth. Samson stirred restlessly and Rafe ran one hand down the bay's sweaty neck until he relaxed again. Still stroking, he examined the area that had been under the saddle cloth until he found what he sought. A small metal object was lodged in Samson's hide, and the horse jerked when it was removed, a sluggish line of blood trickling down his brown flank.

The object Rafe had pulled from the wound had four spikes joined in the center, rather like a miniature version of the caltrops that were used to cripple horses in warfare. He showed it to the groom, who had gone beyond surprise to anger.

"Someone wanted to hurt his lordship." The boy's mouth was hard. The lad was no fool, and must know something of the tense political situation in Paris.

"Who usually handles Lord Castlereagh's horse?"

"The head groom, Mr. Anthony, but he's not here now. He had to go to Saint-Denis this morning."

"Do you know who would have saddled Samson today?"

The groom thought, then shook his head again. "Not exactly, your grace. I was cleaning tack and didn't see who it was. Didn't know nothing was wrong until I heard Samson screaming."

"Could you make a guess? Has there been anyone suspicious about the stables?" Rafe questioned.

A gleam of excitement came into the groom's eyes. "I can't swear it was him for sure, but there's been a Frenchy groom working here 'cause we're short-handed. It was probably him that saddled up Samson and took him out. One of the regular grooms had to go back to England 'cause his father died, and another one was beat up in a street fight and can't work for a few days."

"What did this French groom look like?"

The boy said, "Medium height, dark, a scar on his face. Brown eyes, I think. He kept to hisself, and I never really talked to him. His name was Jean Blanc."

"Don't be surprised if you don't see or hear of him again," Rafe said. He looked hard at the young groom to impress him with his seriousness. "Don't tell anybody what we have found. I'll talk to Lord Castlereagh myself. Do you understand?"

The boy nodded. Rafe looked at him for a moment longer until he was sure that the groom understood the seriousness on his words, then he left the stables and joined Maggie and Lady Castlereagh as they waited for the physician's verdict on the foreign minister. The news was good; Castlereagh had several cracked and broken ribs and a mild concussion but was already planning on holding meetings in his bed-chamber, to his wife's considerable exasperation. After Lady Castlereagh had given Maggie and Rafe her heartfelt thanks for their part in preventing the accident from being more serious, the duke extracted his dusty and bedraggled lady-bird to take her home.

Maggie didn't speak at first. Finally she said, her voice stark, "He could have been killed right in front of us."

"I know," Rafe said bleakly. "It speaks poorly for our abilities as spies and bodyguards."

"What did you discover in the stables?"

The duke briefly described the cutting bit, the spike in Samson's side, and the mysterious French groom, Jean Blanc.

Maggie thought a bit, then said, "He probably chose to-day because the head groom was away and the stables were understaffed. I suppose Blanc jerked on the bridle, cutting Samson's mouth. Then when the horse reared, he slammed his hand onto the saddle cloth, driving the spike in. He was on Samson's far side, where no one could see him. Then he ran away."

"He might have run away because we were there and things weren't going according to plan," Rafe suggested. "If Castlereagh had been trampled, he might have been killed outright. There would have been such an uproar that Blanc could have stayed around long enough to remove the cutting bit and spike, and the death would have seemed like an accident.''

"That sounds plausible," she agreed. "I thought something looked wrong about that groom." Maggie tried to remember her brief glimpse of the man. "He didn't carry himself like a groom," she said slowly. "He looked like a soldier. That may not mean much, since so many Frenchmen were in the emperor's army at some point, but he didn't quite have the look of a servant."

"I didn't notice him myself, but from the description, he could be one of the men on your list of secondary suspects, Captain Henri Lemercier. I met him at the Café Mazarin."

"Indeed?" Maggie's eyebrows lifted. "It didn't seem important enough to mention to me, even though we had a report of an assassination being discussed there?" Her voice was icy.

Rafe considered explaining that he had not mentioned the meeting because Lemercier had ended the evening with Robert Anderson, but decided to avoid the topic altogether.

"He was drunk and had nothing to say of any interest," he said shortly. But underneath his impervious face, Candover's thoughts were churning. Unless he had undisputable evidence of Anderson's guilt, there was no point in confronting Maggie about the man. After today's attack on Lord Castlereagh, more than ever they needed to be able to work together. Work together? He forced himself to face some unpalatable facts. Perhaps it would be more accurate to say that he needed her skills.

Maggie was regarding him suspiciously but did not pursue the topic. Rafe wished he knew just what thoughts were passing behind those wide, smoky gray eyes. Her golden hair was tangled after the incident in the stableyard, and the low-cut blue satin dress caressed the sensual body that was so incredibly good at distorting a man's judgment. If she were really his mistress, he would take her right here in the carriage. Instead, he forced himself to re-evaluate what he knew.

Castlereagh's near-disaster had shaken Rafe badly, and brought home to him the dangers of this business as nothing else had. For the first time, the duke questioned whether Maggie was really the loyal British citizen he had blindly supposed her to be. She had helped save Castlereagh this morning, but that did not mean that she wasn't selling information or plotting against her country. There were too many hidden years lying between Margot Ashton and Magda Janos to take her on trust. She might be a mercenary, working for whoever would pay her, or she might be loyal to someone or something inimical to Britain.

The most damning evidence against Maggie was her association with Anderson, who visited her in the dead of night. The blond, bland Anderson, who looked like a choirboy or Lucifer fallen, a man whom Rafe was now convinced must be an agent against Britain. Had Anderson been arranging Castlereagh's "accident" that night he met Lemercier at the Café Mazarin? And was Maggie his dupe or his accomplice?

In one way, it didn't matter. Rafe wanted her, no matter what she was or what she was doing. If he exposed the conspiracy and Maggie proved to be a traitor, she might have to choose between accepting him or going to the gallows. He would prefer that she chose him willingly, but if necessary, he would take her by any means short of violence.

It was not a thought the duke was proud of.

The Englishman was becoming accustomed to these trips to *Le Serpent* and no longer worried as he had the first times. Still, on entering the darkened room where his master waited, he reflected that his blond hair would make him a clear target even in this dimness. Had he known the murky paths he would be treading, he might have had the foresight to be born dark.

The failure of *Le Serpent*'s attempt on Lord Castlereagh had made the masked man less fearsome. The Englishman couldn't help thinking there were surer ways of killing a man than with a horse, and he made the mistake of pointing that out to his dark host.

"You presume to criticize me? You, who have no idea who I am or what my objectives are? You're a fool." The sibilant voice hissed like wind over ice. Then with a ghost of cool humor, he continued, "You should be pleased, *mon*

Anglais, to learn that the next plan will have less element of chance, and will require more of your participation.

"As of tomorrow, the important diplomatic sessions will be held in Castlereagh's bedchamber, since he is injured. I will need complete floor plans of that part of the embassy. Every room, every corridor, every closet, with accurate measurements of each. Plus, information on the staff and their movements.

"Is that all?" the Englishman asked with veiled sarcasm.

"No, *mon ami.* I also need to know who will be attending each session, as soon as the information becomes available. I *must* know that, without fail, no later than the evening before." He stood, a looming figure in the shadows. "And you will tell me, *mon petit Anglais.* Every evening, without fail."

The Englishman nodded reluctantly. He was already in too deeply to withdraw. But he needed time, time to trace the crest he had seen on *Le Serpent*'s hand, and he needed to allay any suspicions of himself. Thinking quickly, he decided to offer a piece of information that he had been keeping in reserve.

"You heard about the Countess Janos, who drove the horse away from Lord Castlereagh before the job was finished?"

"I heard. A pity that she and her lover were there, but one cannot plan for everything." *Le Serpent* gave a slight, worldly shrug, implying that minor impediments might delay but never defeat him, then added, "Rather a beautiful woman. There is no one quite like a Hungarian in bed."

It was a perfect opening. The Englishman said, "She isn't a Hungarian. She's an Englishwoman named Margot Ashton, an impostor, a whore, a spy."

"Indeed?" The breathy voice held menace, but not directed against his visitor. "You interest me, *mon Anglais.* Tell me what you know about this woman. If she is working for the British, it may be necessary to . . . deal with her."

Triumphantly, the Englishman proceeded to tell everything he knew about the Countess Magda Janos, who had once been known as Margot Ashton. It would be a pity if all that luscious blond beauty was wasted, but one's own interests must come first.

Chapter 12

The next morning Maggie and Hélène Sorel went to the home of Mme. Daudet, who had now listed all the French family crests that showed serpents. After an obligatory half-hour over the teacups, the guests were presented with a lengthy list of names written in script as fragile as the old lady herself, then given the freedom of the library, which turned out to be a treasure trove. Huge leather volumes stamped in gold contained exquisite hand-colored plates of heraldic devices and family crests. The two women looked up all of the names on Mme. Daudet's list, and in the most promising cases they traced the crest on sheets of translucent parchment that Maggie had brought with them. While they rejected dragons and medieval creatures of dubious ancestry, they studied anything that was clearly snakelike, including the crest of the d'Aguste family, which bore a twining three-headed serpent that looked like a hydra.

Two hours exhausted their researches, but as they prepared to leave, Hélène noticed a book titled in German which proved to be on the Prussian aristocracy. Turning to Fehrenbach, the Frenchwoman became so still that Maggie came to stand beside her, then inhaled in surprise. The Fehrenbach crest was a lion holding a spear with a snake twisted along the shaft. Looking at the Latin motto, Hélène translated in an unemotional voice, "The cunning of a serpent, the courage of a lion."

Maggie was shaken. "Of all our prospects, I thought Colonel von Fehrenbach was the least likely. In fact, I had eliminated him."

"This proves nothing," Hélène said, an edge in her soft voice. "We copied a dozen other crests as likely."

"But none of them belonged to suspects." Maggie

paused, then said, "Hélène, I asked this before and I will ask again. Is there something between you and Colonel von Fehrenbach?"

Hélène slipped back into one of the leather-upholstered chairs, her eyes not meeting Maggie's. "There is nothing except . . . an attraction. We have met several times, always in public, and have said nothing that anyone might not hear."

Maggie sat also, brushing her hair back with fingers dusty from old books. Like herself, Hélène acted on instinct, usually a more reliable guide than logic. "Do you think the colonel could be involved in a plot against France?"

"No," Hélène said flatly, then raised her eyes to Maggie's. "I will investigate him more closely for you."

Maggie sat forward in her chair with misgivings. "Hélène, what do you have in mind? If the colonel is really *Le Serpent*, he is a dangerous man. In fact, he might be anyhow."

Hélène smiled faintly. "I will do nothing that will endanger either myself or your investigation." Seeing the mutinous expression on her friend's face, she added, "You can't stop me, you know. I am not your employee but a free agent who works with you because we share the same goals."

Maggie sighed, eyeing Hélène's soft features and gentle face. Her friend looked as innocent as a lamb, but Hélène was both tough and intelligent. Since she was determined to approach von Fehrenbach, Maggie could only hope that something worthwhile would be discovered.

Summoned by Maggie, Robert Anderson came late that night to her house. The moon was only half full, but bright enough that the man watching from the alley had no trouble making an identification. Blond and handsome as Lucifer, just like the duke had said. The watcher settled back in the shadows philosophically. Fortunate the weather was warm; it wasn't likely that a midnight visitor to the luscious countess would be in any hurry to leave. He had no idea that another pair of hidden eyes was watching the same house.

Maggie slept badly after Robin left. He had found the sketches of crests very promising and intended to show them to members of the Parisian underworld in the hopes that tongues might be loosened. Von Fehrenbach's crest made him very thoughtful. Robin had little to say in return, which made Maggie nervous since she guessed he was withholding something. Most likely, he was trying to protect her, which reinforced the idea that this was a dangerous business.

Fervently Maggie wished that the treaty was settled and she could go back to England, to peace and quiet and safety. Then her eyes opened wide in the dark and she stared unseeing at the ceiling. The little cottage in England was less appealing than it had been a few weeks before. While she would welcome the peace, the days stretched empty and uneventful. She could walk and read, make friends and pay morning calls on them, day after day, month after month . . . the prospect seemed rather dull.

Duller, or more lonely? She would be very much alone in that life of blameless respectability that she had been looking forward to. There would be no men like the Duke of Candover to verbally fence with her, or make disgraceful proposals.

At that thought, she laughed softly in the darkness. Based on history, there would be no shortage of men to proposition her; there just wouldn't be any that she would want to accept. And that, finally, was the core of her restlessness. Rafe Whitbourne was still the most fascinating man she had ever met, intelligent, a little arrogant, alternately tender and enigmatic. And damnably, maddeningly attractive. He had been charming women since he was in leading strings, and it was hardly surprising that she should be among his legions of admirers.

From the vantage point of thirty-one, she could see how fortunate she was that they hadn't married. They had been such children then; she had been utterly in love with Rafe, and it had never occurred to her that he would have mistresses, like most men of his station. The first time that happened, she would have been shattered. Rafe would have reacted with incredulity and embarrassment, regretting that he hadn't taken a wife from the upper levels of the nobility, a woman who would understand such things. Maggie knew she would have turned into a rampaging virago, unwilling either to let Rafe go or accept his infidelities. In the end, they would both have been miserable.

It was all so tragically clear. Since she had just proved to herself how lucky she was that Rafe broke their engagement, why didn't that conclusion make her happy? Despairingly, Maggie laid her forearm over her eyes in a vain attempt to block out images of Rafe, and the memory of how his touch dissolved her common sense and self-control. It was poor comfort to know that the greatest significance she would ever have in his life was to be the one woman he had propositioned who hadn't accepted. But was that really better than nothing?

Maggie's and Rafe's visit to the Louvre with the Roussayes turned out to be educational in quite unexpected ways. Napoleon had looted art treasures wherever he went and installed them in the old palace, naming it the Musée Napoleon and holding state receptions in the magnificent galleries. Art had become a major point of contention during the treaty negotiations. Not surprisingly, the conquered nations wanted their paintings and sculptures back, while the French royalists and Bonapartists were united in their desire to retain the fruits of conquest. The issue was unresolved, though the Allies were bound to win in the end; only the Russian tsar, who had lost no art himself, was in favor of letting the French keep their spoils.

The only reference to the ongoing dispute was Roussaye's comment in front of a magnificent Titian. "It is well that we see these while we can. Never has such a collection been seen before, and perhaps there will never be its equal again."

The two couples were regarding the superb canvas respectfully when an unexpected voice came from behind them. "You are quite correct, General Roussaye. This museum is one of the finest fruits of the empire."

The dark, whispery voice made the hair on Maggie's neck prickle and she turned to see the Count de Varenne. Michel Roussaye said coolly, "I am surprised to hear a royalist approve any of Bonaparte's acts."

The count smiled faintly. "I am a royalist but not a fool,

General. The emperor was the colossus of our age, and only a fool would attempt to deny that."

Rafe touched Maggie's arm lightly, and she felt that they were sharing the same thought. Varenne might be many things, but a fool was not one of them. His words had produced a noticeable thawing in the general's expression.

Varenne continued, "Like you, I am here to say goodbye to some of my favorite paintings."

The words were hardly out of his mouth when a commotion sounded further down the gallery. Amid French shouts, the stamp of marching feet heralded the entrance of a company of soldiers. Maggie recognized the uniforms as Prussian, and as the numerous museum-goers watched in frozen shock, the Prussians started unhooking paintings from the wall.

General Roussaye swiftly crossed to the Prussians and demanded furiously, "By what authority do you do this?"

The Prussian commander turned, and Maggie recognized Colonel von Fehrenbach. Here were all three of their suspects in one place, all of them angry. With a touch of dark humor, she wondered whether if the three men killed each other on the spot that would end the assassination plot. She was so intent on observing every word and nuance of the confrontation that she started to follow the Frenchman across the gallery but Rafe stopped her in her tracks by clamping his hand above her elbow.

"Keep out of it," he said, his low voice allowing no argument. Glancing up at the stern, dark face, Maggie considered disputing him but common sense made her concede the point.

Thirty feet away, as the soldiers lifted down paintings and packed them in the cases they had brought, von Fehrenbach answered with bored precision. "By the authority of ownership. Since the negotiators are no closer to a just settlement now than they were in July, Prussia takes what is hers."

The Count de Varenne had gone to stand by his countryman. His tone was less fierce, but nonetheless hostile when he said, "The Congress of Vienna allowed France to keep her treasures, and it is by no means certain that the decision will be reversed. What you are doing is theft."

The tall, pale Prussian was unmoved. "Say what you will, I am here by my king's orders. We have both might and right on our side, and will brook no interference."

A circle of French citizens had drawn around the disputing men, sullen fury on their faces. Briefly, Maggie wondered if they might rush the soldiers but the moment passed and the bystanders remained passive. Varenne's sibilant voice said, "Do not be so righteous, Colonel. Many of the art works that the Allies are so virtuously reclaiming were stolen in the first place, like the bronze horses of St. Mark's, plundered from Constantinople."

Von Fehrenbach looked cynically amused. "I don't deny it, but the nature of loot is such that it defies easy moralizing."

Roussaye said tightly, "Many countries are looters, but only France has made such beauty available to all. Even the poorest of the poor can come here to glory in the sight."

"Quite right, the French are the most efficient thieves in history," the colonel agreed. "You studied guidebooks and sent artists to ensure that you missed none of the best pieces. The emperor even made the Vatican pay the cost of shipping his spoils to Paris. But don't forget what the Duke of Wellington himself said. Loot is what you can get your bloody hands on and keep."

Von Fehrenbach turned away to his men, but said over his shoulder, "And France bloody well can't keep these."

It was fortunate that the colonel had brought such a sizable troop of soldiers, because his words caused a rumble of impotent rage to rise from the watchers. After a frozen moment, General Roussaye spun on his heel and returned to his companions, saying with a set face, "I think it best we leave now." He took his wife's arm, leading her down the gallery away from the soldiers as Maggie, Rafe, and Varenne silently followed.

Word of the assault on the Louvre had spread quickly, and outside a crowd was gathering in the Place du Carrousel. Under the shadow of the great victory arch that carried the bronze horse of St. Mark's, Maggie and her companions were privileged to see the Venus de Medici being carried out feet first, followed by the Apollo Belvedere. Nearby, a young man in a paint-smudged smock gave a howl of anguish. "Oh, that Wellington would only order the removal to take place at night, that we should be spared the horror of seeing them torn away!"

The artist's anguish was vivid, but Maggie could not help thinking that the Venetians and Romans and Prussians and other victims of Napoleon's greed had felt equal pain. Behind her, Rafe said softly, "Wellington is being blamed for this, more's the pity. His popularity with the French will vanish quickly."

General Roussaye turned to face them, his wife clinging to his arm with distress in her huge black eyes. "I hope you will forgive me if we take our leave now. I fear that I will not be good company for some time." In spite of his anger, Roussaye was impeccably polite, and Maggie admired his control.

Varenne spoke up for the first time since they had left the Prussians. "All France shares your anger, General."

The two Frenchmen shared a look of understanding, and it occurred to Maggie that France would again be the most dangerous country in Europe if the royalists and Bonapartists were united. Thank God that too much hatred lay between the factions for that to be likely. These two men might be in temporary harmony, but France was still a nation divided, and it was better that way.

Rafe said, "Of course, General. We can meet again for a less controversial engagement, perhaps a picnic in the country."

The general bowed to Maggie, then said, "Nothing in France is without controversy." Then he and his wife left.

Varenne looked after the Roussayes, then turned to Maggie and Rafe. "I am sorry you were subjected to such a scene. I had heard rumors that the Prussians were growing restive, but no one expected them to move so quickly."

Rafe shrugged. "It will be worse before it gets better. The art controversy is becoming a symbol of all the conflicts of the peace conference. I can only hope that no blood will be shed."

Varenne nodded gravely. "The situation is very volatile. As I'm sure you know, the king's government is in disarray and I fear that Richelieu is not strong enough to maintain order."

The count put aside his dark mood. Smiling at Maggie, he said, "I should not talk of such things before a lady."

Maggie supposed acerbically that he meant she was too much of a lackwit to understand politics. Still, the less intelligent he thought her, the better. Fluttering her eyelashes, she cooed, "It is all so dreadful. Since the wars are over, one would think there should be no more problems."

Varenne shook his head. "I'm afraid matters aren't quite so simple. I look forward to the day when I can retire to my estate and concentrate on my own affairs, but it will not be soon."

"Is your estate near Paris?" Maggie asked, though she knew the answer from her research.

"Yes, near the emperor's house at Malmaison. Chantueil is much older, perhaps the finest medieval chateau in France."

Maggie smiled with innocent enthusiasm. "It sounds wonderfully romantic."

"It is." Varenne replied with a smile that would have been charming were it not for the ice in his eyes. "I would be delighted to show it to you. Perhaps next week?"

Maggie's answer was forestalled when Rafe put his arm around her waist. "Perhaps later. The countess and I are much engaged for the near future."

Varenne seemed amused by the duke's show of possessiveness. He took Maggie's hand and squeezed it meaningfully as he brushed a kiss above it. "You and the enchanting countess would be welcome at Chantueil at any time, *monsieur le duc.*"

Then he too disappeared into the restless crowd of angry Parisians. Maggie watched his broad back retreat with disquiet. The count had behaved flirtatiously, yet she sensed that he wasn't really interested in her. It was disquieting.

Before she could analyze her unease, Rafe said brusquely, "Time to leave, Countess. This crowd could turn ugly."

His words made her aware of the angry mutterings around her, and she felt the familiar touch of panic that crowds always produced in her. As people fell away from Rafe, she was grateful for his presence; anyone would think twice or thrice before accosting the Duke of Candover, not just because of his obvious wealth but because of his faintly dangerous air. Rafe made a far better friend than enemy. In a few minutes they were free of the crowd and Rafe summoned a cab to take them to Maggie's house.

Secure in the privacy of the cab, Rafe echoed Maggie's earlier thought, saying, "Interesting to have all three suspects together, but I can't say that I have any better idea of who is guilty of what. Do you have any thoughts on the subject?"

Maggie sighed as she analyzed the swirl of nuances and impressions she had observed during the confrontation in the museum. At length she said gloomily, "The same thoughts I had before, only more so. Colonel von Fehrenbach despises the French and enjoys their humiliation. While I still don't see him masterminding a plot, it is possible that he could be used by someone of more devious temperament. General Roussaye . . ." she hesitated, then continued slowly, "behaved with unusual restraint. He was so furious with the invasion of the Louvre that I wouldn't have been surprised if he had rallied the French mob to attack the Prussians."

"Surely he wouldn't have risked that with his wife there."

"I'm sure that was a factor," Maggie agreed. "Also, he's an intelligent man and must realize that driving the Prussians out would do no real good. But as I watched him, I had the feeling that it was very difficult for him not to fight back. Remember I said once before that I thought he was up to something secret? Perhaps he left rather then act in a way that might jeopardize another project. I would lay any odds you like that he is involved with something that wouldn't bear the light of day."

"What about Varenne and his so-romantic chateau?" Rafe inquired sardonically.

Maggie chuckled. "I wouldn't trust the man further than I could throw his drawbridge, and I suspect that he is so devious by nature that it would be impossible to determine if he is conspiring or just obfuscating on general principles."

When the cab pulled up in front of Maggie's house, they alighted and Rafe paid the driver. The premature end to the expedition had gotten them back hours early, so the duke followed her inside, determined to take advantage of the opportunity to confront Maggie about her association with Robert Anderson. Time was too critical to avoid the topic any longer. As they entered her salon, he said, "We haven't played chess lately," and crossed to the table where the pieces were frozen in mid-game.

Maggie's heart wasn't in chess, but she thought it might serve as a good distraction, so she ordered an afternoon tea and sat down opposite Rafe. She was playing badly, and it came as no surprise when the duke said, "Check."

That got Maggie's attention, and she saw that one of the black bishops was threatening her king. After a moment's thought, she moved one of her knights into the bishop's path. Rafe could capture the knight, but then Maggie would take his bishop, restoring the balance of power. "I like the knights," Maggie said absently. "They move in such a deceptive manner."

"Like you do, Countess?"

There was a sharp edge to Rafe's voice, and she glanced up at him in surprise. Unalarmed, she said, "I suppose so. Spying is the art of deception, after all."

"Will the white queen sacrifice herself for the white king?"

The duke's gray eyes bored into her, and she realized that he was no longer talking about chess. The lean planes of his face were hard, and she could see the tension in him.

"What are you talking about?" Maggie said in exasperation.

The duke reached out to the chess set and slid his black king across the board to capture the white queen. Maggie said, "You know perfectly well that is not a legitimate move. What obscure point are you trying to make?"

Rafe scooped the white queen and the black king into his right hand, lifting them from the board. "Only this, Margot. I won't let you sacrifice yourself for the white king. With or without your consent, I will take you from the game."

Chilled, Maggie was beginning to guess what the duke meant. Still her voice was steady. "You will have to speak a good deal more clearly if you expect any kind of response from me."

With a sudden, angry gesture, Rafe swept all the remaining chess pieces from the board. The antique enameled figures fell to the oriental carpet and bounced in all directions, thudding and clicking against each other. "We're talking about Robert Anderson, your lover, who is a spy and a traitor."

Maggie stood so abruptly that her chair skidded backward. "You don't know what you are talking about."

The duke stood also, towering over her. The urbane man of the world was gone, and he blazed with angry emotion. "Oh, yes I do, my lady trollop. I know that he comes here late at night, even though Lord Lattimer told you not to communicate with anyone in the British delegation."

Locking her gaze to his, Maggie said softly, "I have been playing dangerous games far longer than you, your grace. I work with those I trust."

"Even if they are traitors? Your lover has been seen surreptitiously visiting General Roussaye, and I myself saw him meeting with the French groom called Jean Blanc at the Café Mazarin. Except that Blanc's real name is Henri Lemercier, and he is on your list of suspects."

For the first time she felt a touch of apprehension, but Maggie said stubbornly, "Spies don't learn anything by talking only to respectable citizens."

"So you admit he's a spy." Rafe stepped around the table until he was only inches away from Maggie.

"Of course he is! We've worked together for years."

"So you've been his mistress for years," the duke mused. "Do you know who he is working for?"

"The British, of course. Robin is as English as I am."

"Which means nothing to a mercenary. He probably sells to the highest bidder, and has been using you as a dupe." He thought a moment, then asked, "Are you sure he is English?"

Maggie exploded. "You ignorant fool! Your accusations are absurd, and I won't listen to them."

She spun away, but Rafe grabbed her by the arm. "Absurd? Who pays your expenses? Who pays for the satin gowns and the carriage and the townhouse?"

She jerked her head around. "I do, with the money I earn from the British government. Now, release me, damn you!"

His grip didn't loosen. "Are you paid directly?" He guessed the answer, but wanted to hear what she would say.

After a pause, Maggie said, "The money comes through Robin."

It was exactly as Rafe expected. "I contacted Lord Lattimer and asked how much the government had paid you over the years. It came to about three thousand pounds, not enough to keep you for a year in the style you live in."

Rafe felt a shudder run through her body but she refused to back down. "Lord Lattimer must not know the whole amount. There is more than one part of the British government that pays for intelligence, and there must be several sources involved."

In spite of her words, Maggie was shaken by what Rafe said. Robin had given her far more than three thousand pounds over the years; if it wasn't from Lattimer, who did it come from?

Rafe's face was dark and implacable, his grip on her arm relentless. "I admire your loyalty. Nonetheless, the odds are that Anderson is a spy within the British delegation, and almost certainly involved in the conspiracy against Castlereagh. The only question is, are you his knowing accomplice or his pawn?"

Her burst of anger gave her the strength to pull out of the duke's grasp. "I won't believe it! Robin is the best friend I ever had, and if I must choose between believing him and believing you, I choose *him*. Now, get out of here!"

Her gray eyes were spitting sparks, and if she had had a pistol it would have been aimed between his eyes. Until now Rafe had restricted himself to telling his suspicions of Anderson's loyalty, but Maggie's refusal to believe ill of her lover destroyed the duke's last vestige of control.

Grabbing her by the shoulders, Rafe shook her and demanded furiously, "Why him, Margot? Why him and not me? Is he such a great lover? Do you think you love him, or is it just that he has supported you in such elegance? If it's money you want, I'll pay your price, whatever it is. If it's sex, give me one night, and then decide who is better." He drew in a raw, unsteady breath, then finished harshly. "And if it's blind loyalty, think hard whether a traitor is worthy of such loyalty."

Maggie looked up at him and laughed bitterly. "You dare ask why I prefer Robin to you? He is the one who saved my life, in every possible sense of the word, and gave me a reason to keep on living. I'd rather be the pawn of a traitor than the mistress of a man who accused and judged me without proof, a man whose insane jealousy drove my father to take me away from England."

Her words tumbled amid angry tears and Maggie cried out an accusation she had tried never to think. "My father never would have have been murdered by the French if it hadn't been for what you did, Rafe. For that alone, I can never forgive you.

"And as for your vain, masculine egotism—I don't care if you've learned your skills in the bed of every slut in Europe—I'd never give myself to a man without love, and you're incapable of loving anyone. You're an arrogant, conceited rakehell, and I don't ever want to see you again. Now let go of me!"

She raised her arms within his and tried to break his grip, but Rafe was too strong for her. He slid one hand behind her head and turned her face up to his, kissing her as if passion would dissolve her opposition. Maggie felt the familiar jolt of physical attraction but her fury was far stronger. She jerked her knee up in a savage street-fighting trick. Rafe's athletic reflexes enabled him to dodge the blow but at the cost of releasing her. Free of his embrace, Maggie whirled across the room to the pier table, pulling out the drawer and grabbing the loaded pistol she kept in it.

Turning to face the duke, her voice trembled but the gun she held in both hands did not. "If you remember, I am an excellent shot. Now get out of here, and don't ever come near me again. If you make any move to hurt Robin, I will have you killed."

She stopped to draw breath, forcing her voice to be level. "I warn you, I know how to arrange such things and I will do so immediately. Even if I am dead myself, retribution will follow you if anything happens to Robin, and there is nowhere on earth distant enough for you to escape. Now, take your clumsy amateur spying and your jealousy and accusations and go back to England."

In his present mood, Rafe considered trying to take the

gun away from her, but there was a wide expanse of salon between them and murder in Maggie's eyes. He damned himself for the idiotic folly of attacking Anderson as he had. It would have been difficult to convince Maggie of her lover's duplicity under the best of circumstances, and letting his own jealousy loose had destroyed any chance that she might believe him.

He took a tentative step toward her but she cocked the hammer and Rafe stopped dead, scarcely daring to breathe. When Maggie first pulled out the gun he hadn't thought she would fire it, but the barrel aimed at his heart was utterly convincing. Under his fear was cool amusement at the thought that the mighty Duke of Candover might be killed in a vulgar lovers' quarrel, with the irony that they were not even lovers.

In the face of her furious eyes and steady hands, he said with as much calm and conviction as he could muster, "For your own sake, Maggie, don't trust Anderson. I may be a jealous fool, but I told you the truth about him. You may despise me all you like, but do you really want to see Castlereagh, and perhaps others, die because you're too stubborn to see Anderson for what he is? He's the only lead to the conspiracy that we have, and we should have Wellington detain him so he can be questioned."

The smoky gray eyes were as hostile as her words. "You haven't convinced me, your grace. As I said, spies must talk to everyone, especially suspects like Lemercier and Roussaye. As for the money—you may be too rich to realize it, but most of the world must be practical about such sordid topics. Selling the same information to more than one of Napoleon's enemies might be simple good business, not treason."

"But you're not sure, are you?" Rafe said softly, sensing the bravado that fueled Maggie's defense of Anderson.

She tensed and he wondered how light the trigger was on her pistol, but she said calmly enough, "You could produce iron-clad evidence and a dozen unimpeachable witnesses that Robin was a traitor and I might possibly—just possibly—believe you, but I would still not come to your bed. Will you leave on your own, or shall I have some of my larger servants throw you out bodily?"

Despairingly, Rafe saw that he had failed. By muddying the evidence with his personal feelings, he had lost any chance of changing Maggie's mind. She might be wrong-headed and loyal to a fault, but he still could not believe that she would condone an assassination plot. Now more than ever Maggie would be hellbent on exposing the conspiracy to prove Rafe wrong; if she got caught in the middle she would be in grave danger and Rafe wouldn't be there to protect her. Even Anderson might be a danger to her, if she stood in his way. Or perhaps not; the blond man could be a traitor and still love his mistress.

The pistol tracked him without wavering as Rafe crossed the room to the door. Pausing with one hand on the knob, he looked back at her, the pistol an incongruous accessory to her lush golden beauty. Neither her anger nor her threats had altered his desire. Quietly he said, "I'm not leaving Paris until this is over. If you need aid at any time, you know where to find me."

Then he left, the paneled door swinging silently shut behind him. Maggie laid the pistol on the pier table and sank into a chair as her knees threatened to give way. Her teeth chattered as if she had a chill and she wrapped her arms around herself as the horrible scene replayed in front of her. While Rafe had made it clear that he desired her, she had not suspected that he felt such violent jealousy. Of course, he had behaved just the same way thirteen years earlier; then she had thought it was from love, but apparently the real source was pride and possessiveness. She had occasionally wondered what lay beneath his air of perpetual calm, and now she wished she hadn't found out.

Could the duke have been lying about Robert Anderson? Robin hadn't mentioned meeting with either Roussaye or Lemercier, but that was not necessarily significant; he seldom discussed his activities in detail. Though Rafe's information was disconcerting, it was hardly evidence of double-dealing.

It was much harder to shrug off Rafe's revelations about the money. While Maggie had not lived lavishly for most of these last years, Robin had given her many thousands of pounds, much more than the amount Lattimer said she had been paid. Some had gone to pay her informants, some for household expenses, and the rest was invested in Zurich, where it drew enough interest to let her retire to England. She had not questioned the amount of money that came to her, assuming that it was the normal rate for spying. Could Robin have been serving more than one master? He had always implied that all of the money was British.

Was it possible that Robin wasn't English? He had the same unerring talent for languages that Maggie did; in fact, he had taught her tricks of listening to perfect her accent. Apart from the bald statement that he was English, he had never talked about his childhood, nor had they ever discussed mutual memories of their native land. He could have grown up anywhere and she wouldn't know it. Though he had come and gone as mysteriously as a cat for years, Maggie had never once doubted that he was honest with her. Now, she was no longer sure. A bare fortnight earlier he had told her never to trust anyone, even him. At the time she had dismissed his comment, but now it haunted her.

With shaking hands, Maggie went over to a cabinet and removed a flask of brandy and a glass, downing half of it at a gulp. It warmed her but gave no clues about what to believe. Rafe might be mad with frustrated lust or wounded pride, but she would wager that he believed the information he had given her. Yet how could she mistrust Robin, her best friend, who had saved her life and sanity?

Her eyes were blind and unfocused as she finished the brandy, oblivious to the way it burned her throat. Strange how much Rafe could affect her, in spite of past crimes and betrayals. He could arouse depths of emotion in her quite different from the solid, warm friendship she shared with Robin. What a pity that Rafe used that power only to hurt her.

Chapter 13

The Englishman provided *Le Serpent* with the requested information about the British Embassy, acquired at no small risk. Twice he had nearly been caught by other members of the embassy staff, and he thought he saw suspicion at his presence in places where he didn't belong. Still, no one had asked any awkward questions, and he had been paid a very handsome price for his pains.

The light was a little brighter this time to enable *Le Serpent* to review the sketched floorplans. After several minutes, he said with a grunt of triumph, "Perfect, absolutely perfect. *Le bon Dieu* could have designed it for my purposes."

The Englishman had no desire to know more of the conspirator's plans so he straightened up to leave. "If you have no more need for me, then . . ."

Le Serpent straightened also, his eyes a hard glint behind the mask. "I have not dismissed you, *mon petit Anglais*. My plan requires your willing participation. Do you see that closet there?" A blunt finger tapped the floorplans.

The Englishman glanced down. "Yes. What of it?"

"It is right below Castlereagh's bedchamber. It is seldom used, always locked. And when it is filled with gunpowder and exploded, it will blow that end of the embassy to flinders, along with everyone meeting with the British foreign minister."

"You're mad!" the Englishman gasped. Now he understood why *Le Serpent* had wanted to know who was attending the various meetings; if he chose the right day, he could destroy Wellington and all the chief Allied ministers along with Castlereagh.

"Not in the least," the hooded man said calmly. "My

plan is audacious but wholly workable. The most difficult part will be getting the gunpowder into the embassy, but since you are on the staff, that presents no insurmountable problems."

"Just how do you intend to set the explosion?" the Englishman asked with unwilling curiosity.

"A candle will do the trick nicely. A slow-burning, hard wax candle will take hours to melt down, and you can be safely out of the way. No one will suspect you."

"No! I want no part of this madness! If Allied ministers are killed, Paris will be taken apart to find the culprits."

"There will be an uproar, but the Allies will be like beheaded chickens with their leaders gone. By the time the dust settles . . ." he paused dramatically before finishing, "there will be a new order in France."

"What do I care about France? I'll not put my neck in the noose for it!"

The Englishman tried to move away, but *Le Serpent* reached out and seized his wrist with an iron grip. In a voice from a nightmare, he said, "I will tell you once more, *mon ami*, you have no choice. To defy me means death. On the other hand, I reward my underlings very generously and your cooperation is vital for this particular project." He paused to let his words sink in, then continued softly, "Notice I make no attempt to buy your loyalty, because I know you have none. Greed is the best lever with creatures such as you, so I make you a promise: help me to success and you will be rich and powerful beyond your wildest dreams."

The Englishman glanced at the hard hand clamped on his wrist. It was the hand that wore the signet ring, and this time he could see the crest clearly enough to identify it precisely. At the moment, he was unsure whether he wanted to work with *Le Serpent*, expose him, or fly from France. He was uneasily aware that he would have to choose sides within the next few days, and if he chose wrong he was dead. Of course, he might die anyway if he betrayed *Le Serpent*, or if the British discovered his treachery. Harshly he said, "Release me. Once more I find the brilliance of your logic convincing."

Le Serpent let go with a sigh of satisfaction. "Very good. I like a man who learns quickly. Now sit. I have some more questions for you. There are several British agents sniffing at my heels, and it will be necessary to remove them from my path. Tell me everything you know about the people in question."

Two of the names *Le Serpent* gave were expected, but one was a surprise. A most pleasant surprise, and quite logical when he thought of it. The Englishman suppressed a smirk of satisfaction; he could think of no one he would rather see removed.

The staff had long since retired and Maggie had been sitting alone in her kitchen for hours, with only a candle and an aloof kitchen cat for company. Robin had said he might stop by if he had anything new to report, but he would not come this late. Maggie was desperate to talk to him, to hear his explanation of the points Candover had raised. There was surely a reasonable explanation . . . and if he lied to her, she would know it.

She could not possibly sleep with so much unresolved, with treacherous doubts about Robin, with the echoes of the horrible fight with Rafe. Impulsively, she decided that if Robin wasn't coming here tonight, she would go to him. It would not be the first time she had walked the streets of Paris after dark.

Upstairs she swiftly changed to dark men's clothes, glad that the September night was cool enough to justify the form-concealing cloak. As always when she traveled alone, she carried a small pistol and a knife, plus her own fighting skills. While she preferred to avoid trouble, if necessary she could startle and slow an attacker down long enough to enable her to escape.

It was well past midnight when she set out. Robin had rooms near the Place du Carrousel, adjacent to the Louvre and the Tuileries. And if he wasn't there, she would wait until he returned. She needed most desperately to believe in him again. After all, if she didn't have him, who did she have?

Rafe should have turned around and headed back to London as soon as he learned that Lattimer's beautiful spy was Margot Ashton. Certainly his sojourn in Paris had been of no great help to his country and it had wreaked havoc on his calm, orderly life. The simple-minded schoolboy love he had felt for Margot had been replaced by the dark strains of obsession. She was the only living creature who could destroy his prized detachment, and he hated her for it, even as he compulsively imagined what it would be like to make love to her. He already knew the taste of her mouth and his mind supplied vivid images of how she would look, the feel of her skin, of how she would respond . . .

Once more he jerked his thoughts from their unhealthy circle. Maggie had accused him of wanting her because she was unavailable, and there was some justice to that. After all, she was just a woman, and all women were made much the same. He knew from experience that the most beautiful women were seldom the best mistresses; women who were less blessed usually tried harder. If he could just once make love to Maggie, it would free him of his obsession, which was rooted in his youthful memories. No chance of that happening; she would put a lead ball in him if he came within fifty feet of her again. He wondered, briefly, whether he was capable of rape, if the opportunity presented itself. Wondered, then shied away from looking at the answer.

The duke had dismissed his man who usually watched Maggie's house, taking that post himself. He was glad Anderson hadn't visited her tonight, or he might have killed him out of hand and the blond man was much more useful alive. Tomorrow the duke would notify Wellington of his suspicions and suggest that Anderson be questioned, but tonight Rafe kept his morbid watch. The townhouse was dark except for a light in the kitchen, and he wondered if Maggie was sleeping, or whether she was as restless as he was. The accusations against Anderson had upset her, and perhaps she was suffering doubts. Savagely, he hoped so.

It was very late when he saw the dark figure slip from the townhouse, a shadow that moved with catlike stealth and grace: Margot Ashton, alias the Countess Janos, leaving on some secret business. He was about to follow when he saw two figures exit the building on his left and follow her. Frowning, he wondered who else might be watching her. Had his own men missed the competition or was this a new development? He was abruptly glad for the impulse that had made him take tonight's watch; if she was in any danger, at least he would be there, and he trusted his own ability to protect her more than that of any of his hirelings.

The streets were almost empty and Rafe worried that he might be conspicuous. Mindful of the farcical aspects of several people trailing each other, he checked his own back to be sure that no one was behind him, but he seemed to be the last of the parade. The two men ahead of him were skilled at their tracking, and both were substantial figures, possibly professional toughs.

Maggie led them a merry chase and Rafe had to admire the speed she made while at the same time being almost invisible. Avoiding the well-lit boulevards, she was just one more shadow in the dark back alleys. Occasionally she glanced back, but the same dark that shielded her passage concealed the followers, and presumably she had no reason to suppose anyone was behind her.

With a sick feeling in the pit of his stomach, Rafe soon realized that she must be heading to Anderson's. A planned assignation, or was she going to challenge the man with what the duke had told her? He wasn't sure he wanted to know.

Ahead of him, he saw Maggie stop at the mouth of one of the streets leading into the Place du Carrousel, and even at a distance it was possible to read astonishment in her reaction. Looking beyond her, Rafe could see the great victory arch that Napoleon had built in the middle of the plaza and crowned with the four bronze horses taken from St. Mark's in Venice. Torches flared around the monument and by their flickering light Rafe could see workmen standing on top of the arch. The clink of chisels and hammers echoed around the plaza, and he could see a supervisor in the uniform of a British officer.

The duke gave a noiseless whistle of admiration. It appeared that Wellington had heard of the disturbance at the museum and tactfully decided to spare French feelings by removing these most visible examples of loot by night. Rafe hoped that old Louis would sleep through it; the work was taking place literally under the king's windows in the Tuileries.

Maggie seemed to hesitate, as if wondering whether to

cross the busy plaza. Then a clatter sounded behind Rafe and he looked back to see a large detachment of the French National Guard surge from a cross street and hurl themselves toward the Place du Carrousel along the road he stood in. In the snarl of small streets around the plaza, they seemed to have materialized from nowhere. As the Guardsmen ran by shouting, Rafe darted up several stone steps into the shelter of a deep doorway. The Guards were followed by an angry mob, and he realized that there had been shouting audible for some time but the jumbled medieval streets had made the noise seem distant. The duke had heard mobs before in London, and they all sounded the same: like a ravening beast that was all teeth and claws and no mind.

No one paid any attention to him in his vantage point above the swirling bodies, and he could see over the crowd to the plaza. The men on the arch spotted the Guards and the mob and abandoned their tools to beat a hasty retreat, dashing for the Tuileries where a door opened and the workers escaped inside. Fortunate that Louis's people weren't letting the workers be torn to pieces; Wellington would have taken an exceedingly dim view if the king had let British soldiers and workers be murdered.

In the moments his attention was on the plaza, Rafe had lost sight of Maggie, and he felt a clutch of fear as he thought of her caught in the turmoil. Running down the steps, he forced his way through the mob to where he had last seen her, keeping a wary eye out for the two men who had been following but making no special attempt to conceal himself. He was just one more person in the crowd and speed was more important than security.

At the edge of the plaza, he looked around but saw no sign of Maggie until he heard frenzied shouts from the mouth of a small alley to the right. A familiar French voice yelled hoarsely, "It's an English spy, one of Wellington's thieves!"

Balked of the workmen, those members of the mob close enough to hear started moving toward the fracas. Then a woman's scream of sheer, mindless terror cut through the general rumble. It was Maggie's voice, and with a surge of panic Rafe started fighting his way toward her, ruthlessly using his size and boxing skills to elbow, kick, and shove his way through as quickly as possible. He was followed by curses but no serious retaliation as the crowd assumed he was just another rioter keen on a front-row view. As he fought toward the center of the disturbance, there was a sharp sound of ripping fabric and the voice cried out excitedly, "Ai, it's a woman!" The animal cry of the mob took on a dark new tone.

As Rafe came to the inner circle of men, he made sure one of his pistols was ready to hand in the pocket of his greatcoat. Shoving aside a heavy-set man in the clothing of a laborer, he was finally able to see the writhing figure on the ground. Maggie was fighting, twisting and kicking and slashing with a knife, forcing some of the men back from her whirlwind defense. Her shoulder and part of her chest showed white against the torn fabric of her clothing, and in the uncertain light her face was distorted by horror such as Rafe had never seen before.

In the moment after he arrived, her nerve-shattering scream was cut off abruptly as a heavy boot caught the side of her head. She slumped into unconsciousness, the knife falling from her nerveless fingers. The man behind her reached down to lift her from the pavement and pull her against his chest, one hand casually fondling her exposed breast. "You'll have to wait in line, lads," the man said genially, "I saw her first, but don't worry, there's plenty to go around."

The surrounding rioters fell back a little, aware of the practical difficulties of more than one man raping a woman at a time. Rafe looked at who held Maggie, and recognized the scarred, triumphant face of Henri Lemercier.

Boldness was the only possible strategy, and Rafe paused only a moment to collect himself. Lemercier's attention was on his captive as he dragged her backward toward the alley where he would have more room. Summoning all of the strength of an athletic lifetime, Rafe bolted out of the crowd, chopped the side of his hand across Lemercier's throat, and grabbed Maggie as the Frenchman's grasp loosened. Stooping, he threw her over his shoulder, then raced down the alley away from the plaza.

There was a bellow of fury behind him and he turned to see the astonished crowd catch its breath, then flow down the alley in pursuit, Lemercier in the lead. Rafe stopped and turned, knowing he would have only one shot; if he didn't use it well, they were both dead. He had been careful to put Maggie over his left shoulder, and now he pulled his pistol from his coat, cocked it, and took aim with the same deliberation he used shooting wafers at Manton's. The priming fizzled oddly and for a heart-searing moment Rafe thought the pistol had misfired.

Then the gun kicked in his hand. Time seemed to slow, and he could almost see the ball spinning through the air until it struck Lemercier dead between the eyes. Rafe saw the man's expression change from vicious lust to disbelieving shock, saw the small spurt of blood and bone as the force of the ball drove Lemercier back into the arms of the rioters, saw the mob's surprise and confusion as a bit of good fun turned lethal.

The duke wasted no more time in observation. He turned and escaped into the maze of alleys that surrounded the plaza, dodging first left, then right, then left again. The unexpected shooting had slowed the mob down long enough for him to get out of the original alley, and after five minutes of lung-searing running with no signs of pursuit, he stopped, gasping for breath with great wrenching gulps. He laid Maggie on the pavement and tried to examine her, though it was too dark to determine much. She was unconscious but her breathing and heartbeat were strong.

In the distance, he could still hear shouts from the Place du Carrousel, and as soon as possible he lifted her in both arms and started walking again. In a few minutes he emerged into one of the boulevards and was able to flag down a cab, curtly ordering the driver to take them to the Hotel de la Paix. In the dank privacy of the cab, he cradled her in his arms, praying that the heavy boot hadn't hit her squarely, and there were no other serious injuries. He couldn't forget the horror on her face, and realized with distant wonder that for the moment, at least, tenderness had replaced his lust.

When they reached the Hotel de la Paix, Rafe stepped out of the carriage, tossed a gold piece to the surprised cabby, and carried Maggie up the steps without looking back. The doorman looked startled but said nothing. One doesn't question a duke, even one with a ragged person of indeterminate sex in his arms.

One kick at the door of his apartments brought his valet on the run. Carrying Maggie inside, Rafe said harshly, "Wake one of the maids immediately, and tell her to get down here with a clean shift. Then go for a doctor. I want one here within half an hour even if you have to kidnap him." The apartment was small, with no guest room, so Rafe carried her into his own bedchamber, where her black-clad figure was dwarfed in the huge four-poster. The irony did not escape him; when he had dreamed of having her in his bed, these circumstances had never occurred to him.

Lighting a large candelabrum, he set it by the bedside table. Maggie's smudged face was oddly peaceful as he pulled the torn shirt over her exposed breast. Her hat had been lost in the plaza but a dark scarf was tied around her head and with some difficulty, he untied it, releasing her tangled golden hair to fall over the pillow. A purple bruise was starting to form on one side of her head, but it seemed as if her heavy hair had cushioned some of the effect of the kick.

A yawning maid scurried into the room in her dressing gown, a white garment over her arm. She was French, employed by the hotel, and seemed accustomed to the vagaries of guests. Rafe glanced up at her and said. "I'll buy the shift from you. Undress this lady and put it on her."

The maid's eyes widened slightly; when gentlemen guests brought women here, they were usually far more interested in undressing them themselves. She gave a very French shrug and set to work. Rafe left the room; after what Maggie had gone through tonight, it would have been an unforgivable violation of her privacy to have watched or undressed her himself.

A few minutes later the maid left, her sleepy eyes widening at the size of the tip the duke gave her. When he reentered his chamber, Maggie lay beneath the covers as if asleep. The maid had combed her hair out and it lay around her shoulders in a fine-spun golden mist. The soft muslin shift had delicate embroidery around the neckline and Maggie looked like a schoolgirl, the only sign of her ordeal a slight graze on her left cheekbone. As he waited for the doctor, Rafe studied her face hungrily. She looked now like the Margot Ashton he had loved, and he wondered at the twists of fate that had brought them here, so far in time, space, and circumstance from that original innocent love.

The doctor arrived quickly, a tribute to the persuasive powers of Rafe's valet. Told only that the patient had been caught in a riot, the physician examined her while Rafe paced restlessly in the overfurnished drawing room. After an endless time, the doctor emerged to say, "The young lady was very lucky. Apart from some bruises and the devil of a headache, she'll be fine. No broken bones or signs of internal injuries."

Examining his disheveled patron, the doctor added, "Should I examine you also? You don't appear to have escaped unscathed."

Rafe made an impatient gesture with his hand. "There's nothing wrong with me. Or at least, nothing to signify," he qualified. Now that his anxiety for Maggie was allayed, he was beginning to feel aches and bruises all over, rather like the time he had been thrown from his horse during a steeplechase race and half the field had galloped over him.

Sending his valet back to bed, Rafe settled down with a glass of brandy to sit with Maggie through the rest of the night. Given what she had been through, he didn't want her waking in a strange place with no familiar faces. As he stretched his long legs out before him, he thought tiredly that she might hate him, but at least he was familiar.

He was dozing a little when restless movements woke him. Leaning over Maggie, he saw that she was beginning to writhe back and forth, images of fear rippling across her face. Her breath came in gasps, as if she had been running, and as Rafe watched, she twisted violently and began to scream, the same shattering cry of panic that she had made in the plaza.

Sitting on the bed, he leaned over and pulled her into his arms, saying urgently, "Margot, it's all right! You're safe here, it's just a bad dream." As she started to scream again, he shook her slightly, hoping to penetrate the nightmare.

The scream faded and he held her away from him, searching her face for signs of recognition. As he watched, her gaze came into focus. "Rafe?" she asked in confusion, her mind knowing him but unaware of how she came to be there.

"Yes. Don't worry, apart from a bang on the head nothing happened to you." He spoke softly, as if he was gentling a frightened horse, but his words brought back the memory of what had happened in the plaza and she started to cry, bending forward with great racking sobs that shook her whole body.

Rafe drew her against his chest, stroking her neck and back as she clung to him. In a remote corner of his mind he was surprised at how distraught she was; the tough-as-leather countess had seemed equal to anything. But this wasn't the countess, it was Margot, achingly vulnerable, and he continued to hold her, talking platitudes and reassurances, letting the tone of his voice speak to her fear. When her sobs abated, he said, "It was Lemercier. Did you see him?"

She nodded, her face hidden. He continued, "If it is any comfort, justice caught up with him rather quickly."

Startled, she lifted her head to stare at him. "Did you. . . ?"

Rafe nodded. A brief expression of satisfaction flickered across Margot's face, but then it crumbled, and he saw her struggling with the panic again. She gasped, "I keep seeing them, the faces and the hands, all reaching for me . . . No matter how hard I try, I can't get away. And then, and then . . ." Her body convulsed again in an involuntary attempt to escape her memories and imagination.

Grasping her shoulders, Rafe said urgently, "Margot, it's over, you're all right. I won't let anything happen to you."

She gulped, drawing deep drafts of air into her lungs. Her eyes had been closed but now they opened, the smoky gaze meeting his as she struggled to find words. Finally she managed to say in a wavering voice, "Rafe, please. I want you to make love to me. I want to forget."

He was stunned at her request. With all that lay between them, the mixed attraction and denial, the explosive fight the day before, he doubted what he heard. Hesitantly, Rafe asked, "Margot, do you know what you are saying?"

She nodded, her lovely face open and pleading, the high cheekbones sculpted by candlelight. Her long fair lashes were clumped with the tears she had shed, but her eyes were aware and transparently vulnerable. "I know what I am asking, and I know it isn't fair, but . . ." Her voice trailed off and she shuddered, closing her eyes for a moment before opening them to renew her plea. "Please, Rafe, if you have ever cared for me at all . . ."

Still he held back. For all of his lurid fantasies, he found that he didn't want to take her like this, when she was fragile and terrified. Rafe wanted her to desire him as he desired her, not to use him to block out unbearable memory. Then Margot reached out and laid her hand against his cheek, saying, "Please . . ."

Rafe couldn't bear to see all her pride and vitality broken, nor could he resist the banked passion that flared to life at her touch. Turning into her hand, he kissed her palm and whispered, "Oh God, Margot, I've waited so long, so very, very long . . ."

Over the years his dreams of her had been a product of his own desire, but now his needs were secondary. When he leaned over to kiss her, there was desperation in her response and he used his lips and tongue and hands to transmute fear to passion. He could feel the fear drain from her body, replaced by the tension of growing desire. All the subtle skills of love that he had ever learned became a gift to her, as Rafe sought to sever Margot Ashton's awareness from her tortured memories.

Slipping the thin shift over her head, he exposed her lovely body to the soft candlelight and wondered that he could ever have thought that all women were made much the same. For Rafe, Margot was the essence of femininity, and she aroused him as no woman ever had. Using every shred of control at his command, he forced himself to hold back, bringing her to such a prolonged height of intensity that she was aware only of desire.

When finally Rafe permitted them release, it was a bitter victory; so successful had he been at freeing her from her mind and fears that she whispered, "I love you," the husky sweetness of her words hurting him more deeply than he would have dreamed possible, because they were meant for another man.

Afterward, Margot slept against him, utterly still in the

depths of exhaustion, her tangled hair adrift on his bare chest, her face relaxed. Rafe himself was so tired that he could barely find the strength to raise his hand and brush the dark gold strands from her eyes, to trace the fine bones of her face.

He wished the night would never end. He had wanted Margot Ashton back, and with the bittersweet treachery that marked the gods' answers to human prayers, he had gotten what he wanted. What Rafe hadn't realized was that if he found Margot again, he would once more be as blindly, helplessly in love with her as he had been when he was twenty-two.

The obsession he had felt for the Countess Janos was just another name for that love, but he had been too cynical and adult to name his emotions truly. In the dark, with the palest of dawn light etching the windows, he knew that he loved Margot, the brave and beautiful woman who lay in his arms. No matter what her betrayals and lies, no matter how many beds she had passed through, he loved her, more than wisdom, more than pride, more than life itself.

And in the morning, she would leave him. He had been no more than a convenient substitute for the man she loved, and she had taken him as an invalid takes opium, for oblivion. In the delirium of passion, Margot had whispered words of love that she would deny in the daylight, words whose poisoned sweetness haunted him because they were not meant for him. Tomorrow, all the barriers would lie between them again, with perhaps an additional layer of shame on her part, for what she had done so shamelessly.

The irony was crushing. Rafael Whitbourne, fifth Duke of Candover, had been beloved of the gods, blessed with health, intelligence, charm, and wealth beyond imagining. Those who crossed his path gave him love and admiration, or at the very least, respect. Yet he damned his fate with dark, despairing anger that Margot, who mattered more than anything else in his life, could not love him. She had cared for him when she was young, surely, but not enough to be faithful through the short months of the engagement. He had never come first with her, not then, and not now, when a traitor and spy held her allegiance. Staring upward into the softening dark, Rafe wondered what deep, hidden flaw made him unable to love any woman except one who could not love him back.

Tomorrow would be time enough to ponder that; for now, he would try to hold back sleep so he could savor this handful of moments with the only woman he had ever loved. With the bleakness that lies beyond hope, he knew it was all the time he would ever have.

Chapter 14

Maggie was deeply relaxed when she awoke, though from the angle of the sunlight on the wall it must still be early. She remembered the night before with sharp clarity, her journey through the streets, the unexpected crowd, then Lemercier's denunciation and the slavering mob as it turned on her. . . . She forced the panic back, trying to think calmly of what had happened, but the last she remembered was being down on the ground, fighting for all she was worth, without a prayer of success.

Then a blow on the head had knocked her into darkness, and she remembered nothing more until she woke here, screaming. Everything after that was etched on her brain forever: Rafe holding her, fighting the demons, the doubts on his face as she asked him to make love to her. What followed had been the most intense experience of her life, driving away both panic and inhibition. The warm length of his body lying against her made Maggie feel safe and protected. Among other things.

Turning her head slightly, she studied Rafe's sleeping face. A shadow of dark beard showed, and she could see bruises on his bare torso and the strongly muscled arm that held her close to him. God only knew how he had gotten her away from the mob. Take away his title and his wealth and his power, and he was still a man among men, strong and brave and incredibly beautiful, in an entirely masculine way.

Her body tingled at the memory of their lovemaking, and she closed her eyes in pain. Maggie had always known that if they became intimate, she would be helplessly in love with Rafe again, and it had happened. The love had always been there, since she had first met him thirteen years ago. Perhaps that was why she had never been able to love Robin as much as he deserved. She opened her eyes again, seeing the strong profile, and the lips that could be both tender and wild.

No, the problem was not how *much* she loved Robin, but *how* she loved him. Rafe she loved with conflict as well as harmony, challenge as well as understanding. Odd to think that it was the harsher elements between them that gave her feelings for Rafe such depth and profundity. With Robin there was only harmony, and their feelings were those of friends, almost siblings.

She swallowed hard and slid away from Rafe's arm, careful not to wake him. Rafe she wanted as a mate, the archetypal male that made her feel most deeply female. Though she would like nothing better than to stay in bed with him and spend the rest of her life there, that was impossible. Conspiracy and death still surrounded them, and there were the charges against Robin.

One way or another, the business would be resolved, and then she would never see Rafe again. Possibly he would still be interested in having her as his mistress for a time, if his pride wasn't too deeply injured by the way she had used him, but she would never dare accept. The memory of last night's loving made it almost impossible to imagine life without him; if she became his mistress, she would never survive the end of the affair. The duke would be perfectly charming, of course, kind and a trifle bored. She could imagine it already.

Laying the back of her hand against his cheek, Maggie said a silent farewell to their brief hours of intimacy, resisting the temptation to kiss his chiseled mouth. Her clothes were neatly folded on a chair and she dressed, wincing over the incredible variety of aches and bruises she had. By turning the shirt inside out under her coat, the ripped places didn't coincide and she was more or less decent, apart from being dressed as a boy. Then she went to the window seat and curled up, hugging her knees to her chest as she waited for the duke to wake.

It was perhaps half an hour until Rafe stirred, and his first movement was toward the side of the bed Maggie had occupied. The emptiness woke him, and he pushed himself up on one elbow, his gaze scanning the room until he found her on the window seat. Relaxing fractionally, he looked across the intervening space, his face wary. His torso was bare as he lounged there and Maggie found herself distracted by the elegant patterns of dark hair. Last night she had experienced it as a texture, but now sight provided a different kind of pleasure.

She swallowed and said, "Good morning."

He looked at her with those damnably cool gray eyes. "Is it a good morning?"

With resignation, Maggie realized that he was going to make it difficult for her. She swung her feet to the floor and forced herself to meet his gaze. "Well, I'm alive, and I wouldn't be if it weren't for you. There wouldn't have been much left of me after the mob was done, and if there was, Lemercier would have made sure I didn't survive to carry tales."

Rafe flinched at her words. As soon as he woke and saw her curled up on the window seat, her tight body rejecting him, he had known that there had been no miraculous transformations in her feelings for him. Her terror of the night before had vanished, and with it all traces of vulnerability. The countess was back in control. In the same detached tone that she had used to refer to her death, Margot said, "There are no words strong enough to thank you. I don't know how you found me and got me out of there, but it was an astonishing feat."

In a few words, the duke sketched out what had happened. Margot shook her head in amazement. Tactfully ignoring the fact that he had been having her watched, she said only, "You're a wonder, your grace. I apologize for having called you an amateur—you could have had a splendid career as a spy."

Rafe was silent, wondering if she was going to pretend

nothing else had happened between them. Something in his face must have warned her that if she didn't speak, he would. Her voice a little uneven, she said, "I owe you an apology. You saved my life, and I used you in an unforgivable manner. Asking you what I did was an offense against honor and good taste."

She paused, her smoky eyes searching his, then ended quietly. "You helped me survive a nightmare. I hope you can also find it in your heart to forgive me."

Apologies and gratitude were not what Rafe wanted from Margot, and he was unable to keep a caustic edge from his voice. "Think nothing of it, Countess, I'm sure a woman of your experience knows that men don't mind servicing distraught females."

He was angry, very, the gray eyes like ice chips. Maggie suspected that pride was the deepest of his emotions and she had gravely wounded that. No man would like the idea of being used as an anodyne against pain, and this one would like it less than most. At least he didn't taunt her with the words of love that had escaped last night, when all her defenses were down and her heart spoke uncensored. If he had mocked her unguarded declarations, the pain would have been unbearable.

Well, it was impossible to change last night, and in her secret heart Maggie was glad of that, in spite of what it would cost her in the future. She could only repeat sadly, "I'm sorry," as she stood and turned to leave.

"Just where do you think you are going?" His voice lashed across the bedchamber.

Maggie stopped but didn't turn to face him. "To Robert Anderson's. I must talk to him."

"Do you mean I actually managed to raise a few doubts in your irrational female mind?" The bitterness was unmistakable.

Turning to face him, she snapped, "Yes, damn you, you did. I must give him the chance to defend himself."

Rafe was sitting fully upright now, the covers spilling across his lap, his eyes boring into hers. "And if he has no satisfactory explanation?"

Maggie's shoulders sagged and she whispered, "I don't know."

The duke's voice was calmer now. "Ring for breakfast when you reach the drawing room. I'll join you in fifteen minutes."

When Maggie started to protest, he cut her off. "You're not leaving here without some food in you. Then I'm taking you to Anderson's myself."

Maggie felt herself starting to sputter, unsure whether to be amused, alarmed, or outraged at the duke's high-handedness. Fixing her with a gimlet eye, he said, "If you think I will let you walk the streets alone in that outfit, that blow on the head did more damage than the physician thought. Every night men are killed in the streets of Paris—two bodies were found near the Place du Carrousel just the night before last. Speaking of physicians . . ." he picked up a small bottle and tossed it to her.

As Maggie automatically caught it, Rafe said, "The physician left those for what he assured me would be the devil of a headache. Now, will you get out of my bedroom so I can dress?"

Her predominant feeling was amusement, Maggie decided as she left the room. That, plus the headache which his words made her sharply aware of. She was grateful for the tactfulness that kept Rafe from dressing in front of her; she doubted that modesty was part of his nature. Perhaps now that he had taken her once, his desire was quenched and he feared that if she saw him naked she might become inflamed. The damned man knew too much about women.

There was little discussion over the excellent coffee and rolls, or on the ride to Robin's, until Rafe's carriage was stopped at the edge of the Place du Carrousel. People were milling about, though it was nothing like the riot of the night before. As the driver turned the carriage, Maggie and Rafe could see that the plaza was sealed off by thousands of Austro-Hungarian troops, the sunlight dazzling on their white uniforms and brass cannon. With such protection, the task of removing the bronze horses of St. Mark's was proceeding without incident. As the first horse was swung down from the arch, the soldiers cheered delightedly while the French crowd howled in anguish. This time, Napoleon's loot was leaving for good.

Rafe smiled grimly. "Wellington must have been furious

when he heard about last night and decided on a show of force. Paris might not love him now, but by God, she will respect him!''

Maggie's flat voice drew him back to the implications. "Let us hope this won't increase his chances of being assassinated.''

The rest of the journey was made in silence as they swung around the Place du Carrousel and the Louvre to reach the small hotel where Robin had rooms. The duke waited in the carriage while Maggie went in, saying tersely that he would follow her if she was gone more than ten minutes, but no such action was required. There was no answer when she knocked on Robin's door, and the concierge told her that Monsieur Anderson had not been home in the last thirty-six hours. Indeed, the British delegation had sent to inquire his whereabouts.

When she went back outside to the duke's carriage, Maggie's stomach was twisted into an anguished knot. She could think of only two possibilities: if Robin had heard that there were suspicions about him and run away, he was guilty. If he was innocent, he never would have left Paris without notifying her. Therefore, since he had disappeared, he was probably dead.

The duke was silent as he returned Maggie to her townhouse, his brows drawn like thunderclouds, and she could only be glad that he refrained from saying, "I told you so." Maggie was so wretched and confused that she had no idea what to think about Robin's disappearance, except that it was ominous. As soon as she reached home she withdrew into her bedchamber for three hours of pacing and intense, unhappy thought. She would prefer that Robin was a live traitor rather than a dead loyalist—but if he had betrayed his country, she never wanted to see him again.

Before withdrawing, she sent a message to Hélène Sorel, asking her friend to come for lunch if at all possible. Hélène appeared promptly. Maggie had arranged for a cold collation so they wouldn't be disturbed, and as soon as the edge was off the women's appetites, she began to talk over the dining room table. She told Hélène everything—about her background and her involvement with Robert Anderson and the British intelligence network, about the plot that Lord Lattimer had wanted them to investigate, about their suspects, about the Duke of Candover, and finally, about Robin's disappearance. About everything, except the relationship between her and Rafe. With matters reaching a crisis, she felt the need of a confederate who might be able to see something she had missed. Besides the fact that they had been friends for a long time, Hélène had experience in spying and would make a good sounding board.

Hélène listened carefully, her brown hair drawn back in a modest chignon, resembling any other pretty young French matron except for her precise, intelligent questions. When Maggie ran out of words, Hélène said, "Some of what you say I had guessed, but the picture is much larger and darker than I knew. Since Talleyrand is out of the government and Castlereagh is confined to his embassy, it would seem that Wellington is the most likely target for assassins, *n'est-ce pas?*"

Maggie nodded. "I believe so. Candover has gone to speak to Wellington, to warn him to take special care. They know each other, so Wellington may listen, but he is notorious for ignoring danger. He thinks it would damage his dignity to seem afraid."

"It is time we reduced the number of suspects," Hélène said, her brown eyes thoughtful. "I have finished my inquiries about Colonel von Fehrenbach, and this evening I will call on him. When I am done, I think he will no longer be a suspect."

"Promise me you will take an escort, Hélène," Maggie said urgently. "I can't afford to lose more friends. Candover is asking Wellington for the use of some soldiers if we need them."

Hélène's rounded face showed amusement. Carefully selecting a pastry from the tray between them on the dining table, she said, "If you insist. But they must wait outside in a carriage, and not come unless I summon them. They will not be needed."

Maggie wished she shared her friend's faith. If Maggie could be disastrously wrong about Robert Anderson, Hélène could certainly be wrong about a man she barely knew.

"If he is eliminated, that leaves General Roussaye as the

most likely prospect." Maggie sighed. Her head throbbed from the blow she received the night before and she wanted to retire to her room and sleep forever, and not have to face a world where she had lost Robin, and Rafe despised her, and the fate of European peace might be resting on her tired shoulders. Planting her elbows on the polished mahogany table, she buried her face in her hands, telling herself not to be melodramatic.

A knock sounded, followed by her butler with Cynthia Northwood. The butler apologized. "I know you didn't wish to be disturbed, my lady, but Mrs. Northwood said it was most urgent."

Pulling herself together, Maggie stood and said, "Quite right, Laneuve."

As the butler stepped clear of her guest, Maggie gasped in shock. Cynthia's face was violently bruised, her left eye blackened and swollen shut. She carried a small portmanteau, and after Laneuve had left the dining room the girl said in a shaky voice laced with appeal, "I didn't know where else to go."

"My dear child!" Maggie was appalled, and walked over and put her arms around her guest. Cynthia shuddered for a moment, then resolutely pushed herself away. "I'm sorry, I didn't mean to do that. I must talk to you." She looked uncertainly at Hélène, who had poured a glass of brandy and now offered it. Maggie said, "Don't worry, you can speak freely before Madame Sorel. She and I work closely together. Now, what has happened to you?"

Accepting the assurance, Cynthia slumped into the chair Maggie offered. "I was able to search my husband's desk."

"Did he find you doing it and beat you?" Maggie exclaimed. Even though she had warned Cynthia to be careful, she felt horribly guilty that her words had precipitated such a result.

"Oh, no, he beat me for quite other reasons," her guest said bitterly. "I had ample time to find a hidden drawer and copy everything I found there." She leaned over her portmanteau, then pulled out half a dozen sheets of writing paper. Handing them to Maggie, she said, "I didn't dare bring the originals, but I thought you might be able to make some sense of this."

Maggie accepted the papers but didn't look at them. "If he didn't know of it, why did your husband beat you?"

Cynthia swallowed. "I had decided to leave him. To stay was insupportable, and Gregory swore that he was willing to face the consequences, no matter what Oliver did." She paused and glanced at Hélène, then continued, "Gregory has been sent to the fortress at Huninguen and won't be back for several more days. When he returned, I was going to . . . tell him about the baby, and go to him. Having made up my mind, I was almost giddy with relief, and Oliver guessed something was in the wind."

Looking down at her hands, she continued, her voice a little unsteady, "He came into my room unexpectedly when I was dressing, and immediately saw that I was increasing. He knew the baby couldn't be his, and he was enraged. He . . . he made my maid leave and started beating me, calling me horrible names and saying he hoped I'd lose the filthy brat, and if he was lucky, I'd die, too. Then he locked me in my room."

She broke down, but managed to say desperately through her tears, "I can't go back there, he'll kill me! Please, Maggie, can I stay here until Gregory returns?"

Maggie went to stand next to her, holding the girl's head against her breast. "Of course you can. He'll never find you here. Tell me, how did you escape from the locked room?"

The question helped Cynthia collect herself, and she smiled with a touch of pride. "I was quite the tomboy when I was a girl, and I tied the bedsheets together and climbed down after he had left to go to the embassy, then caught a cab over here."

"Goodness!" Maggie said with a smile of approval. "You are a most resourceful woman. I'm glad you are on our side."

Seeing how gray-faced her guest was now that she had reached safety, Maggie installed her in a guest room and sent her groom for a physician to check that she had no serious injuries. Then she settled down with Hélène in the dining room to look at the papers Cynthia had copied. They consisted mainly of cryptic phrases, the kind of jottings a person doodles while thinking, and which are almost impossible for another person to decipher. There was one list of gambling vowels, and another detailed sums of money in francs, possibly from winnings or losses.

Maggie was disappointed but supposed that even a dolt like Northwood was unlikely to leave anything very incriminating around, assuming that he was guilty of anything more than garden variety beastliness. Secret compartments were common in desks, and one of the first places that would be searched. She had a secret drawer herself and had filled it with some scorching but synthetic love letters, so that if anyone ever discovered them it would merely support her reputation as a brainless doxy.

Then buried in the middle of the next to the last page a phrase jumped out: "Anderson—spy? Possible danger."

Hélène saw it at the same time. In an expressionless voice, Maggie said, "This doesn't prove anything about Robin."

"No, it doesn't," Hélène agreed. In a soft voice, she added, "You still believe in his innocence, don't you, *mon amie?*"

"Yes," Maggie said bleakly. "I think he disappeared because he got too close to the fire once too often." Her throat tightened, so she laid out the last sheet of paper. The drawing on it caused both women to stare in surprise and speculation. In Maggie's hand was a copy of the three-headed serpent crest of the d'Aguste family she had traced at Mme. Daudet's. Underneath was written, *Le Serpent*, and a triumphant *Eureka!*

After a long moment, Maggie said, "Obviously, Northwood is involved in some secret work. The question is, for whom?"

"And what did this crest suggest to him? If this is indeed the crest of *Le Serpent*, the puzzle is solved once we understand who it is connected to," Hélène said thoughtfully.

"Perhaps we are finally making some progress," Maggie said wearily. "But I feel more as if we are opening Chinese boxes, and each contains another."

At that moment, the butler announced the arrival of the physician, and Hélène rose to take her leave, promising to return that evening after her confrontation with Colonel von Fehrenbach. Maggie could only pray that her friend's initiative would bring them closer to their goal before disaster fell.

Chapter 15

Hélène dressed carefully for her confrontation with Colonel von Fehrenbach, choosing a blue dress that was feminine but unprovocative. Though she had two reasons for visiting him, neither was seduction in the usual sense. Candover had lent her his carriage and arranged for four British soldiers to come up the back stairs of the colonel's building and wait out of sight in case she needed assistance. As a signaling device, she had been offered a pistol small enough to fit into her reticule, an offer she rejected with distaste. Instead, she had a whistle whose shriek could penetrate several walls if necessary. She carried it to appease Maggie and Rafe but was sure it wouldn't be required.

The duke had grave doubts about a woman confronting von Fehrenbach alone, saying that the colonel would deny any involvement in a conspiracy, so Mme. Sorel's visit would do no good and might endanger her as well. Both women had politely listened to his arguments, then Maggie had endorsed Hélène's right to follow her instinct. Nonetheless, Hélène was sure that Candover would be with the British soldiers, just in case.

Candover and Maggie . . . an interesting topic of speculation, and Hélène considered it now. She could feel the tension between them and wondered if it was because they desired each other and had done nothing about it, or because they had. . . . Wondering about them made a refreshing change from worrying about her own concerns, because in spite of her surface confidence, this upcoming interview with the Prussian officer terrified her.

The carriage halted in front of an elegant mansion on a quiet street in the Marais district, not far from Mme. Daudet's. The building was divided into apartments and the colonel lived here with only a manservant, who should be off tonight. Von Fehrenbach avoided the temptations of Parisian night life, going out only when his duties demanded it, so Hélène should find him alone.

After touching a nervous hand to her hair, she stepped down from the carriage. When she told the concierge whom she was calling on, his look was first surprised, then lewdly speculative as he directed her to the second floor, front apartment. The mansion had been built in the early eighteenth century, and it retained much of its grandeur even after its conversion to smaller units. As she stood in front of von Fehrenbach's door, Hélène glanced down the short hall to the door which concealed her soldier bodyguard, then knocked at the door.

After a delay of some moments, the colonel answered the door himself. Good, the servant was off this evening. Von Fehrenbach was not in uniform, but even in his severely cut blue coat he was unmistakably a soldier. The pale blond hair shone silver; altogether a very handsome man, in the fashion of an ice prince.

When he saw who had knocked, his face reflected shock and a complex mixture of other emotions. "Madame Sorel. What an unlikely pleasure. What brings you here this evening?" He stood in the doorway, his tall figure as cold and unyielding as his voice.

Meeting his gaze required her to tilt her head rather far back. "A matter of some urgency. If I promise not to compromise you, will you let me in so I may discuss it?" A hint of color touched his cheeks and he stepped aside so she could enter. The rooms were well-proportioned and impeccably neat, but apart from the well-filled bookcase there was an unwelcoming austerity. It was as Hélène expected; a person's interior state was mirrored in his surroundings and the colonel had winter in his soul.

Inclining her head in thanks, she stepped into the drawing room and accepted an offered chair. Von Fehrenbach seated himself some distance away and waited for her to begin. Hélène spent a moment studying his face, feeling the tension that lay beneath his impassive expression. In a stab of self-doubt, she wondered if she was wrong about the source of that tension. Perhaps he really did make dark and dangerous plans to injure others, and she was suddenly glad of the whistle in her reticule.

When the silence reached the snapping point, Hélène plunged into what she had come to say. "There is a conspiracy to destroy the peace conference by assassination. An attempt was made on Castlereagh's life and Wellington may be the next target."

Von Fehrenbach's pale brows rose marginally. "Indeed? Paris is rife with plots, and I understood that Castlereagh was injured in an accident such as might happen to anyone. What has either of those things to do with me?"

Her hands lay loosely in her lap, but her thumbs twisted around each other. "There is some reason to believe that you might be behind the conspiracy."

"What!" The impenetrable calm was shattered now. The colonel stood, his face furious. "How dare you come here and accuse me of such a thing! What perversion of logic could lead anyone to suspect me?" With a flash of pale blue fire in his eyes, he finished in a soft, dangerous whisper. "And why do I hear it from you, of all people?"

Hélène remained still. In the moments after he spoke, she could hear his angry breathing, could almost hear the sound of his heart beating, or perhaps it was hers. "That is three questions, none of them simple to answer. If you will sit and listen for a few minutes, I will explain." As he hesitated, she added, "It is in your best interest to hear."

Eyes narrowed, he said, "Are you threatening me, madame?"

She shook her head. "Not at all, Colonel. What threat could I possibly pose to you? You are one of the victors, a man of wealth and position, while I am but a widow from a defeated nation. If you are threatened, it is not by me." As he stood uncertainly, she added impatiently, "Come, surely you do not fear me personally. It will cost you nothing to listen."

He sat then, this time in a chair closer to Hélène. The tension vibrating in his body would now be obvious even to the least observant, and he said so softly she might have imagined the words, "In that you are wrong, Madame Sorel. I do fear you."

With sudden relief she knew that she was right, that every

exchange between them took place on more than one level, but she said prosaically, "First, you wished to know why you are suspected. Considerable effort has gone into investigating this plot, and you were one of a handful of possibilities thought to have the intelligence, skill, and motive to organize it."

"I am flattered by your assessment of my ability," he said. "But what would my motive be?"

"You are known to hate France and everything French. Twice you have killed French officers in duels. You have also said repeatedly that the proposed settlement is too moderate. If Wellington or Castlereagh are killed, what will happen to the treaty that is so close to acceptance?"

After a moment of surprise, the colonel said, "I begin to understand. If either of the British leaders were killed, the voices of moderation would be dead, and all of Europe would demand reprisals. France would be dismembered and impoverished."

"Does that thought please you, Colonel von Fehrenbach?" Hélène asked in her gentle voice.

Flushing he said, "It might please me, but I am a soldier, not an assassin. I killed two French officers who had challenged and killed several junior Allied officers. I would do so again if such action was warranted, but that is a very long way from plotting against your country. My duty is to follow my sovereign's orders, not to make policy."

"I believe that, and that is one of the reasons I am here." She sat without flinching as his gaze examined her with new thoroughness. He was beginning to really hear what she was saying, and that was what she had hoped for.

Slowly, he asked, "Are there other reasons I am under suspicion? I am not the only Allied officer who hates France."

"There is another reason, circumstantial but strong. We have learned that the man behind the plot is called *Le Serpent*."

"Again, what has that to do with me?" he asked impatiently.

"The cunning of a serpent, the courage of a lion," she quoted, watching his reaction closely.

He sucked in his breath. "Of course, my family motto.

Interesting, but as you said, entirely circumstantial. Many family arms carry serpents. In fact," he added after a moment's thought, "it needn't refer to family arms. There is a French general who was called *Le Serpent,* and for all I know the Parisian king of thieves is called that as well."

Ignoring his later words, Hélène asked with sudden excitement, "What general is that?"

The colonel gave her a hard look. "Michel Roussaye. A friend of mine tried to capture him and a small force of French soldiers after the Battle of Leipzig and Roussaye slithered away time and again, very much like a serpent. He's a fine soldier," he added with professional respect.

Hélène made a lightning decision to tell him more. "General Roussaye is another leading suspect."

"How could he benefit by seeing France crippled by the peace settlement?" von Fehrenbach said with a touch of exasperation. "You people, whoever you are, are guilty of massive illogic."

"A revolutionary might welcome a settlement that would anger France to the point where she would once more take arms."

The effect of Hélène's words on the colonel was immediately visible. His face closed and he seemed to almost forget she was there. Finally he returned his gaze to her and said, "Why have you come here to tell me this? If I am truly under suspicion, why didn't Wellington just arrest me?"

"There are political realities," Hélène pointed out. "Marshal Blücher would be furious if one of his most valued aides was arrested on such flimsy evidence. Indeed, there is no real evidence to speak of, merely possibilities. That is one reason why this business is being handled with as much discretion as possible. Besides, if this becomes a *cause célèbre,* the effect would be almost as disruptive as an actual assassination."

"As you say," the colonel said dryly, "there is no real evidence. There could hardly be any since I have done nothing, but what has happened to convince you there is some great plot?"

Hélène turned one hand up in a dismissive gesture. "Rumors and small inconsistencies that would never stand up in a court of law. The only truly solid evidence is the attack on Lord Castlereagh, and the fact that a British agent may have been murdered because he was getting too close to *Le Serpent.*''

"Or else he got into a fight over a woman," von Fehrenbach said caustically. "I have never heard that spies were a very honorable lot. Which brings us to you, Madame Sorel. You have answered my other questions, but not why you, of all the men and women in France, have come to accuse me."

Now the conversation was going to become really difficult. Hélène's palms were moist but she replied equably. "I have an unofficial connection with British intelligence and have been involved in the investigation."

"So the lady is a spy," he said with disgust. "Or is that a contradiction in terms? Spying is just another form of whoring, and I understand that female spies sell themselves in many ways."

She had known that something like this would be said, but even so it stung. "I have never sold myself in any way, Colonel, and I accept no money for what I do. Someone else could have come to question you, but I wanted to."

"Why?" He leaned forward in his chair, his hands linked together, his eyes narrowed and hostile. "Once again, why you?"

"You know why, Colonel." Her brown eyes were open and full of warmth as they met his. His eyes might be the pale, cold blue of northern ice, but underneath she could see the pain in him.

He wrenched his gaze away from her and stood, turning to move toward his bookcase. She could see some of the titles from where she sat. Philosophy and history, mostly, with a number of Latin and Greek texts. The colonel was a man of parts. Without looking at her, he said, "You speak in riddles, Madame Sorel."

"No," she said, shaking her head and rising. "I am speaking very clearly, though it might not be a language you wish to hear." Crossing the room, she stopped several feet away from him. "Even if you will not admit it, there has been something between us since the first time we met."

He faced her then, anger melting the ice prince's calm.

"Very well, I admit it. You arouse me, like a mare in heat inflames a stallion. You must feel it too, or you would not be flaunting yourself here. Have so many Frenchmen died that you must seek farther afield for a stud? Shall I take you here on the carpet, do to you what I want the Allies to do to France?"

Hélène's face whitened. She had expected him to fight her and knew that his cruelty was a measure of how much she affected him. Even so, his words cut too close to the bone to ignore, and her voice had a slight break as she said, "If casual fornication was all I wanted, I could find it easily enough without coming to a man who insults me."

"Then why *are* you here, madame?" His words were bleak, yet not so bleak as his haunted eyes.

"I want you to look at me, just once, without remembering that I am French and you are Prussian." Hélène's soft voice held a touch of steel.

The colonel looked down at her for a long moment, a blue blood vessel throbbing visibly under the fair nordic skin. Then he whirled away from her, taking long strides as if he could escape her words. "That, madame, is quite impossible."

He turned now, a safe distance between them, and began to hurl bitter words at her. "I look at you and see my burned home, my murdered wife and son and sister. Murdered by the French, madame, by your people, perhaps by your brother or husband. I can never forget that we are enemies."

"I am not your enemy."

He stared at her, his face working, then said flatly, "Yes, you are. The only worse enemy I have is myself, that I should be attracted to a woman of a race I hate and despise. You have given me many sleepless nights, madame. Does it please you to know how much you have made me despise myself?"

Hélène made no attempt to close the distance between them. Standing before the bookcase, she was a small, gently rounded figure. Soft, yet unyielding. "I can never be pleased at another's pain. I became involved in spying to make what small contribution I could to peace. I did have brothers, Colonel. One died in the retreat from Moscow, the other under torture by Spanish partisans. I was told it took him two days to die. That was my younger brother, who wished to be a painter.

"And I had a husband, too, killed at Wagram, two months before my younger daughter was born. You fought at Wagram, Colonel. It might have been your troops that killed him."

"Splendid, Madame Sorel, we have both suffered." His voice was a lash of bitterness. "You have my permission to hate the Prussians as much as I hate the French. Will that satisfy you?"

"No!" she cried, her pain finally overcoming the hard-won serenity she had learned in a lifetime of loss. "I want to see an end to hating. If Prussia had been the aggressor rather than France, would my husband be any less dead? I want my daughters to live in a world where their husbands will grow old with them, where boys like my brother can paint flowers and pretty girls and write silly love poetry, instead of dying screaming."

She looked at him pleadingly, wondering if there were any words that would melt the ice around his heart. "As a Christian, I have been taught to hate the sin but love the sinner. I hate war and the unspeakable evil it brings, but if we cannot love one another, we are doomed to fight and die again and again."

"And you think that if I could love you, that would put an end to war?" His voice held pain but also a yearning to believe.

"I don't know if we can love one another, perhaps there is nothing between us but physical attraction." The tears flowed unheeded down Hélène's face. She knew her words were reaching him, but feared it was not enough. He had lived in his pain and loss too long to risk life again. Her voice breaking, she continued, "If two individuals cannot even try, there is no hope for mankind—we will be condemned to suffer our mistakes forever."

Von Fehrenbach turned away to drift uncertainly across the room, his broad shoulders tightened defensively against her, then stopped by a table where a small portrait, perhaps six inches high, stood next to a closed Bible. From where she stood, Hélène could see that the painting was of a blond woman seated with a small boy at her side. Looking down at it he said, his voice husky, "You are a brave woman. Perhaps women are braver than men. If a body is injured badly enough it dies, but with an injured heart one survives to suffer pain without end."

Reaching out one finger, he gently touched the woman in the portrait, then looked up at Hélène, his face deeply sad. "You ask too much, Madame Sorel. My strength is not equal to the task."

She had failed, then. Closing her eyes against the tears, she said with infinite sadness, "It is not that women are braver, Colonel, but that we are more foolish."

Turning away, she fumbled in her reticule until she found a handkerchief. The mundane business of blotting her tears and blowing her nose gave her a chance to establish a fragile self-control, and now she crossed the drawing room to the vestibule. His words followed her.

"What will you tell your masters about my villainy?"

Her hand on the doorknob, Hélène said without turning to face him, "I will tell them I think you are not involved in any way, and I will be believed. You will be closely watched until the conference is over, so even if I am wrong, your opportunities for villainy will be reduced." She looked at him now, her wide brown eyes resigned. "Farewell, Colonel von Fehrenbach. I think we will not meet again."

Then he did something that surprised her. Crossing the room to stand by her, he looked searchingly into her face, as if trying to memorize what she looked like. Finally he repeated, this time with a note of wonder, "You are a very brave woman indeed." Bending over, he lifted her hand and kissed it, not romantically, but with a kind of sad respect.

Hélène managed to walk out with her head high as the colonel held the door, but after it had closed she leaned against the paneled wall of the hallway. She was so incredibly weary . . .

Finally she walked to the door at the end of the hall and opened it. As expected, the Duke of Candover was there, his stern face registering relief that she had emerged intact. Four soldiers were engaged in a friendly card game on the floor, and they scrambled hastily to their feet as Hélène appeared. They all looked so very young. She smiled at them, and the gangling young lieutenant blushed and bobbed his head.

The duke said, "All is well then, Madame Sorel?"

Sighing, she said, "As well as can be expected."

Inside the austere apartment, Karl von Fehrenbach moved around restlessly, picking objects up and setting them down, pulling out a volume by Fichte and replacing it unread, then opening a volume of Virgil at random. Looking down, he read, *"Omnia vincit Amor: et nos cedamus Amori."* Love conquers all: let us too give in to Love.

He slammed the book shut and reshelved it so violently that he dented the leather binding. Leaning his head against the books, he thought of Hélène Sorel standing where he stood now, small and sweetly feminine, and didn't know if she was an angel from heaven come to redeem him, or a demon from hell sent to seduce him out of what was left of his immortal soul. Whatever else she might be, she had courage, to open herself to such rejection.

Finally he went to the portrait of Elke and Erik, lifting it to study their beloved faces. His wife, who had had the gift of laughter, and his son, who had inherited his father's height and his mother's sunny nature. Inge had sent it three months before they were killed. The house had been burned around them and he prayed they had died of the smoke rather than the flames.

He could feel the grief welling up in him, dissolving all the defenses he had built to dam the pain, and in desperation he flipped open the Bible that lay on the table and glanced in, hoping for some guidance. The verse that leaped out at him read, *"Her sins, which are many, are forgiven, for she loved much."*

If it was a message from God, it was one too painful to be borne. He sank onto his knees by the brocade-covered Louis Quinze armchair, burying his head in his arms and giving way to the gut-wrenching sobs of a man who had forgotten how to cry.

Chapter 16

This visit to *Le Serpent* was a short one. The Englishman no longer cared that his dread host was masked; he knew now whom he served and at the right time he would reveal that knowledge. *Le Serpent* was curt, not even rising from his chair. Glancing at his visitor, he said, "The gunpowder is now secured in the closet?"

"Yes. I brought it in over several days and it's in an area that few people frequent. Unlikely anyone will discover it by chance, and even if someone looked in the closet, the gunpowder is in boxes that should arouse no suspicion."

"Very good." The masked man was silent for a moment, then said, "Thursday is the day."

"Day after tomorrow?" The Englishman was startled; all of a sudden, it seemed too close.

"Yes. The gunpowder must go off as close to four o'clock as possible. The wax candle I gave you should burn eight hours, so light it at eight in the morning. I trust that presents no problems for you." The last sentence was not a question.

The Englishman paused uncertainly. "Could be difficult. I've been playing least-in-sight the last few days and it might seem suspicious if I'm at the embassy, and so early."

"I am not interested in the complications that your personal life is causing you," *Le Serpent* said coldly. "I pay you for results. Once the candle is lit you can run as far as you wish, but the explosion *must* take place on Thursday. That's the only day the king himself will join the ministers. There may never be another time when they are all gathered in one accessible place."

"Don't worry, I'll manage." The Englishman knew who would be there, and understood the urgency of the situation. The British foreign minister's bedroom had become the axis around which the conference revolved, but that would end when Castlereagh was able to get up. When he had realized the scope of the destruction that would be caused, he decided to cast his lot in with *Le Serpent*. The conspirator's boldness of vision and strength of will could take him to the very top during the chaos that would follow the explosion, and those who had assisted would go with him. It was an intoxicating prospect. But he wished to inquire about another subject, not vital in the long run but of interest just now. "About the British spies . . ." he began.

Le Serpent looked up impatiently from his desk. "They are being dealt with. Do not concern yourself."

"I'm interested in the woman, Countess Janos."

The masked man leaned back and laced his fingers across his ribs, and his voice was amused. "Oh, do you want her for yourself, *mon petit Anglais?* She's a handsome piece, I admit."

"Yes, I want the bitch. At least for a while."

"Very well, you have done your job well—I will give her to you as a bonus. Now, leave me, there is much else to be done."

The Englishman was almost purring with pleasure as he left. He had never forgotten how Margot Ashton had scorned him, and now she would pay for that and every other humiliation a woman had ever given him. She would pay, and pay, and pay.

Maggie started the day early with a trip to the British Embassy. The night before, she and Hélène and the Duke of Candover had spent some time discussing the implications of what the Frenchwoman had reported. From the gray look that Hélène wore, it was clear that she had failed in any personal hopes she might have had; it seemed kinder not to ask.

Rafe had sent a note to Michel Roussaye, asking permission to call at his earliest possible convenience, and had received a courteous reply suggesting eleven o'clock the next morning. Clearly, the next order of business was to confront the general, perhaps hurl some accusations, and watch his reaction.

Before the evening was over, Maggie had contacted one

of her informants and received independent confirmation that Roussaye had been called *Le Serpent*. She had almost hoped that von Fehrenbach had fabricated the story, because if what the colonel said was true and Robin had been paying surreptitious visits to Roussaye, it seemed likely both men were conspirators. The general might be considered a patriot, albeit a misguided one, but it was hard to judge Robin's collaboration as anything other than treason. Maggie's emotions fought that conclusion, but her mind made it hard to deny the mounting evidence against him.

This morning's visit to the British Embassy was ostensibly a courtesy call on Lady Castlereagh, but in fact Maggie's prime purpose was to deliver a report on her suspicions of Oliver Northwood. She explained her doubts to Emily, urging that the information be passed on to her husband as soon as possible. A worried Lady Castlereagh had promised to do so immediately, but also told Maggie that Northwood hadn't been at work in the last two days. A note had been delivered saying that he had acute food poisoning and would be back as soon as possible.

Maggie was thinking hard during the ride home. Northwood's "food poisoning" had coincided with his attack on his wife. Fearful of what Cynthia might say about him, had he decided to run after he discovered that she had escaped her prison? Or was he seeking her himself, intent on forcing her to return to him? Thank heaven Cynthia was concealed at Maggie's; as long as the girl was willing to stay hidden, she would be safe.

Keeping her mind on business helped her avoid thinking about Rafe. He had treated her with chilly politeness since the night they had made love, but she could feel his anger and contempt. Whatever warmth had been between them had vanished.

Maggie had needed him so desperately to help her through that night, but the price was even higher than she had thought it would be. With a touch of asperity, she thought that most men would not consider it a horrible fate to make love with her; even the duke had not seemed to regret it at the time, but with daylight his invincible pride had reasserted itself. She could only hope that the plot would be neutralized as soon as possible, so they would never have to see each other again.

The carriage dropped Maggie off in front of her house, then continued around to the mews in back. In less than half an hour, Rafe was due to pick her up for the visit to General Roussaye, and her thoughts were on the upcoming interview as she put one foot on the first of the marble steps. When a carriage pulled up behind her, Maggie turned, thinking the duke had come early, but the luxurious dark blue berlin was unfamiliar. However, she recognized the man who climbed out smiling expansively, and she greeted him with practiced charm. "Good morning, Count, you are out early today. If you were calling on me, I fear I must disappoint you—I am going out again immediately."

"What a pity, Countess." Varenne contrived to look suitably crestfallen. His broad figure was garbed with his usual discreet elegance, but the coldness of his eyes caused Maggie to take an involuntary step back from him. He continued, "When I saw you here, on impulse I decided to invite you to my estate at Chanteuil if you have no other pressing engagements today. The gardens will not be at their best much longer."

"I'm sorry, my lord, but. . . ."

The count interrupted her to say jovially, "Really, my dear, I will accept no excuses. It is scarcely an hour's drive from here, and I can guarantee you an interesting visit." He laid a casual hand on her waist, as if to help her to his carriage, and Maggie froze. Varenne had a knife in his hand, and he held it against her with such force that the point penetrated her green muslin dress and stabbed into her flesh. "I really must insist."

If she tried to call her servants, the knife would be between her ribs before the first sound escaped. Stony-faced, Maggie climbed into the carriage, where a wizened man dressed in dark clothes like a clerk sat with his back to the horses. Still pressing the knife into her side, the count took the seat next to her as the door was closed and the carriage started up. The whole business was over in less than a minute, and even the woman watching from the window above noticed nothing amiss.

The count withdrew the knife once the carriage was under

way. "You're a prudent woman, Countess; it would have done you no good to attempt a scene. Or should I call you Miss Ashton?" he asked, his sibilant voice menacing in its amusement.

Furiously angry at having been so easily taken, Maggie refused to drop her eyes before his. "I see my instincts were correct. It was obvious from the first that you were despicable, but I was unable to imagine any possible reason for an Ultra-Royalist to plot against the British leadership."

Varenne was expansive in his self-satisfaction. "Lack of imagination is a dangerous failing, as you are about to find out." He nodded to the clerk, who poured a few drops of liquid from a bottle onto a scarf. "Pray forgive my rudeness, Miss Ashton, but I have a great respect for your abilities and don't wish you to be damaged prematurely. You acquitted yourself well in the Place du Carrousel, though your efforts would have done no good if your muscle-bound lover hadn't been on the scene."

The clerk leaned forward and pressed the rag over Maggie's nose and mouth, his other hand clamped behind her head so she couldn't turn away. She struggled against the sickly-sweet drug, but she was trapped in the tight confines of the carriage. As her consciousness slipped away, she heard the count say amiably, "Candover cost me the services of Lemercier, which I cannot easily forgive. Still, I am a flexible man, and since you survived that little altercation I have found a use for you. I have promised you to an associate of mine. He admires that lovely flesh, and doesn't care whether it is willing or not."

His last words produced a wave of horror in Maggie but her muscles were no longer responding to her will, and in a few more moments blackness overcame her.

Rafe was on edge when he arrived at the Boulevard des Capucines townhouse, uncertain whether he was more upset at the thought of confronting General Roussaye or at having to spend more time with Margot. Impossible to think of her as Maggie any longer; that name belonged to the elusive, maddening countess. After their intimacy she had become Margot Ashton to him again, and he didn't want to let go of that, even if she no longer wanted to be called by her real name.

Already the memory of the night they had spent together seemed incredibly distant, as if it had happened years earlier rather than a scant day. He wondered if there was any chance Margot might come to want him if Robert Anderson was now out of her life. It might take a long time, but he was prepared to wait; God knew, he'd waited thirteen years already.

Frowning at the butler's statement that the countess had not yet returned, Rafe waited for ten restless minutes before calling for Cynthia Northwood. Margot had told him why the girl was staying there, but even so Rafe was shocked by her bruises. Bowing over her hand, he asked, "How do you feel today, Cynthia?"

With a smile, she replied, "Better than I have in years, Rafe. I only wish I had dared to leave sooner."

Returning her smile, he said, "It must have taken a great deal of courage to leave at all." He was glad to see that she was not cringing or bemoaning her fate. They had not been lovers in years but he was fond of Cynthia and her sometimes reckless spirit. She would need all her courage in the scandal to come; he hoped her major would prove equally strong. "I'm sorry to have disturbed you, Cynthia, but I wanted to know if the countess said she was going anywhere besides the embassy. We have an urgent appointment, and it surprises me that she is not here."

Cynthia frowned. "That's odd—I shouldn't think she would forget that you were coming. Maggie did return from the embassy about half an hour ago, but left again without re-entering the house. A man pulled up in a carriage and talked with her for a moment, then she went off with him."

Rafe felt sick to his stomach. "You saw this happen?" At Cynthia's nod, he asked flatly, "This man . . . was he blond?"

"No, dark-haired. He wasn't much taller than she, and he looked French. Were you expecting someone else to go with you?"

Rafe forced himself to quell the rising jealousy and confusion he felt. It was conceivable that Margot might have gone off with Anderson like that, but it seemed unlikely that anyone else could persuade her to break the engagement to visit Roussaye. Therefore, she might not have gone willingly. "Tell me *exactly* what you saw, Cynthia; it might be important."

She described what she had seen but could add little but the color of the coach. The sheer window curtains had obscured details, and her description of the man Margot went off with would have fit half the men in France, including Michel Roussaye.

Anderson had disappeared, and now Margot. Rafe felt the beginnings of fear, and the best antidote for that was action. It was more important than ever that he talk to Roussaye, and if the general turned out to have kidnapped Margot. . . . He stood and said crisply, "I must keep our appointment by myself. Please send a note around to Madame Sorel and ask her to meet me here. I should be back in an hour or so, and it is urgent that we talk."

Then he left, leaving a worried Cynthia Northwood. On the drive to Roussaye's house, Rafe decided that the best strategy with the general was to shock him with accusations, hoping the man would give something away if he was guilty. In his present mood, it would be very easy for the duke to appear accusing.

Roussaye received him affably from behind the desk in his study, standing and offering his hand. "Good day, your grace. Good of you to call, though I am sorry the countess is not with you. My wife was hoping to visit with her."

Rafe said harshly, "This is not a social call, Roussaye. I have been conducting a secret investigation for the British government, and I am here to tell you that the game is up. Even *Le Serpent* cannot escape this time."

The general's face paled and he dropped his hand. Slowly he sat down again behind his desk, absently reaching to open a drawer. Rafe swiftly reached under his coat for one of the two loaded pistols he carried. Cocking it, he snapped, "Don't do it, Roussaye. You're under arrest. I have British soldiers waiting outside. Even if you could shoot me, you'll never escape."

The general looked up in surprise and a hint of amusement. "Such fierceness, your grace. I was reaching for a cigar. If I am under arrest, this may be my last opportunity to partake of civilized pleasures. Care to join me?'' Moving with exaggerated care, he removed an inlaid walnut humidor and placed it on the desk, then took out a cigar. He clipped the end and lit it with leisurely grace, as if he had all the time in the world.

Rafe refused the offer impatiently but took a seat in front of the desk, the pistol still aimed at Roussaye. There would be time enough to call the soldiers in later: before that happened the general had some questions to answer. He felt reluctant admiration for Roussaye's *savoir faire* when faced with the wreck of all his plans and the likely loss of his life as well.

The general inhaled the smoke with pleasure, then let it out with a sigh. ''There is one thing I would ask of you, Candover, as one gentleman to another. I swear my wife knows nothing of this. Please do what you can to see that she does not suffer for my sins.'' Scanning his visitor's hard face, Roussaye added gravely, ''After all, Filomena is your kinswoman. That should mean something, even if someone of your distinguished lineage cannot accept a man of my birth as a gentleman.''

The duke's lips thinned at the gibe. ''I will use what influence I have. Unlike you, I do not make war on women.''

The general scowled, showing anger for the first time. ''That was quite uncalled for, Candover. While no officer can always control the men he commands, I did what I could to prevent the atrocities that occur too often in war.''

''I'm not talking about war, I'm talking about today, and the Countess Janos.'' The duke stood and leaned over the desk, his tall frame taut with threat. ''She's disappeared, probably kidnapped. If anything happens to her and you are behind it, I swear you will not live long enough for the firing squad.''

The general removed the cigar from his mouth and looked into the furious gray eyes of his visitor with astonishment. ''I haven't the remotest idea what you are talking about. Why should I have any desire to injure the countess? My interest now is in preserving life, not destroying it.''

''Fine words, General,'' Rafe said bitterly. ''After you have told me what you have done to Margot, perhaps you can explain how you rationalize assassination as preserving life."

Tapping the cigar ash into a china dish, Roussaye studied his visitor intently. After a long moment he said, "Do you know, your grace, I am beginning to wonder whether we are speaking at cross purposes. Just what exactly are you accusing me of, and why should your lady be involved?"

Rafe was beginning to loathe the calm he had admired. Had his own imperturbable control maddened others as much over the years? "The countess is a British agent and has been instrumental in uncovering your conspiracy. I assume you realized what she was doing and decided to remove her, but it's too late. We know about the attempt on Castlereagh's life and that Wellington was your next target. After you tell me what you have done to her, I want to know what your future plans were. I shot your confederate Lemercier, and by God, I'll put a bullet in you if I have to!"

Roussaye stared at him, then threw his head back and began to laugh bitterly. When he regained control over himself, he said with wry self-mockery, "This would be hilarious, except that I will probably end up just as dead as if I was really doing what you accuse me of." Taking another pull of his cigar, he glanced at the duke and said, "My villainy, which it now appears you were ignorant of, was an attempt to help some of my distinguished colleagues who are on King Louis's death list."

As Rafe stared at him, the general elaborated. "Come, Candover, surely you know about the death list—the names of many of the chief imperial military men are on it. It is just a matter of time until Marshal Ney and Lavelette and a score of others are executed. They are considered traitors. It is the sheerest chance that I am not in prison with them."

There was a dark, brooding look on his face. "Treason is so often a matter of dates. They are all honorable men, whose only crime was to serve the losing side. I had hoped I might help some of them escape." With a bleak look at the duke, Roussaye added, "Even some of your countrymen agree that the king's reprisals are outrageous. Indeed, one of them has been aiding me."

He drew in on the cigar, then exhaled a thin wreath of smoke. "I won't give you his name, so don't waste your

time with threats. Though I doubt your superiors would ex-
ecute one of their own nationals for participating in a foiled
plot.''

His mouth dry, Rafe asked, ''Was it Robert Anderson?''

Roussaye paused, then said slowly, ''You are well informed.''

The duke was stunned, rapidly rearranging everything he
knew. If Roussaye was telling the truth, it removed a major
piece of the evidence of Anderson's treachery. Many men,
Rafe included, disagreed with the vindictiveness of the royalists. Anderson's money might be suspect, but as Margot
had defensively suggested, her lover might have been selling
the same information in several places without actually betraying his own country.

As for the general, his nickname of *Le Serpent* could be
a coincidence; after all, the three-headed serpent crest found
among Northwood's papers was still unexplained, and it
might well be the symbol of the true Serpent. The only
other possible link was from Lemercier to Roussaye, and
the fact that both were Bonapartist officers didn't mean they
were co-conspirators. Rafe asked abruptly, ''Was Henri
Lemercier also working with you?''

The general wrinkled his nose as if a bad odor had forced
its way through the cigar smoke. ''You insult me. Lemercier
is a jackal, who was the worst kind of officer. He would
never lift a finger to help anyone unless he was very well
paid. If the price was right, he'd strangle his own grandmother.''

Numbly, Rafe lowered the gun, uncocking and thrusting
it beneath his coat. He had been wrong, and now it seemed
likely that both Anderson and Margot were kidnapped and
possibly dead at the hands of the real conspirator. Roussaye
might be a fluent liar, but Margot had doubted that the general had the temperament of an assassin, even though she
suspected that he was involved in something secret. Her
instincts were proving to be remarkably sound. Rising to
his feet, he said woodenly, ''I owe you an apology. I hope
you will forgive my accusations.''

''Wait.'' The general raised his hand. ''Why did you think
I would want to murder Castlereagh or Wellington? Without

them, France would be forced to accept a much more punitive peace.''

"Exactly. It seemed possible that a true revolutionary might want to see France humiliated, to the point where she would be willing to take up arms again. Now if you will excuse me, I must leave and start looking for Margot.''

Roussaye shook his head. "Ingenious thinking, but I assure you, I would do nothing to prolong my country's suffering—France can afford no more Waterloos. If there is a conspiracy that threatens the peace, I am as interested in uncovering it as you are. If you will tell me what you know, perhaps I can help.''

Rafe hesitated, then sat down. At the moment, he had no idea where to look for Margot, and any assistance was welcome. Briefly he outlined what they knew or guessed, then listed all of the primary and secondary suspects they had been investigating.

The general listened attentively, his face darkening at the news of Robert Anderson's disappearance, but he interrupted only when the duke mentioned that the Count de Varenne had been a suspect. "Excuse me, your grace, why was Varenne on your list? The Ultra-Royalists have the greatest stake in the status quo.''

Rafe had to think back to remember. "At the beginning, there was some thought that the Ultra-Royalists might want to assassinate the king so Count d'Artois could succeed him.'' He shrugged. "Once it became clear that the attack was aimed at the British leaders, we eliminated Varenne from our list.''

In retrospect, the duke cursed himself for being so bewitched by Margot that he hadn't asked more questions. Now it was too late, and with both Anderson and Margot out of the picture, he was crippled by his own ignorance. Without access to their information sources, he had no idea where to turn.

Roussaye nodded. "I had never met him before our encounter at the Louvre, so I made a few inquiries. Varenne was heavily involved with royalist intelligence work during his exile, but his activities are now legitimate. Pray continue.''

When Rafe was finished, the general pondered while the

air became blue-gray with smoke. Brows furrowed with thought, Roussaye finally said, "I am familiar with most of those men, and of them all, Lemercier was the most likely to be involved in a conspiracy but he wasn't intelligent or ambitious enough to be the mastermind. We need to discover who he was working for . . ."

After a few more moments' thought, he said, "I might be able to discover that. If we know the identity of Lemercier's employer, you may have your Serpent. I'll begin inquiries this afternoon and notify you if I learn anything significant. What will you do, ask Wellington for men to search for the countess?"

"No," Rafe said with a shake of his head. "Without an idea of where to look, we could set all of the Allied troops in France to searching and not find her. Still, you have given me an idea. If Varenne was involved in royalist intelligence work, he might know how to get information now. Perhaps I can convince him to help me, for the countess's sake. He seemed to admire her."

"What man wouldn't?" Roussaye said with his first smile since the duke had made his accusations. Then seriousness returned. His voice was calm but his fingers on the cigar stub were tense as he asked, "Do you intend telling the royalist government about my interest in freeing political prisoners?"

The duke shook his head as he stood up. "No. I will not turn a man in for being loyal to his friends. But have a care, General, your wife deserves your loyalty, too."

"I know." Roussaye stopped, then said softly, "When you told me I was under arrest, I had a vision of my wife a widow, my unborn child an orphan. I will not subject them to that. Besides," he added with self-mockery, "I would be a liar if I did not admit that life is sweet to me, now more than ever."

Rafe offered his hand. "There is nothing wrong with enjoying life. God knows there is enough misery in the world."

Michel Roussaye shook his hand, then watched the powerful, driven figure depart. He murmured, "You are carrying more than your share of misery, my friend. May heaven protect your countess, if it is not already too late."

For himself, the general felt as if he had fallen over a fatal brink, then been pulled back at the last moment. With a shake of his head, he started thinking who to ask about the late, unlamented Henri Lemercier.

Chapter 17

Consciousness returned slowly to Maggie, accompanied by a feeling of nausea that she vaguely identified as an effect of the drug they had used on her. She lay on what felt like a bed, but her eyes were so blurred and the light level so low that she saw only dim shapes when she opened her eyes. Slowly she lifted her left hand toward her head, exploring her surroundings and feeling a bolt of sheer panic as she brushed a hairy object beside her. The panic cleared her wits even as her stomach turned. If a man was lying there, what had happened while she was unconscious?

Before her fearful speculation could go any further, she twisted her head to the left and managed to blink her eyes clear. Then she blinked again at the round object by her head, especially when two reflective gold circles materialized in the blackness. After a moment of near hysteria, she realized that a cat had chosen to share her imprisonment. A very large, very shaggy black cat that had curled into a ball on her pillow. Cautiously pushing herself upright, Maggie said in a croaking voice, "What was your crime, Rex, are you a spy too?"

She stroked the cat and was rewarded with a purr so vibrant she felt it through the mattress. The silky fur was very unlike human hair; her confusion and underlying fear had thoroughly misled her. The animal must have slipped in when they deposited her here. "By the way, your name *is* Rex, isn't it?"

Since the cat didn't disagree, she considered the matter

settled. Swinging her legs over the edge, Maggie stood and made an inventory. Aside from light-headedness, she seemed well enough. Her green muslin dress was rumpled but intact, and she didn't feel as if she had been mauled while she was unconscious.

Leaning on a corner of the wide four-poster bed, she surveyed the sparsely furnished bedchamber. Once, a very long time ago, it might have been attractive but now the wall-coverings were dingy, the blue bed-hangings threadbare. The darkness was caused by equally shabby draperies drawn across the window so she crossed the room and pulled them apart, blinking in the blessed sunshine that poured in. From the angle of the light, it must be early afternoon and she had been unconscious two or three hours.

The window overlooked a sheer two hundred foot drop to a river, and looked down brought back a touch of nausea. So Varenne had brought her to Chanteuil, his estate on the Seine. Maggie spent some time exploring her surroundings but found nothing of interest. Naturally the heavy door was locked, there was nothing that could be easily converted into a weapon, and there would be no escape through that window.

Sitting on the bed, Maggie scratched the cat's head and considered what she could do. The answer was, not much, so she swung her legs onto the bed and leaned against the headboard while she evaluated the situation. For whatever reason, Varenne must be *Le Serpent* and he was a dangerous and powerful man. Interesting that a Bonapartist like Lemercier had worked for him, but apparently the captain was just a mercenary.

Since she and Rafe had been engaged to visit Roussaye, her absence would already have been noted. However, Varenne had picked her up so quickly that it was unlikely anyone had seen what happened; her coachman had been out of sight and the street otherwise empty. She should never have let logic overrule instinct; Varenne's lack of apparent motive was less important than her distrust of the man.

Rex was now flopped across her leg, his dark furry weight threatening to cut off the circulation as he snored happily away. Still, as she sat there, Maggie did think of one possible silver lining; if Varenne had kidnapped her, he might have done the same to Robin, who might be under this same roof, alive and not a traitor. The thought made her feel much better.

Over the next hour, the only excitement occurred when Rex jerked his head up, then hurled himself across the room with a turn of speed surprising in a creature so somnolent. A sharply cut-off squeal told her that he had caught lunch. Maggie shuddered as he settled down with the limp little body and proceeded to eat. While she couldn't blame the cat for being a predator, she found herself identifying with the mouse.

The rays of the sun had shifted to mid-afternoon when a heavy grating in the door lock was followed by the Count de Varenne. He was accompanied by a bully boy carrying a shotgun that was trained on Maggie while an elderly man-servant placed a tray of covered dishes on the one table. At least they weren't planning on starving her; in another few hours Rex's mouse would have started looking good. Urbane as always, the count stopped a dozen feet away. "I hope you won't feel offended if I keep my distance, Miss Ashton. You see what respect I have for you."

"I can hardly imagine why," Maggie replied calmly. "I haven't demonstrated any great brilliance on this case. I still can't understand why you would be behind this particular plot."

"The usual reasons, Miss Ashton: power and wealth." The count's half open eyes had a reptilian look; perhaps that was the origin of his nickname. "I confess, you had me convinced you were just a Hungarian doxy looking for a rich protector. It was something of a surprise to discover who and what you are."

While Maggie was wondering just what she had done to give herself away, the count strolled over to the window and gazed out absently. The burly gunman with his remorseless weapon discouraged any idea Maggie might have about making a dash for it. Varenne turned back and asked with polite curiosity, "By the way, my information about you is spotty. Is Miss Ashton the correct appellation, or have you acquired some husbands over the years?"

"Not legal ones," Maggie replied shortly.

The count chuckled. "No doubt there have been a number of the left hand kind, like your blond friend."

Maggie's pulse speeded up but she kept her voice calm. "I suppose you mean Robert Anderson. Do you have him too?"

To her intense relief, the count nodded. "Yes, though his quarters are less comfortable than yours. He is almost directly below you, five levels down. Castles have certain drawbacks as living quarters, but they do have excellent dungeons."

Looking into the emotionless dark eyes, Maggie asked, "What are you going to do with us?"

Varenne gave a faint, chilling smile. "One of my associates wants to play with you and the fellow has earned a reward, at least for a while. After that, it depends on how cooperative you are. You could really be quite an asset, my dear."

Controlling her repugnance, Maggie asked, "And Robert?"

Shaking his head with feigned regret, he answered, "I have hoped he might prove useful but he's a remarkably stubborn young man. I can't imagine there is much point in keeping him around indefinitely." The guard shifted restlessly and the count said, "But I fear I bore you by thinking out loud. If there is anything you would like to make your visit more comfortable . . ."

Apparently he didn't expect her to take his ironic suggestion seriously, and he was halfway out the door when her voice stopped him. "Actually, a hairbrush, comb, and mirror would be nice. Also a washbasin and water and something to read."

Varenne turned back to her with amusement. "You are a most adaptable woman, Miss Ashton. Do you wish to make yourself presentable for your new paramour?"

Maggie wanted to spit at him. Instead, she smiled and said, "Of course. One must make the best of circumstances."

Glancing at the guard, Varenne said, "Get her what she asked for." When they had left, Maggie doubled over on the bed and buried her face in her hands as she struggled with her heaving stomach. She had tried so hard not to be a victim and had been successful until these last few days. Now she was caught in events that might have been designed to prove that she was as powerless as she had been a dozen years earlier, fodder for a mob or a helpless prize for a conspirator, and this time there was no Rafe or Robin to free her or obliterate her fears.

The first small victory was controlling her nausea. Then she stood and walked to the window and opened the casements, drawing the cool air into her lungs. Looking down at the river far below, rocks visible around the base of the cliff, Maggie thought, I can always jump. But that was a coward's way out, and she had not lived through what she had to die without a fight.

Turning away from the window, she went to the tray and found a bowl of tasty-smelling stew, a small bottle of wine, and bread and fruit. Determinedly she sat down to eat; she would need all her strength to seize any advantage that occurred.

A soft "Mroowp" beside her announced Rex, clearly willing to share her meal. He had the pushed-in face of the true Persian, and his fluffy black tail switched back and forth hopefully. With a faint smile, Maggie spooned out several lumps of meat for him. He was the only ally she was likely to find here.

Mme. Sorel was waiting when Rafe returned from seeing Roussaye, and as the duke had feared, there was no word from the missing countess. Having heard about Maggie's disappearance from Cynthia, Hélène's usually calm face was taut with anxiety and she wasted no time on preliminaries. "Is the general your man?"

Rafe shook his head as he paced the room restlessly, unable to sit still. "No. He convinced me that his interest in peace is as great as ours. He's going to try and find out who Lemercier was working for."

Hélène sighed. "I pray he is successful. We have no other leads now, do we?"

Succumbing to a morbid curiosity about how Margot did her work, Rafe asked, "Not unless you can go to the same information sources that the countess used. Is that possible?"

With a shake of her head, Hélène replied, "Not really. She knows dozens, perhaps hundreds, of women throughout the city—laundresses, servants, prostitutes, street peddlers. All across Europe, actually. I was merely one of them, except that we became friends. We each needed a friend, you see." She halted after that too-revealing statement, then continued, "Somewhere there might be a list of her informants, but it would be well hidden. Even if we could find and decipher it, most of her women would not talk to a stranger. Our loyalty was to Maggie personally, and to her cause. Money was secondary."

"That was how she did it, by talking to women?" Rafe asked incredulously. In his jealousy, he had assumed that Margot traded her body for information, with the cynical encouragement of Anderson. It was another shock, in a day full of them. How many other things had he been wrong about?

"Think about it, your grace," Hélène advised with a faint smile. "Women are everywhere, yet they are often ignored as if they were invisible. Men speak of secret plans in front of maids, throw vital papers in the trash, brag of their achievements to prostitutes. Maggie's genius was in collecting so many pieces of information, then making sense of them."

Hélène was getting a sore neck watching the duke prowl around the salon. Obviously he had shared Colonel von Fehrenbach's belief that the only way a female spy could work was on her back. The thought produced a twist of sadness. Putting it aside, Hélène said, "What will you do now, go to Wellington?"

Rafe turned from the window where his pacing had taken him. "No, the most he could do would be to lend some troops, and without knowing where to search, that would do no good. The duke's time is fully occupied with overseeing the Allied military forces; he doesn't have the information sources that might be able to discover who took the countess, and where."

His voice detached, Rafe continued, "If Roussaye is successful at discovering Lemercier's employer, we may be able to go right to the source of the conspiracy. Apart from that . . ." he shrugged, "I'm going home to rack my brains.

Write down your direction and I'll contact you if I come up with anything."

Hélène nodded and went to the escritoire for pen and paper and ink. As she wrote her address for the duke, she said, "I, too, shall see if I can think of anything else. There must be someone who could help, if I can only think who it would be."

The two shared a bleak look, then Rafe left to return to his hotel. It was on the carriage ride that he abruptly decided to go to Varenne. If the count had been active in royalist spy work during his exile, he must have contacts throughout Paris. Briefly Rafe considered taking some soldiers with him, but he had taken them on enough wild goose chases, and he could travel faster alone. Varenne had only been a suspect until they had realized who the conspiracy was aimed at, so there was no danger.

At his hotel he asked the knowledgeable concierge for directions to Chanteuil, then set off on the fast new stallion he had bought the first week in Paris. The road led west past the imperial palace of Malmaison, which Josephine Bonaparte had bought as a quiet country retreat. Josephine retired there after the emperor had divorced her for failing to produce an heir, and it was to Malmaison that Bonaparte had come to spend his last free hours on French soil, near the spirit of the woman he had never stopped loving. It was a romantic story, and as Rafe passed the estate he felt a twinge of sympathy for the Butcher of Corsica, who had continued to love where it was neither wise nor expedient. It was something they had in common.

The concierge's directions were excellent and Rafe arrived at Chanteuil in just under an hour of fast travel. The gates were somewhat rusted but solid enough, as was the gray stone wall that protected the estate. An ancient gatekeeper examined the duke with deep suspicion before consenting to allow him entrance.

Once inside the walls, Rafe could see the chateau looming in the distance as dramatically as Varenne had promised. The original fortress lay within a bend of the Seine with water on three sides, having been built on a rocky upthrust that stood above the surrounding fields. Over the centuries, new buildings and wide formal gardens had spread out below the turreted keep.

As he cantered up the long gravel drive, Rafe could not help thinking that Chanteuil looked like a setting for one of Mrs. Radcliffe's lurid melodramas. Close up, the estate showed the effects of years of neglect. The gardens had become jungles of unkempt plant life, and many of the outbuildings were in a poor state of repair. Attempts were being made to return Chanteuil to its former grandeur, but it would take Varenne a substantial fortune and years of time to finish the task.

When Rafe reined in before the main entrance and dismounted, a servant appeared quickly to take the reins and confirm that the count was in residence. Impatient with the sense of valuable time slipping away, Rafe took the steps two at a time and wielded the massive knocker vigorously while he prayed that the visit would produce something of value. The elderly butler who admitted him consented to take the duke's card to the master after subjecting the visitor to another dubious scrutiny. The servants appeared to date back to pre-revolutionary days. Perhaps the count had left them in storage when he fled France, then dusted them off and reactivated them on his return.

The Count de Varenne was in his library amid the musty odor of ancient books when the card was presented to him. When he saw it, his thin lips formed a smile of cool pleasure. The gods were on his side; who would have dreamed that the next fly would walk right into the web and offer the spider a card? And this fly was solid gold. He asked the butler, "The duke is alone?"

"Yes, milord."

Glancing at the wizened clerk who was his companion in the library, Varenne said, "Grimod, go up to the gun room in the west turret and bring down another shotgun and ammunition." Turning back to the butler, he said, "Fetch Lavisse, then wait ten minutes and bring up Candover."

The vast hall where Rafe waited was cold and drafty even in the last days of summer. As the duke watched a mouse scamper across the uneven flagstones, he wondered what it would be like in winter, with cold wind and river damp. Eventually the old butler shuffled back and gestured for the visitor to follow, leading the way along uneven stone passages and narrow stairs. Walking behind the bent figure, Rafe was glad his family seat had been modernized over the years; Candover Castle was equally old but infinitely more comfortable. Varenne would have his work cut out for him making his dank medieval fortress habitable.

The library was bright after the dark halls and Rafe paused at the door so his eyes could adjust. In that moment, hard objects were shoved into his sides as an amiable voice said, "Put your hands up in the air, Candover. Those are fowling pieces. At point-blank range, they won't leave much left of you."

After a moment of furious shock, Rafe slowly raised his hands. A man had been waiting on each side of the door with a shotgun and he could never reach one of his pistols quickly enough to prevent himself from being blown to pieces. Directly in front of him, leaning against an elaborate desk, waited the Count de Varenne. As one of the servants searched him and removed the two pistols, the duke said with admirable coolness, "I assume one could say I have found the Countess Janos, in a manner of speaking."

"You have indeed, your grace, and I assure you she is quite well. In fact, she is adjusting to her captivity with remarkable speed." The count gestured for Rafe to sit down while he sat behind the desk himself. The servants remained near the door, their shotguns trained on the duke. "Indeed, your fraudulent countess is quite the little survivor. Did you know that she is as English as you are, without an aristocratic bone in her delightful body?"

Taking Rafe's stony face for shock, the count chuckled and said, "Don't be too hard on yourself, Candover, I didn't guess either. I had to have inside information before I realized what the little trollop really was. But enough of these pleasantries. I have a few questions for you. First, does anyone know that you came out here?"

Rafe considered lying and saying yes, but he hesitated too long. Varenne seized on the pause and interpreted it correctly. "Good, you didn't. This close to the critical hour

I would not like to waste my men's time in hunting down whomever you told.''

So the plot was on the verge of execution and Rafe and Margot couldn't do a damned thing about it. He asked, ''Satisfy my curiosity, Varenne. What are you up to? If I'm going to die, I'd like to know why.''

The count looked shocked. ''"Going to die? Whatever made you think that I would unnecessarily eliminate a man of your wealth? It would be most profligate of me, and I did not get where I am by wasting my opportunities. This brings me to the other question I had. You are reputed to be worth between fifty and sixty thousand pounds a year. Is that correct?''

Rafe shrugged. ''Near enough. It varies a bit from year to year, depending on how different business interests are doing.''

''Splendid!'' The count positively beamed, his cold black eyes sparkling like agates. ''Since I have a few minutes to spare, I will satisfy your curiosity, or at least part of it. By the way, would you join me in a glass of burgundy? This is a rather fine vintage.''

The duke felt like he had wandered into Bedlam, but he nodded his agreement. Quite apart from maintaining Varenne's social pretenses, he could use a drink. A few minutes were spent in ordering glasses and pouring the wine. Rafe took a sip, and conceded that the vintage was excellent.

After a deep draft of his own wine, the count said musingly, ''You wondered what I am about. Actually, it is quite simple. France needs strong leadership and will not get it from the decadent remnants of the Bourbon line. When my plan is executed there will be chaos, and I am prepared to step in to sort it out. I have royal blood in my ancestry, some of it even legitimate, certainly enough to appease the royalist factions. After all, I served my time in exile, I am one of them.''

''Given the quality of the Bourbons, it should be possible to convince the royalists,'' Rafe admitted with some interest, ''but what about the Bonapartists? They will never accept a member of the old order who wants to turn back the clock.''

''But I do not wish to turn back the clock, my dear duke,

that is what makes me unique," Varenne said complacently. "I am a flexible man, I can prate of the rights of man, of 'liberty, equality, fraternity,' as well as any revolutionary. I already have Bonapartists working for me. Remember, Napoleon spoke of liberty and created the greatest tyranny Europe has ever known. If one tells a great lie boldly, one can do almost anything."

Reaching across the table for the wine bottle, Rafe topped up both their glasses. He wasn't sure whether Varenne was insane or a genius, or if there was a difference between the two things.

The count nodded his thanks for the wine and finished, "Under Napoleon, France became the greatest power since Rome. No true Frenchman wants to give that up, even the royalists."

"So you will rally the nation together *'pour la gloire'* one more time," Rafe said musingly. "But there is one constituency that you have forgotten. What of those people who are tired of fighting, who want to live in peace?"

"The wolf will eat the lamb every time, Candover."

Looking into those gleaming black eyes, the duke saw that Varenne believed his own words. Yet when Rafe thought of Margot and her army of women, of Hélène Sorel, of the tough pragmatism of Michel Roussaye, who had seen enough of war, he was not sure he agreed. Enough brave lambs might overwhelm even the most ruthless of wolves. However, argument was pointless so he asked, "If you aren't going to kill me, what do you intend?"

"You are insurance, Candover. My plans should be successful but I could fail since chaos is inherently hard to control, even when one is expecting it. If someone else rises to the top, I will need a great deal of money."

"I thought you had a great deal of money," Rafe said dryly.

"I have tried to convey that impression," Varenne said. "However, you see the condition of my estate, and conspiracies are expensive. At the moment I am almost penniless. If my *coup d'état* succeeds, I will have all the wealth I need, and you will be returned to England unharmed. If not . . . ." he shrugged. "You will prove useful. I am sure you are willing and able to pay a substantial price for your life and freedom?"

"For mine, and the countess's as well."

"You are that fond of the little trollop?" Varenne said with surprise. "I really should find out just what she does that is so special. She's just a woman, after all."

At that moment, Rafe discovered that the expression "to see red" was not a metaphor. If a small fragment of common sense hadn't reminded him of the armed men at the door, he would have taken Varenne apart with his bare hands. Some of that must have showed in his face, because the count said smoothly, "If you feel that strongly, I'm sure something can be arranged. Of course I would not free you without your word as an English gentleman not to retaliate in any way. It is one of the delightful things about Englishmen, that they take such promises seriously."

At that moment, a knock sounded at the door and a courier entered with a message. Varenne looked at it and frowned slightly, then said, "Sorry, Candover, but I really can't chat any longer. Matters require my attention." He glanced over at one of the gunmen. "Lavisse, escort the duke to the dungeon."

As the taller of the gunmen jerked his shotgun in a gesture for Rafe to precede him, Varenne called after, "I apologize for the quality of the accommodations, but if you are too comfortable, you may be in no hurry to pay your ransom and leave."

Rafe's thoughts were jumbled as he was herded down a winding flight of narrow stone stairs. Varenne might be mad, but quite effectively so; given the precarious political state at the moment, a well-chosen blow might indeed take him to ultimate power. Louis's throne stood on sand and a strong leader who could unite the factions would be welcome. The rest of Europe was tired of fighting and would accept any French leader who had a fig leaf of respectability and who seemed unlikely to lead France into more wars. It was diabolically clever.

The upper castle was dank and unpleasant but the dungeons were far worse, stinking of death and ancient evil. Eventually they reached a bare, dismal antechamber containing a massive iron-bound door and a battered wooden chair. Lavisse took a rusted key from a hook by the door and inserted it in the heavy lock. As his companion kept the duke covered with the shotgun, Lavisse struggled with the ancient mechanism until it turned. Swinging the heavy door out just enough to admit a body, the jailer said with heavy sarcasm, "Enjoy your visit, your bloody grace."

As Rafe walked through, Lavisse gave him a shove that sent the duke tumbling out of balance to his knees. Even before he hit the stone floor, Rafe realized that he was not alone.

Chapter 18

Rafe caught himself swiftly and drew his body into a wary ball, crouching on the floor as he scanned his surroundings. The cell was roughly cubical, about a dozen feet in each dimension. It was partly carved from rock with other surfaces of coarse stonework, and the scant light came from a narrow, barred window above head level. The only furnishings were a slop bucket in one corner and a pile of straw with a couple of blankets. The light was sufficient to burnish the blond head of the man reclining on the straw, who was watching the duke's entrance with interest.

Rafe drew in a breath and stood up. While he supposed he should be glad Robert Anderson was alive and apparently no friend to the Count de Varenne, he could think of many people he would rather be imprisoned with than Margot's lover.

It was Anderson who broke the silence. Without rising, he said, "I see they got you too, your grace. What has been going on?"

Leaning over to brush the dirt from his pantaloons, Rafe said shortly, "Riots, kidnappings, conspiracy—the usual sort of thing.'' Straightening up, he said, ''He's got the countess.''

A black look crossed Anderson's face and he sat up, then winced at the sudden movement. ''Damnation, I was afraid of that. Do you know if she's all right?''

''Varenne says so, for what it's worth.'' As his eyes became accustomed to the light, Rafe realized that his companion looked considerably the worse for wear, his left arm cradled awkwardly in his lap and his face visibly bruised. Forgetting his sense of rivalry, he exclaimed, ''Good God, man, what did they do to you?''

Anderson smiled faintly. ''In a tribute to my legendary ferocity, Varenne sent four bruisers to invite me here. I attempted to decline, but they overcame my demurrals.''

Rafe was moving restlessly around the cell, but he turned to look at Anderson as something clicked in his memory. Tentatively he said, ''The morning after you disappeared, the bodies of two unidentified Frenchmen were found near your lodgings.''

Anderson nodded. ''That sounds about right.''

Surveying the slight build and almost feminine good looks of his companion, Rafe realized that he had been guilty of still another misjudgment. With a half smile, he said, ''Remind me not to get into any arguments with you.''

''I doubt I'd be a danger to a husky sparrow at the moment.''

Rafe realized that Anderson's pallor was extreme even for someone of such fair coloring, so he crossed the cell and knelt in the straw, saying, ''Better let me take a look at that arm.''

He whistled softly at the purple swelling running from Anderson's hand into his sleeve. ''Did you hit someone too hard?''

''No, actually I was fairly intact when I arrived here, but Varenne was interested in chatting and I wasn't.''

After gently examining the swollen limb Rafe glanced at his companion's face. The sheen of sweat indicated how much Anderson's studied casualness was costing him, and the duke's reluctant admiration for his rival increased. He said, ''One of the bones in the wrist is probably broken, and three of the fingers. They seem to be fairly clean breaks. Let me help you get your coat off so I can bandage the area.''

Removing his own coat, the duke took off his waistcoat and tore it into strips. While there was no material available for splints, binding the wrist and hand should immobilize the bones and reduce the discomfort some. As he did the basic medical work learned in the hunting field, Rafe was suddenly struck with images of that same elegant hand caressing Margot and he stopped dead for a moment, fighting his sick jealousy. It was neither the time nor the place for such self-indulgence and after a moment he resumed his ministrations. For his own self-respect, the duke did his best to make the bandaging no rougher than necessary, but even so the procedure nearly broke the younger man's stoicism. By the time it was over, Anderson was lying full length in the straw, perspiration damping the edges of his hair.

Finally he said rather breathlessly, "Since he ended up getting Maggie anyhow, maybe I should have just written the damned note.'' When the duke gave him a questioning look, he elaborated. "Varenne wanted me to write Maggie and coax her out here. Said he'd keep breaking my left hand until I agreed. After he'd broken three fingers, I explained that I was left-handed and he'd wrecked any chance of my handwriting being normal. He really should have been working on the right hand.''

Rafe found himself chuckling at the dark humor of it as he settled down to make himself comfortable on the straw at Anderson's feet. "This really is Bedlam, isn't it?''

"That's as good a description as any. Still, I've been in worse prisons. The straw is fresh, the blankets clean, and since this is France, they serve quite a tolerable wine with meals. At this season, the temperature is reasonable, though I'd rather not winter here.'' After a moment of silence, Anderson said, "Tell me, did Varenne give any clues as to what he's up to and why?'' When Rafe glanced over at him, the blond man said apologetically, "Professional curiosity dies hard, you know.''

Anderson certainly deserved what answers Rafe had so the duke brought his companion up to date on the interviews with von Fehrenbach and Roussaye, mentioning the death of Lemercier without elaborating, then repeating what Varenne had said about his motives. After asking several probing questions, Anderson sighed and closed his eyes briefly. Opening them again, he said ruefully, "We are too soon old, and too late smart."

"For what it's worth, you have plenty of company in not deducing what was going on," the duke said bleakly. After that, there was little to say and the two men sat in the gradually fading light without talking. After two hours or so, Rafe decided that the worst part of imprisonment must be boredom. The cell was too small to stretch one's legs, the stone walls were singularly unstimulating, and if he had to spend any length of time here, he'd be raving. He envied Anderson's peacefulness. Worn out by pain, the other man slept some but even awake, he had a philosophical relaxation Rafe doubted he could ever match. Of course, based on his own words, Anderson had prior experience of incarceration; perhaps practice perfected one's skills.

Dinner was delivered with the usual caution as one man set a tray inside and another stood guard with a shotgun. It was quite efficient; a shotgun blast wouldn't need to be accurate to stop a charging prisoner. The meal was a very reasonable stew with bread and fruit, accompanied by a jug that held about a gallon of red wine. Besides pewter bowls and mugs, the only utensils were soft, easily bent spoons that wouldn't make effective weapons. When the tray, bowls, and spoons were collected later, the prisoners were allowed to keep the wine and drinking vessels.

It was the wine that induced the conversation. Sitting in the fading light with nothing else to do, it was easy to keep drinking, and while the amount of wine wasn't enough to render an experienced drinker foxed, it was enough to loosen tongues.

The two men were talking in a desultory fashion about what Varenne might be planning when Rafe asked abruptly, "Why is Margot the way she is?"

After a long pause, Anderson said, "Why don't you ask her?"

Rafe laughed harshly. "I don't think she would tell me."

"If she won't, why do you think I will?" For the first time there was a note of hostility in Anderson's voice.

Rafe hesitated, trying to think of a compelling argument. Instead of a direct answer, he said, "I know I have no right to ask, but I want—rather badly—to understand her. I knew her very well once, or thought I did, and now she's a mystery to me."

Now the hostility was obvious. "Ever since Maggie heard you were coming to Paris, she's been different—edgy and moody. I met her when she was nineteen and I know very little about her earlier life, but I do know that someone started a job of wrecking her that the French bloody near finished. If you're the one who did that, I'll be damned if I'll tell you anything."

The darkness was nearly total now, only a faint glow of moonlight illuminating the cell. Anderson's figure was barely hinted at, gray against black to the duke's right. In the dark, the pain of thirteen years ago was very close. Reaching out to find the jug by touch, Rafe poured them both more wine, then asked softly, "She never told you what happened?"

"No."

Anderson's voice was flat, but Rafe could hear an undertone of curiosity. If the other man was in love with Margot, he must also be interested in her past. In the anonymity of the dark, it was easy to make a suggestion that never would have occurred to him by the light of day. Choosing his words, Rafe said, "Each of us holds a key to part of Margot's past. Why don't we exchange information?" Anticipating possible objections, he added, "I know it's ungentlemanly, but I swear I don't mean her any harm."

Rafe could almost hear the factors weighing in Anderson's mind. Finally the other man sighed and said, "My father always said I didn't have a gentlemanly bone in my body, and he was right. But I warn you, it's not a very pretty story."

Rafe knew he must begin, but even in the dark it was hard to speak. Sipping the wine, he said, "Margot Ashton made her come-out during the 1802 Season. Her birth was no more than respectable, her fortune negligible, but she could have had any eligible man in London."

He stopped, remembering his first sight of Margot, when she was entering a ballroom. One look and Rafe had walked away from the group he was in and gone directly to her, cutting through the crowd like a hot knife through butter. Margot's chaperone recognized the heir to Candover and made an introduction, but Rafe was barely aware of that. All he remembered was Margot, gently amused at first by the expression on his face. Then her smoky eyes met his and changed as an echo of his own feelings flared in her, or so he supposed at the time. Only later did he question the fact that her response had come after she learned who he was.

What he said now was, "It appeared to be a perfect fairy tale, love at first sight and all that nonsense. Colonel Ashton wouldn't let us become formally betrothed until after the Season, but we had an understanding. I have never been so happy as I was that spring. Then . . ." He halted, unable to continue.

"Don't stop now, just when we're getting to the crux of the matter, Candover. What happened?"

The dry edge to Anderson's voice cauterized Rafe's memories to the point where he could continue. "It was simple enough. I was out with a group of friends one evening, everyone was drunk enough to be indiscreet, and one of them told how . . . how Margot had given herself to him a few weeks before." He drained his wine, feeling the bite of the young vintage in his throat.

Anderson swore softly as Rafe continued, "In retrospect, I can see how badly I overreacted. I was young and idealistic and completely unbalanced by love. Instead of accepting her actions as curiosity or experiment or whatever, I acted as if she had committed the greatest crime since Judas when I confronted her the next morning. I would have been happy to accept any defense or show of remorse, but she made no attempt to deny it, just threw my ring at me and walked out.

"I decided that the people who had told me she was a fortune hunter were right and she was just sorry to be balked of her quarry, but then, within a fortnight or so she and her father had left England to travel on the Continent. I don't think that would have happened if she wasn't as distressed as I was, so I suppose you could say we wrecked each other."

With an angry rustle of straw Anderson shifted position.

"Let me see if I have this correctly. You asked if she had been carrying on with this friend of yours and she didn't deny it?"

In the interests of accuracy, the duke said, "Actually, I didn't ask her. I told her what I knew."

A stream of profanity was accompanied by sounds of Anderson getting up and moving around the cell, too angry to sit still. When he had calmed down some, he said with disgust, "Given the stupidity of the British nobility, I can't believe the whole lot hasn't died out already. If you took a drunken sot's word without questioning it, you never knew the first thing about Maggie. You deserved what you got, though she certainly didn't."

Rafe flushed in the dark, angry but not entirely able to dismiss Anderson's words. "You can't know much about the nobility or you wouldn't make such sweeping statements. No young man of honor would lie about such a thing. Even dead drunk, it was surprising anything was said, and that wouldn't have happened if Northwood had known about my involvement with Margot."

Anderson stopped in his tracks. "Northwood? Would that have been Oliver Northwood?"

"Yes. That's right, I forgot that you knew him."

A new burst of profanity put the former one to shame. Then Anderson said, "If you aren't stupid, you must be too naive and honorable to live in this highly imperfect world. I still can't believe you would accept the word of a man like Northwood against Margot's, but maybe he was more believable in those days than he is now. Obviously he was no more honest."

"You're assuming he was lying? Why on earth would he do a thing like that?" Rafe demanded defensively. It is not easy to change one's mind about something that one has believed without question for thirteen years.

"Any number of reasons, Candover," Anderson said with exasperation. He was standing under the narrow window and his pale hair shone in the faint moonlight. "Maybe he was jealous of you. It doesn't sound like it would have required a very discerning eye to observe that you and Maggie were thick as inkle weavers. Or it could have been spitefulness because she had scorned him, or immature male boasting.

Maybe you never had to invent exploits, but plenty of young men do. Knowing Northwood, he might have lied from sheer bloodymindedness."

Feeling compelled to offer some rebuttal, the duke said, "Why are you so hard on Northwood? He's a boor, but that doesn't mean he's a liar. I don't know where you grew up, but where I come from, someone is assumed honest until proven otherwise."

"What a wonderful standard. Why didn't you apply it to Maggie?" Anderson said caustically. He sat down again, the straw rustling beneath him. "This 'boor' you are so anxious to defend has been selling information about his country for years to anyone who will buy. From what I've seen of him, I doubt he has an honest bone in his pudgy body."

"What . . . ?" Rafe felt as if he had been pole-axed. He had never been close to Northwood, but he had known him for twenty years. They had gone to the same schools, been raised by the same rules. While he had thought the man coarse, there had never been reason to doubt his honesty. And yet, it explained so much.

Margot's white face when he had accused her of infidelity swam before him. How would he have felt if the person who should have most trusted him had accepted slander without question?

He would have felt just as she had: furious, and hurt beyond words. What had she said then, something about how fortunate it was that they had discovered each other's true characters before it was too late? At the time, he had taken her words as an admission of guilt, and that admission had confirmed his belief in Northwood's accusations. Now her answer took on a whole new connotation. Burying his face in his hands, Rafe groaned, "Bloody, bloody hell . . ."

Even when Rafe had felt the most desperate pain at her imagined betrayal, he had been soothed by his belief that he was the injured party. Now that comfort was gone and he saw his actions as Margot must have seen them. Whatever she was now could be traced back to his betrayal of her, to his own jealousy and lack of trust, and any dim hopes he had of regaining her love now lay crumbled among the ruins of his pride. How could she ever trust him when he had so utterly failed her? By his own actions Rafe had lost what was most important to him, and there were no words strong enough for the bitterness of his guilt.

Seeing the despair in that dark figure, Robin Anderson felt unwilling sympathy for the duke's pain. It must hurt like hell to be knocked off the moral high ground by the realization that he had caused his own suffering, and Maggie's as well. In spite of Candover's accusation, Robin was very familiar with the world of aristocratic Englishmen, with their infernal games and clubs and gentleman's code. It was natural to believe a companion, and Northwood would have seemed bluff and honest.

On the other hand, a young woman would have seemed to be a strange, almost magical creature to a romantic young man. It took maturity to learn that the similarities between men and women were greater than the differences. Given the passion and possessiveness of first love, one could see how Candover had blundered, his emotions swamping his judgment. Robin had never fallen victim to that kind of helpless, mind-distorting desire, but he had seen it in others often enough to recognize it.

It wasn't as if the duke was a bad fellow—who wasn't a fool when he was young? Robin certainly had been, though his foolishness had taken a different form. He knew Maggie well enough to be sure that her temper had contributed to the problem; if she had had the sense to burst into tears and deny the accusation, the breach could have been patched up in half an hour and the two of them might have been happily married these last dozen years. In that case Robin would never have met Maggie, which would have been his loss but her gain.

Robin sighed and said half to himself, "You poor bastard." Fumbling in the dark, he located the duke's mug and presented it into Candover's hand, adding, "It's a little late to be suicidal, if that is the direction your maunderings are taking you."

Rafe straightened up enough to drink, wishing he had something stronger. Over the years he had prided himself on tolerance, thinking that he should have accepted Margot's infidelities in return for her charm and companionship.

He had even felt regret that she had been more in tune with the morals of their order than he, and had attributed his violent emotional reaction to immaturity. Instead, he had been closer to the truth with his youthful idealism than with all the fashionable cynicism he had cultivated over the years. Margot Ashton had been as true and loving as he had believed her; it was Rafael Whitbourne, heir to the dukedom of Candover, universally respected scion of the aristocracy, who had been unworthy of such love.

Anderson said with clinical detachment, "No wonder Maggie didn't want to have anything to do with you when you came to Paris. If she had told me about your past relationship, I would never have suggested that she get within seven leagues of you."

He reached for the wine and Rafe helped him pour another mugful since the heavy stone jug would be difficult to handle with a broken hand. Of course, it was much less heavy than it had been; the last of the wine emptied into Anderson's mug. They must have put away the equivalent of two or three bottles each. The duke could only wish there were more, though there wasn't enough alcohol in France to drown the way he felt now.

"I suppose this question is redundant, but I gather you are still in love with Maggie," Anderson mused.

"I'm just as unbalanced about her now as I was when I was twenty-two." Rafe drew in a shuddering breath. "I had always rather prided myself on my balance." Finishing his own wine, he said softly, "She's too good for me."

"I wouldn't argue the point," his companion said acidly.

"What has happened in the years since then?" Rafe asked. "How did Margot come to be the Queen of Spies? You said you'd explain." Now that he saw clearly how her journey had begun, he could better understand the beautiful, slightly brittle woman she had become then, with her toughness and suspicion, her flashes of humor and vulnerability.

"There's been enough rampaging emotion in this cell for one night," Anderson said as he rolled up in one of the blankets. "I'll tell you the rest of the story in the morning, when I should have slept off my residual desire to kick you in the teeth." Burrowing into the straw, he added, "If you're going to spend the night flagellating yourself, kindly be quiet about it.''

Rafe could just make out the outlines of the other man's body in the starlight. Anderson was right, enough had been said for one night, and he wrapped himself in the other blanket against the increasing chill. However, unlike his companion, Rafe strongly doubted that he would sleep.

Chapter 19

Considering how much wine he had drunk the night before, Rafe felt fairly well the next morning. He had even slept a little and by the time Anderson stirred, the duke had come to terms with his new knowledge. It was too much to believe Margot would ever forgive the past but he hoped he would have a chance to beg her pardon for his criminal misjudgment. It seemed very important that he do so.

Anderson claimed that his arm was feeling better this morning, even though his face was flushed and he seemed feverish. Breakfast proved to be fresh bread, sweet butter, strawberry preserves, and a large quantity of excellent hot coffee. As Rafe spread preserves on the bread, he said, ''I have eaten a good deal worse at respectable English country inns.''

Anderson chuckled. ''A pity Varenne's ambitions aren't aimed at the restaurant trade rather than at dictatorship.''

As the duke glanced at his companion, he was nagged once more by a fleeting sense of recognition. The more he saw of Anderson, the more familiar the man seemed, but the memory was elusive.

They had finished eating when the door opened. Rafe expected a servant to remove the tray but instead Varenne himself entered, the usual shotgun-carrying guard behind him. This morning the count was less the affable host as more of the underlying steel showed through. Speaking in a clipped voice, he said to the blond man, "I suppose Candover has explained what I am about?"

Sitting relaxed in the straw, Anderson nodded and finished his coffee. "He did. I was curious where I went wrong."

"Good." Reaching under his black coat, Varenne drew out a pistol. Aiming it at the precise center of Anderson's forehead, he said, "I would be reluctant to kill a man who doesn't know why he is dying. It seems a pity to do this, but I have been unable to come up with any possible scenario where you might be useful to me, and as long as you are alive you may be a danger. A pity you could not be brought over to my side, but even if you pretended to do so now, I would not trust your promises."

As Rafe watched in frozen horror, Varenne said, "Do you have any last prayers or messages you would like to make, Anderson? I shall permit them as long as you are quick about the business; it is going to be a busy day for me."

His face pale but imperturbable, Anderson glanced at Rafe. His eyes were very blue as he said, "Give Maggie my love."

In the silence that followed his words, the sound of the hammer being cocked was as loud as the anvil of doom.

The hour was very early but the British Embassy buzzed with activity and Oliver Northwood was greeted with relief by several of his fellows, who had worked all night. Even bed-ridden, Lord Castlereagh was generating enough letters, proposals, memos, and draft treaties to keep a dozen men fully occupied, and being short-handed was taking its toll on the staff. There was concern about Robert Anderson, who had been missing for several days. No surprises there, since Northwood had a very good idea what had happened to him. Served the supercilious puppy right.

Shortly before eight o'clock Northwood excused himself and made his way to the passage that ran beneath Castlereagh's bedroom. After checking both ways to be sure the corridor was deserted, he unlocked the closet door and entered, closing it behind him. He hadn't considered how nervous he would feel carrying a candle into an enclosure filled with gunpowder and his hands were sweaty as he made the necessary preparations.

First he used his regular candle to create a pool of melted wax on the floor, then set another candle of dense beeswax firmly into the puddle. When the wax had cooled and the candle was secure, he used a pocket knife to gouge a hole in the corner of one of the boxes of gunpowder, then took a small bag of gunpowder from his pocket and laid a careful trail from the box to the candle, ending with a mound of powder around the base.

He let himself out very, very cautiously, making sure that no draft would bring flame and gunpowder together prematurely. *Le Serpent* had said it would take about eight hours for the candle to burn down. Except for the wildly unlikely chance that someone would notice the scent of a burning candle in this seldom used part of the embassy, the explosion would go off around four in the afternoon and Northwood would be long gone by then.

When he was clear of the corridor he dug out his handkerchief to wipe his brow. He deserved every franc he had been paid, and then some. In the last couple of days security had gotten very tight at the embassy, with British soldiers at every entrance checking the credentials of strangers. As a regular employee Northwood had gotten in easily; *Le Serpent* could never have brought this off without him.

Returning to the clerks' copying room, Northwood settled down to make a fair copy of one of the interminable letters. The only other person there was a senior aide called Morier, who looked up with a tired smile. "Glad to see you, Oliver. Are you sure you're well enough to work? You look a little gray."

He couldn't look half as bad as Morier would after the explosion. The other man would certainly be present at the meeting this afternoon and would be blown up, a minnow dying with the big fish. Northwood suppressed the thought uneasily; Morier had always been pleasant to him and it was too bad he would be caught in the conflagration. Still, it couldn't be helped. Smiling bravely, he said, "I still feel pretty beastly, but I thought I could manage at least a couple of hours of work. I know how overworked the rest of you are. Rotten time to be ill."

Morier smiled gratefully and murmured, "Good show," before returning to his own document.

Northwood worked for two hours, the back of his neck prickling with the knowledge of the candle burning toward that lethal trail of gunpowder. He excused himself when he could bear no more, having no trouble looking ill. Morier and the other clerks who had come in commiserated on his illness and thanked him for making the effort. As he left, Oliver reflected that it was enough to make even a man without a conscience squeamish but he repressed his uneasiness as he went into the Rue du Faubourg St. Honoré and hailed a cab. In spite of casual friendliness, he knew the other members of the delegation looked down on him, thought they were more intelligent than he was. Well, they were wrong; he would have more power and wealth than any of them.

As he arrived home and changed into riding dress, Northwood's mouth was a thin, hard line from thinking of his sluttish wife. When he sued Westford for criminal conversation, the major would be ruined and Cynthia with him. But that was for later. Now he was going to visit the Count de Varenne and let him see just what a knowing one Oliver Northwood was. If he was lucky, *Le Serpent* would have the promised bonus waiting; the gorgeous, unobtainable Margot Ashton would be in Oliver Northwood's power.

As early as was decent, Hélène Sorel sent a messenger to Candover's lodgings to see if he had learned anything, then fidgeted as she waited for a reply. Less than three quarters of an hour later her groom returned with the unwelcome news that the duke had not been seen since the previous afternoon.

Sitting in a brocade chair in her drawing room, Hélène could feel her hands growing cold in her lap as she considered the implications of the duke's disappearance. It might not be significant, but given the disappearances of Maggie and Robert Anderson, one could only assume the worst. If the unknown *Le Serpent* had seized the other three, was Hélène also on his list?

For a moment she was tempted to flee back to the country, to her two daughters and safety. With the conspiracy so close to culmination, *Le Serpent* would never bother to follow her there. What could she do alone, without help? Her hands curled into fists as she rejected that solution. If worse came to worst and she too disappeared, Hélène's own mother would take care of her granddaughters faithfully and well. But if there was any action Hélène could take, she would do it rather than live a craven.

But *was* there anything she could do? She was too insignificant to convince any government officials that danger was imminent even if she had been well informed about the plot, which she wasn't. As Hélène thought, her hands unclenched and she rose. There was something she should have thought of sooner, and she would do it right now.

The sound of the hammer being cocked freed Rafe from his momentary paralysis. More than that, the stark resignation on Anderson's face caused an elusive memory to click into place, and the duke was reasonably sure he knew who the blond man was. Even if he was wrong, the information might be enough to stave off execution for the time being. His voice crackling with authority, Rafe said, "Varenne, shooting Anderson would be a big mistake. Remember that you said you were never profligate?"

The finger that had been tightening on the trigger loosened, but the count was annoyed as he glanced over. "Don't interfere, Candover. You are worth keeping for your potential value, but a spy is not in the same category."

"If he was only a spy, that might be true," Rafe drawled, drawing himself to his full height and keeping his eyes steady on the count. "But the man you are so wastefully going to kill happens to be Lord Robert Andreville, son of the Marquess of Wolverton, one of the richest men in Britain."

"What!" Varenne's eyes narrowed and he looked down at his intended victim. "Is that true?"

When Rafe had dropped his bombshell, Anderson's face had reflected as much shock as the count's, but he answered Varenne's question. "I'm a younger son, which reduces my market value, but I imagine the family would be willing to pay something to keep my hide unperforated, at least until my brother produces an heir."

For a long, tense moment, Varenne looked down, judging the potential benefits against the risks. Then he uncocked the pistol and thrust it back under his coat. "Very well, I can always eliminate you later if you're lying."

"It's the truth," Rafe said shortly. "I went to school with his older brother."

Varenne nodded absently, his mind already on other matters, then exited with his gunman. Rafe felt a shudder of distaste as he wondered how many of the brute's other chores were going to be casual, efficient murder. He supposed Varenne had intended to carry out the shooting in front of the duke as a show of ruthlessness; it would have been a very effective demonstration.

As the sound of steps disappeared from the anteroom, the blond man let out an explosive breath and slumped back against the stone wall, his eyes closed from reaction. After a moment of visible struggle to control his emotions, he said with commendable calm, "I thought my sins had caught up with me that time. I owe you a considerable debt, Candover."

As he recovered from his close brush with death, curiosity returned and he asked, "How long have you known who I was? For that matter, how did you know I was not one of the late marquess's bastards?"

"I wasn't certain, it was just an educated guess that occurred to me when Varenne cocked the hammer of the pistol." Rafe was feeling a bit weak in the knees himself, and he folded down in his usual spot in the straw.

"I'm glad your mind worked faster than mine did," Anderson, or rather Andreville, said fervently. "It never occurred to me that my connections would make any difference." After another moment's thought, he added, "If you know the family, you must know that my father died about two years ago."

"I did know, but it seemed a poor time for a genealogy

discussion," the duke said. "You might have been illegitimate, or not even an Andreville, but there was a look on your face when he had the gun on you that reminded me of your brother Giles."

Leaning his head against the stone wall, Rafe continued, "Giles was a year ahead of me in school and we've never been close friends, but we run into each other once or twice a year and generally have dinner and a good conversation. Occasionally he mentioned his scapegrace younger brother Robin." The duke smiled. "You don't really look much alike or I would have made the connection sooner. Some of the stories he told me . . . Did you really manage to get expelled from Eton your very first day?"

Andreville chuckled. "It's true. I wanted to go to Winchester but my father insisted I follow in the footsteps of countless Andrevilles to Eton." Smiling reminiscently, he added, "It was a busy year. The old boy didn't want to be defeated by an eight-year-old, so I had to get myself expelled from three other public schools before he let me go to Winchester."

Curious, Rafe asked, "What made you so set on Winchester?"

Robin shrugged. "I had a friend going there, and my father wanted me to do something different. Either reason would have sufficed." Wryly he added, "You were stretching a point by assuming my family would be willing to ransom me, by the way. Given my checkered past, they might be delighted if I vanished without a trace before I embarrass the clan any further."

"That might have been true of your father, but certainly not Giles. Besides, even if the family wouldn't pay, I thought you had inherited considerable property from someone else."

Andreville nodded. "From a great-uncle. The Andrevilles throw up a black sheep every generation or so. Uncle Rawson was the last one before me, so of course we got along very well. I have some illegitimate half-brothers, though. If I had been one of them, it might have been difficult to raise the blunt."

Rafe shrugged. "The Candover estate could have

stretched to another twenty or thirty thousand pounds if necessary.''

Andreville looked at him with surprise. ''You would have done that for someone you hardly know, and don't much like?''

Uncomfortable that his companion had picked up that concealed resentment, Rafe said shortly, ''Margot wouldn't have liked it if you had gotten killed.''

The blond man was looking at him speculatively, so the duke continued, ''Speaking of Margot, you were going to tell me what has happened in the years since you met her.''

Andreville sighed and looked tired. ''If you're really sure you want to know. Some of it is hard to hear.''

''If it's a difficult story to listen to, it must have been a damned sight worse for Margot to live through,'' Rafe said grimly. ''I want to know everything.''

''If you insist.'' Andreville shrugged, then pushed himself upright and crossed the cell to lean against the wall under the window. ''You know that Maggie and her father and his servant were set on by a gang of former soldiers going to Paris to volunteer their services when the Peace of Amiens ended?''

Nodding, Rafe said, ''Yes, it was quite a scandal in England. However, there were no details known, which is why Margot was thought to have died.'' Briefly he explained how he had come to France looking for her and ended by taking two coffins home.

Knowing just how difficult that journey must have been, Andreville gave the duke a very respectful look before he said, ''The details are important. Colonel Ashton and his party were eating in a country auberge when a dozen or so soldiers arrived, already drunk and bullying everyone in sight. Ashton tried to get his party away but someone recognized his accent as English, they were accused of being spies, and the fight was on.''

''Anyhow, Ashton and his man put up one hell of a struggle, but they were greatly outnumbered and never had a chance. At the end, the colonel threw himself across his daughter to try to protect her, hoping that they might not kill her after the mob spirit wore off.'' His voice harsh,

Andreville said, "Maggie's father died lying on top of her, Candover, bleeding from a dozen knife and bullet wounds. Try that on for a nightmare."

"God help her," Rafe whispered. Margot had adored her father. Having him die like that . . . he shook his head, not wanting to think of it, but he was sure now there was worse to come. Well, Andreville had warned him. Steeling himself, he looked up and asked, "Then what happened?"

"What the hell do you think happened, Candover?" Andreville's voice was violent with barely controlled anger. "A girl who looks like Maggie, in the hands of a mob of drunken ex-soldiers?" He turned away from the duke, his good arm braced against the wall, his shoulders rigid and his head bowed. It was several minutes before he spoke again, minutes while Rafe remembered the blind, hysterical panic Margot had exhibited in the Place du Carrousel and after. He stood, no more able to sit quietly in the face of such an atrocity than Andreville was.

The blond man's voice was ragged when he began speaking again, still turned away from Rafe. "Since they had a beautiful girl and a cellar full of wine, they were in no hurry to move on, so they stayed and prepared to enjoy themselves."

The fingers of his right hand were splayed in front of him on the wall, stiff with fury. "I came along, traveling in the uniform of a French grenadier captain. When the villagers saw me, the mayor came out and begged me to get the soldier-pigs to move on before they destroyed the whole village.

"I was going to pass on by. After all, I was alone and not even a genuine officer. But when the mayor said they had an English girl . . ." Finally turning to face the duke, Andreville shrugged, the fair skin drawn tight over the fine bones of his face. "I couldn't leave. So I went into the inn, praised the soldiers for their patriotism and cleverness in catching spies, chided them for overzealousness, and made them get moving to Paris because the emperor needed them."

Rafe imagined that slight, elegant figure facing down a taproom full of armed drunks, and could understand why

Margot had fallen in love with him. Lord Robert would have been hardly more than a boy himself. Shaking his head in awe, the duke asked, "How did you get them to let Margot go, rather than taking her?"

"Sheer force of personality," Andreville said with even more dryness than usual. "Also, I said I would take the English spy to Paris myself for questioning. Her horse and luggage were in the stable, so I got her mounted and both of us the hell away from there." The tight face eased a little. "It didn't take long to realize what kind of girl I'd rescued. She was half-dead from what they'd done to her, and wearing a ragged dress covered with her father's blood. Any other woman would have been raving mad or unconscious. But Maggie . . ." He smiled at the memory.

"When I stopped the horses a mile down the road to introduce myself and explain that she was safe, I found her pointing a pistol at me. She had gotten it from her saddlebag. I'll never forget the sight: her hands were shaking, her face was so bruised her own mother wouldn't have recognized her, and she'd been through an ordeal that I wouldn't have wished on Napoleon himself, but she was unbroken." Softly he said, "She's the strongest person I've ever known."

Rafe realized that he was pacing his end of the cell, his hands clenched, his eyes unseeing. Never in his life had he had a stronger desire to be alone, to assimilate the horror of what had happened to Margot, yet he was trapped here. Andreville had warned that it was unpleasant hearing, but as Rafe had said then, experiencing it would have been infinitely worse.

On top of the helpless pain he felt on Margot's behalf was the crushing knowledge of his own guilt. If he hadn't hurt Margot so badly, she would not have been in France. No wonder she had accused him of being responsible for her father's death: it was true, and there was no way he could make amends for the disaster he had unwittingly sent her to.

The frantic energy churning inside him was unbearable and Rafe wished he could do something physically violent, ride suicidally fast or destroy an enemy with his bare hands.

Most of all, he wanted to kill the men who had hurt Margot. Andreville must have read his feelings because he said, "If it's any comfort, anyone who went with the *Grande Armée* then is probably long since dead. One can only hope that they died slowly and painfully."

"One can only hope," Rafe said raggedly. Drawing a deep breath, he tried to steady himself. If he didn't, he'd go mad.

Finally relaxing, Andreville went back to his corner and sank into the straw, the emotions of his story etched on his face, shadows showing under the blue eyes. Having reestablished a fragile control, Rafe said, "I suppose that after that, things had to get better."

Andreville nodded. "Yes. It was a bit of a quandary for me, of course. I couldn't just leave her in the middle of France but I was engaged in some rather vital business I couldn't walk away from. When I explained, Maggie said she didn't want to go back to England, so why didn't I take her along? So I did.

"I took a flat in Paris and we stayed there. I told everyone Maggie was my sister, and no one questioned it." He studied his cellmate, wondering what reaction his next statement would evoke. "I asked her to marry me. It would have helped her reputation in the future, and if something happened to me, she would be a considerable heiress."

"And?" Rafe asked woodenly.

"She refused. Said we shouldn't marry just because of some unlucky circumstances." The blue eyes were narrow and unreadable now. "Instead, Maggie said she would be my mistress."

Rafe just nodded. So that was how it had begun. Still . . . "I'm surprised that she could bear having a man near her."

Robin hesitated. They were getting into an area that was too personal to discuss. Certainly he would not speak of the screaming nightmares Maggie had had for years, or the gentleness and patience that he had needed with her, or the pleasure and deep affection that had grown between them. Still, something should be said if the duke was to understand what events had shaped Maggie. Since Robin owed the duke his life, he felt some obligation to provide the information Candover desired. Clearly the duke was genuine in his feelings for Maggie, and perhaps that gave him some right to know.

Choosing his words carefully, Robin said, "She wanted some more pleasant memories to help her forget what had happened. I had some doubts about the arrangement—remnants of a proper upbringing, no doubt—but I agreed. I was only twenty years old myself and really didn't want to be married. On the other hand, I would have had to be an absolute fool to pass up an offer like that from a girl like Maggie."

Making a vague gesture with his unbandaged hand, he said, "We've been working together ever since. I would move around Europe as necessary, sometimes for months at a time. I've traveled with armies, sailed across the Channel with smugglers, and generally did a lot of other hare-brained, uncomfortable things that seem like great adventures when one is young and foolish." He smiled faintly. "As a child I had always rebelled against staid English respectability, but I must say the idea has gotten considerably more appealing since I turned thirty.

"Anyhow, home was wherever Maggie was, and that was where I always returned. Most often she was in Paris, living quietly, not like now when she's playing the countess and moving in society. She developed her own network of informants, and turned out to have a really spectacular talent for spying. The rest I think you know."

Rafe sighed. If his self-esteem took any more of a beating, it was never going to recover. "To think that I had decided that you were the spy in the delegation."

"You what?" Andreville asked, his eyebrows rising.

"I've had some of my own men over here watching." Rafe explained how he had set up his own watchers, how he had discovered that Andreville visited Margot, Roussaye, and Lemercier, and the inferences he had drawn from the amount of money Margot had received from her partner in spying.

Andreville was amused. "Even though your conclusions were wrong, you do have talent for this work; you just asked Lord Lattimer the wrong questions. If you'd asked him about me directly, he could have told you who I was. You know why I was communicating with Roussaye; as for Lemercier, I was suspicious and trying to find out what he was up to.

"Perceptive of you to wonder about the amount of money, though; spying really isn't all that lucrative a career. Fortunately, Margot accepted whatever I gave her without questioning. I never mentioned that much of the money came from me—she would have gotten all prickly and independent if she knew I was supporting the household, even though it was my home, too. Also, since she wouldn't marry me, I wanted to make sure that she had enough to live on comfortably if my luck ran out."

He stopped, temporarily out of words, then thought of something else. "Did you tell Maggie your suspicions of me?" When the duke nodded, Andreville asked curiously, "How did Maggie react when you tried to convince her that I was a traitor? She doesn't really know anything about my background, and there was some strong circumstantial evidence against me."

"She flatly refused to believe it and threw me out of her house at gunpoint. And if you are thinking of saying that Margot could teach me a few lessons in loyalty, don't bother—I already know," Rafe answered. He stopped, then said stiffly, "Thank you for telling me all that. I needed to know."

There had been enough talk, so Rafe sat down on the straw, his back braced against the cold wall, and gazed blankly into space as he tried to deal with the grief, guilt, and anger he was feeling. Now that he understood the depth of the bond between Andreville and Margot, he realized how minuscule the chance had been that she would turn to him. Amazing how arrogant he had been, blandly thinking he could seduce her to win her loyalty. She had turned to him that one night only because of the horror of memories aroused by the mob in the Place du Carrousel.

Sighing, he ran his hand through his black hair. As Andreville had helped her forget a dozen years earlier, Rafe had been there to help her that night. She had indeed used him but she was entitled to that, given the amount of damage the duke had inflicted on her. Ironic that in helping her forget, he had found a magic and a memory that would always torment him. If Margot had ever desired vengeance, she had achieved it.

The only other thing he could do for Margot was to keep the episode from Andreville. Lord Robert might be a tolerant man but he wouldn't like hearing about that night, and Rafe had no desire to sow discord between Margot and the man of her choice. He had already done far too much to hurt her.

Tiredly he asked, "If we all get out of this alive, are you going to marry her, Lord Robert?"

"Well, I intend to ask her again," Andreville replied. "And I'd rather you didn't call me Lord Robert—that name belongs to another life, just as the woman who is Margot to you will always be Maggie to me."

Rafe glanced across the cell. "What do you prefer to be called?"

"My friends call me Robin."

It was said with an engaging smile. Were they friends, then? Rafe wasn't quite sure, but there was certainly a bond, composed of respect, of shared danger and emotion, and of loving the same incomparable woman. With a trace of a smile on his own face, he said, "I'm usually called Rafe. The actual name is Rafael, but as Margot said when I met her, naming me after an archangel was singularly inappropriate."

His cellmate laughed. After that there was silence, but it was a comfortable one.

Chapter 20

"Don't worry, Varenne will see me," Oliver Northwood assured the decrepit butler who answered the door at Chanteuil. The servant eyed him doubtfully but toddled off into the depths of the castle as Northwood quietly followed. He didn't want to give the count time for too much thought. When the butler entered a room, the Englishman entered, too. Varenne was receiving the news of his visitor with an expressionless face, but Northwood's entrance into the library provoked a narrowing of the eyes. Haughtily he asked, "Do we know each other, monsieur?"

"Of course we do, *Comte le Serpent*. Or shouldn't I call you that in front of your servants?" Northwood said boldly. He was here to be accepted as a valuable associate, not just the pair of hired hands that he had been in the past.

Varenne stared at him for a moment, then began to smile. Dismissing the butler with a wave of his hand, he offered the Englishman a chair and sat down again at a desk covered with stacks of reports and papers full of figures.

"No need to worry about the servants. Every man on the estate, from my cook to my little army, is personally loyal to me, and all of them look forward to a better day for France." The thin lips curved into a smile. "I see that I have underestimated you, Monsieur Northwood. Tell me, how did you discover my identity?"

"Your signet ring. I traced the crest." Deciding it was time to put his insurance policy into effect, Northwood added, "Incidentally, a sealed envelope with what I know is with someone who will take it to the authorities if I should disappear."

Varenne gestured gracefully. "Come, there is no need for such precautions, just as there will be no need for secrecy soon. You *have* done as we had discussed at your embassy, I assume?" The black eyes were fixed intently on his guest.

"Yes, everything went according to plan. In about four hours, half the diplomats in Paris will be only a memory."

"Good, good, you've done well, *mon petit Anglais*. I regret that I have little time to socialize, but this is a most busy day. My soldiers must be made ready for whatever comes, I have been receiving information about matters that must be attended to after the explosion . . . a thousand things." Varenne was expansive again now that he was sure this oaf of an Englishman had not compromised the plan. "Have you come here for your bonus?"

"Partly that, partly to make sure that I am not forgotten

in your rise to power." Northwood was beginning to relax; this was much easier than he had expected. The masked *Le Serpent* had seemed much more threatening than this affable aristocrat.

"You will not be forgotten. There will be ample rewards for those who supported me." The count smiled pleasantly. "As I said, I am very busy just now. Perhaps you would like to spend the next few hours amusing yourself with the countess?"

It was the right diversion; Northwood's expression altered and he ran an eager tongue along his lower lip. "I was hoping you had her. I can see her now?"

"But of course. As I said, you have done well; it is right that you enjoy the fruits of your labors. If you will follow me?" Varenne led his guest up the stairs and along a dusty corridor, stopping before a door with worn gilding. Pulling a key from an inside pocket, he handed it to Northwood and said, "Enjoy yourself. Just two things: be sure to lock the door behind you when you enter, she's a tricksome wench and I don't want her loose in the castle."

Northwood looked greedily at the key. He had waited a long time for this. "And the other thing you want me to remember?"

"Don't damage her too much, Monsieur Northwood. I may have use for her myself."

Nodding in acknowledgment, Northwood put the key in the lock and turned it.

It had been maddening to wait two hours at Mme. Daudet's for the old lady to wake up, but her servant had been adamant about not waking the mistress. Hélène had scarcely been able to contain her impatience. Apart from finding the book that contained the three-headed serpent crest of the d'Aguste family, she had nothing to do but worry. When Mme. Daudet finally emerged, she smiled gracefully and said, "What can I do for you today, my child? Is your pretty blond friend here, too?" The old lady seemed scarcely more than black lace and delicate bones, but there was still strength and the ghost of beauty in her face.

"No, Madame, I am here because I am worried about her." Hélène's voice was tense. "The Countess Janos and some other friends have disappeared, and the only clue I have is that a d'Aguste might be involved. Can you tell me anything about the family?''

Mme. Daudet peered nearsightedly at the colored plate, then said, "I'm sorry, child, but the direct line is extinct. There have been no noble d'Agustes in about, oh, fifty years or so.''

Hélène's disappointment was so bitter she could taste it. If Mme. Daudet could give no lead, there was nowhere else to turn. Desperately, she asked, "What happened fifty years ago?''

Mme. Daudet pursed her lips as she cast her memory back over the years, then her face brightened. "It comes back to me now. The last d'Aguste was a daughter, an only child named Pauline. She married the Count de Varenne. Pauline was the mother of the present count. An odd girl. Bad blood in the d'Agustes.''

Hélène waited for no more reminiscences. After thanking Mme. Daudet, she flew out of the apartment and down to the street. She still didn't know what to do about it, but at least she now knew who *Le Serpent* was.

Michel Roussaye was growing more and more concerned. The previous evening had been spent visiting the haunts of Bonapartist military men, the clubs and cafés where they gathered to drink and gamble and reminisce about the glorious days of the empire. Mention of Captain Henri Lemercier had produced blank looks, expressions of distaste, or occasionally a hard stare followed by a disclaimer of any knowledge of the man.

What alarmed him were the fragmentary rumors of a possible change in the wind. There was mention of a man called *Le Serpent*, who would lead France once more to the glory she deserved. Remembering his own army nickname, two or three men had even asked indirectly if he was the coming leader. Roussaye had vehemently disclaimed any such role, but the hints were worrisome. While most of the officers were like him, tired and willing to give peace a chance, there were still a few hotheads whose truest happiness had been in the days of the great victories, who refused to see what a high price their country had paid for a fleeting taste of *la gloire*.

Even more alarming was the news his servant brought back from a visit to the Duke of Candover. The duke had gone out the previous afternoon and not returned. Roussaye swore softly, then decided to go to Silves's, another popular Bonapartist café. It was nearly time for the midday meal and perhaps he could find someone who would know who Lemercier's employer had been.

Maggie was sitting in a shabby wing chair attempting to read a lurid French novel as Rex sprawled on the floor by her chair. He lay on his back, curled sideways like a comma, his massive furry feet in the air. If he wasn't snoring she would have worried whether he was alive. During the past twenty-four hours she had made what plans she could, and now there was nothing to do but wait. The cat was really better entertainment than the book; the servant who had filled her request for toiletries and reading matter must have assumed that ladies never read anything but the most arrant tripe. The novel even had a spy subplot that was the veriest idiocy; really, the author didn't have the least idea what an unglamorous business spying was.

With a sigh, she laid the book on the table next to her and leaned over to scratch Rex's neck. At the moment, she would have been delighted to embrace the most boring spy work in existence. Being kidnapped might be glamorous in a book, but it was a combination of terrifying and tedious in real life.

When the key grated in the lock, her hand tensed and the cat looked up in irritation as the stroking stopped. Lunch had already been served, so a visitor must mean either Varenne or, much worse, the associate he had promised her to.

When Oliver Northwood came through the door, Maggie was unsurprised and a little relieved. The man was a coarse brute, a wife abuser, and a traitor to his country, but at least he was a known quantity, with neither the intelligence nor the calculated wickedness of Varenne. As he relocked the door, Maggie readied herself to play the role she had chosen. If she made a mistake, there would be no second chance. Northwood turned to face her, his broad, slightly fleshy face openly gloating. He would expect her to be frightened; in fact, he was probably looking forward to it, so Maggie was going to surprise him. She stood and offered Northwood her hand and a broad smile, for all the world like a hostess in her own drawing room. "Mr. Northwood, what a pleasure! I did so hope it would be you, but the count wouldn't tell me, naughty man. Do sit down. Would you care for some wine?"

Northwood looked confused as he automatically accepted a seat in the other brocade chair by the table. If the countess had cowered or begged, he would have been on her in an instant, but receiving charm and social amenities made him respond in kind. Maggie poured some of the lunchtime carafe of wine into her one glass, then handed it to her visitor. He accepted the glass, saying uncertainly, "You are glad to see me?"

"But of course! I've always fancied you, you know."

"No, I didn't know," he said belligerently. "You picked a damned funny way of showing it, Margot Ashton. You always treated me like dirt." Northwood used her name deliberately, flaunting his knowledge and power over her.

Maggie settled herself gracefully in the chair opposite him, soft folds of green muslin settling around her feet. Her gown was slightly rumpled but still presentable, and that morning she had spent considerable time on her hair, combing it into a loose style designed for the boudoir. Sighing a little, she said, "Oh, dear, I was afraid you might have taken it that way. I had always hoped that you would understand. We are kindred spirits, you know, I have always sensed that."

Northwood was beginning to relax and enjoy himself. It was undeniably flattering to be waited on by a woman like this, with her wide gray-green eyes and her luxuriant body, and she seemed genuinely happy to see him. Nonetheless, he would not let himself be appeased too easily. "If we're such kindred spirits, why were you always so rude to me, both when you made your come-out and these last weeks? You never treated Candover like that."

"Well, of course not," Maggie said, a trace of exasperation in her voice. "The man's insanely jealous, and it wouldn't do to show favor to anyone else when he's around. You're much cleverer than he is, though. He still thinks I'm a Hungarian countess."

Gulping a third of the wine, Northwood said, "Oh, I'm clever all right, though I never let that lot at the embassy know. They all think they're so bloody superior." He brooded for a moment, then said, "So why did Candover get the royal treatment, not me?"

"Why, because he's rich, of course," Maggie said, making her eyes wide and indignant. "Surely you don't think women would waste time on the man for any other reason?"

"You're gammoning me," Northwood said gruffly. "He always had any woman he wanted." Viciously he added, "Even my wife."

"Well, he's always been very, very rich, hasn't he?" Maggie said reasonably. "Oh, he's not bad-looking, but amazingly stiff-rumped." She gave a bawdy chuckle, and asked silent forgiveness for the enormous lie she was about to utter. "Really, Oliver—do you mind if I call you Oliver? I always think of you that way—if Candover had to rely on his physical attributes to keep a mistress, no girl would go back for a second round."

It was what Northwood wanted to hear; he had the kind of small soul that rejoiced in seeing others maligned. Leaning forward greedily, he asked, "How much of a man is he, then?"

Maggie giggled, undulating in her chair a bit, the lines of her body signaling her availability. "Well, a girl really shouldn't talk of such things. Let's just say that where she would hope to find the most, she would have to be content with the least." Looking pensively off into space, she added, "He's a thirty-second wonder, he is, and absolutely no imagination. Why, he won't even . . ." Maggie listed several exotic variations on the common theme and had the satisfaction of seeing Northwood's eyes nearly bulging from their sockets with fascinated lust.

Tilting her head to one side, she said, "In spite of losing all that lovely money, I'm almost glad I didn't marry him. Besides everything else, he was boring and madly jealous.

239

But when I was eighteen, I was so pleased to have attached the heir to a dukedom that I didn't realize what he was like."

Northwood crossed his legs, the wineglass loose in his hand. "You have me to thank for his breaking the engagement."

Maggie felt a cold chill on the back of her neck, but she purred, "Do I? How did that happen?"

"It was easy. You're right, Candover isn't very clever. Anyone could see he was head over heels for you even without an announcement." He sipped more wine, saying musingly, "I always despised him. We were in school together, my birth is as good as his, but he was always too high in the instep to associate with the likes of me." A surly note entered his voice as he went on, "Just because he had a fortune and was heir to a grand title, he acted as if that made him better than me. But I watch people, you know, I know what their weaknesses are."

Cutting off the flow of self-congratulation, Maggie coaxed him back to the original topic. "What were his weaknesses?"

"Why, his weakness was you, of course. He thought you were so pure and perfect. I decided to let him find out that you weren't." Northwood looked at her challengingly. "Even though you had him flummoxed, I knew you were too good to be true."

Her throat was tight but Maggie managed to say admiringly, "That was very perceptive of you. So, what did you do about it?"

Smiling maliciously, Northwood said, "A group of us had been out one night, drinking and carrying on. When I knew that Candover—or Wilton as he was then, his father was alive—was within earshot, I told what I had done to you in the back garden of one of those balls. I pretended I was too drunk to know that I was being indiscreet, but I knew exactly what I was saying. Wilton looked as if he'd been kicked in the stomach, got up and left right away. The next I knew, you had left London."

Staring at the florid, self-satisfied face and thinning blond hair, Maggie felt an icy hand on her heart. Her opinion of Northwood had never been high, but it was still a shock to hear him boast of a vicious, cold-blooded act that had had such catastrophic repercussions on her. While intelligence wasn't his strong suit, he had a genius for low cunning; something overheard from a man in his cups was far more convincing than a direct slander would have been. No wonder Rafe had come to her that morning, half mad with pain and jealousy. His lack of trust in her was still a betrayal, but a far more understandable one. Maggie felt ill, but daren't give in to it. If she lost her self-possession now, she would be at the mercy of this beast.

Before Northwood could register her appalled expression, she shaped her face into a pout. "Really, Oliver, that wasn't at all a nice thing to do. It injured him, and believe me, he took it *very* badly, but you caused all kinds of problems for me, too. If you'd wanted me for yourself, all you would have had to do was wait a decent interval after the wedding."

"Really? You would have been interested in an affair?" Northwood was skeptical but willing to be convinced.

"Of course I would have been," Maggie laughed. "Once I had the ring on my finger, I could have done anything I wanted. Candover is far too proud to sully his name with divorce, no matter what his wife did. Oh, I would have given him an heir, of course; but after that . . ." Her smile was infinitely suggestive.

She stood and poured the last of the wine into his glass, letting him get a good look down the low-cut neckline of her dress, then sat again, pulling her chair closer to her guest.

"Before we get down to pleasure, could you satisfy my curiosity? What is it that you and Varenne are up to?"

Northwood reached over and roughly squeezed her breast. If she had flinched it would have roused his doubts but the tart gave him a sensuous smile, her catlike eyes full of promise. He wanted his cleverness appreciated, so he was willing to tell the story. "We're blowing up the British Embassy this afternoon."

Maggie's eyes widened involuntarily. "Is that possible? Surely it would require an enormous amount of gunpowder."

"Well, actually we're only blowing up one section, but

that is where everyone important will be.'' He stretched out his hand and fondled Maggie again. ''There's a closet right under Castlereagh's bedchamber, where they've been holding all the important meetings since he got kicked by the horse. I filled it with gunpowder and it will go off this afternoon at four o'clock. Nobody will find it, either. I have the key to the closet right here.'' He patted his jacket pocket complacently.

''Oh, then you'll have to leave soon!'' Maggie exclaimed in disappointment. ''I was hoping you could stay.'' After a moment, she added, ''Won't it be dangerous for you to set it off?''

''That's where the real cleverness comes in,'' Northwood said, not mentioning whose idea this had been. ''I set a candle in the closet. When it burns down, it will hit a trail of gunpowder, run over to the boxes and, *Boom!* Castlereagh's bedchamber and everyone in it will be blown to bloody shreds.''

Maggie shuddered, then tried to make it appear that she was excited by the idea. ''That's remarkable! I wish that I had been involved in something important like that,'' she said wistfully.

Northwood's eyes raked her. ''Oh, really? I thought that you were quite the loyal little British spy.''

''Whatever gave you that idea? If you're a girl of no fortune, like me, you have to take what money comes. And I've taken it from everyone.'' Maggie decided that she had probably learned everything that she was going to from him, and that if she didn't move quickly, he would pounce on her and she would lose the initiative. While she knew something of rough and tumble fighting, her chances would not be good against a man as large and heavy as Northwood. She stood and stretched languidly, watching the way his eyes followed the movement of her breasts.

''I've done what's needful for money, Oliver.'' With a rich, bedroom chuckle, she closed the distance between them and stretched out her hand. ''But some things I do for pure pleasure.''

He reached up and grabbed, pulling her onto his lap. Maggie had expected that and as he pressed his lips to hers, she was perfectly positioned to lift the pitcher from the china washing set and smash it into Northwood's head. The pitcher was half full of water and she hit as hard as she could. There was a horrible sound, pulpiness mixed with shattering china. While water cascaded over them, Northwood's eyes showed a flash of surprise as he fell over sideways, taking the chair and Maggie with him.

The impact knocked the breath from her, but she scrambled up quickly, equally fearful of having killed him and of not having hit hard enough. A quick check showed that he was still alive, and from his slight movements, not deeply unconscious. Maggie gave a sigh of relief. Much as she despised Northwood, she had never killed a man and didn't want to begin now.

Earlier Maggie had disconnected the drapery cords and she used them to tie his wrists and ankles, with another length securing him to the heavy table. She also tore a length of fabric from the drapery lining and gagged him, then searched his pockets. Besides the key to this room, he had a ring with several other keys in his coat. Not knowing which was the key to the closet in the embassy, Maggie took them all.

After unlocking the door, she peered cautiously into the corridor. It was deserted, and from its dinginess either the castle had few servants or this area was seldom used, or both. All to the good. Glancing at the black cat pressing against her ankle, she said, "Come on, Rex. We're going to find Robin."

At Silves's cafe, Roussaye settled at the table of a man he had served with in Italy, Raoul Fortrand, and raised the subject of Henri Lemercier. Fortrand spat on the floor. "That swine. He was always a swine, but lately he proved it by working for the Ultra-Royalists."

His pulse speeding up, the general leaned forward. "Really? What was he doing? And for whom?"

"God only knows what he was doing—something illegal." Fortrand shrugged. "I heard he worked for the Count de Varenne. They say Varenne expected to be prime minister after Talleyrand and that he was furious when the king picked Richelieu. Maybe Varenne wanted Lemercier to assassinate the new prime minister."

The words were casual but uncannily close to the truth. Roussaye thought for a moment. Varenne's estate lay scarcely an hour outside Paris, convenient for plots and prisoners. The general might be wrong but his soldier's instinct demanded he investigate. Rising, he looked around the café at the two dozen men there, many former comrades-in-arms. Pitching his tone above the voices, he called out in a battlefield voice, *"Mes amis!"*

After a few seconds, silence settled on the room as everyone turned to the general. Climbing onto his chair, Roussaye said, "I have evil news of a royalist plot against the Duke of Wellington, a soldier second only to Bonaparte himself. They say the Duke will be assassinated and Bonapartists will be blamed. Men like us who have faithfully served our country will be persecuted, and France herself may be driven to the brink of civil war."

The silence was absolute. Roussaye looked at the familiar faces: at Moreau, who had lost his arm at Waterloo; at Chabrier, one of the handful of survivors of the disastrous Moscow campaign; at Chamfort, with whom he had shared a billet in Egypt. His voice soft now, he said, "We may find the answers, and perhaps even a beautiful lady to rescue, at Chanteuil, the estate of the Count de Varenne. Will you come with me?"

After a moment of silence, the men began to rise to their feet, coming to him and offering their arms. Pitching his voice above the babble, the general said, "All of you who have horses and weapons, follow me. We will have one last ride for France."

Hélène Sorel had hurried two blocks before fatigue and common sense made her slow down. She was sure that Varenne was *Le Serpent* and his lack of obvious motive had shielded his activities. But what should she do now? As Hélène stood on a corner of the Faubourg St. Germain, agonized indecision on her face, the clattering hooves of a passing horse suddenly stopped beside her and she looked up to see Karl von Fehrenbach swinging down from his mount, an uncertain look on his face. He said, "Madame Sorel, I am glad to see you. I have been thinking . . ."

Then he saw her expression and said sharply, "What is wrong?"

Hélène knew the colonel lived nearby and it was just luck that he was passing, but as she looked at his broad, capable shoulders she decided he had been sent by heaven. There might be nothing personal between them but the colonel was an influential man who might be able to help, and since he knew of her spy work he might believe her. Taking a deep breath, she poured out the story of the conspiracy, the disappearances of the three British agents, her realization that Varenne must be the master plotter, and her belief that Chanteuil contained the answers.

The colonel listened without interrupting, his light blue eyes intent on her face. When Hélène came to the end of her story, he swung onto his horse, then extended his hand to her. "Come, there is a Prussian barracks near the St. Cloud road. I will be able to get some men there to investigate Varenne's estate." As Hélène hesitated, he said impatiently, "To save time, you must come and show us the way to Chanteuil. If you are right, there is no time to be wasted."

Hélène took his hand and he lifted her easily up onto the horse. As she settled sideways in front of him, she said anxiously, "But what if I am wrong?"

The grave Prussian colonel did not quite smile, but he had a mischievous glint in his eyes and she recalled that he was the same age she was, only thirty-three years old. "If you are wrong," he said, "there are compensations."

Hélène suddenly realized how close she was to his lean, athletic body, and how warm was the arm that held her steady. For a moment, the serene and worldly widow disappeared and she blushed like a girl. After a lingering appreciative glance at her, von Fehrenbach put his heels to the horse and they were away.

Chapter 21

As the heavy key rattled in the lock the two men took their positions, Robin on the straw in plain sight and Rafe against the wall where he would be concealed by the door. If there was any chance of a successful attack on whoever entered, Robin would signal the duke. If resistance would be futile, Rafe would be innocently pacing and they would try again the next time.

The flicker of shock on Andreville's face was not what Rafe was expecting. A moment later, Margot hurtled into the cell, her golden hair loose around her shoulders and her overall aspect rather like that of a Valkyrie. Hugging her partner, she said, "Robin, thank God you're all right! I was so frightened . . ."

Putting his good arm around her, Andreville hugged her back but his eyes went up to meet Rafe's. "I'm well enough, Maggie. We have reinforcements, too."

Margot stiffened in his arms, then turned to follow the line of Robin's sight. She gasped, her eyes rounding, and whispered, "Rafe," as she stepped toward him. Then she stopped and smiled uncertainly. "I'm not sure whether I should be glad to see you, or sorry that you're a prisoner too."

Her first reaction to seeing him had been pure uncomplicated joy that was quite unconnected to the circumstances in which they found themselves. Rafe, however, was looking at her with his usual expression of cool detachment, the same he had shown ever since they had spent that night together. Sharply tamping down her reaction, Maggie turned her attention to the present. Looking at Robin, she realized that his expression was strained and the only color in his face seemed feverish. Then she noticed the crude bandages on his hand and asked, "What happened?"

Rafe described Varenne's ambitions and Maggie tersely outlined what Northwood had told her about the gunpowder plot, adding that she had the key to the embassy closet in her reticule. Both men tightened, each showing anxiety in his own way. His mouth set, the duke said, "I presume that means that the next priority is escape. Have you seen enough of the castle to have an idea of how to get out?"

Margot shook her head, her eyes going from one man to the other. "Not really, since I was brought here unconscious. I do know there aren't many people about—no one saw me even though it took forever to find my way down here. Varenne had said Robin was being held directly under where I was, but there's a real labyrinth of service stairs and passages on the lower levels of the castle. Thank heaven the dungeon key was hanging outside."

Robin said crisply, "It's less than two hours until four o'clock, so all we can do is try to steal horses and get to the embassy in time. Rafe, could you give us a general idea of the grounds? If we're discovered, we'll need to scatter and hope one of us can get through alone."

Margot nodded, and after a pause, the duke did also. Rafe found the professionalism of his companions unnerving. While preventing the embassy explosion was more important than any of them individually, he couldn't bear to think of abandoning Margot—even though she had looked at him like a woman finding a spider in her tea when she first entered the cell.

As Rafe opened the door, he felt a pressure on his ankle. In the midst of high melodrama, it was a shock to see a fluffy black cat brushing against him coquettishly. "What the devil. . . ?"

"Oh, that's Rex," Margot said, leaning over to scratch the cat's broad head. "He kept me company when I was locked up, then followed me down here."

After one last ankle thump, Rex pattered down the corridor on some mysterious cat business. Margot made an instinctive move after him, but Rafe shook his head. "Better let him go. He's in a lot less danger than we are."

* * *

Oliver Northwood regained consciousness quickly to find himself wet, bound, and gagged. Rage from that discovery cleared his mind and as he pulled at his bonds, he swore mentally at the little slut who had done this. He should have raped her as soon as he came in rather than falling victim to her cozening ways. The bonds on his wrists stretched as he strained at them; the old drapery cords had been softened by the water. He swore some more, this time in gratitude that luck had turned his way again. He'd get the bitch if it was the last thing he ever did.

After some minutes of struggle, Northwood freed one wrist and it took only a few moments to get rid of the other bonds and the gag, stagger to the door, and start yelling for help. Once again he was in luck; a servant was passing nearby, and in a short time Northwood was free of his prison.

Northwood remembered the way back to Varenne's library and he burst into the room without knocking to find the count still seated behind his desk, working at his infernal plans. As Varenne glanced up, the Englishman gasped, "She's gotten away! The little bitch is loose somewhere in the castle!"

Varenne stared at his bloody, disheveled visitor with distaste, saying coolly, "You let a female half your size do that to you? I have overestimated your abilities."

Northwood flushed angrily. "No need to be insulting; that brazen-faced hussy could bamboozle a saint. She's dangerous."

"Quite deliciously so," Varenne murmured, more amused than alarmed. Reaching for the velvet cord behind him, he said, "She won't get far, you know. What can one woman do alone? Your Miss Ashton won't even be able to get past the guard at the gate."

Northwood growled, "She knows what's going to happen at the embassy this afternoon."

"What! You fool, why did you tell her that?" Varenne's lip curled in disgust. "You needn't answer. Obviously, you were boasting. My respect for Miss Ashton grows greater hourly."

The butler hurried in, too quickly for it to be a response to the count's summons, but before the man could say anything, Varenne drawled, "The countess has escaped. Set all the servants searching for her." Glancing at Northwood's bloody head, he added, "Tell them to carry shotguns and travel in pairs; she is quite a ferocious wench."

The butler said urgently, "Milord, I was just coming to inform you . . ." He faltered under Varenne's sharp attention, then continued, "The lady has freed the two Englishmen. They are loose somewhere on the lower levels."

The count swore, his air of perpetual calm disintegrating. Standing, he said harshly, "Alone she was a minor threat but the three together are a significant problem. Tell the searchers that while I would prefer to have the spies captured alive, they should shoot if necessary. They must *not* be allowed to leave Chanteuil."

The butler nodded and left. Northwood turned to follow the servant, but Varenne stopped him. "Where are you going?"

Northwood glanced back with an ugly scowl. "To help search. I want to be the one to find her."

"Considerate of you to help undo the damage you have caused, but I have a better plan." The count's voice was dispassionate again. "The lower castle is a maze of passages and the prisoners might conceal themselves indefinitely, which is a nuisance but not a disaster. The real threat comes if they escape the house and get to the stables. If they manage to steal horses and escape within the next hour, they could conceivably reach Paris in time to undo my plan. Therefore you and I shall wait in the stables until it is too late for the explosion to be stopped."

Brushing blood from his forehead with his sleeve, Northwood growled, "Very well. Just as long as the bitch is punished."

"Have no fears, she will be," Varenne said coldly. He reached into his desk and brought out a box containing two dueling pistols that he expertly loaded. Offering one to Northwood, he said sarcastically, "I trust you know how to use this?"

The Englishman glowered but said only, "Don't worry, I'm a crack shot with any kind of firearm."

As Varenne led the way downstairs the distant boom of a shotgun blast was heard from somewhere below. With a faint air of satisfaction the count said, "Perhaps our vigil in the stables will be unnecessary. Nonetheless . . ." Before they went outside, he gave terse orders that his small troop of soldiers should surround the stables but stay concealed. The three Britons might make it that far but they would never make it out again.

The count took a footpath down to the stables, which were built on a lower level of the hill. Inside the stone building, the main room stretched back with box stalls on each side of a wide central area. Most of the stalls were occupied and the earthy scents of animals and sweet hay were heavy in the air. A couple of horses whickered in recognition but Varenne ignored them, turning to the right to enter a long, narrow harness room.

Northwood had been following without comment, but now he asked, "Why are we going to wait in here?"

"Because I have some hopes of capturing them alive, imbecile," the count snapped. "Come over here."

Unsuspecting, the Englishman followed him to the far end of the room and glanced out the window the count was indicating. Only when he heard the click of a pistol cocking did he swivel his head around to see the weapon Varenne was aiming at him.

As Northwood stared at him in disbelief, the count said evenly, "You have ceased to be an asset, Northwood. You are too stupid to know your place, and I greatly disliked your attempts to coerce me. As a last gesture for services rendered, I was willing to allow you your fling with the countess, but you have bungled even that. I really cannot waste any more time on you."

Northwood reached for his own pistol but he never had a chance. Aiming at the chest, Varenne calmly pulled the trigger. The pistol jerked in his hand, the sound of the shot shatteringly loud in the enclosed space. The Englishman spun around to this left at the impact of the bullet, falling face down on the stone floor in an ungainly sprawl.

Varenne walked over to the body and prodded it with a toe, but the only response was the slow spread of blood from under the body. The count regarded his victim emotionlessly. He had shot Northwood out here to avoid ruining the library carpet and his only regret was having to share this room with the body for the next hour or so. In general he was not involved with death directly; it was such a messy business. Northwood had fallen on the second dueling pistol and Varenne had no desire to move the body to recover it; servants could do that later.

Reloading his own firearm, he reflected that one gun and the element of surprise were all that was needed against the escaped prisoners. He need only threaten the *soi-disant* countess and her lovers would fall into line immediately. The fools.

Rafe led the little party, since he had the most knowledge of the castle and its grounds. They would have to go up at least one level, then to the right. Leaving by the main entrance was too much of a risk so he hoped they could find a side door. They moved as quickly as they could, making little sound in the endless stone passageways. The castle seemed almost deserted and they went up one flight of stairs and turned right into another passage without seeing anyone.

Then their luck ran out. They had almost reached the end of the corridor when two hulking men with shotguns came around the corner right in front of them. Making a lightning judgment, Rafe yelled, "Get Margot out of here!" as he threw himself forward in a flat dive, barreling into the man in the lead.

Summing the situation up with equal speed, Robin barked, "Come on, Maggie!" and grabbed her arm, pulling her back the way they had come. She resisted for an agonized moment, terrified to leave Rafe behind, but the pressure on her arm left her no choice. She fled with Robin as the blast of a shotgun echoed through the halls.

Because the Prussian barracks was off the main St. Cloud road, Colonel von Fehrenbach's Hussars came by a different route and didn't intersect the French party until they were a bare half mile from Chanteuil. The Prussians entered into the main road at a right angle from a lane they had taken as a shortcut.

Both groups came to a halt in a moment of explosive mutual suspicion and hostility, the uniformed Prussian cavalryman facing the former French officers. A Hussar started to raise his musket but von Fehrenbach threw one hand up imperiously. "No!"

Hélène had gotten a mount at the Prussian barracks, complete with sidesaddle, though since she wasn't wearing riding dress there was still an indecent amount of leg showing. Recognizing Michel Roussaye, she urged her horse into the open ground, crying, "Don't shoot, we're friends!"

Having a woman ride between the groups released the tension and von Fehrenbach trotted out after her, meeting Roussaye in the middle. It took only a few moments for them to compare notes as to where they were going, and why. The colonel said judiciously, "Perhaps we should join forces, General Roussaye."

Roussaye raised his brows, his dark face skeptical. "Frenchmen and Prussians riding together?"

The colonel's eyes flickered over to Hélène Sorel, tensely sitting on her horse at the third corner of their triangle. "Such a thing should not be impossible when men share the same goal." He offered his hand. "Shall we try to go forward together?"

Roussaye smiled and took the Prussian's hand. "Very well, Colonel. Instead of looking back we shall go forward, together."

The shotgun firing by his ear nearly deafened Rafe and a pellet grazed his cheek, but the speed of his attack took the two searchers by surprise. The balding man whose shotgun had discharged tried to club him with the weapon, but while the man was swinging it back Rafe kicked him in the groin, and he staggered into his companion, throwing him off balance. Rafe snatched up the two shotguns and ammunition pouches the men carried, then hared his way down the hall after Margot and Andreville.

The whole encounter had taken less than a minute and the duke caught up with his companions easily around the next bend. Maggie threw him a quick glance as they raced toward the west side of the house, and between gulps of breath she said, "I thought we had agreed on no heroics or martyrdom."

Rafe grinned at her, his dark hair rumpled and a trace of blood on one lean cheek where the pellet had nicked him. "Sorry, I forgot. Remember, I'm just an amateur."

Rafe's fleeting humor disappeared when two more armed men appeared in front of them, drawn by the sound of the earlier shotgun blast. These men were too far away to attack and they could hear more men emerging from the room behind them. Rafe lifted the loaded shotgun he had appropriated, cocked both barrels, and let loose with one barrel ahead of them and one behind. He took no time to aim, relying on the scattering effect of the shot to discourage the searchers.

The three of them had halted by a door in the middle of the passage. While Rafe was blasting the pursuers, Robin opened the door, exposing another service stairway, gray and dark, and they raced up single file, Robin in the lead. The door at the top opened into a hall that was wider and better kept than the service passages below; they were now in the section of castle where the masters lived. It was quieter here, as the pursuit seemed to be focused on the ground levels.

As they hesitated in the hall, Rafe said, "This way," nodding to the right. As he recalled, the left side of the castle had a sheer drop to the river and there would be no escape there. This long corridor looked familiar and he thought it was the one that ran past Varenne's library. If so, at the end should be steps that would take them downstairs some distance away from the beehive they had stirred up below.

Taking a momentary pause, Rafe reloaded both shotguns from the spare ammunition and Maggie fished a large key from her reticule, locking the door they had just emerged from. "There," she said with satisfaction, "that should slow them. This was the key to my room, but I'll wager it will work on every interior door in the castle."

As they headed down the corridor, angry pounding came from the door Maggie had locked. The stairs were where Rafe remembered and they hurried down. Since the windows of the ground floor were not far off the ground, the duke had decided that their best bet lay in finding a room on the eastern wall and escaping that way since the doors were likely to be guarded.

It was a good decision. The first downstairs room they found had leaded casement windows overlooking level ground and the drop was no more than five feet. Rafe smashed the glass with the stock of his shotgun, then helped Margot and Robin out before dropping lightly beside them. "Shall we see if the stables are being guarded by Varenne's army?"

"They had better not be," Maggie said grimly as she hoisted the second shotgun. "We're running out of time."

It was a sobering remark. While saving their own lives had high priority, it was far from their only concern.

When the combined French and Prussian force reached the gates of Chanteuil, there was no one in sight and the gate was locked. Von Fehrenbach dismounted and rattled the gate, and eventually an ancient gatekeeper creaked out to meet him. The old man had a look of terror on his face at the sight of so many mounted men, half of them in the uniforms of Prussian Hussars. "Open this gate in the name of Marshal Blücher and the Allied Army of Occupation," the colonel said crisply.

The gatekeeper seemed rooted to the ground so Roussaye called out, "You will not be harmed if you do as you are commanded." The Frenchman's reassurance succeeded where the Prussian order hadn't and after a minute of fumbling the gate was opened and riders began to stream through. As the last rider entered, the flat, deadly rattle of gunshots came from the castle a quarter-mile ahead. Amid fading echoes, von Fehrenbach wheeled his horse to face Hélène. "You had best wait here, Madame Sorel. We can handle whatever rabble Varenne has."

She nodded, her tired hands clutching her horse's reins. "I'm sure you can. Just . . . please be careful."

He nodded and touched one hand to his forehead in a salute, then was off to lead the force toward the sounds of firing. As Hélène watched the men go, she prayed they had come in time.

Maggie and company saw no one on the shrubbed path between house and stable; most of Varenne's men must still be searching in the castle. The open yard felt horribly exposed and it was a relief to get to the barn door. Rafe unlatched the door, then kicked it open, his shotgun in readiness for possible danger within. The precautions seemed unnecessary: there was nothing inside but horses. Perhaps the grooms had been pressed into duty elsewhere. After glancing around, Rafe said, "Robin, select the best horses. Margot, look for the harness. I'll stand guard."

The other two nodded and moved off, meshing together into a smoothly working team. As she turned right to look for the harness room, Maggie thought it was remarkable how well they were getting on considering that all three people were by nature leaders, more accustomed to giving orders than receiving them.

Her thoughts were abruptly cut off as she entered the side room and was seized in an iron grip. Maggie tried to scream a warning and break away, but a hand was clamped over her mouth while her wrist was wrenched until she had to drop her shotgun.

Twisting her head around, she found herself looking up into the black eyes of the Count de Varenne. He smiled at her, his usual congenial social smile, as he pulled her back against him. His left arm was tight around her waist, pinioning her own left arm to her side, and his right hand lifted a cocked dueling pistol to her temple. He said, "Congratulations on escaping my men in the castle, though I am not entirely surprised. You and your gentlemen friends are formidable adversaries."

The pistol was jammed so hard against her temple that there would be bruises, if she lived long enough. Forcing her ahead of him, the count went into the main stable block. Robin saw them first and his soft profanity caused Rafe to turn and look. The count smiled coldly and said, "I'm sure that neither of you gentlemen wishes any harm to come to your lovely, fraudulent countess. Drop the gun, Candover.

Both of you raise your hands above your heads and move into the center of the floor.''

After a frozen moment, Rafe tossed the shotgun aside as Robin came forward to stand by him. Margot's face was white and he could see fear in her eyes, but she said in a detached, steady voice, "Don't let him stop you—he has only a single-shot dueling pistol so he can't get all three of us.''

The count gave an admiring chuckle before saying, "While the countess shows an admirable willingness for martrydom, I wouldn't advise you to try anything, gentlemen." He started to back toward the door, still holding Maggie firmly against him. "My men are concealed outside at both ends of the stable and you would never escape. I have gone to this effort because I prefer to capture you alive, but I warn you, at the least move from either of you, I will blow the countess's head off.''

When Oliver Northwood swam dimly back to consciousness, he knew he was dying. There was too much blood puddling below him and the final chill was reaching into his bones. But even though the smallest effort exhausted him, he still had a little strength left in him and by God, he would use it.

An eternity was required to struggle to his knees, another to gain his feet. Northwood was gratified to discover that he still had Varenne's pistol thrust in his waistband. He pulled it out, a time-consuming act since his fingers had no sensation.

The wound in his chest wasn't bleeding much; he must be running out of blood. Northwood's mind was perfectly clear, in a distant way. There was one thing that he must do. He hated Margot Ashton but that was a pale emotion compared to how he felt about the Count de Varenne. He blinked, trying to clear his eyes, then slowly wove his way the length of the harness room toward the sound of raised voices that came through the open door from the main stable. One of those voices was Varenne's.

As Varenne mentioned his men outside the stable, Rafe could sense the tension draining out of Andreville and wondered if the other man had been planning an attack that would cost Margot's life. Thank God he had been forestalled by mention of the men outside; Rafe would let the embassy blow to the moon and Europe go up in flames before he would do anything to endanger her.

In a detached corner of his brain, Rafe saw it as a tableau, he and Andreville motionless with their hands up, Varenne inching back to the door, Margot's golden hair falling about her shoulders, the high cheekbones stark and dramatic in her rigidly calm face. Rafe was almost consumed by his fury, yet he remained absolutely still, unwilling to risk angering the count.

Then a blood-soaked figure slowly emerged from the harness room just behind Varenne. Oliver Northwood could barely stand and his face was contorted with an ugly blend of fury and concentration as he tried to raise his pistol, his hand wavering feebly in an attempt to center the weapon between the count's shoulder blades. In eerie silence, Northwood lifted his other hand to steady the pistol, then carefully squeezed the trigger.

The blast shattered the tableau. Varenne was knocked forward by the impact, his weight carrying Maggie with him. Falling, his finger tightened on the light trigger of the dueling pistol and it discharged, but Maggie had twisted away, ducking her head below the muzzle of the weapon. It fired so closely that her hair must have singed and she hit the floor hard, Varenne's heavy body on top of her.

Maggie lay there for a moment, wondering whether she had been hit and was too numb to feel it. Then the count's body was dragged from her and Rafe was pulling her up in his arms.

"Oh, God, Margot, are you all right?" He was holding her close, touching her hair to see if the blood that had come from somewhere was hers, his long fingers probing gently as he swore and prayed under his breath. As she listened dazedly, it was impossible for Maggie to tell the prayers from the profanity.

She managed to nod, saying through dry lips, "I'm fine, the gun missed me." Then Rafe was crushing her so tightly Maggie thought her ribs would break and she had trouble breathing because her face was buried against the scratchy wool of his coat. In spite of the discomforts of her position, she wanted to stop the world right now and stay here forever, safe and warm.

Glancing over at the tender scene between Maggie and Rafe, Robin said pragmatically, "In a very short time Varenne's men are going to decide to come in here and investigate."

Brought back to the dangers of the moment, Rafe released Margot and stood up, then helped her to her feet. Grimly he said, "Margot, get the other shotgun and stand guard with Robin while I saddle three horses. Possibly if we ride out together and fast, one of us may get through."

For just a moment his eyes met Margot's. The smoky depths were dark and unfathomable and for an instant Rafe wrestled with the temptation to pour out his feelings for her since there might not be another chance. Then he swallowed hard and turned to the harness room. At a time like this, he had no right to burden her with his emotions.

Rafe quickly saddled three horses. It must be three o'clock by now, and if they didn't break out almost immediately and ride like the wind, they would never make it to the embassy in time.

As Margot and Robin crouched behind thick stone columns with the shotguns, a shot crackled outside, then a multitude of guns were firing. A bullet came through the upper part of the door and Rafe instinctively ducked, swearing under his breath. Varenne hadn't been lying about having an army out there!

Then the sounds of firing diminished, as if the fighters were moving away from the stables. Puzzled, Rafe led two of the horses forward into the front of the barn. Before he could go for the third, the door swung open and Margot raised her shotgun. Rafe leaped over to Robin's side, ready to take the firearm away if the other man's injured hand couldn't support it properly.

With the bright sunshine behind, it took a moment to identify the tall figure in the door. Maggie was steadying her weapon when she recognized the fair hair of Colonel von Fehrenbach, his own pistol drawn and ready. When she realized what his presence meant, she dropped the muzzle of her shotgun to the floor in a rush of relief so great that her muscles went limp. She stood and said unsteadily, "I hope you are here to rescue us, Colonel, because we certainly need it."

Recognizing her voice, he lowered his gun and stepped into the stable, Roussaye at his heels. The Prussian smiled slightly and said, "Then we are in time? Madame Sorel will be pleased."

"You are in time for us, but if we can't get into Paris before four o'clock, the foreign ministers meeting at the British Embassy will be blown to kingdom come." Rafe's words were staccato as he led the horses outside. As the three Britons mounted, they quickly outlined the situation to their rescuers.

The sound of firing still came from the right, away from the main road out of the estate. Roussaye glanced in that direction. "Our men are herding Varenne's back to the river. They won't last long without a leader. Some have already surrendered."

None of the horses carried sidesaddles and Maggie was astride, most of her long legs visible. The animals pranced nervously in the lingering scents of gunsmoke as von Fehrenbach asked, "Should I send an escort with you?"

Rafe shook his head. "They couldn't keep up with fresh horses. Wish us luck. I'll send word if we're successful."

With that, the three Britons put heels to their horses and galloped out of the stableyard. The colonel shook his head. It didn't need to be said that if the three got to the embassy at the wrong moment, they would be in no position to send messages without angelic assistance. He shrugged fatalistically, then turned back to supervise the end of the skirmish.

Chapter 22

Afterward, Maggie never remembered that ride clearly. She had waved reassuringly at Hélène as they dashed by the gatehouse but hadn't stopped for explanations. There was a mad exhilaration in this race toward Paris with the two men she loved most in the world. They had survived one set of horrors and for the moment she felt invincible, as if no amount of gunpowder on earth could harm them. Distantly she knew her relief was premature, but she might as well enjoy the euphoria while it lasted.

They made excellent time through the countryside but were slowed by the heavy afternoon traffic from the city. Rafe was in the lead, pushing for the fastest possible pace. Time was too short to hold back for a slow rider, but all three were expert equestrians and they stayed close together. Though Robin was pale and held the reins in his right hand, his face showed a grim determination to finish the job he had set out to do.

As they got closer, Maggie could feel her nerves tightening like steel wires, the exultation of the early ride shredding away. As they finally cantered down the Rue du Faubourg St. Honoré, their horses sweaty and exhausted, she heard a distant clock striking four times.

They jolted to a halt in front of the embassy and swung off their horses, leaving the reins for any street boy close enough to grab them, then raced up the steps, Rafe in the lead. The guard at the door recognized all three of them in spite of their dishevelment, Robin as a member of the delegation, Rafe and Maggie as recent guests. As the soldier saluted, Rafe snapped, ''There's a plot to blow up the embassy, and the explosion should go off at any moment. Go upstairs with the countess and start evacuating people from Castlereagh's chamber.''

Then he swept on by, leaving a slightly befuddled rifleman. After tossing Northwood's keys to Rafe, Maggie ran inside to start the evacuation. Robin, who knew the embassy layout, took the lead now as the two men went left, then down a flight of stairs in a run that was hauntingly like the escape from Chanteuil. This time, however, they ran *to* something, not away.

''Here,'' Robin said tersely, stopping in front of a door. It was a heavy interior door that opened outward and would be impossible to break down, so Rafe jammed one of Northwood's keys in the lock. He had to force himself to be calm as he searched for the right key, knowing that too much haste could bring disaster. The acrid scent of a guttering candle was noticeable and if the flame reached the gunpowder before the closet was open, they would be gone before they knew they had failed.

The third key was the one. Rafe twisted it savagely, then flung the door open. For a frozen moment time seemed to slow as the men saw the tendril of flame flutter in the draft from the door, dipping lazily toward the mound of gunpowder.

Then Robin dived into the closet, his right arm sweeping across the line of gunpowder the instant before the flame touched the explosive and flared down the powder trail faster than the eye could follow. Half a second later would have been too late. The burning powder scattered and for a moment both men were busy slapping the red-hot particles that scattered across the floor of the closet. The odor of sulfur hung in the air and dense white smoke puffed in eye-stinging clouds. Remarkable how much smoke a small amount of gunpowder could generate.

And then, with startling anticlimax, there was no more fire and it was over. Robin slumped onto the floor, his head bent between his knees as he struggled for breath, and Rafe leaned heavily against the door frame, scarcely able to believe they had made it in time and that they were alive and reasonably well.

Several members of the embassy staff had followed them and were drawing near, their voices murmuring in confusion. Rafe waved his hand vaguely at the onlookers. "It's safe now; you can tell the ministers that the evacuation isn't necessary." One of the men nodded and turned to go upstairs.

Andreville looked up, a wry smile on his fine-drawn face. "I am ready for a new career. I'm getting too old for this."

Rafe returned the smile tiredly. "I think I was born too old for this." He felt an intense sense of comradeship with this man who was both friend and rival. No, not his rival, for that implied the issue was in doubt; Andreville was not a rival but the victor. Well, the duke prided himself on good sportsmanship so he would try to live up to his own standards. Reaching down, he helped Robin to his feet, catching him as he swayed.

Then Margot was forcing her way through the onlookers. The wheat-gold hair was disastrously snarled from their ride, her green dress had taken such a beating that it was barely decent, and her face showed the same stress and exhaustion that the two men were experiencing. Rafe thought she had never looked more beautiful. She walked up and mutely put her arms around both men, burying her face between them.

After a moment of giving way to her feelings, Margot raised her head and stepped back. With a slightly unsteady smile she said, "It is fortunate that you reached the closet in time, because I had not even persuaded the guard to let me into the conference chamber, much less gotten any of the august personages to move. Considering how long it has taken them to agree on a treaty, they would have been debating whether to evacuate the chamber from now until Twelfth Night."

Rafe had thought there might be a problem; one of the reasons he had directed her upstairs was to get her farther away from the blast if they were not in time to stop it.

Then the onlookers parted and another man joined them. The Duke of Wellington was of only average height and the famous hooked nose was more striking than handsome, but even the dullest of mortals would know immediately that this was a man to be reckoned with. He nodded at Rafe and said, "I understand that you uncovered a conspiracy in the nick of time, Candover."

Rafe smiled back and said, "I deserve very little of the credit. My companions here did more than I."

Margot had stepped aside and Robin was standing under his own power now. Rafe considered introducing them but had no idea what names they would prefer, or if introductions were necessary. The Iron Duke solved the problem by offering his hand to Robin and saying, "This must be Lord Robert. I've heard of you, sir."

Robin looked startled but nothing like as much so as Margot, who shot an incredulous sidewise glance at him. Wellington now turned to her and said, "Would this be," he paused for a moment, "the Countess Janos?" in a tone that said he knew that it was a *nom de guerre*.

Margot smiled and offered a hand. "I have been called that."

Wellington bowed over her hand, then gave the smile which had enraptured so many female hearts. "Lord Lattimer was right."

"In what way, your grace?" Margot asked in puzzlement.

"He said you were the most beautiful spy in Europe," the Duke responded with a twinkle in his light blue eyes.

Margot Ashton, dauntless in the face of death and disaster, blushed a most becoming shade of rose. While she recovered, Wellington's voice turned serious. "There is no way to underestimate the importance of what you have done. Besides Castlereagh, Richelieu, and myself, all of the Allied foreign ministers were upstairs, plus," he paused significantly and lowered his voice, "King Louis and his brother."

Maggie gasped. If the explosion had killed the king, his nearest heir, and the chief minister, France would have been ripe for chaos indeed. Varenne might well have emerged a victor in a struggle in which all Europe would be the loser.

Wellington said, "None of our visitors know that anything was amiss and perhaps it is best this way. We wouldn't want anyone to think he is unsafe in the British Embassy, would we?

"Castlereagh will want to see you, but another day will be better. Get some rest; you all look rather the worse for wear."

He started to turn away, then stopped. "I must return to the conference, but there is one other thing. The foreign minister was concerned that one of his aides, Oliver Northwood, might have been involved in this affair. Is that true?"

Rafe hesitated, glancing at his companions. Robin's face was noncommittal while Margot's smoky eyes were trying to convey some message. Picking his words carefully, he said, "Northwood apparently had suspicions that something was amiss and came out to Chanteuil to investigate. His timely intervention was instrumental in foiling the plot, and his was the hand that felled the Count de Varenne, the man behind the conspiracy. Unfortunately, he was killed as a result of his activities."

Wellington's shrewd eyes studied him. "That's the story?"

"It is," Rafe said firmly.

Wellington nodded in acceptance and left, cutting his way through the remaining staff members who hovered outside of hearing range. In the silence after he left Robin said, "Getting some rest is the best suggestion I've heard in some time."

Margot glanced at him. "You, my lad, are not going back to that dismal little hole you call home. I'm taking you to my house so you can be waited on hand and foot for a while."

Robin smiled tiredly. "I am at your command."

With sudden pain, Rafe felt very much the outsider, and the bond that connected the three of them shivered and dissolved. Margot hesitantly invited him back to her house, but he firmly declined, saying that he must send a messenger to Chanteuil and write a report for Lord Lattimer and a thousand other things.

Margot looked at him for a moment with some indefinable emotion in her eyes. Surely it couldn't have been pain. With a graceful bow, Rafe put her and Robin in a carriage and sent them away together. It was the hardest thing he had ever done.

* * *

Before Maggie could rest, she had to break the news to Cynthia Northwood. Speaking gently, she outlined both the facts of the case and the official story that they had all tacitly agreed to. To the rest of the world, Oliver Northwood could be a hero, but Cynthia knew better and deserved the truth.

After Maggie had finished speaking, Cynthia bowed her head, her fingers restlessly twisting the fringe of her shawl. Finally she said with only a faint tremor in her voice, "I didn't want it to be like this. I never wanted to see him again, but I didn't want him dead." She looked up, her eyes meeting Maggie's. "That may be hard for you to understand, after all that he did to me."

Maggie shook her head. "No, I think I understand. He was part of your life for seven years. Surely there are some good memories."

Cynthia closed her eyes for a moment, a quick spasm of emotion crossing her features. The heedless girl was becoming a woman. In a soft voice she said, "There are only a handful of good memories, but there are some. And truly, for all the things he did wrong, he was not really an evil man, was he?"

There was a plea for reassurance in Cynthia's voice. Maggie was silent, thinking of Northwood's act of casual malice that had brought so much pain to her and Rafe. It had changed her life forever and it was done from the meanest of motives. Was that evil? She wasn't objective enough to judge. By Northwood's actions she had lost Rafe and gained Robin. She loved both men in different ways and would rather not decide if her life was better or worse for the path Northwood had forced her to take.

Instead, Maggie said, "Whatever his motives, it is true that his intervention helped bring off a fortunate result. Perhaps, at the end, he was trying to make amends for what he had done."

"Perhaps." Cynthia smiled faintly. "It was generous of you and your friends to give him the benefit of the doubt."

"Blackening his reputation would have done no good and saving it does no harm." Maggie stood and gave Cynthia a sympathetic hug before withdrawing. Alone in her own chamber, she wearily fell back on her bed without changing from her ragged dress, eyes open and staring upward in spite of her exhaustion. It was true that she had no desire to see Cynthia and the Northwood family suffer the public humiliation of their villain. Their shame would not repair the damage he had done.

She thought of Rafe, then closed her eyes against the sharp sting of tears. The moment of time when they had loved was as dead as the flowers that had bloomed in that spring. It was mere unlucky chance that those feelings had been rekindled in her. No, they had not been rekindled, they had never really died.

With a sob, Maggie rolled over and buried her face in the pillows. In the future she would let herself cry no more tears at the injustice of it all. She had learned to live without Rafael Whitbourne once before, and she would again. But for this one hour, she would allow her emotions free rein. She rather thought she had earned the right to some self-indulgence.

Hélène Sorel sat in her drawing room sipping a late morning cup of coffee and going through her correspondence. With the shafts of early autumn sunlight illuminating the graceful room, the high drama of the day before seemed no more than a fever dream.

Hélène told herself that her feeling of depression was merely the sense of letdown that came at the end of a great enterprise. Now it was time she went back to her daughters. The basic terms of the treaty had been agreed upon and it was just a matter of working out the details. In a few weeks or months it would be safe to move her household back to Paris.

As Hélène stared at the coffee grounds, her maid entered to say that a gentleman was calling. A Prussian gentleman, very tall.

After a frantic thought for her hair and the fact that this was only her third-best morning gown, Hélène touched tongue to dry lips and bade the maid bring in her visitor. The colonel had returned her to her home yesterday with a respectful bow but had said nothing about calling. No doubt he was here to be sure she had suffered no ill-effects from that frantic ride.

Karl von Fehrenbach looked very tall and very handsome, his fair hair gleaming in the morning light. He was also very grave as he bowed over the hand Hélène offered.

There was an awkward moment of silence, then Hélène bid him take a seat. The colonel's eyes studied Hélène's face intently as he said slowly, "I have thought about what you said that day you called on me." He halted, searching for words.

As her pulse quickened, Hélène said, "Yes?" encouragingly.

"You said that someone must stop the hating, and that you wanted me to look at you without remembering that you are French and I am Prussian." His light blue eyes were clouded by this attempt to express his emotions, something he had never found easy and which had become almost impossible these last years.

Hélène said nothing. She just sat still, her face as warm and open as she knew how to make it.

After another long pause, the colonel said with difficulty, "I had tried to cut myself off from all feeling, but I was unsuccessful. The pain was still there. Yet surely if a heart can feel pain, it can feel happier emotions."

There was a question in his tone, and Hélène suggested softly, "Emotions such as love?"

His eyes held hers as he nodded. "Exactly. If you are willing to forgive my coldness, perhaps . . . perhaps we can try."

Hélène gave him a brilliant smile. "I should like that above all things."

The tension went out of his face and he looked much younger as he said, "In that case, would you be free to take a drive out to Longchamps now? My carriage is outside."

Hélène blinked a bit in surprise; the colonel certainly didn't waste any time! But then, why should he? She stood and said, "My time is at your disposal."

With a smile he offered his arm, but just before they reached the drawing room door he stopped and said with a touch of hesitation, "There is one thing . . . with your permission?"

He bent over her slowly, giving Hélène ample time to pull away, something she had no desire to do. The kiss was quite a surprise; given the grave politeness with which he had asked permission, his embrace was surprisingly thorough—not just surprising, but downright exciting. As she looked up at him a little breathlessly, Karl said with the mischievous gleam she had seen once before, "I have wanted to do that since the first time I saw you. You said there was something between us, and you were quite right. That is just one thing, but I'm sure there will be others."

With an irresistible bubble of laughter, Hélène took his arm again and they went out to his carriage. The colonel would always be a reserved man, grave rather than effervescent, but that was all right; she was emotional enough for both of them.

A special messenger arrived in mid-morning with a small package for the Duke of Candover. Rafe stared at it for a moment, guessing what it contained. Inside the velvet box were the ill-fated emeralds and a note that said, *"The masquerade is over. Thank you for the loan. Always, Margot."*

She had signed it "Margot," and he wondered if there was any significance to that. Doubtless it was just an acknowledgment that he no longer called her Maggie. Rafe lifted the emerald necklace out, admiring the delicacy of the gold settings and remembering how lovely she had looked in them. He had spent some time choosing the gems and could not imagine them on anyone else. On impulse he decided to go to her house and return them; perhaps she would accept them as a wedding gift. He wanted Margot to have something that had come from him.

It seemed that even that simple ambition was to be frustrated. When he arrived at Margot's house a short time later, he was shown into the salon but the only occupant was Lord Robert. Robin was looking much stronger today, his left arm professionally bandaged in a sling, his impeccably tailored blue coat and buff pantaloons unexceptionable. He rose and greeted the duke with every evidence of pleasure.

After returning the greeting and accepting a seat, Rafe asked, "Is Margot in?"

Robin shook his head. "No, she's gone out to Chanteuil." At the sight of the duke's raised brows, he grinned and added, "Something about a cat."

"Good lord, is she going to bring that mangy beast back here?" Rafe said, unable to resist an answering grin.

"No doubt. The Prussians will not neglect the horses—probably the stables are empty already—but she was afraid that since the servants had all fled, the cat might be abandoned."

Rafe shook his head admiringly. In spite of all that had happened, trust Margot not to forget the cat, which, to be fair, was not at all mangy. His amusement evaporated, leaving emptiness in its wake. So he wouldn't even get a chance to say good-bye. He stood and said, "I'm sorry to have missed her. I'm returning to London tomorrow, so will you give her these? I'd like Margot to have them. That is, if you don't object," he added after Robin had cast a startled look into the box.

Robin looked at him appraisingly. "Why should I object?"

Rafe felt a flash of irritation at the other man's willful obtuseness, almost as if he was rubbing salt in the wound. "As her future husband, you might not like her accepting anything so expensive from another man," he said shortly.

"As her husband. . . ?" Robin tossed the box lightly in his right hand, then set it on a pie-crust table. "What makes you assume that we are getting married?"

Rafe was feeling increasingly angry. Lord Robert was playing with him, and it was damned unpleasant. He hadn't thought the other man would gloat. "If you recall, you said that you were going to ask her to marry you."

Robin gave him a long, level look, his face for once serious. "I said I was going to ask her. I didn't say she was going to accept. Frankly, I doubt that she will."

The duke felt as if he had been clubbed in the midriff: numb, confused, and unsure what the blow meant. "Why wouldn't she accept you? You've been lovers for the last dozen years or so, and from what I can see, you're on the best of terms.''

Robin stood suddenly and walked over to a window and stared out as if he was thinking. Coming to some decision, he turned to Rafe, leaning against the window sill, his face and body dark against the outside light. ''That is not precisely accurate. We have not been lovers for over three years. Three years, two months, and,'' he thought a minute, ''five days, to be exact.''

Rafe stood also, his muscles and emotions equally churning. ''What is that supposed to mean? You certainly act like lovers, and I saw you enter her house late one night myself.''

Robin shrugged. ''Professionally we have continued to be partners, and friends as well.''

Nonplussed, Rafe said, ''Then why. . . ?'' He stopped, aware of how shockingly intimate was the question he had almost asked.

Unfazed, Robin said, ''Why are we no longer lovers? Because Maggie no longer felt right about it. She wouldn't marry me in the beginning because she wasn't in love with me. Many things changed over the years, but that didn't.''

When Rafe said nothing, simply staring incredulously, Robin continued, ''I was sorry, of course, but made no attempt to change her mind. Except in that one way, our relationship stayed the same. If you know anything at all about Maggie, you will know one does not compel or coerce her. Until this last year or so, when she became the Countess Janos in Vienna and here, we continued living together when I wasn't out risking my neck. It was only in these last three months since I attached myself to the British delegation that we have pretended to be only acquaintances.''

''And you really didn't mind when Margot no longer. . . ?''

''Oh, I minded,'' Robin said shortly, ''but as long as we were still friends, I could accept it. One can always find women for physical relationships, but there is only one Maggie.''

There was only one Maggie, as there was only one Margot, and they were one and the same. Rafe's thoughts were jumbled. He said, "Surely you thought there was some chance that she might accept you or you wouldn't have planned on offering again."

With a mocking half-smile the blond man said, "Once I thought there was a chance. She intended to go back to England to a quiet life in some genteel place like Bath. I thought I would wait about three months, then show up and offer again. Maggie would have been so bored that she might have accepted. It could have worked very well. I'm rich, she's beautiful, and we are the best of friends. Most marriages have much less."

It was time for the ultimate question in this extraordinary conversation. Rafe had been prowling restlessly, but now he turned to the other man. "Are you in love with her yourself?" He had thought that he knew the answer, but was no longer sure.

Robin was very still, silhouetted against the bright window. Musingly he said, "In love? I'm not quite sure I know what that means. Perhaps I lack the temperament for grand passions. Certainly, I am not in love as Maggie would define it." He stopped a moment, then said in a voice meant more for himself than Rafe, "I would go through fire for her, but that's not quite the same thing."

Rafe felt as if his heart was being constricted. He crossed over to the window and stood close enough to really see the other man's face. Quietly he asked, "Why are you telling me this?"

Robin's blue eyes were steady as they met Rafe's. "Because I think Maggie is in love with you. I knew she had loved someone before we met and I have seen how she has been since you came to Paris."

The aching confusion began to disappear, washed away by a feeling of warmth. Rafe said, "If you hadn't spoken, I would have gone back to England without seeing her again."

"I know. That is why I spoke."

After a shaken pause, Rafe said, "You're a generous man."

Robin's gaze was very direct. "I want Maggie to be happy."

As he looked at Lord Robert's handsome, collected face,

Rafe felt a dizzy sense of déjà vu. Somewhere he had experienced this scene before, from a different point of view, and after a moment he remembered Lady Jocelyn Kendal, or rather Lady Presteyne as she was now. My God, was it only three weeks since he had been with her, pleasurably anticipating the beginning of a new affair, when her husband "of convenience" had appeared and it had been very obvious that the bond between them was piercingly alive? Lady Jocelyn had been shattered and confused and it was Rafe who had helped her retrieve what she had almost lost. With a sense of awe, he wondered if some underlying law of universal order was repaying him in kind for what he had so casually done then.

Rafe had no words to express such a thought and the only ones he could think of were shockingly inadequate. Still, he said them. "Thank you." He opened his mouth to say more, then closed it. Perhaps there was nothing else to be said. Shaking his head, he turned and picked up the emeralds as he left the room. By the time he reached the carriage outside, he was running.

Holding the sheer drapery aside at the window, Robin watched the duke turn his carriage for the ride to Chanteuil. With a wry, self-mocking smile, he dropped the drapery and turned away. He was indeed a very generous man. He was also a damned fool.

After the terror of what had happened, Maggie would never have returned to Chanteuil if it hadn't been for Rex, and for her desire to be away from home if the Duke of Candover called. In spite of her reluctance to come back, it was very pleasant in the Chanteuil gardens and she found no lingering trace of Varenne's evil. The sunny day was as warm as high summer and the flowers showed the flamboyant splendor of the last days before frost.

Maggie sat under a rose-covered arbor in a small enclosed garden with a fountain centered in the lush green grass. A cupid cavorted in the fountain while Rex slept with his head on her lap, the rest of him sprawling onto the stone bench, one back paw in the air. The cat had a truly extraordinary talent for relaxation and his soft snoring combined with bird songs and the hum of insect wings to produce a sense of deep peace. Rex would be an excellent tutor as she learned to live a normal, quiet life.

As Maggie absently scratched behind Rex's ears, she congratulated herself on her self-possession. The wild grief of yesterday was behind her. Even when she was eighteen and in the first throes of love, she had not quite believed that Rafe would ever be for her, and sure enough, fate in the malignant personage of Oliver Northwood had intervened. Still, she had at least one night of tenderness to remember; had it not been for this disastrous last investigation, she would not have had even that.

Her self-congratulations were premature. The crunching of footsteps on the gravel path sounded over the garden noises and she looked up to see the Duke of Candover walking toward her. Maggie stared at him, her heart behaving rather strangely and her hand motionless on the cat. Rafe was dressed with his usual casual, damn-your-eyes elegance, and he looked so handsome that after a moment she realized that she was forgetting to breathe.

Swallowing hard, Maggie donned a bright social smile. "Good afternoon, your grace. What on earth are you doing out here?"

Sitting next to her on the lion-footed bench, he smiled and said, "Looking for you, of course. Apart from the Prussian guards at the gatehouse and the one at the front door that sent me out here, the estate seems deserted."

She nodded. "It is—not so much as a cook or a scullery maid left. It's fortunate I came for Rex. He might have been able to survive on castle mice but he would have been lonesome."

Maggie's word were said almost at random; even though it meant another night of tears, it was impossible not to respond to Rafe's heart-melting smile. His clear gray eyes were striking in his dark face, and his expression was more intent than she had ever seen it. As their gazes locked, she thought there was something different about him this morning. Had he lost some of that unshakable pride and confidence that was so integral a part of him? No, it was not that he had lost anything, but rather that he had gained something new. Hard as it was to believe, Maggie's instinct insisted on labeling it as humility.

They had been looking at each other silently for some time and it was not entirely comfortable. Rafe's eyes turned away and he pulled a velvet box out of his pocket. Clearing his throat, he handed it to her. "I wanted you to have these."

Maggie immediately handed the box back. "I can't possibly accept them, they are too valuable."

His eyebrows lifted. "If I gave you flowers you would accept them. What is the difference?"

Her heart thudding uncomfortably, Maggie pointed out, "The difference is about five thousand pounds, if not more."

He put his hand over hers on the velvet box, and the warmth of his touch spread up her arm. His voice serious, the duke said, "The cost is unimportant. What matters is that they are from the heart, no more and no less than flowers would be."

Maggie stared down at their joined hands, his dark against her creamy English blond complexion. "Very well," she said in a low voice. "If you really wish me to keep them, I will."

"I would like to give you a great deal more."

Rafe's face was so close that she could feel the faint brush of his breath on her forehead as she looked at the velvet box. At his words, Maggie felt a rush of fury. Why did he have to say that and spoil everything? She jumped up, jerking her hand away from his and leaving both jewels and an indignant Rex on the bench. Her voice was edged as she said, "I don't want you to give me anything more. This is already too much."

She stepped out of the arbor into the sunshine and plucked a rose, twirling it between her hands and telling herself that she was *not* going to lose her self-control. It was another resolution doomed to failure as Rafe stepped up behind her and put his hands lightly on her shoulders. There was nothing overtly sensual or coercive in that contact, but Maggie felt the same sense of melting that his touch always induced in her.

In his deep, beautiful voice, he quoted, *"Come live with me and be my love, And we will all the pleasures prove . . ."*

It was unendurable. He must have felt the tremor that ran through her as Maggie jerked away, whirling only when she was safely out of his reach. "Damn you, Rafe Whitbourne, we've been over this before! I won't be your mistress."

He made no move to close the distance between them so that he could persuade her with all the intoxicating weapons of the senses. Rafe just stood there, tall, handsome, and formidable, yet somehow vulnerable. He said quietly, "I'm not asking you to be my mistress. I'm asking you to be my wife."

Maggie felt as if the two of them had stopped in time while the sounds and sights of the garden continued around them. The wind soughed through the high hedges that surrounded this little garden and the lush scent of sun-baked roses was almost palpable.

Her heart felt as if it was bleeding. Maggie had thought that she was resigned to losing him, and she was not. She had thought that matters could not be worse, and now they were. Rafe was offering the deepest desire of her heart and she had just enough wisdom left to know what a mistake it would be to accept.

Using all her reserves of self-control, she gave a brittle laugh. "You do me great honor, your grace, but we both know that when men like you marry, they choose rich, beautiful, eighteen-year-old virgins. I am none of those things. Don't let the last few days of high adventure warp your judgment."

Margot was staring up at him, anguish and confusion on her lovely face. In spite of her words, Rafe felt a flowering of joy. She had said nothing about not loving him, which was why she refused Robin, and which was the only reason that really mattered. If he could discern her true reason for refusing, surely he could change her mind.

In his most reasonable tone, he said, "I have quite enough money for any two people, or even any hundred people, so that is hardly an issue. Beauty? That is in the eye of the beholder, and in my eyes you are the most captivating, irresistible woman in the world. You always have been. You always will be."

Closing the distance between them, he lifted one hand to

her face, lightly caressing her cheek. "As for age, the only eighteen-year-old I have ever met who didn't bore me to paralysis is you, and the woman you have become is even more fascinating than the girl you were." Her lips parted and he laid his forefinger on them. "That being the case, why won't you marry me?"

Tears started in her wondrously expressive eyes and she turned her head away. After a shuddering moment she faced him again, her voice as low as his own but filled with bleakness. "Because I know myself too well, Rafe. I can't live by the rules of your order—I could never share you with another woman. If you had even the most casual of affairs, I would turn into a raving shrew and we would both be wretched."

Swallowing hard, Margot stepped away from his hands as she finished, "I suppose you could keep your affairs from me but I will never live a lie, be it ever so charmingly told."

Rafe caught her gaze with his, knowing that his future happiness depended on how well he could convince her. "I'm not asking you to be a complaisant wife, because I could certainly never be a complaisant husband. God knows that I have been punished for my unreasonable jealousy. I didn't trust you once, and it was the greatest mistake I have ever made."

He tensed, remembering what had happened to her as a direct result of that betrayal of trust. "I know that Northwood lied, and I know what happened in Gascony as a result." As her eyes darkened, he added, his words slow and distinct, "I know all of it, Margot."

"Robin told you?" Margot's eyes narrowed at his statement and she stepped back from him. Until now, only Robin had known the horror of what happened at that infamous inn.

"Yes, when we were in the cell together."

"If you know that, then you know another reason why I can't marry you, your grace. A duchess shouldn't be damaged goods." The bitterness of memory overflowed into her voice, as tears did in her eyes.

"Margot, don't do this!" Rafe begged. "Not to me, not

to yourself. No one could ever blame you for what happened."

She twisted away from him and folded down on the marble edge of the fountain, burying her face in her hands. "If you think no one would blame me, you are more naive about society than I would have believed possible. Of course, your view of the *ton* has always been from the top, not the lower fringes, where I grew up. The daughter of a duke might— just might—survive the disgrace, but not an impoverished orphan who had been jilted by the greatest prize in the Marriage Mart."

Her voice broke and she had to pause before continuing, her face still hidden. "I would have been a pariah. Even if no one ever found out, how could I go back and pretend to be an innocent girl? I had changed too much."

He went and knelt in front of her, gently peeling her hands away from her face and holding them as he brushed the tears from her cheeks with his other hand. His voice soft, Rafe asked, "Is that why you never returned to England and let everyone think you had died?"

She nodded, her eyes still not meeting his but her tears under control. "There was nothing for me there. I wouldn't even let Robin tell Lattimer who I was. Margot Ashton was dead. I wanted her to stay that way."

The duke sank back onto his heels, holding her chilled hands between both of his. Bleakly he said, "Your whole life was misshapen by my stupidity. If it hadn't been for me, your father wouldn't have died, you wouldn't have suffered as you did. I understand now why you can't forgive me."

Margot shook her head fiercely. "You blame yourself too much for the end of our engagement. Northwood told me how cleverly he contrived to let you hear his lies—it is not surprising you believed him." She looked deep into his eyes, level with hers as he knelt before her. "If I had denied the charges, would you have believed me?"

Rafe nodded. "Yes. Even as mad with grief as I was, I never thought you would lie. When you made no attempt to refute the charges, I was sure they must be true." He stopped, then said slowly, "Even worse than believing you had betrayed me was thinking that you cared so little that it wasn't worth the effort to deny it.''

She closed her eyes, her face reflecting that long-ago misery. In a whispering voice she said, ''My wretched, wretched temper. I was so angry and hurt that you could blindly accept such a thing . . . I could think only of running away. Later I realized that I should have fought, that I should have made you believe me. If there is blame, I must share it with you.''

Her hands clenched around his. ''In spite of what I said when we had that horrible fight, I never really blamed you for my father's death. We did leave England because of the broken engagement, but that's not why we spent so long in France.''

Her smoky eyes opened now. ''Remember, my father was a soldier. He knew the peace wouldn't last long, and he took the opportunity to observe the French troops and armaments. He was sending reports back to the Horse Guards. That is why we waited too long to leave the country. You see, I come by my spying abilities naturally.''

She smiled tremulously. ''If we hadn't come to France, if Father hadn't died and I hadn't ended up working with Robin . . . who knows what would have happened in Paris this week? Perhaps Varenne would have been successful and Europe would be tumbling into war again.''

He was unbearably moved by her gallantry. ''I hope that is true—there is comfort in believing that a greater good has grown from the sorrows of the past.'' Then he raised her hands and kissed first one, then the other. ''But now that Europe is saved, Margot, what about us?''

She shivered at the touch of his lips and regarded him sorrowfully. ''Is it possible to go back, to love each other without the shadows of anger and pain between us?''

''Why go back when we can go forward? Surely now we can bring a depth and wisdom to loving that we could not have done all those years ago.''

Seeing the doubt still on her face, he continued hesitantly, ''I loved you with all that was the best in me. At the same time, I was frightened at how much I was in your power. I thought I loved you more than pride and honor. When I lost you, only pride and honor were left, and I slid into all their traps. If I was always polite, it was because it was beneath me to be rude. When I saw lovers, I held them in contempt, thinking they were victims of self-delusion."

"Do you believe that now, Rafe?" she whispered.

He shook his head and stood, effortlessly raising Margot to her feet as well. "Now that I see the man I had become, I don't much like him. When I am with you, I am most alive, most whole. Once again, you are bringing out the best in me. All of which is a very long way of saying that I love you, and only you."

The struggle between doubt and desire to believe was clearly mirrored on her face, and he laughed, his mood lightened as he sensed that he had won. "As for your fear that I will be unable to resist the charms of other women . . ."

He put one hand under her chin, saying teasingly, "I have always liked women in direct proportion to how much they reminded me of you, but no one else has ever held a candle to the original Margot. Will you find it easier to believe me if I say that I have been in enough fields to know that the grass is *not* greener?"

Margot's face was startled, and then, with dazzling suddenness, it shone with joy and laughter. With a catch in her voice, she said, "Why is an ignoble assertion so much more convincing than a noble one?"

"Human nature, I'm afraid." Cupping her face in his hands, he asked, "Do you believe me now when I say that I love you and will never knowingly do anything to hurt you again?"

She searched his handsome, beloved face, hearing the words she had longed for in a thousand dreams, seeing the open, caring young man she had fallen in love with so many years ago. Rafe was waiting for some signal from her and Margot was grateful that he did not try to seduce her or coerce her in any other way. He had learned a great deal, understanding that she was too much a product of her past to let any man compel her. But where love led, she would always follow.

Sliding her arms around his neck, she said with a catch in her voice, "Perhaps because we loved truly when we were young, we molded each other so that no one else can ever suit so well.''

Holding his clear gray eyes with her own, she whispered, her words a pledge, ''I love you because you are you, and no one else can ever fill my heart in the same way. Even though I wanted to deny it, the words spilled out when we made love. I was so afraid that you would hear. . . .''

He pulled her tight against him, wanting to keep her so close that he could never lose her again. ''I heard what you said and couldn't believe your words were meant for me. Margot . . . Margot, my love . . .''

Her joyous laughter chimed through the garden as she lifted her face to Rafe's, running her fingers through his black hair, molding her body against him in the sheer delight of closeness. As their lips joined, she had a fleeting moment of gratitude that this garden was so very private.

On September 26, the Tsar's Holy Alliance, that bit of ''sublime mysticism and nonsense,'' was signed and the Allied monarchs went home. Paris breathed a sigh of relief to be rid of all that so its citizens could get on with the serious business of pleasure.

The notice in the London paper said that the Duke of Candover and Miss Margot Ashton had been lately married in a private ceremony in Paris. As the former Lady Jocelyn Kendal read it, the notice brought first surprise, then a long-buried memory. She had been a twelve-year-old walking in the park when she saw two people riding together, so patently in love with each other that it made her long to grow up so she too could be in love.

Her governess, who knew such things, said it was the heir to the Duke of Candover and the Incomparable Miss Ashton, and perhaps that was the moment when Candover became the image of all romance to the young Lady Jocelyn. Meeting him as an adult, she had been infatuated with him until she had met David, and had speculated that the duke had been disappointed in love. Comparing the notice with her memory, any romantic was bound to put two and two together. Lady Presteyne smiled in delight; she was nothing if not romantic, and she hoped that Rafe would be as happy in his marriage as she was in hers. But of course, no one could be.

Major Gregory Westford and his bride Cynthia accepted a posting to India. By the time they returned to England, the unusually rapid appearance of their first child would have been forgotten. Meanwhile, on cold French autumn nights Gregory proved to be as good at keeping feet warm as Cynthia had hoped.

Hélène Sorel became engaged to a Prussian colonel, and acquaintances wondered how the prospect of marriage to such a cold stick of a man could put such a satisfied look on her face, rather like a cat that had been in the creampot. When she heard their doubts, she just purred.

When the first son of Michel and Filomena Roussaye was born, he was named Rafael, after his mother's cousin. The general thought it would be a good name for the lad to live up to.

Exhausted by the strain of being carried across the Channel in a velvet-lined box and fed Dover sole and salmon, Rex spent a great deal of time sleeping.

Lord Robert Andreville found Paris sadly flat with Maggie gone. They would always be friends, and Candover knew better than to try to change that, but of course it would never be the same. When the final peace treaty was signed on November 20th and his job was over, Robin decided with a mischievous glint in his eye that it was time he returned to England to shake the family tree. After all, what good was a black sheep to a family if it didn't come around and say "Bah" now and then?

Historical Note

While the Congress of Vienna is relatively well documented, the Paris peace conference of 1815 is much less known but equally vital since it represents the real end of the Napoleonic Wars. I have taken some authorly liberties, but the background events of the story are true. Paris in the summer and autumn of 1815 was a hotbed of conspiracies, assassination plots, and political cross currents. Lord Castlereagh was indeed kicked by a horse in mid-September, and for some days after the important meetings took place in his bedchamber at the British Embassy.

Both art and Bonapartist political prisoners became topics of great controversy, and the events at the Louvre and the Place du Carrousel are accurately depicted, including Wellington's show of force to remove the bronze horses after the mob drove the workmen into the Tuileries the night before. The French, however, had the last laugh on this; while the final treaty sent the stolen art treasures in Paris home, no one thought to include the many fine works that had been sent to provincial museums.

Some of the top Bonapartist military men were indeed executed, causing outrage throughout Europe. Marshal Michel Ney, "the bravest of the brave," died with great courage before a firing squad. However, the other man mentioned, Lavalette, escaped from prison dressed in his wife's clothes and aided by three British subjects, proving once again that art has nothing over life when it comes to farce.

While the Congress of Vienna and the peace settlement of 1815 are often called reactionary, that is twentieth-century hindsight. The tsar's nonbinding Holy Alliance was signed by the despots of Russia, Prussia, and Austria, but not by Great Britain, since the Prince Regent came up with a clever constitutional argument for not signing. President James Madison was also invited to sign but declined.

The Holy Alliance, which came to be used as a tool of reactionary forces, is often identified with the Quadruple Alliance, which was the actual peace treaty signed on November 20th. The Quadruple Alliance had one vital new idea: that in times of future trouble, the great powers would get together and talk about it. This agreement, which came to be known as the Concert of Europe, was the seed that flowered into the League of Nations and the United Nations in this century.

The statesmen who engineered the settlement were tough, pragmatic men who sought to have peace in their time and had to work with the materials available on a shattered continent. They succeeded better than any of them dreamed: Europe did not experience another continent-wide conflagration until 1914.

Meanwhile, the British Embassy is still housed in the mansion that Wellington bought from Pauline Bonaparte, the Princess Borghese, and I'm told that on great occasions her plate still graces the table.

There's an epidemic with 27 million victims. And no visible symptoms.

It's an epidemic of people who can't read.

Believe it or not, 27 million Americans are functionally illiterate, about one adult in five.

The solution to this problem is you... when you join the fight against illiteracy. So call the Coalition for Literacy at toll-free **1-800-228-8813** and volunteer.

Volunteer Against Illiteracy. The only degree you need is a degree of caring.